MARYLAND

Promises Kept
in Three Romantic Novels

LOREE LOUGH

BARBOUR
PUBLISHING

Pocketful of Love © 1994 by Loree Lough
Pocketful of Promises © 1995 by Loree Lough
The Wedding Wish © 1998 by Loree Lough

ISBN 1-59310-909-1

Cover art by Getty Images.

Scripture quotations are taken from the King James Version of the Bible.

Published by Barbour Publishing, Inc., P.O. Box 719, Uhrichsville, Ohio 44683, www.barbourbooks.com

Our mission is to publish and distribute inspirational products offering exceptional value and biblical encouragement to the masses.

 Member of the
Evangelical Christian
Publishers Association

Printed in the United States of America.
5 4 3 2 1

POCKETFUL OF
LOVE

To my family, who fills all the pockets of my heart with love. TMM:YKW

Chapter 1

Thick, dark hair swirled around her shoulders as she turned toward the sound of his closing car door.

"Who do I see about having a sign painted?" he asked.

She dropped the weed she'd just picked onto the pile with the others then stood and brushed the dirt from the knees of her jeans. "That'd be me."

He pocketed both hands and focused on the small child who ran toward them, a Popsicle clown-grin on her tiny face. "Mommy," she giggled, "it's leaking."

"What's leaking, Annie?"

"The place where the water comes out." Her pudgy hands flapped, imitating the flow of water.

Annie's mom closed her eyes and tilted her face toward the late afternoon sun, then took a deep breath. When she looked at him again, her face brimmed with amusement. "You'll have to excuse me, but I'd better see about this before we flood the valley."

He followed Annie and her mom into the backyard. Bright splashes of color shocked his senses. To him, planting involved only the seeds that became food. He was totally unfamiliar with those that produced such beauty. Subconsciously, he compared it to his own stark yard.

"See?" Annie squeaked, pointing to the spray of water coming from the hose. "It looks like a fountain, doesn't it, Mommy?"

He guessed the child's age at four or five. Lindy would have been seven. The big ache in his heart throbbed as he watched Annie break off the end of her Popsicle and watch the crimson line that crept toward her elbow. The last time he'd seen Lindy, he'd snapped a picture of her spaghetti-sauced grin. For an instant, he wondered where he'd put that photograph.

Annie's mom turned off the water, adjusted the hose more tightly to the spigot, then twisted the squeaking handle until the end of the hose spurted water once again. "You're right, sweetie. It did look like a fountain. Maybe you ought to stand under it and rinse off that sticky Popsicle juice."

When she faced him again, her brown eyes seemed to smile as brightly as her lovely mouth. "Sometimes I feel like Captain Kangaroo. . .without benefit of pocket entertainment," she said. "It's a madhouse around here, isn't it?"

Standing this close to the petite woman made him feel like a linebacker. "Not at all," he said, assessing the freshly mowed lawn and the tidy flower beds. "Things seem very organized. Your husband must have ten green thumbs. I don't

5

think I've so many flowers—"

"My mommy calls them little presents from God," Annie injected, chewing the tip of one blond braid. "But she doesn't have a husband. First he runned away. Then he died."

He tried not to stare at the agonized, embarrassed expression, partially hidden behind the mother's hands.

She took a deep breath and said, her voice trembling slightly, "Annie, go inside and ask Emi to stir the soup."

Annie glanced toward the screen door. "But, Mommy. . .she's right there. You could tell her yourself."

The gentle smile vanished. Her left brow rose high on her forehead as she tucked in one corner of her mouth. Then, aiming her pointer finger at the child, she said, "I'd like you to tell her. And ask her to call the Becks and have them send Danny home. It's nearly supper time."

Annie stuck the dry braid into her mouth, wide blue eyes deciphering her mother's demeanor. Without a word, she looked at her bare toes, then turned and disappeared into the house.

"Twin Acres Signs comes very highly recommended," he said, closing the subject of her missing-then-dead husband. "I saw the one you painted for the Becks. Good work." He wondered how her husband could have left a woman with such a sweet, innocent face.

But her past really didn't matter one bit to him. He'd decided long ago that living life alone was far easier than loving—and losing. Her business was painting signs. He wanted one. Period. "Cabot Murray," he said, extending a hand.

She grasped it firmly and without a moment's hesitation. "Elice Glasser." She nodded toward the garage. "That's my workshop." She headed for the double-doored building. "Follow me," Elice said, "and we'll see about that sign of yours."

Inside, Cabot surveyed the clutter-free workbench. Inventoried power tools. Saw tape measures and wood files that hung in order by size on the pegboard behind the slanted draftsman's table. On the opposite wall, jars of paint thinner and cans of varnish stood in orderly rows on metal shelves. On a big drafting table across the room, lay a sign in progress. Clean paintbrushes of all shapes and sizes poked out of a tall tin can. Here, as in the yard, perfection.

"Can you really use all this equipment?"

She dropped onto the squeaking seat of an ancient secretarial chair. "Yup."

His heart did a little flip when she punctuated her answer with a merry wink. The reaction surprised him, since he'd always been partial to tall, blue-eyed blonds.

Still, something nagged inside him. Except for the husband story, things seemed entirely too perfect in Elice Glasser's world. And, if his former cop-life had taught him anything, it was that perfection didn't exist. He wondered what Elice Glasser was hiding behind that perfect façade.

"What kind of sign did you have in mind?" Her hair hid her face as she rummaged in a desk drawer. It seemed to annoy her. She grabbed a rubber band from the table top and pulled her thick hair into a loose ponytail.

Cabot shrugged, strangely disappointed that she'd imprisoned all those gorgeous curls. "Something that says Foggy Bottom Farm."

She looked up and met his eyes, then smiled. "What a nice, peaceful name."

His heart did the little flip again. Without all that hair around it, her face seemed more noticeable. He'd heard of heart-shaped faces and guessed they'd be pointy-bottomed, horrid little things. He'd been dead wrong. Cabot pocketed both hands. "My dad named the place. I'm just carrying on tradition."

"You take a look at that," she said, handing him the booklet she'd pulled from the drawer, "while I whip up a sample sketch." Using her foot, she slid an old metal stool closer to her drafting table. "Make yourself at home."

As he took the booklet, he couldn't help but notice her rough, reddened hands and closely cut fingernails. He hung the heels of his scuffed work boots on the stool's bottom rung and pretended to study lettering styles. But Cabot never really saw the pages; he was too busy remembering the pained expression that darkened her bright eyes when Annie blurted out all that stuff about her daddy. Elice obviously still felt the pain of his leaving quite intensely; the look on her face had been proof enough of that. Cabot wondered what kind of man would leave a gorgeous wife and three kids.

"How's that?" she asked.

He'd been staring, and she'd caught him at it. Cabot coughed to hide his blush and took the sketch from her work-hardened hand. In just over a minute, she'd centered the words "Foggy Bottom Farm" in a bold arch, the western lettering so precise it reminded him of the sign above the blacksmith's shop in Williamsburg, Virginia. Elice's husband and why he left grew less and less important as Cabot added "talented" to his growing list of her attributes.

"I guess you'll want the standard size—two feet by three—same design on both sides?"

Cabot nodded.

Elice nodded, too, as if she'd expected him to agree. "Just a plain rectangle, or some fancy curves?"

"Plain and simple, that's my style." *Plain and simple is your style?* he repeated mentally. Where'd that come from!

"I'll put your family name here," she said, reaching across his chest to point at the space she'd left beneath "Foggy Bottom."

Cabot forced himself to stare at the drawing. Being a cop all those years had honed his ability to see many things at once. His eyes were on the drawing, but it was Elice he saw. Her dark hair made him think of his grandmother's old mink stole, gleaming with red and gold highlights. He inhaled the clean, fresh scent of her shampoo and wondered if the curls would feel as soft as they looked.

He cleared his throat. "How soon will it be ready?"

She lifted the calendar page and squinted at the bold, black numerals. Clicking the pencil's eraser against her bottom teeth, she said, "Two weeks, give or take a day."

But she was a widow. With three kids to raise, a house and two-acre spread to tend, and a business to run. "There's no rush. I'm back in Freeland for good."

He watched as her brows knitted, as if she didn't understand what his being back in town had to do with how long it would take to complete the sign. But then, he wasn't surprised. Everything about her was a contradiction: soft hair, rough hands; velvety eyes, hard life; sweet voice, tough businesswoman. The contrasts caused a bubbling warmth deep in his stomach, and Cabot didn't know what to make of it. *Nothing ventured, nothing lost,* he reminded himself. "Just call me when it's finished," he said, sounding more abrupt and harsh than he'd intended.

She leaned back in her chair. The clock on the wall said tick-tock, tick-tock. In that instant, he recognized the look on her face as one he'd seen hundreds of times as he had interrogated witnesses. It told him she was trying to figure out whether or not his tone had been one of anger.

"Standard price is a hundred dollars." Her voice sounded as smooth and sweet as honey, despite her businesslike words. "Half down, to get me started, the other half when I'm finished."

They faced each other for a long, silent moment, like old West gunfighters, waiting to see who'd draw first. He reminded himself he'd come here to order a sign. He hadn't had a decent night's sleep or a real meal in days and had avoided any semblance of family for years. The romantic stuff tumbling around in his head he chalked up to deprivation. But he knew he'd better get away from this place, fast, or his life's motto would be a distant memory.

"Sounds like a fair price to me," he said.

The guys on the force had nicknamed him Speedy Gonzales because he'd always moved with lightning speed. When he reached for his billfold, Elice flinched. Cabot froze. He'd seen that reaction, too, in his street cop days. It told him she'd been abused. He wanted to tell her he wouldn't dream of hurting her. At the same time, he wanted to throttle the man who'd put such fear into those beautiful brown eyes. The clock tick-tocked some more while he tried to think of something clever, something soothing to say. His big hands trembled as he thumbed through the bills in his wallet. "I. . .uh. . .I seem to be a little short. . . ."

"You're not short," Annie said. "You're tall. Very tall."

He'd been so involved in Elice's fright that Cabot hadn't even noticed the little girl enter the workshop. As she stood there, looking up at him with those big blue eyes of hers, he wanted to scoop her up, give her a huge hug, and kiss that Popsicle-red smile of hers. He met Elice's eyes. She'd composed herself quickly, he acknowledged. If he hadn't seen it himself, he'd never have guessed that only moments ago, she had looked for all the world like a terrified child. "It won't take but a minute to run home and get my checkbook. My cupboards are as bare as Old Mother Hubbard's," he said, chuckling, "and I have to do some grocery shopping anyway; I'll be passing right by—"

" 'Old Mother Hubbard went to the cupboard to get her poor dog a bone,' " Annie said, grinning, as she recited the Mother Goose nursery rhyme. "Do you have a dog?"

Cabot laughed. "No. I don't."

Annie shook her head and frowned. "Me, either. Mommy says she doesn't have time for a fuzzy kid with four legs." She headed for the door, stretching the pink straps of her bathing suit. "Emi says to tell you the table is set and Danny's on his way home." She gave Cabot a quick once-over, then looked back at her mother. "Is he eating supper with us, Mommy?"

She glanced from her daughter to Cabot and back again. "He just stopped by to order a sign, sweetie," Elice said. "I'm sure he has better things to do than eat day-old bread and soup."

Maggie had called Lindy "honey" in exactly that same motherly tone of voice. The dull ache in Cabot's heart grew as Annie planted herself directly in front of him and asked, "Do you have any kids?"

Cabot shook his head, then squatted to make himself child-sized. "I had a little girl once, but she died." It surprised him how easily the words came tumbling out. What surprised him more was that saying them didn't hurt this time.

"Couldn't you and your wife get another one?"

He swallowed hard. "I'm afraid she's dead, too."

She placed a tiny hand on his cheek. "That's too bad," she said, blinking her huge blue eyes, the blond brows above them rising in sympathy.

Cabot didn't dare look at Elice. If he saw even a trace of pity on her face, he'd flee the workshop like a man being chased by a nightmare. Because that's exactly what he was, and he knew it.

Her hand clamped on her daughter's shoulder, the sweet, maternal tone replaced by one of no nonsense: "Annie, go inside and wash up for—"

Annie's brows rose high on her forehead as she folded her tiny hands in front of her chest. "Oh, Mommy," she said, turning to hug Elice's knees, "he's all alone. Can't the nice man stay for supper? Please?"

Cabot resisted the urge to bolt from the workshop, fire up his Jeep, and head back to Foggy Bottom as fast as he could. Then he realized he was still holding his wallet. Standing, he closed it and cleared his throat. "I'll. . .uh. . .I'll stop by later with the money," he stammered, stuffing it into his back pocket.

Annie's bare feet made tiny slapping sounds on the concrete floor as she followed him to the door. "What's your name?" she asked, grabbing his big hand.

He stared at the tiny hand in his. "Cabot. Cabot Murray."

Frowning, Annie looked at the big hand that surrounded hers. "How'd you get so dirty, Mr. Murray?"

"Annie, if I have to tell you one more time to go inside. . . ," Elice warned.

Smiling, he met Elice's eyes at last. "It's okay. I don't mind." He faced Annie. "This stuff is called axle grease. You see, I've been working on my tractor all day."

Annie shook her head and frowned. "Mommy doesn't like dirty hands. 'Specially at the table." She glanced at Elice, then whispered, "Grandma gave me some neat soap for my birthday. It will make you smell like flowers. Maybe once you're clean, Mommy will let you stay for supper."

"Annie. . ." Elice's voice was a mixture of warning and amusement. "I'm going to count to three, and if you're not inside washing those hands by the time—"

Immediately, the child released Cabot's hand and headed for the door. "Okay, okay, I'm going."

When she was out of earshot, Elice frowned. "Sorry about that. I don't know what gets into her sometimes."

"There's absolutely nothing to apologize for. I think she's adorable." *And so are you,* he thought. Twin Acres had a strange and mystical hold on him. He knew if he didn't get out of there, and quick, he'd lose all control over his emotions. He needed time to get things straight in his head. Lots of time.

"I'll stop by in the morning with the deposit," he promised. And then he left, without a word, without so much as a backward glance. Cabot had faced armed gunmen in dark alleys, stood eye to eye with drug dealers, thieves, robbers, killers. But none had caused such a mixture of confusion and fear in him because while he could easily explain his feelings toward the bad guys, he sensed that one more moment in her company, and he may as well kiss his life's motto good-bye. Doing that scared him more than any of those bad guys.

When Maggie and Lindy died, he rewrote the old cliché to fit his new, solitary lifestyle and "Nothing ventured, nothing gained" became "Nothing ventured, nothing lost." He threw himself so completely into his work that the loneliness didn't attack—until darkness closed in. Sometimes a good mystery novel or a spirited baseball game on TV knocked it out. But now, for the first time since their deaths, loneliness attacked in the daytime, too. And it was harder, more painful to look at in the bold light of day.

When his farmhouse finally came into view through the windshield, emptiness echoed loudly within him. "Find something to take your mind off it," he told himself, parking the Jeep, then slamming its door. "Just get busy and you'll—"

Cabot noticed it the moment he started up the back walk. He'd locked that door. He was certain of it. A familiar tension knotted in his gut as he hurried inside and peered around. The kitchen looked exactly as he'd left it, right down to the half-filled coffee cup and slice of cold toast he'd left on the table.

Except for the blue slip of paper that leaned against the salt and pepper shakers in the middle of the table. On it was the message: *Go back where you came from, cop, before innocent people get hurt.*

No matter how busy she kept herself, Elice couldn't get Cabot Murray out of her mind.

She'd been a widow for nearly three years and had been without a husband two long years before that. In those first lonely days, her solitary status frightened her. But soon, as she began taking on more and more responsibility—and succeeding—she began to like being on her own, being in charge of her own destiny. She learned that the more she concentrated on the many things about her life for which she could be thankful, the happier she felt. Her dad willed her the house and two acres upon which it sat. Her kids were physically fit, well behaved, and well adjusted; Twin Acres Signs was a thriving business. She'd accomplished a lot, all on her own, but Elice never let a day begin or end without thanking God for her many blessings.

It hadn't always been that way, of course. When Bobby first left, she couldn't understand how God could have let a man leave his pregnant wife and two small kids to fulfill a silly dream of driving race cars. She'd been hanging on by a thread, praying that God would guide Bobby home, when the call came informing her that Bobby's souped-up car had exploded, killing him instantly. When he died, a little bit of her innocence died with him. But with that death came maturity and wisdom—something else for which to be thankful.

Yes, she liked her solitary lifestyle just fine. Elice came and went as she pleased, answering to no one but the Lord. She worked hard, and it showed. What had started as a hobby grew into a bustling business that sent the bill collectors packing and kept the kids well fed and clothed. Her first sign painting jobs were simple entrance signs for friends' and neighbors' farms. Gradually, her reputation had grown, until the little company she'd started from scratch on her dining room table was being commissioned by business and industry in northern Maryland and southern Pennsylvania.

Several eligible men had tried, unsuccessfully, to woo her, saying she was far too young and pretty to stay footloose and fancyfree for long. But Elice had no intention of marrying again. She'd made a huge error in judgment when she'd put all her faith and belief in Bobby Glasser. It had been at his graveside that she'd promised herself she'd never again put her children or herself through the kind of torture that goes hand-in-hand with the cold, self-centeredness of a non-believer.

And then Cabot Murray waltzed into her life, tall and blond and bronzed, with those glowing, knowing, hazel eyes.

She'd never liked the strong, silent type, but something about him appealed to her. Elice suspected he hid a softer, gentler side beneath that rough-and-tough exterior. She'd seen a glimmer of it in his golden eyes when he had squatted to talk with Annie in the workshop.

Marge King, who knew everything about everybody in Freeland, had told Elice that Cabot had earned a full academic scholarship to attend the University of Illinois. He'd been the school's starting quarterback for three years running. After graduation, he had become a uniformed Chicago street cop. He'd only been on the force two weeks when he sent for his fiancée, Maggie, and they were married in the Windy City. Five years later, he made detective. And he'd just celebrated his fifth year at that rank when his wife and daughter were killed in a car accident on the Dan Ryan Expressway.

Elice told herself God had allowed her to experience such full-hearted warmth toward the big stranger because Cabot had been away from his home town for such a long time and hadn't had a chance to rekindle old relationships. The Lord wanted her, she believed, to extend a hand of friendship to the sad-eyed, lonely man.

Cabot had left Freeland when Elice was still in junior high school and though they'd shopped in the same stores, attended the same schools, even gone to the same church, their paths had never crossed. Now that they had, Elice felt obligated, being the first person he'd made real contact with in town, to be a good Christian in every sense of the word and help him make the adjustment from the hustle and bustle of the big city to the slow-paced life of a farm community.

She decided that when he stopped by in the morning with the sign's deposit, she'd invite him to lunch or supper or maybe Sunday dinner. She giggled to herself as she thought, maybe all three; it's what any decent Christian would do, after all.

Elice pictured his broad shoulders and barrel chest. . .his narrow waist. . .the thick blond curls atop his handsome head. . .those piercing, dark-lashed, golden eyes, and the wide smile he seemed cautiously determined to keep all to himself. Her stomach fluttered and her heart pounded as she remembered the power of his handshake and the warmth of his big, calloused palm. Though she'd turned thirty-two on her last birthday, Elice had never experienced such a physical reaction to a man in her life. The feelings scared yet intrigued her, and she realized it would take all the strength she could muster to maintain her steady, independent lifestyle. "Lord," she said aloud, grinning, "I have a feeling I'm gonna be callin' on You a lot in the days to come."

❧

He'd run into Marge King at Nardi's grocery store, and now that Cabot had been told Elice Glasser's history, he knew why he'd been so attracted to the petite brunette. He'd always admired people who turned negatives into positives. And he'd never met an individual who'd turned a bigger minus into a plus better than Elice Glasser had.

According to Marge, everybody loved Elice and her kids. She'd become a legend of sorts, having survived what only a few others could have.

As the days passed, Cabot chopped enough wood to last six winters; he also thought of her. As he plowed the garden, he pictured her. While he mended fences, he heard her musical voice in his memory. No matter what task he undertook or how hard he worked at it, Cabot couldn't get her out of his head.

The top of her curly head barely reached his shoulder. From the looks of her, she couldn't weigh more than a hundred pounds, yet he'd seen her lift Annie, a hefty child of five or six, he guessed, as if she'd been light as a feather. Elice had grit. She was a marvelous blend of tender and tough, and he liked that. . .liked it a lot.

She moved like a fashion model, destroying the stereotype that only tall, willowy women carried themselves with grace and dignity. He liked that, too. When she smiled at Annie, her whole face got involved, from those dancing brown eyes to that adorable, dimpled grin. He'd never seen longer eyelashes on a human being. . .or creamier skin. And those freckles, sprinkled across the bridge of her nose, gave a little-girl quality to her womanly features. He liked that best of all.

Cabot dragged his shirtsleeve across his perspiring brow and leaned on the gate he'd just repaired. A movement in the pines at the north end of Foggy Bottom caught his attention. He'd seen a similar movement earlier and had dismissed it as a deer. Now, curiosity propelled him forward, and he ran toward it full throttle, big booted feet thudding across the grassy meadow, eyes riveted to the spot where he'd last seen it. When Cabot reached the row of evergreens, he found nothing but confusion and fear, for no animal had caused the branches to move in that lazy, bouncing way, nor redistributed the fallen pine needles, nor cast that eerie, ghost-like shadow.

The chill had been gnawing at him like a hungry rat for weeks, ever since Clancy's call. "Deitrich is out," his former partner had said. "They released him more than a week ago. Just thought you oughta know."

Cabot had shrugged off the warning. Surely Deitrich wouldn't carry out the threat he'd made that day in the courtroom: "I won't rest till I see you dead, cop," he'd seethed as the guards dragged him, handcuffed and kicking, toward the paddy wagon that would deliver him to Joliet Prison. Chuckling, Cabot wished he had a dollar for every bad guy who'd threatened him that way. Once they got out of jail, convicts were usually too busy reconnecting with friends and loved ones, trying to make a go of the straight life to be bothered with making good on stupid threats.

Still, Deitrich had been different from most. His eyes bore no trace of human compassion; his smile never quite reached those steely gray orbs. And when he'd promised to see Cabot dead, his words hung in the muggy air for what seemed like a full minute before being swallowed up by the footsteps, paper shuffling, and muffled whispers.

Cabot had used the last of his energy speeding toward the shadow. Thirsty, he headed slowly back to the farmhouse. Then, standing at the kitchen sink, he gulped three glasses of cold water, one right after the other. Deitrich's threat was gonging in his head when the phone rang. It startled him so badly that he splashed the contents of a fourth glass down the front of his plaid work shirt.

"I hope I'm not interrupting your. . . ."

It had been nearly two weeks since he'd heard that musical voice, yet he recognized it immediately. Suddenly, Deitrich, the note, and the shadow in the pines were forgotten. "Not at all," he said, unaware of the width of his smile. "In fact, I just quit for the day."

"I wanted to let you know your sign is finished," Elice said.

"Already?" He tugged the front of his shirt to keep the cold, wet material away from his skin. Cabot checked his watch. If he didn't fool around, he could be showered and changed in half an hour. "I can pick it up this evening, if that's convenient."

He wished he could retract what he'd just said. Toss some warmth into his voice. Replace the formal vocabulary with friendlier, chattier talk. Cabot heard Annie's voice in the background: "Can he have supper with us tonight? Please, Mommy?"

Her voice was muffled, and Cabot could almost see Elice standing there, one hand over the mouthpiece, the other holding the phone to her ear. "What is it with you and that Mr. Murray?" he heard her say.

"I like him," was the child's response. "He wants us to be his friends. I can tell."

When everything got loud again, he knew she'd uncovered the phone. She sighed deeply, then said, "If you're not busy, maybe you'd like to join us for supper tonight."

Nothing ventured, nothing lost, he thought. He considered telling her he already had plans. That he had a pot of stew on the stove. "What's on the menu?"

"Stuffed, roasted chicken. Mashed potatoes and gravy. Green beans," she recited, her voice a monotone. "Nothing fancy."

"I'll bring dessert. What time should I—"

"Six o'clock. And you don't need to bring anything. I just took an apple pie out of the oven."

He couldn't remember what she said after that, or what he'd said in response. Cabot could only concentrate on the fact that he was going to see her again.

The minute she said good-bye, he showered and shaved. He stood in his closet for fifteen minutes, trying to decide what to wear. He decided casual would send the best message, and chose blue jeans and a starched white shirt. But he'd polish his cowboy boots.

As he paced from the living room to the kitchen, Cabot glanced at his watch. Its hands seemed stuck at four thirty. He considered taking it off, thinking maybe time would pass more quickly if he couldn't see the second hand flick slowly, slowly around the dial.

He sat at his desk and shuffled papers and refused to look at his watch. Cabot balanced his checkbook, paid a few bills, started a letter to Clancy and his fiancée then wadded it up and tossed it in the trash when he noticed he'd doodled "Elice" in the margin. When the mantle clock signaled five thirty, his heart pounded.

She'd told him not to bring anything, but he wanted to stop at Nardi's and buy a bouquet of flowers, at least. Elice seemed to love them. Why else would she have surrounded the house with colorful blooms of every variety?

As he drove toward the neighborhood grocery store, "Nothing ventured, nothing lost" echoed in his mind. He drove straight past Nardi's. The smart thing to do, he told himself, is give the pretty lady her money, grab your sign, and tell them you forgot a previous engagement. And then get on out of there. . .nice and neat. . .and safe.

But he'd forgotten what a fool he'd always been for big, sad eyes. His weakness seemed to have grown stronger as he aged for as he stood in the middle of the Glassers' sunny kitchen and made his rehearsed announcement, Annie's lower lip jutted out. Elice's bright eyes dimmed with disappointment. He felt like a heel. So he agreed to stay. *But just this once*, he promised himself. *As soon as you clean up your plate, you'll hit the road.* Hate to eat and run, he'd say, smiling politely, but I have a million things to do. . . .

Why did they have to be such nice kids? And why did their mom have to be so pretty? She was a good cook, too; he couldn't remember when homemade apple pie had tasted as good. Cabot found himself clearing the table, then standing beside her, towel drying each dish she washed. It was as if someone had buried a giant magnet under the tidy little house and he had a huge core of ore in the middle of him, because he couldn't seem to pry himself from the place.

When the dishes were done, she handed him a glass of iced tea and invited him to join her on the covered back porch.

"How old are they?" he asked, nodding toward her children, playing in the yard.

"Emily is ten. Danny's nine. And Annie's five."

He'd guessed eleven, eight, and six. Satisfied that his guess had been fairly accurate, he grinned. "It's hard to believe you're their mom. You don't look old enough to have kids at all."

"That's the oldest trick in the book," she teased.

Both blond brows rose in sincere confusion. "Trick?"

"I'm thirty-two, to answer your unasked question. Until next week, that is." He grinned. "I don't believe it."

The phone rang, and she dashed inside to answer it. He focused on Annie, digging happily in the sandbox, and Emily and Danny, who dangled from the tire swing that hung from a giant oak. When she returned, he saw a worry frown on her face. Impulsively, Cabot took her hand. "Hey, what's the matter?" he said, concern edging his voice as she sat in the lawn chair beside him. "Looks like you've seen a ghost."

She took a deep breath and squared her shoulders. "Oh, it was nothing.

Just another one of those prank calls. It's been going on for a week or so. I wish parents would teach their kids that a telephone is not a toy."

Elice fidgeted, staring at their entwined hands. He let her go and leaned his elbows on his knees. "What does the caller say?"

"Nothing." The brave smile dimmed slightly. "I feel like I know the person, though. Isn't that strange?"

It wasn't the least bit strange. Plenty of ordinary folks had what cops referred to as "gut instinct," and he told her so.

"I wonder," she said, more to herself than to Cabot, "if the phone calls have anything to do with the doorbell—"

"Doorbell?"

She met his eyes briefly. But in that instant, he read her fear.

"Night before last, it rang in the middle of the night. When I looked outside, no one was there. That was the second time in two weeks—"

He was all cop now, his brows drawn together in concentration. "How many calls, altogether?"

"Ten. Fifteen, maybe." She shrugged helplessly.

"And two doorbell incidents in as many weeks?"

She nodded.

"When did all this weird stuff start?"

Her eyes locked with his as a grin formed on her lips. "You have too much hair to be Kojak, but you sure do sound like him."

Cabot blinked, stunned by her comment. Her smile was contagious. "Old habits die hard, I guess," he said. "Sorry. I was a cop—"

"In Chicago. I know," she finished.

He could tell by her tone that Freeland had been buzzing and that he'd been the main subject in the hive. He liked the way she looked when she smiled, and wanted to encourage more of it. "So tell me. . .how do you manage? It can't be easy, running a business, taking care of the house, raising three kids all by yourself. . . ."

She took a deep breath. "It was tough for a while there, but the Lord has been very good to us."

He wished he could accept what happened to Maggie and Lindy as well as Elice seemed to accept her lot in life. The accident had rendered him helpless. When the helplessness passed, bitterness set in. He'd been a devout Christian all his life, and his faith only got bigger with Maggie at his side. But without her. . . . How could he believe in a Being who would allow two generous, loving people to die needless, horrid deaths? Every day, Cabot saw the innocent victims of violent crime. Where was God when all that mayhem was going on? he wanted to know. He must have demanded an answer to that question a hundred times. But his question always went unanswered.

When he couldn't take any more death and suffering, he quit. Not just the police force, but God, too. Then he headed back to his birthplace, where life promised to be peaceful. And now Elice was being harassed by prank calls and a doorbell nut. Tranquil Freeland was beginning to sound an awful lot like Chicago, New York, L.A. *And what are You gonna do about it, God?* he wanted to know.

"Can I freshen your iced tea?" she asked, interrupting his reverie. "It's decaffeinated."

Cabot glanced at his empty glass. The sun had set and dusk surrounded them. It would be dark soon. He knew he should leave so she could tuck her kids in and get some much needed rest. But he couldn't break away from that powerful magnetic force that was distinctly Twin Acres. Maybe if he hung around, whoever was pestering her would get scared and cut it out. He wasn't exactly a midget, after all. He grinned, admitting the real reason he didn't want to leave was standing beside him, hand extended to accept his empty glass. "I'd love more iced tea."

Once she'd refilled his glass, Elice led him into the living room and turned on the ball game. "The Orioles are playing Toronto tonight," she said. "I've been looking forward to this all day." Elice grinned and handed him the TV's remote, then turned her attention to the kids' bedtime ritual.

Elice had it all, all right. She was a terrific mom, a talented artist, a successful businesswoman. In addition she was pretty, sweet, a great cook, and a baseball fan, too! He didn't think a more perfect woman existed. From where he sat in the overstuffed forest green chair, he could see all the way to the other end of the house. His eyes rested for a moment on the stove, its chromed parts shining in the dim light. She had waxed the floor recently—had missed a spot. So, he thought, smiling, she's not perfect after all.

Listening to the giggling and babbling of her kids, Cabot recalled what Marge had said about Elice: "No matter what anybody else said, she insisted something good and decent lived in Bobby Glasser."

Helen, the cashier at Nardi's, had been listening: "She'd give you the shirt off her back, even if it meant she'd have to go without."

The women shook their heads. "She deserved better than that low-life," Marge added.

"She'd trust a rattlesnake," the older woman put in. "I used to think she was addle-brained, she was so sweet."

Marge concluded: "They don't make 'em like Elice anymore."

They sure don't, Cabot thought, closing his eyes. Being in her house, surrounded by the laughter of children and the warm family atmosphere had forced him to reexamine his solitary lifestyle. At that moment, he didn't miss Lindy and Maggie in the same old hurting way. Rather, being at Twin Acres made him yearn for that companionable feeling that only a home filled with loved ones can bring.

"Resting your eyes?" Elice asked. She was standing in front of him, holding a mug of hot coffee. "It's safe," she said, putting it on the table beside him. "I drink only decaf."

He sat up and ran a hand through his curls, embarrassed that she'd caught him nearly napping. "I really ought to hit the road. I don't want to overstay my welcome."

She ignored his comment and sat cross-legged on the floor in front of a chair exactly like his. "This is my favorite time of day." Elice leaned back, her hair fanning across the cushion.

"Have you lived here long?" he asked.

Elice sat up. "Nearly all my life." She drew up her knees and hugged them to her chest, then rested her chin there. "My folks bought this house when I was in elementary school. I'm an only child, and Mama died when I was ten. Daddy died during my senior year of high school and left me the house and everything in it. Made me quite attractive to certain. . .gentlemen."

A strange, spiteful tone cut into her usually sweet voice. Then, meeting his eyes, she grinned. "I don't know what it is about you. I've told you more about myself tonight than I've told anyone in a lifetime."

Marge and Helen hadn't looked closely enough at her. They'd described a simple young woman, one so good and decent she didn't even recognize evil when she saw it. He knew better. She not only recognized it, she'd built a barricade to protect herself from it. He knew, because he'd built one exactly like it around his own life.

"I'm curious," she said.

"About what?"

"Why did you become a cop?"

He sipped his coffee. "Lone Ranger Syndrome," he said, smiling. "I believed I could clean up the mean streets. But by the time I grew up enough to see how foolish that ideology was, I was hooked." He took another sip of the coffee. "When Maggie and Lindy died, I had nothing to go home to. So I didn't. Work became my whole life." Cabot sighed.

"And what brought you home?"

He sat forward and firmly planted both big feet on the carpet. "Back to Freeland, you mean?"

Elice nodded.

He shrugged. "Guess I just got sick and tired of death and dying. I wanted to see things grow and live for a change." He sat back again and rested an ankle on a knee, and balanced his coffee cup there. "But enough about me. You said earlier that you never share your troubles with anyone. I just want you to know one thing. . . ." Cabot met her eyes and held the gaze for a moment before saying, "Ditto."

Elice didn't speak. Instead, she continued looking into his eyes.

The day he met her, he reminded himself he liked 'em tall and blond, blue-eyed and pretty. He'd been suspicious of Elice because nobody, he thought, could be that good. And she seemed too good to be true. He'd told himself she wasn't his type. But he'd been wrong. She was his type—exactly.

She stared into space for a long, silent moment, then put her mug on the table and extended her hand. "If you ever need a friend, Cabot, you have one, right here."

The moment their fingers entwined, the high wall he'd built around himself began to crumble. He felt it as surely as he'd have felt an earthquake. Somehow, this diminutive woman had shaken his whole world. And she'd done it with nothing more than a quiet offer of friendship.

Chapter 2

Guess I'd better hit the road." Cabot looked at the mantle clock, unable to believe it said eleven fifteen. "The sign looks great," he added, hoisting it from where she'd leaned it near the front door. "It's going to look terrific at the end of my drive."

Elice felt as though everything stopped as he stood there, looking at her.

"Supper was delicious. I'm glad Annie insisted. . . ."

"We'll do it again sometime," she promised.

"Soon, I hope."

Side by side, they walked to the end of her long, gravel drive, where he'd parked his Jeep. Carefully, he slid the sign into the back seat. "You have a fantastic family," he said, closing the door. "And you're quite a woman, you know that?"

"Cabot. . .stop. You're embarrassing me."

"The truth shouldn't embarrass you, Elice."

He'd never said her name before. Coming from him, it sounded musical, poetic. His face loomed nearer hers, but when his lips made contact, it was with her forehead. Elice pretended she wasn't disappointed.

She watched him climb into the front seat, realizing this tender but tough guy had touched a distant, forgotten chord inside her. He hadn't even left yet, and already she was trying to think of a way to ask him back without appearing overly eager.

Cabot crooked his forefinger, beckoning her near. She took a step closer to his car door, and he stuck his head out the window. "If you get any weird calls, or if the doorbell rings in the middle of the night, I want you to call me."

She hoped the darkness would hide her blush. "That's not necessary. I shouldn't have bothered you with that—"

"Yes. You should."

"Someone's got their calendar mixed up. They think it's Halloween or something. They'll get bored and stop soon, I'm sure."

"Maybe."

Elice realized he wasn't going to take no for an answer. "I can take care of myself." She said it with conviction and hoped he'd believe her. Because she could, usually.

"It's not a sign of weakness to ask for help, Elice."

Lord, she prayed, *if I had a dollar for every time I heard that since Bobby left,*

I'd have. . .a couple hundred dollars.

"So, you have a character flaw after all," he said.

"I beg your pardon?"

"You're stubborn."

She grinned and wondered how many dollars she could have stacked up for that one. "Perfection is boring."

He reached through the opened window and gently stroked her cheek. "I don't think you're the least bit boring." With that, he winked and backed out of her driveway.

She stood in the driveway, her fingertips resting on the spot he'd touched, until his tail lights were nothing more than tiny red dots in the darkness.

�

"I want Sugar Pops." Annie stood in the middle of the hallway, rubbing sleep from her eyes.

"Okay, sweetie." Elice hugged her tightly. "Wet or dry today?"

The child put a finger against her pursed lips and gave the question a moment's thought. "I want my milk in a glass and my cereal dry." Then, grinning impishly, she added, "I'm going to wake up Emi."

"Oh, no, you don't," Elice chided. "You let your sister sleep. Just because you're up with the birds is no reason the rest of the house has to chirp."

Annie followed Elice into the kitchen. "Mommy, do you think Mr. Murray is a nice man?"

Her heart thudded. "Why, yes. I do." *He's a very nice man,* she thought, smiling as she remembered his compliments.

"Then. . .could he be my daddy?"

Her heart pounded harder. "Mr. Murray is a friend. That's all."

"But he doesn't have any kids. He's very lonely. And we need a daddy."

Elice took the cereal box from the pantry shelf and poured golden nuggets into a blue plastic bowl. "You're right. He's lonely. Which is exactly why we're going to be his friends."

She could almost hear the gentle grate of his voice, the deep growl of his laughter. She pictured the shining waves of his hair and his wide, easy smile.

"What's to eat?" Danny asked, stifling a yawn, "I'm starving."

"Sugar Pops," Annie said around a mouthful.

"You're going to turn into a Sugar Pop," he observed. "That's all you ever eat." He turned to Elice. "Can I fry myself an egg, Mom?"

"If you clean up after yourself this time," she said, pouring milk into two plastic cups.

"We're going to be friends with Mr. Murray," Annie announced.

"Good," Danny said. "He's got the best fishing pond around for miles."

Emily plodded into the kitchen and stretched. "I had the most wonderful dream last night," she sighed dreamily. "Mr. Murray and you got married and we all went to live at Foggy Bottom. I had a big sunny room, and we each got our own pet, and Wally worked for us." She lifted her shoulders in a dainty shrug. "Imagine having a father who looks like a movie star."

"Get real," Danny said, jabbing the egg turner into the egg yolk. "He doesn't look like a movie star. He looks like a quarterback."

"A daddy!" Annie squealed. "Mr. Murray looks like a daddy!"

Emily and Danny exchanged "good grief" glances. "You say that about every man you see," Danny said, rolling his big brown eyes. "I don't want him to be my daddy."

Elice was about to tell Danny he had nothing to worry about, that Cabot Murray certainly didn't want to saddle himself with a frazzled widow and three active kids, when Wally knocked on the back screen door.

"You're early today, Walter," she said, smiling.

"The robins was fightin' up a storm outside my window," he explained, sidestepping into the kitchen, "an' woke me up. They sure can make a racket for such li'l things."

Wally tugged the pockets of his faded army fatigues and shuffled from one booted foot to the other. "What can I do for you today, Miz Glasser?" he asked, combing his fingers through thick, gray curls.

Wally had been helping her ever since Bobby left. He had no family and few friends. People feared him because of his unusual appearance and behavior. But she'd decided long ago to live by The Golden Rule. Where Wally was concerned, it had certainly paid off, for in the five years she'd known him, Elice came to think of him as a fourth child. He looked to her for guidance and comfort, attention and advice.

"I think we'll weed the vegetable garden today," Elice said.

A big, gap-toothed grin split his ruddy face. "I'll get started."

"Not before you have some breakfast, Walter." She pulled out a chair. "How about scrambled eggs and toast?"

"Thanks, Miz Glasser. That would be real nice." He took off his grimy Baltimore Orioles baseball cap. "Did I tell you about my new pet?"

Elice grimaced as he described his latest acquisition. He'd built a cage for it out of soda straws and string, exactly like the ones he'd built for his other "pets." He'd named this bug Happy and had gone to great pains to find the proper diet for his newest insect. Later, as they knelt in the garden, he told her about the job Mr. Olson had given him. "He says he'll give me an extra five dollars a week if I clean out the chicken coops every Saturday. I can buy lots of stuff for my pets with all that extra money."

Before she had a chance to congratulate Wally, Cabot's Jeep pulled into the driveway.

"Hey, Miz Glasser. There's that Murray feller. I heard 'bout him down at the store. They say he ain't very friendly. What do you suppose he's doin' here?"

Elice stood and waved at Cabot. "You can't always believe what you hear, Walter. People don't think Mr. Murray is a very nice man, but I happen to like him." Playfully, she jabbed him in the ribs. "He loves knock-knock jokes."

Wally met her eyes and grinned. "Really?"

The moment Cabot stepped out of the Jeep, her heart began beating double-time. The closer he got, the faster it beat. He seemed taller, broader, more hand-some, if that was possible, dressed in neatly creased jeans and a pale blue shirt.

"Forgot my pictures last night." He'd taken snapshots of his wife and daughter out of his wallet so she could see them better and, in their excitement about a wild pitch during the Orioles' game, forgot all about them.

"They're still on the end table," she said. Then, one hand on Wally's shoulder, she added, "Cabot Murray, I'd like you to meet Walter Hedges. Walter is my right-hand man."

Wally glanced at Elice, his blue eyes filled with pride, then grasped Cabot's extended hand. "She's the only one in town who calls me Walter. Everybody else just calls me Wally."

Elice tucked in one corner of her mouth and overlooked his comment. "Cabot just moved back to Freeland. He lived here when he was a boy."

"I used to live in York. Moved here after the war. Did you leave town to fight in the war?"

"Not exactly. I was a cop. In Chicago."

"Wow." Wally nodded, then held a finger to his temple. "Got shot in Korea. That's why I'm so dumb."

"Walter!" Elice scolded, taking his hand. "You're not dumb, and we all know it."

Beaming at her, he said softly, "Well, you're the only one who feels that way, Miz Glasser, but I sure am glad." For a moment, he stared at their hands, clasped in friendship. He seemed to have more to say. Instead, he dropped to his knees and resumed weeding.

Elice and Cabot chatted for a few more moments before she tapped Wally's shoulder. "You've worked hard enough for one day. Why don't you get out of the hot sun and feed your pets now." When he got to his feet, she added, "Supper is at six o'clock. We're having roast beef and all the trimmings tonight, and I'd like you to join us."

She'd done it with her usual gentleness, but even Wally knew he'd been dismissed. And he sensed that Cabot was the reason. Leaning close to Elice's ear, without taking his eyes from Cabot's, he whispered, "Watch out for this guy, Miz Glasser. I heard he's mean." With that, he hurried through the backyard and disappeared into the trees.

"Mean?" Cabot repeated, feigning hurt and shock. "Who? Me?"

"He thinks everybody is as honest as he is, so he believes everything he hears," she explained.

"But 'mean'? Where would he hear something like that?"

Elice shrugged and headed for the house. "Why don't you get your pictures while I pour us some lemonade."

He glanced around the yard. "Where are the kids?"

"Inside. Doing their chores."

As they sipped lemonade at her kitchen table, he could hear the sounds of earnest cleaning made by her children above the friendly chatter he shared with Elice. Suddenly, he said, "You sure look pretty today."

She'd dressed hurriedly in old cutoffs and a white tee shirt. Her hair was pulled back in a loose ponytail, and she hadn't put on any makeup. Elice nervously tucked a wisp of hair behind her ear. "Can I get you another ice cube?"

"Your lemonade is perfect," he said, "like everything else about you."

She hid her hands in her lap, one repeatedly squeezing the other, and flushed in response to his compliment.

Cabot touched her cheek. "You're really cute when you do that. Last time I saw a woman blush, it was my mother-in-law. . .and she was having a hot flash." He laughed heartily. "I didn't stick around to see how long it lasted, but I'd sure like to be here when yours fades." His thumb drew tiny circles on her jaw.

Elice didn't know which she liked more, the sound of his laughter or the feel of his warm skin against hers. She sensed something in this man, something good and decent. Elice hadn't been mindfully advertising for a relationship, but suddenly, she realized that Cabot had applied for the job. One thing was certain: It was wonderful to feel like a whole woman again.

"So your birthday is coming up, eh?"

Nodding, she wished she'd never given him that information.

"In that case, I'm going home to get some work done, and then I'm coming back here to take you out to dinner. I want to be the first to help you celebrate. What's your preference? Italian? French? Chinese?"

She swallowed. "It's sweet of you to ask," she began, "but I couldn't possibly—"

"Why not?"

He reminded her of Danny, sitting there, wide-eyed and expectant. She hated saying no—for herself as much as for him. But she couldn't go out with him. The only people who'd ever cared for the kids in her absence were Bobby's parents. And how could she ask them to baby-sit their son's children while she dated another man!

"Because I don't have a sitter."

He sighed. "Is that all? I thought you were going to say you don't like ex-cops or something." Cabot laughed. "The more the merrier, I always say."

"No. That's out of the question. I couldn't ask you to—"

"You're not asking. I am."

"But—"

"But nothing. Think of it as a 'Welcome Cabot Back to Freeland' celebration if it makes you feel better."

He sat in silence for a long time, his hazel eyes glowing. "I hate to eat alone. Especially when I'm celebrating." He squeezed her hand. "So, what do you say?"

"Say to what?" Danny asked, returning the kitchen trash can to its proper place under the sink.

"A potential ally!" Cabot said, slapping his muscular thigh. Then, focusing on the boy, he added, "I'm trying to talk your mother into letting me treat you guys to dinner. To celebrate her birthday. Help me convince her to say 'Yes.'"

Danny's dark eyes moved from his mother's face to the man's. "Well, there are plenty of things I'd rather do," he began, his voice sullen, "but Mom deserves a treat." He grinned at Elice. "I think we should do it."

"Should do what?" Emily asked her brother as she joined them in the kitchen.

"Mr. Murray wants to take us all out to dinner to celebrate Mom's birthday."

"Oh, Mr. Murray," Emily sighed and clasped her hands in front of her chest. "What a wonderful idea! Can we get all dressed up?"

"Dressed up for what?" Annie wanted to know, climbing onto Elice's lap.

"Mr. Murray's going to take us all out. . .a birthday party for Mom," Danny explained for the second time.

"If I didn't know better," Elice said, smiling, "I'd say this whole thing was a conspiracy."

"Does that mean yes?" Cabot leaned forward as he asked the question.

"Please?" Annie whined.

"It would be so romantic," Emily gushed.

Danny hesitated, then said, "It might be fun."

Elice shook her head and held up her hands in mock surrender. "Okay. All right. I give up. We'll go."

"You're terrific, Mom," Emily said, hugging her.

Laugh lines crinkled around his cinnamon-colored eyes. "Yeah, Mom. You're terrific."

"I suppose you're going to make me wear a tie," Danny complained, following Cabot to the front door.

"Not only that, but you're all going to stop calling me 'Mr. Murray,' too." He looked each child in the eye and grinned. "I want you to call me Cabot from now on. Got that?"

The children nodded and returned his smile.

Wally heard them coming and didn't want Elice to know he hadn't obeyed when she had told him to go home. He'd never deliberately displeased her and didn't want to start now, so he hid behind the big oak tree in her front yard.

"See you at six," Cabot called from the Jeep.

Four smiling faces stared out the picture window. Four hands waved good-bye. Four hearts beat a little faster. . .especially the biggest heart.

He'd been surprising them with visits nearly every day since the birthday outing. And every time he did, Cabot brought little treats for the children. He'd hear none of Elice's objections, insisting that since he had no children of his own to spoil, it was her duty to let him spoil hers. The girls squealed with delight when he pulled hair ribbons or colored pencils from his shirt pocket. And Danny, though he tried to portray an "I don't care" attitude, grinned when Cabot produced a fishing lure or a box of shiny aluminum hooks.

Cabot and the kindnesses he performed seemed to pop into her mind at the strangest moments. As she watered the Swedish ivy plant he'd given her for her birthday, she smiled.

"Mom! Come out here!" Danny's excited voice continued, "Hurry, Mom. You're not gonna believe this."

She dried her hands on the dish towel and went outside and found Danny beside her old yellow Vega, pointing at its tires. "What's goin' on, Mom?"

Elice couldn't believe her eyes. In all the years she'd lived in Freeland, nothing like this had ever happened. She tried to formulate an explanation that would satisfy her frightened son, but nothing made sense.

"Oh no," Emily said, hugging Elice's arm. "Did you run over a bunch of nails or something?"

Elice walked around the car, then bent down to inspect the tires. "I suppose that's possible," she said, feeling around for sharp objects. "But nothing seems to be sticking out."

When she heard his Jeep roar up the drive, she thought she knew how the early settlers felt when they heard the distant notes of the cavalry's bugle. It amazed her how he showed up, just when she needed him most, as if he could read her mind.

"Good morning," he called, smiling. "How's every—" His greeting and his grin died the moment he saw her tires. "What happened?"

"They were fine last night when I took the kids into Shrewsbury for ice cream," Elice said.

Cabot frowned at her, then at the car. He moved in for a closer look. "Just as I suspected," he said, running his fingers along the black rubber, "punctures."

The word frightened her. Broken glass, nails, anything else could have been chalked up to an accident. But punctures, with no telltale evidence, meant someone had deliberately done this. But who? And why?

She saw Cabot's eyes travel to each of her children's worried faces. "Probably some smart aleck teenager pulling a silly prank," he said, forcing a grin. "Say, kids, I've got something for you. On the front seat. Why don't you bring it here."

Immediately, their faces lit up and they ran toward his vehicle. "Strawberries!" they shouted from inside the Jeep. "A whole big box of them!"

"Why don't you take them inside and rinse them off," Elice suggested as they ran toward her and Cabot, "and I'll make some strawberry shortcake for dessert tonight."

The minute the kids were out of sight, she turned her back to the kitchen window, so they wouldn't be able to read the worried look on her face. "This makes no sense, Cabot."

"You'll drive yourself crazy trying to figure out why anybody would do a thing like this. The world is full of loonies and nuts." He pointed at the tires. "You don't need much more proof than that."

She took a deep breath and stood tall. "You're right. What I need to concentrate on right now is getting them replaced. My father always saved the most peculiar things; I seem to recall tires in the shed. I only hope they're the right size." Elice headed for the small, wooden building that sat at the far end of her property.

"Let me do it for you," he said, grabbing her elbow.

"I was hoping you'd say that," she teased. "And when you're finished, I'll fix you a nice big lunch."

"Can't think of anything I'd rather do."

It took him half an hour to get all four tires changed. Cabot was wiping his grimy hands on the old rag she kept in the shed as he joined her in the kitchen. "Where does this Wally character live?"

She frowned, immediately understanding his insinuation. "Walter didn't do it."

He raised his hands defensively. "I'm not accusing him." Cabot continued to run the rag over his hands. "I remember the way he looked at you when I was over here the other day. He's very. . .fond of you."

She lifted her chin in stubborn defiance. "Walter has been a good friend to us since Bobby died. I don't know what we would have done without him."

Cabot tucked the rag into his back pocket, then crossed both arms over his chest. "Is he here a lot?"

"Several times a week." She took a loaf of bread from its drawer.

"He doesn't have a job?"

Elice placed ten slices on the counter, then slapped a piece of bologna onto each. "He does odds and ends at the Olsons' in exchange for the use of a shack out back."

"How does he feed and clothe himself?"

"He gets a pension. 'Bandage money' he calls it." She paused in the spreading of mustard. "You're beginning to sound like Kojak again, and this time, I don't like it one bit."

He'd been hounding her like a spoiled child, and she'd talked to him as if that's exactly what he was. He looked so surprised at her tone that it made her grin.

"Look. What are we making such a big deal about?" she asked. "It's four flat tires, not the end of the world."

Cabot only stood there grinning.

"I know he seems strange," she admitted, filling five glasses with lemonade, "but Walter wouldn't hurt a fly." Laughing, she added, "I mean that literally. He's adopted several, you know."

His brows knitted.

"He collects bugs. Names them. Builds little cages for them and feeds them. If you could see how lovingly—"

"Uh. . .Elice," he said, "I mean no disrespect, but that's. . .that's just plain weird."

Sighing, she looked at the ceiling. *Please God, she prayed, help me make him understand.* "But don't you see?" she began. "If Walter could be kind to a bug, of all things, he couldn't possibly hurt me." She giggled again. "Why, I've baked him brownies—"

"Would he know it if he hurt you? I mean. . .could he have flattened the tires because they made a neat sound?"

The maternal frown returned to her brow as she shook her head. "If you could only hear how ridiculous you sound." Elice sighed again. "Look," she began, "Walter is slow, but he isn't stupid. Nor is he mean."

Cabot pocketed both hands. It was all well and good to believe in people, but Elice carried the idea to a dangerous extreme. "Now you look," he said, no longer caring if she heard the anger in his voice. "Wally may be abnormal by some standards, but he's still a man. And he's been bitten by the Green-Eyed Monster. It's as plain as the mustard on your spoon."

She glanced at the utensil, then dropped it noisily into the sink.

A warm light beamed from his hazel eyes as he took her hands in his. "He's not stupid. . .you've got that right." He took a step closer and drew her into a warm, protective hug. "He has excellent taste, too."

❧

Wally liked this spot under her kitchen window. The shrub was tall and thick, and shaded him from the blistering afternoon sun. It was a good place to hide. Sometimes, he'd sit there for hours, listening to her pretty voice, enjoying the happy banter of her kids. He'd spent many afternoons that way. It was almost as good as having the fun himself.

He'd accepted his limitations. Learned to live with what he'd become. Occasionally, though, in more lucid moments, he remembered what he'd been like before Korea. Before the head injury, when he'd had a fiancée and a good job and a nice apartment in York, Pennsylvania. Wally didn't dwell on those days, though, for the memory of them made a mean mood grow inside him. A stormy, scary feeling, so powerful that he sometimes worried he might do something. . .bad.

Dark clouds formed in his head as he sat quietly in the dirt behind the bush. *That big cop is trying to blame all the bad things on me,* he realized. *He's trying to get Miz Glasser to think I'm the one who's been doing scary things to her.*

She was the most important person in his life, followed only by her children, who called him Big Buddy Wally. At the Glassers' he'd always been treated like family. . .with respect. They were his only real friends. He liked Cabot just fine—as long as he didn't tamper with that—

But Wally had a dream: that someday, Elice would see him as a man, a real man.

❧

"It hurts, Mom," Danny complained.

In less than an hour, she'd unintentionally harmed all three of her children. First, she'd caught Emily's back in a zipper. Then, she'd pulled too hard making Annie's ponytail. And now she was choking her only son with a blue silk tie.

"You look terrific, Mom," Emily said, hugging her from behind.

Elice hadn't paid a lot of attention to her appearance these past few years. But lately, because she never knew when Cabot might drop by, Elice always tried to look her best. "Do you really think so?"

"Aw, Mom. You're gorgeous. And if he doesn't think so, he's a big dumb jerk." Danny was still having a bit of trouble accepting the fact that Cabot could never replace him in Elice's life. She knew he liked the big guy, yet the boy never resisted an opportunity to put him in his place which, in Danny's opinion, was anywhere but near his mother. Elice was about to scold Danny for his disrespectful remark when Annie's excited voice stopped her.

"He's here!" the little girl announced, jumping up and down.

Elice closed her eyes for a moment, tilted her face to the heavens, and took a deep breath. *I'm in Your hands,* she prayed silently. *Please don't let me say anything stupid, or trip, or spill anything in my lap.*

It didn't matter that she'd seen him nearly every day for the past month. Or that this hadn't been the first time they'd gone to dinner. Though they rarely had a moment alone, she had to admit that this dating stuff wasn't as easy as it had been with Bobby.

"Hello, there," Cabot said from his side of the screen door.

The gray suit accented his deep tan and made his pale eyes look more golden than ever.

"I wonder if you'd do me a favor," she said, holding the door open for him. "I'm afraid the authorities are going to prosecute me for child abuse if someone doesn't help Danny with his tie."

Cabot tried not to laugh at Danny's pinched expression. "I'd be honored," he said, his fingertips brushing her cheek. "Come here, Dan," he said. Turning the boy around, he worked from behind and taught him how to tie a perfect Windsor knot. "Guess since I'm responsible for your having to wear one of these things every week or so, the least I can do is teach you how to tie one."

Danny's eyes widened as he realized what he'd done all by himself. "Hey. That wasn't so hard. Look, Mom. I did it myself!"

She smiled. "You look very handsome. And very grown up."

Danny faced Cabot. "I polished my shoes again. Just like for Mom's birthday dinner—"

"Blinding!" Cabot said, shading his eyes from an imaginary glare.

He focused on Emily, then, who stood quietly near the door, her hands folded primly in front of her pale blue dress. She had the loveliest golden hair he'd ever seen, and he told her so. "One of these days, you're going to break a lot of hearts."

She blushed and grinned and stared at her white sandals.

"Hey! What about me?" Annie pouted.

Cabot made note of Annie's frilly lavender dress. "Darlin', you're as pretty as a baby duck."

She gave his comment a moment's thought. Then, hands on her hips and a frown on her face, she said, "Mommy, are baby ducks pretty?"

"All babies are pretty, sweetie."

Cabot pocketed his hands and took a quick inventory of Elice's attire. "You're going to break some hearts, too," he said softly. "Probably mine."

On the way to the restaurant, Annie leaned over the front seat and pointed. "Mommy, look. . .rides!"

"Tell you what," Cabot said. "You'd only get your pretty dress all dirty if we went to the carnival on the way home. So how about if we go tomorrow night?"

Three gasps echoed in the backseat.

"Cabot, you're spoiling us. We can't let you keep—"

"There's something you ought to know about me, pretty lady," he said. "Nobody lets me do anything." Reaching across the space between them, he grabbed her hand. "You'd better wear your sneakers and jeans tomorrow night, kids," he said over his shoulder, " 'cause I like the wild rides."

"That makes one of us," Elice muttered, giving in to his whim.

"You mean. . .that makes four of us," Danny countered.

❧

After he brought them home, Cabot sat on the back porch as Elice tucked the children in for the night. When she joined him, she carried two glasses of lemonade.

"I hope you don't mind my constant intrusion into your life," he said, once she'd settled into the chair beside him.

"Intrusion?" she asked. "I'd hardly call you an intrusion."

"What would you call me, then?"

Elice leaned her head against the back of the chair and squinted as she considered her answer. "I guess I'd have to say you're a very pleasant diversion."

"From what?"

"Everything."

"Hmmm," he said. And after a moment, he said it again. "Hmmm."

She liked the sound of his voice and the way he behaved with her children.

She liked his sense of humor and the easy smile that seemed reserved for the Glasser family alone. "Do you believe this sky?" she asked, hoping to change the subject. "And they were calling for a thunderstorm."

"Let's hope it's this starry tomorrow night."

She stole a quick peek at his profile. "The kids will be disappointed if it rains. We didn't get to go to the carnival last year."

"I'll be disappointed, too. How 'bout you?"

Again she took her time answering. "I'd hate for it to rain."

He sat forward, leaned his elbows on his knees, and clasped his hands. "Elice, I think you know me well enough by now to realize I'm not a man who minces words." He stared at an invisible spot between his polished cowboy boots. "I like you. I like you a lot." He cleared his throat, then met her eyes. "And I think you like me, too. At least," he said, grinning, "I sure hope you do."

Coughing, he shook his head. "So. . .would you mind very much if I. . .if I kissed you?"

She remembered how disappointed she'd been that first night, when he hadn't kissed her good-bye. Ever since then, she'd been hoping to find out if his lips would feel as warm and wonderful as she thought they might.

"We haven't known each other very long," he said slowly, "but then, we're not children anymore. We don't. . ."

He moved in the chair, wincing when it squeaked. "I don't want to do or say anything that would. . .I mean. . ." He combed his fingers through his hair. "What I'm trying to say is that I don't want you to get away. But I don't want to scare you away, either."

"You don't scare me," she said, quietly and without hesitation.

He stood and held his hand out to her. Immediately, she took it, and they walked the perimeter of her two-acre yard, discussing everything from politics to pelicans. Without warning, he put himself in her path. "Do you have any idea what you do to me?"

She looked up at him, the dim light of the quarter moon reflected in her dark eyes.

"It took a while, after Maggie, but eventually I got back on the old horse, so to speak. But those women I dated. . .They were. . ." He glanced around her head, as if the ending to his sentence hung on a tree branch or nestled in a bush. "You're more beautiful on the inside than you are on the outside. And believe me, that's saying a mouthful."

She laughed softly. "Do you enjoy embarrassing me?"

"No more than you enjoy making me repeat myself. The truth shouldn't embarrass you, Elice."

They walked a few more steps before he added, "It wasn't so long ago that I believed I'd never get close to a woman again." He cupped her chin, tilted her face until their eyes met. "Do you believe in love at first sight?"

Cabot watched her as he continued, "I guess I sound certifiable to you. I've known you only a couple of months and already I'm talking about love." His laughter floated across the dew-sparkled yard. "You want to hear something even funnier? I've never felt more sane. . .nor more certain of anything in my life."

He stopped talking then and stopped laughing. His face moved closer to hers. So near that it blurred before her eyes. Strong arms slipped around her, drawing her to him, so that not even the warm summer breeze could have passed between them. Moonlight and starlight and the glitter of dew glowed around them as they embraced, as if God Himself had blessed their embrace.

It had been a long time since anything had touched her so deeply. The heart whose only function, moments ago, had been to keep her alive, now pumped furiously with a whole new purpose. He kissed the tip of her nose, her forehead, her chin. "We'll take our time," he promised, hugging her tightly. "I have the rest of my life. How 'bout you?"

She felt herself relax in his arms and nodded against his chest.

"Is there any more lemonade?" he asked.

"I think I can squeeze one more glass from the pitcher."

Hand in hand, they headed back to the porch. "I've been thinking. . ."

"Uh-oh," she teased. "I smell trouble."

"I'll just ignore that," he said, giving her a sideways hug. "What I was thinking? How would you feel about redecorating my house?"

She stood still and stared up at him.

"Don't give me that 'why me' look. I've seen what you can do. Your place is wonderful. I want that kind of warmth where I live, too."

She lifted her chin and grinned. "I've always wanted to be a designer."

"Then you'll take the job?"

Giggling, she said, "Job. You make it sound like—"

"I couldn't let you do it for free."

" 'Nobody lets me do anything,' " she quoted.

He held up a hand to silence her. "Touché. But you already have enough to do. You can't do it for nothing."

"I wouldn't be doing it for nothing," she said. "I'd be doing it for a friend."

The simplicity of her statement silenced him, and wiped the silly grin from his face. "Friend?" Cabot put his hands on her shoulders and drew her near. "I'd like to be a whole lot more than just your friend, Elice."

Every cell in her body applauded his statement. Enough time had passed since she'd buried Bobby. It was time to begin again. And she felt certain that God would approve. She smiled slightly, imagining God, casually leaning on the Golden Gate, forming the Victory sign, like Winston Churchill.

"What's so funny?" he wanted to know.

"Nothing," she said and slipped her arms around him. "I'm just wondering if you're ever going to kiss me."

Brawny arms held her tightly as his lips covered hers. A quiet groan echoed deep in his chest. "Mmm-mmm," he growled. "You sure taste fine, pretty lady."

"Like lemonade?"

He nodded. "Mmmm. And I'm very thirsty."

Chapter 3

How could Cabot have known that Elice would wear what he had: jeans and boots and a red gingham shirt? They endured the gentle teasing of her kids, knowing full well that anyone who saw them at the carnival would assume their attire had been a calculated, if not silly, plan. Still, it pleased him that they thought so much alike.

While Elice and the children waited in the long line to ride the ferris wheel, Cabot got in another line to purchase tickets.

"Well, looky here," said a deep, gravelly voice. "If it ain't pretty little Leecie." A heavy hand rested on her shoulder. "Why, I haven't seen you in a coon's age."

Elice turned in time to see Jack Wilson ruffle Danny's hair. The boy grimaced and used his fingers to comb his dark locks back into place.

"Whatcha been up to, Leecie?" he asked, dark eyes canvasing her. "I'll say this for you. . .you look fine, mighty fine."

For as long as she'd known Jack Wilson, he'd managed the Hickory Ridge Cannery. She liked him. He'd always treated her with kindness and respect. As far as she could tell, he had two faults: He was a chain smoker, and he couldn't take "No" for an answer. For some time now he'd been after Elice to be his girl. But Jack wasn't her type. Not then and certainly not now that she'd met Cabot.

"It's good to see you, Jack. How have you been?"

"Missin' you," was his simple response.

She couldn't tell if he was winking flirtatiously or merely squinting around the cigarette smoke that encircled his head.

He focused on Emily. "Look at you. Aren't you gettin' pretty?" Jack whistled when he looked at Annie. "Looks like you've grown a foot taller since I last saw you."

Both girls smiled shyly, then pretended to be engrossed in watching the ride. Danny, on the other hand, glared at him openly.

"Here we go," Cabot sang, flapping the tickets. "I got us three books. That way I won't have to stand in that mob anymore and—"

Jack turned, looked from Cabot's shirt to Elice's, and back again. Understanding registered on his weathered, mustachioed face. "Well, Leecie. It's about time, I gotta say. Even if I'd rather you'd chosen me."

Cabot stuck out his hand in friendly greeting and pumped his former schoolmate's arm. "What have you been up to, you old dog?" he asked, grinning.

Jack shrugged. "Working hard. Hardly working. Depends on your point of view," he said, grinding the cigarette into the gravel as he grinned back. But the smile died when he said through clenched teeth, "I was real sorry to hear about Maggie."

Cabot swallowed. *So. It's still like that, is it?* He recalled now what he'd always disliked about Jack: Whatever Cabot had, Jack wanted. He'd wanted to be first string on their high school football team, but skipped practices and broke curfew so often the coach dropped him from the roster. And he'd wanted Cabot's red '67 Chevy; if Jack had worked twenty hours a week, as Cabot had, he could have had one just like it. All through high school, Jack considered Maggie his girl, even though she'd repeatedly said they were just friends.

When Cabot had picked up Maggie at Chicago's O'Hare Airport the day before their wedding, she told him how Jack had followed her to Baltimore's terminal, tearfully pleading for her to stay. He'd promised to be the best husband a woman ever had, if she'd only stay with him in Freeland. She'd heard him say, as she boarded the plane, that someday Cabot would pay for stealing her. For weeks, it bothered Maggie that Jack had been hurt, even if it had only been because of his stubborn refusal to accept facts. Eventually, Cabot convinced her that Jack would soon get over it. He'd marry and have kids, and forget that either of them existed.

But Jack had never married, and he certainly hadn't forgotten that Cabot and Maggie existed.

"Looks like you win again," Jack was saying.

Elice looked from Jack's face to Cabot's, her eyes wide and frightened as she tried to understand the reason for the boiling fury in Jack's eyes.

"Any competition between you and me has always been a figment of your imagination, old buddy, and you know it." Cabot's eyes glowed like hot coals, despite his cool words and careful smile.

Jack shrugged off Cabot's retort and draped a tanned arm across Elice's shoulders. "Well, all I can say is that this is one special lady, fella, and you'd better treat her right." He paused, his dark eyes glittering dangerously, as he lit another cigarette and inhaled deeply before adding, " 'Cause if something like what happened to Maggie should happen to little Leecie, here, you're going to answer to me."

Jack's dark eyes gleamed with quiet longing. Then, hugging Elice, he said, "You deserve to be happy. Just don't let yourself settle for less than the best." He dropped a brotherly kiss on her cheek and walked away.

"What was that all about?" she asked Cabot when Jack was out of earshot. She'd never seen him so angry.

"Don't pay any attention to him," Cabot said. "Jack's been a hothead all his life, and it's gotten him into trouble more times than I care to remember." Then, he noticed the somber, frightened faces of her kids and, to lighten the atmosphere, said, "How are we going to work this out, guys? There are five of us, and they allow only three to a seat up there." He gestured to the highest seat on the big ferris wheel.

"You ride with Mom," Danny said, jabbing his thumb against his chest, "and I'll take care of the girls."

"Now that's what I call an idea, Dan!"

The boy grinned and mimicked Cabot, planting his feet a shoulder's width apart and crossing his arms over his chest. "Know what I like about you?"

"What?" Cabot asked, grinning back.

"You never mess up my hair, and you don't call me 'Danny.' I'm too old for that kind of stuff." He peeked at his mother. "But you can still call me 'Danny,' Mom."

"I'm hurt, kiddo," Cabot said, poking his shoulder. "And here I thought you liked me 'cause I'm such a fun guy."

Danny snickered. "You're okay, I guess."

Cabot patted the boy's back. "And you're okay, too, Dan."

"What about me?" Annie wanted to know.

Cabot lifted her high into the air. "Darlin'," he said, kissing her cheek, "I adore you." Putting her back onto the ground, he gently touched Emily's cheek. "You, too, kiddo."

Cabot slipped an arm around Elice's waist, his lips fractions of an inch from her ear. "But just between you and me," he whispered conspiratorially, "I like you best."

❧

She plopped into a lawn chair and sighed. "They're finally tucked in." Grinning, she turned to him. "When was the last time you settled in after a long hard day. . . with a tall glass of grape Kool-Aid?"

One blond brow rose as he pursed his lips. "It's been a long time. In fact, it's been. . . . Why, I don't believe I've had grape Kool-Aid in my entire life."

They laughed as a roll of thunder sounded in the distance.

"Looks like we're finally going to get that storm they've been promising all week," she said.

"Wonder if it's gonna be an all-nighter?"

"I suppose if it rains tomorrow, the picnic at Foggy Bottom is off."

"My porch has a roof, too, you know."

She shrugged. "Then I guess it depends on which way the wind is blowing."

"It wouldn't dare rain on our barbecue."

As if on cue, the wind kicked up and the thunder echoed closer. A bolt of lightning cracked nearby, brightening the entire yard.

"That breeze feels good." She closed her eyes.

"Smells good, too."

"I like night rain. Puts me right to sleep." She sensed that the atmosphere had changed abruptly and opened her eyes to see why. The reason was simple: Cabot was on his knees, leaning on the arm of her lawn chair, his smiling face just inches from hers. Gently, he kissed her.

Chuckling, he said, "You don't have a romantic bone in your body. You're supposed to close your eyes when I do that."

She closed her eyes and puckered up. And she stayed that way until he'd given her another sweet kiss.

"You're perfect for me," he said.

Silence was her only response.

"What's going on in that pretty head of yours?"

"Well, you were right when you said we're not children, but. . . ."

He sat back on his heels, his gruff yet tender chuckle telling her he understood. "Moving a little too fast for you, am I?" He squeezed her hand. "I'm a man of my word," he said, adding, "We'll take our time." Cabot pulled her into a standing position and hugged her.

Her fingers combed through the soft blond waves that touched his shirt collar. "Thanks for understanding, Cabot."

"A kiss is just a kiss," he sang into her ear. And his next kiss came at the exact moment as a violent clap of thunder. She couldn't be sure which had caused the furious beating of her heart—nature in the sky or nature in her arms.

"Mommy," Annie whimpered, "I'm scared."

The spell shattered, they turned toward the sleepy, frightened child. Something deep inside him ached. Lindy had been afraid of thunder, too. In fact, one of his last fatherly functions had been to comfort her during a storm.

"I'll just rock her back to sleep," she said. "I won't be long."

"Let me. . . ." He carried Annie into the house. "How about we sit in Mommy's chair, and I'll sing you some lullabies."

Annie nestled her face in the crook of his neck and nodded. Less than an hour later, Elice took the sleeping child from his arms and carefully put her back into bed. When she returned, Cabot was fast asleep in the chair, his long legs outstretched and his big hands folded on his chest. Long pale lashes curved upward from his cheekbones as the peace of deep slumber softened the face that, during the daytime, tried so hard to appear cop-hard.

She couldn't wake him, only to send him into a raging thunderstorm. Instead, Elice draped a crisp, line-dried sheet over him and turned out the lights. After one last peek at his boyish position in her chair, she tiptoed into her room.

❧

He woke to the trilling of the phone, and spoke a groggy "Hello" into the mouthpiece.

Her husky voice said, "I hate to bother you, Cabot, but since you were a policeman, I thought. . ."

He'd never heard fear in her voice before. Not when she spoke about the phone calls. Not when she mentioned the doorbell business. Not even when her tires had been slashed. The fact that she'd lost her usual composure at all scared him. "I'll be right there," he promised.

Keep away from the cop, or you'll be sorry, said the note she handed him the moment he walked through the door. It had been typed on the same machine as the note he'd found on his kitchen table. He knew because the *e* was slightly askew. Whoever delivered it had even used the same blue stationery. Cabot tried to keep his hands still as he reread the note. "Where did you find this?"

"It was on the kitchen table when I got up this morning . . .right beside your note."

He remembered the message he'd scribbled on the back of an envelope, using a fat orange crayon to explain that when he woke and couldn't get back to sleep, he'd decided to leave. . .to protect her reputation. But he'd miss her, he wrote, and would call her first thing in the morning. Cabot's hand trembled with anger as he held the threatening message. If he hadn't been so concerned about public opinion, he'd have been there when this lunatic showed up. Perhaps he could have prevented this.

"Did you lock the door before you went to bed?" he asked, suddenly.

"Of course I did. Didn't you have to unlock it to get out?"

Yes. And he'd made sure to lock it behind him, too.

"What about the window?" Cabot walked toward the sink to inspect the lock on the window.

"Everything was fine. Normal. Until I found that." It may as well have been a rattlesnake coiled for attack, the way she looked at the note in his hand.

"Well, whoever wrote it got in through here," he said, indicating the black scuff mark on the kitchen counter. "He pried open the window and stepped right on in."

Her hands flew to her face. For a moment, she shuddered. But almost immediately, she squared her shoulders and got hold of herself. "I'm going to put on a pot of coffee."

"Good. I could use a cup." One hand on the back doorknob, he stuffed the note into his shirt pocket. "I'm going outside to have a look around."

Elice nodded and sent him a trembly smile.

He couldn't stand to see her this way. Cabot gave her a little hug. "You okay?"

Again she nodded. But this time, she made an effort to look brave and strong. He hesitated, not wanting to leave her alone, not even for the few minutes it would take to have a look around outside. He was under the kitchen window when he heard the kids' voices. Emily and Danny were debating between scrambled eggs and Cocoa Puffs, and Annie wanted Sugar Pops. He found several large footprints and one handprint pressed into the red clay dirt. There were smudges on the white window frame, and a few more on the pane itself.

The voice that lived inside him, offering warnings and advice, began to speak. It whispered three names, and Deitrich headed the list. But it wasn't like Deitrich to pull dumb pranks. Pull a trigger, yes, but taunt a widow with notes and phone calls? Deitrich was too savvy a crook for that. And Freeland was too small a town for a "strike now, pay later" guy like him.

Or was it? Maybe he was thinking precisely what Deitrich wanted him to think.

On second thought, Cabot decided to call the police from Foggy Bottom, to keep the kids from overhearing the report. Then he'd come back to Twin Acres and wait. For the first time in his life, he regretted Freeland's rural setting; the Baltimore County police were a full thirty minutes away.

Cabot went back inside and pulled Elice into the living room. "Get the kids out of here," he said. "Take 'em to York. Go shopping at the mall. See a movie. Whatever. There's no sense in getting them all riled up. This could be nothing." But he knew better. And so did she. He could see it in her wide, frightened eyes.

"All right, Cabot. I'll leave. But only if you promise not to keep anything from me. I don't need to be protected, you know. I'm a big girl. I've been on my own a long time. This is my house, after all, and I deserve to hear the truth."

She stood there, chin up and shoulders back, toughing it out, just as she'd toughed out other difficulties in her life. The difference, he decided, was that this time she didn't have to go it alone. Because he'd be there, right beside her, every step of the way.

Suddenly, it struck him that it was because of him that she was going through this whole ordeal in the first place. Spontaneously, he hugged her again. Only then did he notice the trembling in her body. "It'll be all right," he soothed. "I'll make it all right."

❧

He wandered alone through the quiet rooms of her house, waiting for the police to arrive. A place for everything, everything in its place, save a toy here or there to indicate the presence of children. Elice took as much care of her home as she did of her kids, her business, her gardens.

The black scuff on the counter throbbed its presence in the otherwise perfect room, just as the note on the table shouted its existence into the otherwise peaceful atmosphere. The more thought he gave the matter, the more certain he was that someone was trying to get at him through Elice.

And it was working, too. He'd never been more terrified in his life. Not in dark Chicago alleys, where armed robbers hid. Not in dank apartments, where drug dealers did their dirty business. The things that had been going on at Foggy Bottom were unnerving, unsettling. But he could handle that. He'd had his share of self-defense battles over the years and had managed to come through each alive and well.

This was different, completely different. The phone calls and mysterious nonpresence at her door had been tiny warnings. So had the tire incident. But to have entered her home while she and the children slept. . . The thought chilled Cabot to the bone. Whoever had been terrorizing her had stopped playing games; he was serious now.

Cabot ached, deep inside. He'd almost given up hope of ever living a normal life again. . .until Elice. He'd resigned himself to being alone, without children—until her kids. They were his now, in his heart, anyway. He wondered what he'd done to anger God this time. Why else would this be happening now, when he'd come so close to happiness again?

Once the officers arrived, explaining the situation took very little time, much to his surprise. By his recollection, it seemed to take witnesses hours to tell even the simplest stories. Being on the other end of the investigation, he realized that time moves differently when you're the victim.

As the uniformed officers wrote down the facts as Cabot knew them, he realized how vague and useless the information would be. He knew long before they admitted it aloud that the cops were helpless and frustrated. Without concrete evidence, their hands were tied. They left, saying they'd cruise the area several times a day. More than that, they couldn't promise.

Well then, Cabot decided, *I'll just have to pick up the slack.* He'd find the evidence the police needed. He wouldn't rest until he had enough proof to allow them to make an arrest that would stick. Because he wanted whoever was doing this to Elice locked up for a long, long time.

※

"New locks?" Elice repeated. "What good will that do? He didn't even come in through the door!"

Through some miracle he didn't quite understand—or feel he deserved—she'd agreed to come with him to Foggy Bottom. "I can use the time to get started on this redecorating project," she said, stacking the cans of paint and boxes of brushes and rollers she'd brought from her workshop in a corner of Cabot's kitchen.

"I'll pay for the locks. It's just a precaution."

"It's not the money, and you know it. You've got it into your head that this is your fault. And it isn't. Locks can't change that fact."

But he was to blame. If he'd listened to his gut, he'd never become involved with her in the first place. He should have known that threats and violence would follow him wherever he went. And it was killing him that he'd brought it right into her house.

Elice sighed. "You're the most exasperating man, Cabot Murray. Do you honestly think you were such a great cop that every criminal you put behind bars spends every waking moment thinking up ways to get even with you?"

Great cop? he thought. A deep furrow formed on his forehead and his mouth became a taut line. "This has nothing to do with my ego, Elice," he snapped. "I don't need an anti-machismo speech from you right now."

Her left brow lifted. "You're a gentleman, so naturally, you'll listen to anything I have to say." She took a step closer, put her hands on her hips, and narrowed her eyes. "And I say you're not responsible for what's been happening."

Cabot shook his head. "You're the one who's exasperating," he said. "You think you have a direct connection to heaven and God tells you how things are. Well, you're naive. That's what you are."

It was a low blow, and he knew it. But Cabot had to make her realize that their relationship had been a mistake. That it had to end—now. Before the note-delivering lunatic got it into his head to do something really dangerous, something violent.

She took a deep breath and another step closer. "Did the police have anything else to say? Or was 'Get new locks' all the professional advice they had to offer?"

He couldn't believe her. She had more spunk than most men he knew. Somehow, she'd gotten it into her head that everything could be rationalized and explained with one Bible verse or another. What would it take to wise her up. . . death? The moment the word entered his head, his heart thudded wildly in his chest. The very idea terrified him. He looked at her, standing there, not two feet from him, hands on her hips and fire in her eyes. He wanted to take her in his arms and tell her how sorry he was. But he didn't dare. "Do you have any idea how gorgeous you are when you're all fired up like that?" he said. "For two cents, I'd kiss the living daylights out of you, right where you stand."

Her mouth dropped open as her eyes widened. Elice reached into her jeans pocket, withdrew two pennies, and tossed them at his feet. "Put your money where your mouth is, Mr. Murray," she said, grinning.

He couldn't help himself. Cabot laughed, soft and slow at first. "I'm sorry," he said, wrapping her in his arms. "I didn't mean to bark at you. It's just that. . ." He kissed the top of her head. "You don't seem to realize how serious this is. There's a crazy person out there with a fantasy to fulfill. You and the kids could be in real danger."

"What do you take me for," she fumed, pulling out of his embrace, "some kind of addle-brained twit? I understand the seriousness of this situation. What I don't understand is why you blame yourself."

Cabot released a long, whispering sigh, closed his eyes, and shook his head. "I feel like a tape recorder. We went all through this earlier." He faced her, his feet planted wide on the kitchen's shining white linoleum. "I heard a lot of threats while I was on the force. It taught me a thing or two, y'know?" He began counting on his fingers: "Some very peculiar things have been going on at Twin Acres. You're getting weird phone calls, midnight visitors who aren't there, tire slashings, a note with a message very much like mine, yet you can't add two and two."

Elice matched his defiant stare. "I did very well in math, thank you, despite being a girl, and I feel I must point out that you're mixing your variables. What appears to be two and two may very well be nothing of the kind."

The argument was pointless. And nothing annoyed Cabot more than useless conversation. "I love you! I want you safe and happy. Can't you get that through your thick head?" It was neither the time nor the place for such a proclamation, yet Cabot felt relieved to have finally spoken the truth.

She tried to hide her grin behind a stern frown. "Oh, stop looking so red-faced," she said. "I never said I didn't understand your motives." She hugged him tightly and looked up into his face. "But that doesn't mean you're right. And, by the way," she added, "I love you, too."

Cabot met her eyes. "You will put new locks on the doors. On the windows, too."

"I won't."

"It's either that, or we'll just have to get married right away, so I can keep an eye on you twenty-four hours a day."

She tucked in one corner of her mouth. "Don't you threaten me, Cabot Murray." Standing on tiptoe, she planted a quick kiss on his chin. "I hope you've learned something here this morning."

For as long as he'd known her, she'd never been one to keep her opinions to herself. Cabot waited, knowing she'd soon explain herself. He didn't have to wait long.

"Next time you have an attack of Swollen Ego," she said with a smile and a wink, "I want you to remember that the world revolves around no one. Not even someone who kisses as great as you do."

He was about to respond to her blatant invitation when Annie ran into the room. "Mommy, Grandma is on the phone."

"I never even heard the phone ring," he said, stunned.

"I unplugged the one in here so I could paint over the jack," she explained, connecting the wires so that she could talk to her mother-in-law.

"Mrs. Glasser," she said, "how are you?"

"I'm fine, honey. Tried to call last night, but nobody answered. Marge told me you'd be at Foggy Bottom today. Gave me the number. I hear you're helping Cabot redecorate. How nice. . . ."

Why did she feel guilty? She wasn't married to Mrs. Glasser's son any longer. "We. . .uh. . ." Elice didn't know what to tell Bobby's mother. "We were out."

Mrs. Glasser laughed. "So Annie said."

Elice hid her face behind her free hand. If Annie had filled Mrs. Glasser in, there was no telling what the woman had heard.

"She adores him, Elice," her mother-in-law was saying. "He sounds too good to be true." Snickering, she added, "Tall, handsome, funny. . . Why have you been keeping him a secret?"

"I'm not. It's just. . .I've been awfully busy. . . ."

"You'd better grab him before somebody else does, honey. I've seen him in town." Mrs. Glasser whistled. "If I weren't a happily married woman, I'd snap him up myself."

Elice stared into the earpiece, thinking she'd either gone crazy or had a bad connection. Had Bobby's mother actually said that?

"You know, Bob and I were beginning to worry about you, Elice. You spend entirely too much time alone with those kids. It's not healthy. . .for them or for you. You need some adult companionship. Of the male variety, I might add. Which reminds me. From what Annie says, you and that wonderful man never spend any time alone. Tell me it isn't true."

"Well, it's a little hard to find sitters and—"

"Don't you say another word, Elice. I know Bob and I are getting up in years, but those grandchildren of ours are about the best-behaved kids in the state. I think we can handle them for a couple of hours now and then. Having children under foot all the time isn't my idea of romantic."

Romantic? Elice shook her head. She must have inhaled too many paint fumes.

"I'll tell you what, honey. It's been a long time since Bob and I have taken the kids anywhere. We were planning a trip to Ocean City for the week. Won't you let them come with us? We'll come pick them up this evening."

Elice chewed her lower lip. That would certainly solve a lot of problems. For one, the kids would be out of the house. She couldn't believe the melodramatic thought that followed: Out of danger. "I don't suppose Annie mentioned his name, did she?"

"Didn't have to. Every woman in Freeland is whispering about him. It isn't every day a man that handsome rides into town, you know." When Mrs. Glasser laughed like that, it was hard to believe she was in her late sixties. "I can't wait to meet him, though," she added. "What time would you like Bob and me to meet you at your place?"

Elice glanced at her watch. "In an hour or so?"

"It's time you put Bobby behind you. He was my only son, but God knows you deserved better. If being with Cabot makes you happy, Bob and I are all for it."

He was standing there, grinning at her when she hung up. "I take it the in-laws approve of me?"

She pshawed him. "That's only because they don't know you the way I do."

"But they're taking the kids away for a week?"

She ignored his mischievous wink. "I have to get home and pack their things."

He nodded, his grin gone now. "Couldn't have asked for better timing."

"I told you the Lord would take care of things."

He rolled his eyes. "If He was so good at taking care of things, there wouldn't be so many things to take care of, now would there?"

She hated it when he talked that way. Elice had been praying, ever since the relationship began to look like it might become more than a friendship, that the Lord would show Cabot the way back to Him. So far, it didn't look like that was happening. And if he didn't start exhibiting some signs of Christianity soon, she was going to be faced with some very difficult decisions, because Elice had vowed at Bobby's graveside never to involve herself with a non-believer again.

Example. That's what he needs, she decided. She'd just have to set such a good example that he'd have no choice but to see that her way. . .God's way. . .was the only way. She grinned. "Don't get me started," she warned, wagging her forefinger under his nose. "Don't even think about getting me started."

Chapter 4

Elice had just washed the last dish when the phone rang.

"Hi, pretty lady," Cabot said.

She considered saying, "Hi, Mr. Wonderful." "Hi, yourself," she said instead.

"Wally wears black-soled work boots, doesn't he?"

Frowning, Elice said, "I never really paid much attention to the bottoms of his shoes. What a strange question."

Cabot chuckled. "Not when you consider that the scuff mark on your counter was put there by a black-soled boot."

She sighed. "Cabot," she said, her voice a warning, "I told you, Walter didn't have anything to do with what happened here the—"

"You're wearing out my patience. There are footprints under your kitchen window, size twelves. I checked. Wally wears size twelve. The impressions have cleats in them . . .his boots have cleats."

"Well, if you know so much, why bother asking me what kind of shoes he wears!" she snapped. Elice ran a trembling hand through her hair. Walter? Under the kitchen window? She couldn't make herself believe he'd been there at all, let alone believe he could have been responsible for the frightening things that had been happening at Twin Acres lately.

It was Cabot's turn to sigh. "I only called to tell you I might be a little late picking you up for dinner, because I'm going to pay Wally a little visit."

"You're actually going to grill that poor man simply because he wears work boots. . .like almost every man in Freeland?"

"I'm not going to grill him because of his shoes," he said, impatience tingeing his voice. "I'm not going to 'grill' him at all." Cabot sighed again. "Someone broke into your house and, without more evidence, the police can't find out who it was. I'm going to get it for them so they can make an arrest that'll stick."

"This is ridiculous."

"You're ridiculous!" The moment the words were out of his mouth, he regretted them.

"Walter isn't your bad guy, Cabot. I'll bet he doesn't even know how to type. Besides, he adores you, so that blows your 'get even with Cabot' theory right out of the water."

He recalled the argument they'd had last night after they'd left his house to pack the kids' suitcases. The two of them had greeted Mr. and Mrs. Glasser, gave the ocean-bound party hearty good-bye hugs, and warned them not to get too much sun. The house had seemed so quiet and empty after they had left that he'd suggested a drive to Shrewsbury. But not even her favorite—soft ice cream with chocolate sprinkles—brightened Elice's mood. "Stop looking so glum," he'd teased; "they'll only be gone a week." And she'd said, "If I look glum, it's your fault, not the kids', because you've turned your back on God."

The argument had lasted less than a minute, but the stony silence had hung in the air all night. When he'd tried to kiss her good-bye, she offered her cheek. "I love you more than I ever dreamed I could love any man," she'd said softly, "but I love the Lord more. I want to share everything with you, and that includes my faith. If I can't. . ."

He'd taken her in his arms then and explained that old habits die hard; he'd only behaved badly because he felt responsible that his past had put her in danger. As he saw it, Wally was the prime suspect in his "get Cabot" theory. "If you had even a glimmer of faith living inside of you," she'd scolded, "you couldn't say that. You wouldn't even be able to think it."

She'd been praying about it, quite a lot, she'd told him; if Wally had had anything to do with the scary stuff that had been occurring at Foggy Bottom and Twin Acres, she'd know because, as she put it, "The Lord would have shown me the truth."

"Well, what do you have to say about that?" Elice asked.

He'd been so lost in the remembrance of it all that he'd forgotten Elice was on the phone.

"What do I have to say about what?"

"About your 'get Cabot' theory."

"I don't have any answers, Elice. Just a lot of questions."

"Stupid questions, if you ask me."

"Well, I didn't ask you." He didn't know how much more of this righteous indignation he could stand. He'd always been a law-abiding citizen. He paid his taxes, in full and on time, donated a hefty chunk of change to various charities every year, tried to do unto others, and all that. Who did she think she was, anyway, to insinuate he wasn't good enough for her, simply because he didn't believe in God in the same way she did?

"I wish you wouldn't go to Walter's. You'll confuse him. At the very least, you'll hurt his feelings if you tell him what you suspect."

"So now you're an expert in psychology and police work."

She cleared her throat, then said, "You needn't concern yourself with being late, Cabot. I'd rather spend the evening alone. I have a lot of thinking to do."

She didn't want to see him, and that broke his heart. But he was angry, too. No one had ever judged him before. He believed she was doing exactly that. And he didn't like it. Not one bit. "You mean praying, don't you?" His voice dripped with sarcasm. "You going to ask God if He approves of me?"

Silence.

"Well? Are you?"

"Yes, I'm going to pray about you. But mostly, I'm going to pray for you."

He laughed. "I don't need your prayers, Elice. Besides, what makes you think the Big Guy would go to bat for me? He's never done it before. I know, because I've asked. On my feet, on my hands and knees, flat on my face. . . ."

"You're so lost, you're not even aware of it."

One. . .five. . .ten seconds ticked by before he said, "I'm sorry if I offended you. I wouldn't hurt you for the world. You know that, don't you?"

She hesitated a moment, then said, "I know you wouldn't consciously hurt me."

"But I'm not a Bible-reading, church-going, blind follower, like you, so I'm hurting you subconsciously, right?"

"You're hurting yourself far more than you're hurting me. If only you'd—"

"Elice, can't we just agree to disagree on this subject?" he interrupted. "I miss you. I want to see that gorgeous face of yours and spend an entire, uninterrupted evening alone with you."

She hesitated before saying, "I don't think it's a very good idea to—"

That does it! he decided. "All right, then," he said, with all the patience he could muster. "Maybe you're right. Maybe it's best we stop seeing each other, for everybody's sake."

He heard her sharp intake of air.

"But I want you to know that I'm here for you, if you ever need me." Cabot wanted her to say she couldn't live without him, hoped she'd ask him to hurry right over, because she missed him, too, and was waiting for an invitation to spend a quiet evening eating popcorn and watching old black-and-white movies on TV. But, after a full minute of silence, he quietly hung up.

Cabot sat in his easy chair and stared at the phone for a long time. He'd tried everything else, and in his moment of desperation, he tried it her way: "Lord," he prayed aloud, "make her call. Please let her call."

He waited. Five minutes passed, then ten. An hour later, he was still staring at the soundless phone. The longer he stared at it, the harder it got to swallow the sob aching in his throat. "You big jerk," he said aloud, swiping angrily at his tears, "see what you get for not sticking to your motto?"

Cabot gave the still silent phone one last sad glance. Then he got to his feet. He'd talk to Wally, no matter what she said. He'd poke around and dig around and search until he dug up the evidence the police needed to put away the nut who was harassing her. "At least she'll have the good deed to remember you by," he said under his breath, slamming the kitchen door behind him.

※

It didn't matter whether or not he'd done the right thing in ending their relationship. Cabot missed her terribly, missed those kids, too. Eventually, he knew, he'd adjust to their absence. But, like getting used to life without Maggie and Lindy, it would take time, a whole lot of it.

And he spent most of that time on the farm. Foggy Bottom was finally beginning to look like the place where he'd grown up. Orderly precision, from the fences to the barn doors, made it clear to anyone who passed by that someone cared about the place again.

When he wasn't digging or painting or hammering, Cabot was out hunting down clues. One by one, he flipped through the snapshots he'd taken that day of the area around Elice's kitchen window, comparing the black streak on her counter to the one he'd found on Wally's kitchen floor.

Wally had a beat-up portable typewriter, and Cabot rolled a sheet of paper into it and used his forefingers to type "Every good boy does fine." As he'd expected, each *e* tilted slightly to the left, just like the ones in the ominous notes he and Elice had received. And a stack of that same blue paper sat on the table beside the typewriter.

Cabot liked Wally. He hadn't wanted to believe the big guy had been involved in any way with the goings-on at Foggy Bottom and Twin Acres. But every shred of evidence incriminated the slow-witted ex-soldier.

"Where'd you get this old thing?" Cabot asked him.

Wally scratched his head. "Found it in the shed. Mr. Olson said if I cleaned it up and bought a new ribbon, I could have it."

Cabot struck the *e* key again, a small part of him hoping that by some small miracle, it would stand up straight this time. "This is where you keep the type-writer? All the time?"

Wally nodded. " 'Cept for when Mr. Jack borrows it."

He'd been staring at the sentence he'd typed, but at Wally's statement, Cabot's hazel eyes fused to the man's blue ones. "Except for when Jack borrows it?" he repeated.

Wally's blond brows rose. "He don't have a typewriter," Wally explained, "so he borrows mine to write letters to the editor." Smiling, he added, "Did you see the one he wrote in yesterday's paper? About truck drivers speeding up and down New Freedom Road?"

Cabot frowned. "No. I'm afraid I missed it."

"I got it right here," he said. "Want to read it?"

He shook his head. "Thanks anyway; maybe I'll look it up when I get home." Cabot stared hard at Wally. He'd learned to depend on his gut instinct. It had saved his life, and the lives of a partner or two, while working Chicago's streets. Right now, that instinct was telling him that Wally couldn't do a mean thing if his life depended on it. Still, maybe he knew something that would point Cabot in the right direction.

He sat across from him at the table and took a sip of the iced cola Wally had poured for him when he'd arrived. "When was the first time Jack borrowed your typewriter?"

Wally squinted. " 'Bout two months ago, I spoze."

Cabot nodded and absently drew a smiley face in the condensation that had formed on his glass. "How many times has he used it?"

" 'Bout three times, I guess."

"Only three?"

Wally nodded. "Kept it about a week each time. Gave me five bucks when he brought it back, too," he added, grinning. "I used the money for cage supplies. For my pets. Say! Do you want to see my pets?"

Cabot chuckled. "Why not?"

It took a full half-hour for Wally to introduce Cabot to each insect, describe its species and diet, and detail the building of its cage. Cabot found it difficult to pay attention. He was too busy thinking about Jack; about how he'd borrowed Wally's typewriter at almost exactly the same times the blue notes were delivered to Foggy Bottom and Twin Acres. Coincidence? Cabot didn't think so.

As Wally rambled on about his so-called pets, Cabot complimented his attention to detail. "You could probably make a lot of money building dollhouse furniture," he admitted, "as good as you are at building things on a small scale. There are thousands of dollhouse enthusiasts who buy tiny furniture. You could advertise in antiques magazines."

Wally's grin nearly split his face in two. "You really think so? That's a great idea! Will you help me get started?"

Cabot patted his new buddy's back. "Sure. Sure." He sat at the table again and finished his soda. "Tell me something, Wally."

Wally met his eyes.

"How do you feel about Elice?"

Immediately, his cheeks flushed, and he stared at his hands folded quietly in his lap. "She's way too pretty and way too smart for somebody like me." He looked back at Cabot. "Besides," he said, grinning crookedly, "she's in love with you."

Cabot shifted uncomfortably in his chair, remembering their last conversation. "I'm not so sure about that."

Wally nodded. "I am. She said so. I heard her myself."

Leaning forward, he asked, "She did? When?"

The ruddy cheeks reddened again. "When I was. . ." His eyes darted from his fingertips to Cabot's face and back again. "She's got a voice like an angel. Did you know that?"

Cabot smiled.

"She sings while she washes dishes and sometimes when she's making supper. Makes me feel good inside, hearing her pretty voice."

"You heard her from your hiding place under her window?"

Wally's eyes widened. "How did you know?"

Cabot shrugged. "I was a cop, remember?"

Fear widened Wally's eyes even more. "You won't tell her, will you? If she ever found out, she might think I'm weird or something, and quit being my friend."

Cabot stopped smiling. "I won't tell her. But you're going to stop hiding in her bushes. It's against the law, you know."

The blond brows rose again. "Honest? I promise, Cabot. I'll never do it again."

He leaned both elbows on the table. "Good. Now I have something to tell you, Wally, and it's got to stay between you and me. If you repeat this to anyone, Elice's life could be in danger. Will you help me protect her?"

The brows nearly met in the center of Wally's forehead. "Protect her from what?"

It took all of fifteen minutes to fill Wally in on what had been going on at Foggy Bottom and Twin Acres. Cabot didn't leave out a single detail. He discovered that if he spoke slowly, and enunciated well, Wally comprehended everything he said. When he was finished, Cabot held out his hand. "So we have a deal? You'll help me protect Elice and the kids?"

Wally stared at Cabot's big hand, then pumped his arm up and down. "Anything you say, Cabot." He paused, still squeezing the ex-cop's hand. "Say. . . are we friends now?"

Cabot placed his free hand on Wally's shoulder and grinned. "You bet we are."

❧

It was hard to believe that so many days had passed. It had taken every ounce of strength that Elice could muster to keep from picking up the phone and dialing his number. But she'd made the right decision. She was sure of it. As long as she continued to pray hard and long, she'd be able to stick to it.

On the morning the Glassers were to return home from the beach, they called to say they'd booked their condo for an additional week. Elice wanted to protest. "Bring them home right this minute!" she wanted to say, "because I miss them desperately." But Mrs. Glasser put the children on the phone, one at a time, and the joy in their voices was so apparent that she couldn't bear to deny them another week of fun in the sun.

Still, without the children around, Elice had too much time on her hands. With no one to cook for or clean up after, she found herself wandering aimlessly around the house, searching for something to do. She'd completed every sign ahead of schedule and had even finished several that weren't due for weeks. The house sparkled from top to bottom. And a weed didn't dare show itself in the vegetable or flower gardens, for fear she'd be there to snatch it from the ground the moment she got a glimpse of green.

She baked bread, put up thirty quarts of green beans and tomatoes, and made a dozen peach pies and froze them. But, regardless of how busy she kept herself, her mind refused to focus on the task at hand. It seemed to want to think of one thing, and one thing only—Cabot.

She missed his laughing eyes, his merry chuckle, the way he could turn the most mundane moment into a rip-roaring good time. He'd taught Danny to string a fishing line, showed Annie how to tie her sneakers, helped Emily learn to use the computerized card catalog at the library, and had made Elice realize she didn't want to live out the rest of her life alone, after all.

She'd grown accustomed to seeing his big work boots beside the back door, his denim jacket on the hall tree, his broad-shouldered body in her easy chair. She'd gotten used to having him help with the supper dishes, wearing her frilly white apron, his sleeves rolled up to the elbow. She'd even grown to like the way he stacked spoons in the silverware drawer, one on top of the other. She'd even started to think of his phone calls first thing in the morning and last thing every night as part of her daily routine. No amount of hard work could erase the loneliness from her heart. Not even prayer dulled the nonstop ache of his absence.

In six days, she told herself, the kids would be home. God created the entire universe in that amount of time; certainly she could manage to get along—alone—for just six more days. She'd gotten used to life without Bobby in time, and she'd get used to being without Cabot, too. *You just have to keep reminding yourself he's not a believer,* she told herself, *and the Lord will help you get through this thing.*

Elice's inner turmoil became almost too predictable: *He's not a believer, but his patience and sensitivity reminds me of Jesus'.*

He says he's angry with God, but he says just what the children need to hear, precisely when they need to hear it.

He refuses to admit he needs the Lord in his life, but he has no problem admitting how much he wants you in it.

The Lord will get you through this, she told herself again, and again, and again.

⚹

Cabot hadn't had the dream in ages. But the night of their breakup, it came back, like an unwelcome ghost, to haunt him. To Cabot, it was a lot like fast-forwarding and rewinding the scariest part of a horror movie:

He'd heard the call on his police radio and recognized the dispatcher's staccato listing of license plate numbers. He was both thankful and surprised that his car could actually go the hundred and twenty miles an hour promised by the speedometer as he sped from the station to the accident scene. "Please, God," he prayed as he raced through the streets, "let it be a mistake. Don't let it be Maggie and Lindy."

Two fire trucks, three ambulances, and dozens of squad cars blocked his path, and Cabot had been forced to park nearly a block away. He ran the entire distance full-out, and when he broke through the crowd of curious onlookers, he saw Maggie's little red sedan, engulfed in flames. He heard them, calling his name. He saw them, trying to reach for him from behind the smoke-filled windows. Cabot tried to shoulder his way to the front of the crowd. Several officers grabbed him. "Hey, buddy; you can't go in there," they shouted. "You'll be killed!"

He fought them off. "That's my family in there," he screamed. "If I don't go in, they'll be killed!"

A surge of superhuman strength enabled Cabot to free himself from the officers' hold, and he ran up to the car. The only thing that separated him from Maggie and Lindy now was the window. "Can you roll it down?" he shouted at Maggie.

"Stuck," she said, coughing, her sooty hands gripping her throat; her terrified eyes fused to his.

"Dear Lord," he prayed, grabbing the door handle, "help me. Give me the strength to get them out of there." Instinct made him snatch back his hand as the hot metal scorched his palm. He yanked off his suitcoat, planning to use it as a hotpad. "Okay, Lord," he prayed aloud, "it's just You and me now. We're all they've got—"

And then the car exploded.

The huge fireball propelled Cabot backward, rendering him unconscious. When he woke in the hospital, he saw his partner asleep in the chair beside his bed. Cabot ached all over, but his head hurt worst of all. Glancing around carefully, he saw his right arm in a sling, his left hand bandaged. But nothing made sense. Why was he here? Had he been wounded on the job?

"Hey," he whispered, nudging Clancy awake. "Hey, Joe."

The red-haired man came to and sat up.

"I'm gonna report this to the captain," Cabot whispered, grinning as much as his swollen, bruised jaw would allow. "Napping on the job is against regulations."

Clancy didn't smile back. And since Clancy was always smiling, it scared Cabot. "What's going on, Joe? Why am I here?"

"There was an accident," his partner said softly. "On the Dan Ryan Expressway. . ."

It came back in an agonizing flash that was almost as blinding as the fire itself: Red car. Red flames. Maggie's red hair. Lindy's little red lips screaming his name. . .

Cabot sat up, grimacing with pain. "Where are they?" he asked, swinging his legs over the side of the bed. "In pediatrics? In the emergency room?" He grabbed the front of Clancy's shirt, oblivious to the pain of his burned palm. "Where are they! Tell me where they are, before I deck you!"

Clancy gently shoved him back onto the mattress. "They're gone, Cabot."

He blinked up at his partner. "Gone? You mean to Shock Trauma? Well, go get the car. They'll need me. What are you waiting for!"

Clancy only shook his head sadly and repeated, "Cabot, listen to me. Maggie and Lindy are gone."

Gone? he thought. As in dead? But how could that be? *I prayed like a crazy man all the way from the station to the accident. Every word out of my mouth was aimed right straight at God's ear. Surely He didn't let them. . .*

"What do you mean. . .they're gone?"

Clancy sighed heavily. "Why me?" he asked the ceiling. "I mean gone, Cabot. G-o-n-e. Please don't make me say it. . ."

A deep furrow formed on his brow as he tried to fight back the tears. "You're lying. He wouldn't do this to us. To me. All my life, I've believed. He wouldn't do this. He couldn't do this. . . ."

"Who?" Clancy wanted to know. "Who wouldn't do what?"

He lay back against the cool, crisp pillowcase and covered his face with his hands. Nurses, doctors, paramedics—everyone in the E.R.—looked over at him when the mournful wailing began. Then, as though embarrassed to have intruded on his grief, each looked away, and pretended to be engrossed in his work.

It stopped there every time, and just as surely as "The End" showed up at the conclusion of every movie, Cabot woke from the dream, groggy and perspiring, his heart beating fast, tears streaming down his face.

He'd had the dream every night since the breakup with Elice. He believed it was a symbol of sorts. A symbol that proved she was out of his life, just as surely as Maggie and Lindy were out of it, for good.

He'd tried to stave off the horrible nightmare, but nothing worked. Not long days filled with hard work. Not reading until dawn. Not even several days without sleep at all.

Nothing ventured, nothing lost, he reminded himself. *You'd be beyond all this now if you'd only listened to your own good advice.*

The phone rang, and he lay down the hatchet he'd been absently grazing across the pumice stone on the kitchen table.

"Why are you mad at us?"

"Annie? Hey, there! I didn't know you were back. Did you have a good time at the ocean?"

"Yes," she said tentatively. "But why are you mad at us?"

He licked his lips. "I'm not mad at you, Annie. Whatever gave you that idea?"

"You never call. You never come over anymore. And Mommy cries a lot. Every night. She doesn't think we know, but we can hear her in there."

Cabot ran a hand through his hair. "Well, darlin', it's sort of like this. While you guys were on vacation, your mommy and I had an argument."

"What about?"

And what did he say to that?

She started to cry. "Don't you love us anymore?"

His heart ached. He was about to tell her he loved her. That he loved Danny, and Emily, and her mommy, too—especially her mommy—when Annie hung up. He hadn't felt so helpless or useless since the funerals. Trembling, Cabot picked up the hatchet and ran the blade along the pumice stone again. The phone rang again, startling him so badly, he cut his thumb on the hatchet's sharp edge. "Ouch!" he whispered and instinctively stuck the thumb into his mouth.

"Cabot, I want to know what's going on."

"Emily," he said around his thumb.

"Are you and Mom. . . ?" The girl hesitated, as if searching for the right word.

Emily, at nearly eleven, was wise beyond her years. Elice had told him that tests at school showed her to be at least five years ahead of her peers, academically. He realized early on in their relationship that she was at least that far ahead emotionally, too.

"Was it a fight over something stupid, or is this permanent?"

He wanted to slam the phone down, fire up the Jeep, and storm into Elice's house, demanding a reconciliation. But he hadn't found out enough about their mystery visitor yet and, until he did, his presence was a danger to them. Besides, he still hadn't become a blind follower of her God, so such a visit would be pointless.

"It wasn't a fight, Emi," he said. "I prefer to call it a disagreement."

He listened to her long, quiet pause.

"So you're saying you don't love Mom anymore?"

"Of course not!" he said instantly. "I'd never say that!"

What was that he heard—giggling?

"I'll call you later, Cabot," she said, and hung up.

Cabot stared at the phone for a moment before hanging up himself, a confused frown etched on his handsome face. "Now what do you suppose that was all about?" he asked aloud, wrapping his bleeding thumb in a paper napkin.

❧

"We've got to do something. They're too stubborn to fix this all by themselves," Danny said.

"Maybe Grandmom can help," Annie suggested.

"I already talked to Grandmom," Emily said. "She says she'll talk it over with Granddad and get back to us. But grownups talk things to death. We don't have time for that. We have to do something now."

"So, what are we waitin' for?" Danny asked, sitting cross-legged on his bedroom floor. His sisters joined him. Several minutes passed as the children sat in their tiny circle, frowning with concentration. Then, suddenly, Emily's face lit up.

"I've got it!" she said, waving her siblings closer.

The three huddled close, whispering and giggling.

❧

"Now, who can that be so early in the morning?" Elice wondered aloud as she opened the front door.

"Hi, Missus Glasser." Jimmy, Marge King's oldest son, stood on the porch with an armful of red roses. "These are for you."

"What on earth. . . ?" Elice stared at the huge bouquet for a moment, then said, "Danny, bring me my purse, please."

Elice put the big blue glass vase on the coffee table, pulled a dollar from her wallet, and handed it to Jimmy. "Thanks," she told him. "Tell your mom I said hello."

"Sure will, Missus Glasser," he said as she closed the door.

"It isn't my birthday," she said mostly to herself as she reached for the tiny envelope.

Emily grabbed Danny and Annie by their shirt collars and dragged them into her bedroom. "We can't go in there. She'll see through us like window glass. Follow me!"

They thundered toward the back door. "We're going to ride our bikes over to the Becks', Mom," Emily called from the porch. "I'm wearing my watch, so we'll be home by five. I promise."

She'd just unsheathed the card. "Okay," she said distractedly as she read the neat script created by one of Mr. Thompson's florists:

> To my pretty lady,
>   I miss you. I love you. I'm sorry.
>   Cabot

Elice bit her lower lip and held the card against her chest. Tears welled in her eyes. *Could this mean there's a chance for us, after all?* she wondered. She reread the card. *Could it mean he found his way back to the Lord in the weeks we've been apart?*

Kneeling beside the coffee table, she cupped one velvety blossom in her palm and closed her eyes as she inhaled its fragrance. Nothing had ever smelled sweeter. Sitting back on her heels, Elice touched the delicate buds. Ran her fingertip along a smooth green leaf. Smiling, her heart swelled with warmth and love for the gentle giant who'd been responsible for the delivery of this precious and romantic gift.

Suddenly, the doorbell rang, interrupting the touching moment. This time, Billy Beck stood on the porch, holding a long rectangular box. "These are for you, Missus Glasser," he said, poking the huge red satin bow.

She fished another dollar bill from her wallet and exchanged it for the white box. "Thanks, Billy."

"Mom said to tell you she'd see you in church on Sunday," he said as he climbed back into the truck. She watched the white panel van that had Wilhide's in big green letters on its side, back down her driveway, then turned her attention to the card that read:

> To the woman of my dreams
>   With my heartfelt apologies and all of my love.
>   Cabot

She took a deep breath and lifted the lid. Inside, twelve white roses nestled on a bed of green tissue paper, surrounded by feathery ferns and delicate baby's breath. Taking one rose from its resting place, she held it beneath her nose and inhaled deeply. A little giggle popped from her lips. "Two dozen roses, and there's no special occasion!"

No one had ever sent her roses before. Leave it to Cabot to be the first, she thought, flushing like a schoolgirl in the throes of a full-blown crush. *As soon as I put these into water,* she told herself, giggling, *I'm going to give that man a piece of my mind!*

❧

The five of them leaned against Mr. Glasser's big black Cadillac. "You're kidding!" Mrs. Glasser giggled. "But where'd you get the money!"

"It was left over from what you and Granddad gave us at the ocean," Emily explained.

The grandmother laughed. "Do you believe it, Bob? Seems these kids have a lot of their grandfather's blood coursing in their veins!"

Grinning, her husband nodded. "Great minds think alike, I always say."

"Elice is probably dizzy with glee by now," she said, smiling.

"Do you think it'll work?" Danny asked.

"It had better work," said his grandfather, "or the bunch of us just spent seventy-five dollars for nothing!"

"And just wait till Cabot gets a load of what we delivered to Foggy Bottom. . . with your mama's name on it," Mrs. Glasser added.

"Two loaves of honey bread and an apple pie," Mr. Glasser said.

"If you kids hadn't told us they were his favorites, I'd never have known what to bake."

Emily snickered. "I'm scared to go home."

Danny joined her. "Me, too. Will you come with us, guys?"

The grandparents hugged. "I have a better idea," Mrs. Glasser said. "How 'bout you kids spend the night at our house. That way, when they get around to thanking each other for the lovely gifts, they can kiss and make up in private."

All five of them laughed heartily.

They were very pleased with their little matchmaking scheme.

❧

As she dialed his number, her heart raced. How long had it been since she'd heard his wonderful voice? Had it really been nearly three weeks? *Lord,* she prayed, smiling happily, *guide my words. Please don't let me gush too badly.*

After the tenth ring, she hung up, disappointment and a certain sadness registering in her heart. They'd wasted enough time over the silly argument. She didn't want to lose another precious moment.

Elice jumped into the car and headed for Foggy Bottom. Halfway there, she saw him, headed in the opposite direction. They stopped, right there in the middle of New Freedom Road, grinning like a couple of love-starved fools.

"I was just on my way over to your place."

"And I was just on my way to see you," she said.

"I wanted to thank you. Everything was delicious."

She'd imagined it would be wonderful to hear his voice again, to see his handsome face again, but Elice hadn't counted on feeling quite so giddy. She must be hearing things. "Delicious?"

"The bread, of course. And that pie." He smacked his lips. "But I didn't enjoy either nearly as much as this note of yours." Cabot paused. "I didn't know you even had a typewriter."

Elice frowned. "I don't." Then, "What bread?" And after a moment, "What pie?"

His brows furrowed slightly. "When I got back from town a few minutes ago, I found them in a basket on my front porch, wrapped in a red-and-white tablecloth. I followed instructions to the letter." He reached across the front seat and grabbed a sheet of rumpled paper. "'Have a slice of each immediately,'" he quoted, "'because they're symbols of how much I've missed your sweetness and—'"

"I think I smell a rat," she interrupted, narrowing her eyes.

"Anything but, pretty lady. That stuff smelled heavenly."

"Cabot," she interrupted gently, "did you send me roses?"

He laughed. "Roses?"

"A dozen white ones and a dozen red ones?"

"You told me once that you hated cut flowers because cutting them was a waste of their beauty. You said if a man ever sent you roses in a box, you'd box his ears." His left brow rose high on his forehead. "Wait a minute. Who's sending you roses if I'm not?"

A horn tooted behind him.

"We're blocking traffic," he said. "Meet me at the little park up ahead. Seems we have a lot to discuss."

Nodding, she shifted into drive and headed for the children's playground the Chamber of Commerce had constructed last summer. That's when she remembered the silly-yet-guilty expressions on the faces of her children, who'd skedaddled from the house awfully quickly, now that she thought about it.

He parked beside her, and they exited their vehicles simultaneously.

"You were right," she admitted, smiling. "I don't smell a rat. . .I smell three."

He took her in his arms and held her close.

"The kids, huh?"

Elice nodded against his chest. "Um-hmm."

He held her closer. "Feels good to have you back where you belong. I've missed you."

"Feels good to be here. I've missed you, too."

"Then all's forgiven?"

"And forgotten."

"Thank God."

She met his eyes. "Does that mean what I think it means?"

He grinned. "Let's just say you made me realize I have to at least give God a chance."

She hugged him tighter. "Goes to show you, He answers prayers."

His eyes widened. "You mean you've been praying I'd come back?"

"Every morning and every night and every spare minute in between."

Cabot rested his chin on the top of her head. "You say the roses came by way of the florist?"

"How else?"

"Hmmm." He leaned back and looked into her face. "So how'd they get the goodies over to my house? It's too far to go by bicycle."

"Hmmm," she echoed. "It's beginning to look like we're overrun by rats, and some of them drive black Cadillacs."

Cabot dropped a gentle kiss on her lips. "Funny," he said, "but I've suddenly developed a great fondness for the fuzzy little beasts."

Chapter 5

The bed was much too short for Cabot's frame, but it didn't matter. He didn't think he'd sleep much anyway. He clicked on the lamp beside Danny's bed and lay upon the colorful sportscar bedspread, then folded his hands under his head and glanced at the trucks and cars atop the dresser, then at the posters of Air Force jets that hung on every wall. He listened to the electric hum of the alarm on the nightstand. Three o'clock, glowed the dial. Cabot wondered if, down the hall in her own room, Elice thought of him, too.

Cabot sat up with a start. What was that? he wondered. Footsteps? Immediately, he turned out the light.

There it was again. Yes. . .footsteps—definitely.

The kids were safe at the Glassers' house, he'd told her; it's the perfect opportunity to catch whoever is pulling these ridiculous, albeit dangerous, stunts. It had taken nearly half an hour to convince her to let him stay. "The neighbors won't know that you're asleep in Danny's bed," she gasped. "They'll think. . . ." She'd blushed so deeply that he'd taken her in his arms so she couldn't see his grin, and promised to park the Jeep behind the shed out back so the neighbors wouldn't know he was there at all.

He slipped silently out of the bed and into his shoes, glad he hadn't yet removed his pants and shirt, then tiptoed through the quiet hall and into the living room. Someone's out there, all right, he told himself, and not a small someone, either. The silhouette looked strangely familiar, and then he remembered the shadow in his pines.

She'd taken his advice and changed the locks. He tried to remember where she'd put the key that unlocked the double-deadbolt. Once he'd found it, hanging on a tiny nail beside the door jamb, he cautiously stuck it into the lock and turned slowly, wincing when it clicked into the open position and shattered the silence of the night.

His palm was sweating, and when he grabbed the brass knob, it made opening the door impossible. Cabot dried his hand on the seat of his pants, then tried again. He'd thought about oiling that squeak in the hinges several times. Now, as the high-pitched squeal grated in his ears, he wished he'd done it.

Finally, the door was open far enough for him to slip onto the porch. He stood there for a long moment, studying the blackened yard for a sign of that shadow. In the dim light of the moon, he could see the tree swing, swaying slowly in the breeze. Beside it, a red plastic sand bucket rolled lazily left, then right. Annie's tricycle caught a moonbeam and reflected it onto the fender of Danny's dirt bike, leaning on the shed wall. The toys reminded him that three innocent children lived in this house.

Something moved near the clothesline, and his eyes riveted to the spot. Crouching, he made his way into the yard and focused on the thing he'd seen. Then he watched it move steadily closer to the north side of Elice's house, then disappear into the inky darkness.

There were three windows over there: one in Danny's room and two in Elice's. He was on the lawn now, nearly running to keep up with the quickening pace of the shadow and being careful to stay behind shrubs and tree trunks. A bead of sweat stung his eye, and Cabot swiped it away.

Black leather-gloved hands rested on the window sill. One booted foot balanced on the brick garden wall below it. One good push, Cabot realized, and the shadow would be inside. . .in her room. Only the screen separated her from this maniac. He had no choice. If he didn't grab the shadow now, Cabot may not get another chance. He darted forward and lunged at it.

Pain shot through his side. Looking up, he saw the gleaming, curved blade of a hunting knife. As darkness had been his partner up until now, the moon's glow was now his nightlight, and he saw the near-black blood that covered the blade.

Rolling over, he managed to escape further injury. But his wound was more than superficial. He'd been hurt enough times in Chicago to know that much. He'd have to act quickly, before he passed out from loss of blood or shock or both. Before the shadow realized how badly he'd hurt Cabot, it took advantage of his position and made its way into Elice's window.

Did the shadow plan to stab her, too? Had it come here tonight intending to. . .kill?

Cabot did the only thing he could think to do, and threw his weight against the shadow, knocking it off balance. Knocking the weapon from its hand, too. But the would-be intruder was up again, immediately. On its feet and running. Cabot reached for the ski mask, and tried to tear it from the intruder's head. He wanted more than anything, right now, to see who had been responsible for this whole unbelievable mess.

But Cabot's strength was waning. Dizziness crept up, slowly and without warning. He steadied himself against the trunk of a maple tree and breathed raggedly as he watched the shadow scurry, like a cornered rat, along the hedgerow that lined Elice's property, across the road, and out of sight. But not before blasting Cabot's temple with a well-placed blow from his elbow.

Holding his side and head alternately, Cabot limped toward the back porch. Elice, standing there in the doorway, nearly scared him out of his wits. "I heard the noise," she whispered, "and then you screamed."

"Screamed? Who, me? I don't remember screaming," he said, holding the porch rail for support. And then, like a puppet whose puppeteer suddenly let go of the strings that held him upright, Cabot slumped to the floor. "You look like an angel standing there," he said, his voice soft and raspy. Smiling a silly, pained grin, he held his hand out to her, and passed out.

❦

At first, everything was a fuzzy blur. *So. I've made it into heaven, after all,* he decided, grinning crookedly. *Why else would everything be white? And why else would there be an angel standing beside me?* He wondered if he'd see Maggie and Lindy soon. His mom and dad. They were all up here. It could be a regular family reunion.

He blinked, swallowed, tried to sit up and get a better look at heaven and at the angel. But the pain in his side stopped him.

"Now you stop that," the angel ordered. "Lie still or you'll pop your stitches."

Stitches?

She'd placed both hands on his shoulders and held him down. He hadn't realized angels possessed such physical power. But then, he guessed, it took a lot of strength to fly from heaven to earth and back again, maybe dozens of times a day.

"You sure know how to scare a girl," she said. "You've been unconscious for hours."

He thought the angel sounded a lot like Elice.

She fluffed his pillow, then pulled the sheet higher on his chest, and the slight pressure made his side ache. He moaned softly.

"Oh, I'm so sorry. I'll get a nurse."

She turned to leave, but he grabbed her hand. "No. Don't leave me alone up here just yet." He closed his eyes and frowned, wondering why they'd need nurses in heaven. "Boy, am I thirsty," he said.

The angel held a blue plastic cup near his face, then guided a straw between his lips. Her hands were shaking. *Well, what d'ya make o' that?* he asked himself, taking a sip of the cool water. Angels get nervous! Grinning, he said, "I don't get it. My mama told me people don't want for anything up here."

He'd closed his eyes, then opened them at the sound of her laughter. What was so funny? he wondered. But even the angel's laughter, softly musical and sweet, reminded him of Elice. He'd been in heaven only a short time. Hours, the angel had said, yet he missed Elice desperately. The pain in his side didn't begin to compare to the ache in his heart for, if he really was in heaven, it meant she was down there, alone and unprotected.

"Cabot," she said, "drink some more water. You don't want to get a fever. If that happens, they won't let you go home."

Home? Cabot closed his eyes and tried to concentrate. He'd always assumed that once you got to heaven, you were there to stay. Confused by the possibility of a return trip, he opened his eyes and tried to focus. Was he in heaven or not?

Nothing made sense. He felt like a man lost in a fog. And then a deep voice said, "Mr. Murray, I'd like to ask you a few questions, if you feel up to it."

St. Peter? he wondered.

"He's heavily medicated," the angel explained to St. Peter. "Don't pay any attention to that silly grin on his face." She stuffed another pillow under Cabot's head. "There. Is that a little better?"

Cabot nodded. He could see a door, and beyond it, a hallway. There had been a song in the seventies called "Stairway to Heaven." He wondered if he'd missed one called "Hallways in Heaven." The thought made him grin, and soon, the grin became a chuckle. But his merriment didn't last long, because laughing hurt.

The man with the deep voice came closer. He wasn't wearing white, Cabot noticed. He saw the badge first, reflecting the bright overhead lights. Then he recognized the navy blue uniform. This guy wasn't St. Peter. He was a policeman. Cops in heaven? Cabot thought. It seemed even funnier than nurses up there. He stifled the laughter that threatened his side.

"Did you recognize your attacker?" the policeman asked.

"I. . .tried," Cabot answered, "but. . .couldn't get the. . .mask off."

"He was wearing a mask?"

Cabot nodded. "Ski-type. . .black knit. . .red trim around the eye and. . .mouth holes."

The officer scribbled on the small tablet balanced on his palm. "Mrs. Glasser has filled me in on the events that transpired prior to this attack."

He didn't understand why this officer needed to be told what had happened; didn't heavenly beings just automatically know such things? But he started to talk, anyway, and the story tumbled out, from the moment he first heard the footsteps, until he watched the shadowy figure disappear on the other side of New Freedom Road. The officer appeared to have gotten every word down on his little pad, nodding and frowning as his pen scratched the white pages. He thanked Cabot for his help, and then he was gone.

"You look tired, Cabot. I think you should try and get some sleep."

"Don't need sleep in heaven. But then, you're not supposed to feel pain in heaven, either. And my side hurts a lot."

She giggled at that, and gently touched his shoulder. "You're not in heaven, you big nut. You're in the hospital."

Hospital? Cabot ran a hand through his hair and blinked with confusion.

"The doctor said you could go home tomorrow morning," she explained, holding his hand. "But you'll have to stay with us for a few days. We have to keep an eye on that wound so it won't get infected."

Haven't been in a hospital since. . . .

"But even after you're allowed to go back to Foggy Bottom," she continued, "you won't be able to do any heavy lifting. That means no farm work. Maybe we ought to call Walter. . . ."

. . .since the day Maggie and Lindy died. There had been no angel to greet him upon awakening that day. Suddenly, he was very sleepy. "I'm glad I'm not dead," he mumbled. "Even if it means I'm not in heaven."

He heard her giggle again and kissed the hand that still rested on his shoulder. "I love you," he said, his voice raspy with exhaustion.

The last thing he saw before closing his eyes was her angelic smile, and Cabot took her wonderful words with him into his dream world: "I love you, too."

❧

He insisted that the couch would be a perfect bed. "Besides," he said, "I can watch the ball games from here."

"Don't be silly. Your feet will forever hang out of the covers."

"Cooler that way. I don't want to be stuck back there, all by myself."

She shot him a maternal, scolding look. "Well," Elice said, arms folded over her chest, "the doctor did say he wanted you up and about a couple of times a day. I guess you could sleep in there at night, and rest out here during the day."

"I won't take your bed from you—"

In the voice she reserved for the kids, Elice said, "Fine, then. We'll just haul you back to the hospital where they're accustomed to dealing with uncooperative patients."

She wasn't smiling. Without words, Cabot agreed to be agreeable.

Elice let Wally borrow her car twice a day so Cabot's animals would be fed and watered on schedule. The rest could wait until he was better again.

His stay at Glasser Memorial turned out to be rather pleasant, after all. Elice, his ever-attentive nurse, saw to it he had plenty to eat and drink and provided games and books to entertain him when the Orioles weren't playing baseball. And then there was the added bonus of three round-the-clock playmates. Within days, he took meals at the kitchen table with them. He found himself regretting the day when he'd have to return to Foggy Bottom.

On his last night at Twin Acres, Cabot sat in the old brown chair in the corner of her bedroom, watching as she flapped fresh, line-dried sheets onto the bed. "When are you going to marry me?" he asked.

She'd been stuffing a pillowcase, and her hands froze midair. Turning slowly, she met his eyes "You're not kidding, are you? I half expected to see that teasing grin plastered all over your face."

He loved that wonderful smile of hers. "Stop stalling and answer the question, Elice." Cabot watched her cheeks redden, watched those brown eyes blink rapidly, and watched her swallow, hard, then resume her bed-making. She was smoothing the quilt when she said, "Okay Time for you to—"

It startled her when he put his hands on her shoulders and turned her around. "You're not gonna get out of this one, pretty lady. I'm not letting you go until you answer my question. When are you going to marry me?"

When she looked at him like that, he wanted to stop time, because he'd never seen more love directed at him. He'd never loved anyone more; never would love anyone more. It hurt a little, admitting that, because he didn't think it possible to love a woman more than he'd loved Maggie. But the proof was right there in his arms.

He wanted to say it again, but he'd said it so many times that week, he was beginning to sound like a broken record. Instead, he settled for a long, sweet kiss.

"Yuck," Danny said, leaning on the door frame. "Mush. Right here in my own house."

Cabot half expected Elice to pull away, to flush with embarrassment, to try and explain the embrace—and the kiss—to her son.

"That's what you get when you don't knock," she said instead.

"Door wasn't closed," Danny said, his playful grin telling them both that he was pleased to see the warm exchange between his mother and his new buddy. Snickering, the boy repeated, "Yuck. You're never gonna get better if you keep that up."

Cabot laughed and said, "They don't make any better medicine, Dan."

Wally had practically moved into Foggy Bottom. He'd mowed the lawn twice and trimmed the hedges in front of the farmhouse. And Cabot's animals seemed more contented than ever. Cabot decided that a cash payment couldn't repay the man for all the extra things Wally had done in his absence. That's when he got the idea. He left a message at the Olsons for Wally to stop by Foggy Bottom as soon as possible, then got busy preparing his surprise for the old soldier.

Wally showed up at suppertime, knocked on the back door, and waited on the porch, twisting his Orioles cap in his hands. "C'mon in!" Cabot said, waving him into the kitchen. "I'm just about to sit down to a plate of canned spaghetti. Care to join me?"

Grinning and nodding, Wally sat across from Cabot. As they ate, they discussed their plan to protect Elice.

"Guess whoever has been pickin' on Miz Glasser got bored and started botherin' somebody else," Wally said. "When's the last time anything strange happened?"

Cabot held his side. He didn't verbalize his thoughts, but Cabot believed it too much of a coincidence that everything eerie stopped that night. Either the madman in the ski mask had been frightened off by the violence of what he'd done, or he was planning something even more vicious. Much as he hated to admit it, the latter was more likely, considering all the trouble the maniac had gone to to terrify them up until that night.

He gave Wally a slice of the peach pie Elice had baked and frozen for him. When the big guy finished, Cabot led him to the garage. "You took such good care of things around here," he began, opening the huge double-wide doors, "that I didn't think a couple of measly bucks was payment enough." Standing aside, Cabot pointed at a shiny red convertible. He took Wally's hand, turned it palm up, and dropped a keyring into it. "That key starts the motor," he explained, poking the square-headed key, "and this one," he added, pointing at the rounded one, "locks and unlocks the trunk and the doors."

Wally met his eyes, confusion furrowing his brow.

"It's yours, big guy," Cabot said, gesturing toward the car.

It only took a moment for the information to register. "Guess now I'll need insurance," was all he said before he slid behind the steering wheel. He sat there fiddling with the radio dials, turning the headlights on and off, testing the air conditioner and the heater. Then he climbed out of the car and shook Cabot's hand. "I'd give you a hug," Wally said, grinning, "but I'm so excited I'd probably pop your stitches."

When he drove off, his smile was so wide that Cabot could see it when he turned onto Oakland Road. His own satisfied smile was still in place when he answered the phone the next morning.

"It's all over town, Mr. Murray. You're a local legend."

"Why?"

"It's not every man who pays his farm hands in cars," Elice teased. She paused, then added, "Everyone knew what that car meant to you."

"It was in my way. Since the only woman I'd ever consider marrying won't set a date, it doesn't make sense to stockpile useless metal."

"I never said I wouldn't marry you."

"I'll be right over. I want to hear this in person."

It normally took fifteen minutes to drive from his side of Freeland to hers, but Cabot managed it in seven this time. He felt great, healthy and fit, happier than he'd been in ages. The nut who'd been after them must have decided they were no longer worth his trouble. Life was grand.

But when Cabot pulled into her driveway and saw the squad car parked where he usually put his Jeep, his heart began to pound. He slammed on the brakes and threw the car into park, then leaped from the front seat so fast he didn't even bother to close the door. He heard a man's laughter as he stepped onto the porch, then Annie's sweet giggle. Elice was standing just inside the front door, waiting to escort the officer out. "Thanks for stopping by," she was saying. "It's good to know you haven't forgotten about us."

She noticed him then, and her whole face lit up. "How'd you get here so fast? Did you trade the Jeep for a jet?" Suddenly, her smile faded and Elice grabbed his hands. "Cabot, are you all right? You're as pale as a ghost."

"I'm fine. Saw the—"

The officer joined them on the porch. "She's a real cutie," he said, tousling Annie's hair. "Don't you worry. We'll keep a close eye on you guys." He chucked the child's chin. "Wouldn't want anything to happen to this precious angel here, would we?"

Long after the police car was out of sight, Cabot's heart continued to race.

Elice took him inside and sat him in the recliner, then handed him a glass of cold water. Sitting on the arm of his chair, she stroked his blond waves.

"Sorry I scared you," he admitted. "It's just that when I saw that squad car, I thought something had happened to you or one of the kids." He sipped the water.

"Do you intend to have a stroke every time you see a patrolman or a police car?" she teased.

Cabot rubbed his side. He wasn't smiling. "I keep remembering that night. It could have been you—"

"But it wasn't."

He squeezed her hand, then remembered why he'd come over here in the first place. "So, you'll marry me, eh?"

She nodded.

"When?"

She shrugged.

"Soon?"

"Maybe."

"How soon?"

Another shrug.

"Now?"

"No. Not now. I'm in the middle of a sign job. And besides, it's time for lunch."

Cabot laughed and pulled her onto his lap. "Tomorrow, then?"

"Not tomorrow or the next day. . .not until you're completely well."

"I'm fine."

"That's why you're as white as snow."

"I'm only human."

She kissed his chin. "That you are."

"Aw, no," Danny moaned. "Are you guys at it again?"

Cabot laughed. "Dan, I think we're going to have to put a bell around your neck."

❧

Oh, but aren't they just adorable? he asked himself, sneering sarcastically. Cabot and Elice made him sick with all their hugging and kissing. They'd even gotten those kids to accept the whole ridiculous scene. He hoped they enjoyed their little game, because it wouldn't last much longer.

Games had rules, after all, and since he made this game up, he could change them any time he pleased. Like he'd done that night.

Elice had always been so prim and proper. Such a well-bred lady. He'd gone over there only to put a little scare into her, so from then on she'd react with respect to his warnings. Imagine his surprise when he discovered Cabot spending the night!

Well, the ex-cop paid for his sin. Paid with a nice deep cut in his side and a big old goose egg on his head. The town gossips said he'd been laid up for weeks.

And wasn't Elice Glasser a sweet one to take him into her home and nurse him back to health, they'd said. He'd proposed marriage, they added, and Elice had accepted. He wondered if they'd set a date. Wondered if they'd have a big wedding or a small celebration. Wondered where they'd honeymoon, which house they'd live in, his or hers.

She was a sweet one, all right.

Those three nice kids deserved better than that. They'd started out with a bum for a dad. And if Elice married Cabot, he decided, they'd end up with a bum again.

It was pointless, really, to wonder about their plans. He smiled. There'd never be a honeymoon because there would never be a wedding. Not if he had anything to say about it.

They didn't let the rainy weather predictions spoil their plans but went right ahead with the barbecue. God must have sent Cupid to intervene, because it didn't rain a drop until they'd cleared the table. It had been a long, tiring day of playing volleyball and badminton. Annie had been yawning for the past half-hour when Elice said, "I'd better get them home."

"How 'bout if I stop by in an hour or so?"

"Haven't you had enough of me yet?" she laughed.

He drew her into a protective hug. "That day will never come."

Cabot didn't wait quite an hour before heading out for Twin Acres. The kids were asleep when he arrived, though, and, as usual, they sat on the back porch, talking quietly.

"We were meant to be together," he said.

"Is that right?" she asked, grinning.

"Sure." He took her hand and led her into the yard. "Just look at all the patterns we've developed. Like sitting and gabbing for hours."

"And drinking Kool-Aid."

He sat on the wide wooden seat of the tree swing and patted his thigh. She accepted his invitation, slinging one arm around his neck, and holding the thick hemp with her free hand. Raindrops from the rain that had fallen earlier drizzled down upon them from the leaves above, dampening their hair, but not their spirits.

Cabot's big foot, planted firmly in the gravel beneath the swing, stopped their swaying. "I've never wanted anything more in my life than I want you."

His lips were fractions of an inch from hers when she said, "It'll be wonderful, won't it? Being married, I mean."

He kissed her. "Better than wonderful. Spectacular."

It began to rain again, and she started to run for cover. But Cabot caught up with her, stood in her path, and wrapped her in a huge hug. It wasn't a very important gesture, really, yet it seemed to change things somehow. Her lips softened under his, and she returned his kiss—really returned it—for the first time.

Cabot wanted her on every human level. It didn't matter that she wasn't a young thing, or that she had three kids to raise, or that she was stubborn and opinionated. She loved him, warts and all, and that was enough.

Elice ended the kiss and gazed deep into his eyes. He saw the naked vulnerability in the brown spheres. Rain rolled down her soft cheeks and sparkled on her long dark lashes. "You're even gorgeous when you're all wet," he said, tightening his hold on her.

As if on cue, God issued forth a loud crash of thunder and a bright bolt of lightning. Elice hugged him, laughing. "See? He's listening, always. I warned you—"

"Isn't that comforting to know?" Cabot said wryly.

Every weekend, Cabot brought the kids to Foggy Bottom. He and Elice had decided to move into the farmhouse after the wedding, since it was larger and sunnier. The more time the children spent there before the big day, the more quickly they'd adjust afterward. Their delighted squeals changed the atmosphere of the house, reminding him of how it had sounded when he was a boy. His mother would have loved to hear the happy voices of children in her kitchen again. So would his dad, for that matter. He hoped they were enjoying the scene from their places in heaven.

"When do I get to ride a horse?" Danny wanted to know. He'd worn his cowboy hat and capguns, just in case.

"After lunch, we'll saddle 'em up and head for the horizon," Cabot drawled.

"I don't want to sit on any stinky old horse," Annie said. "I'd rather stay here and play with the kittens in the barn."

"You can play with the kittens when we get back from riding," Cabot said. "But right now, I'm gonna rustle us up some grub, pardners. Y'all mosey on outside an' play till it's ready. Stay close by now, y'hear?"

Danny enjoyed Cabot's cowpoke talk, but the girls rolled their eyes. "I'll keep these fillies in line, Cabot," the boy said, sashaying toward the door.

It was going to be some life, Cabot knew, when they became a real family. And it couldn't happen soon enough for him.

It hardly seemed like two months had passed since her house had been ransacked. She'd been grocery shopping. As always, she'd taken the kids. Cabot thanked God that Elice paid attention to details. Small things, like open doors that ought to be closed.

She'd known better than to go inside, and drove straight to his place instead, telling the children to wait in the car while she told him what she'd found upon arriving at Twin Acres: The intruder had broken a window to get into the house this time. But only Elice's room had been disturbed. The contents of every drawer had been rumpled, every shelf on the wall emptied. The clothes in her closet had been pushed aside, and the bed stripped.

Blue paper rested on her pillow. "It's not over till the fat lady sings," the note said, "and she won't be singin' at your wedding."

As before, the police found no evidence. They'd spent countless hours in her house, scouring for clues. Their man was smart, all right. Maybe a little too smart, Cabot hoped; self-confidence had been responsible for snaring more than one bad guy in the past.

※

Since meeting the Glassers, Cabot had been collecting a lot of memorable moments. Christmas morning, in his opinion, was way up there on top of the list. After church, they headed home, where Elice prepared a delicious country breakfast, complete with homemade currant jelly. Only then did they gather in a small circle around the tree.

When most of the hooting and hollering died down, he went out to the Jeep and brought in a gigantic box. "It says 'Mom' on the tag," Emily announced, shaking it gently. "It might be huge, but it's not very heavy."

He'd spent an entire afternoon wrapping it, first in its original box, then larger and larger ones, and finally, in the container his new washing machine had been delivered in. When she finally found the smallest box, wrapped in silver paper and tied up with a red satin bow, she lay on the floor and pretended to be too exhausted to open even one more thing.

The children's groans brought her back to a seated position, and coaxed her to unwrap the last package. "You're a terrible tease," she said, grinning at him as she tossed the ribbon aside. Her mouth dropped open when she lifted the lid.

Cabot didn't know which sparkled more—her eyes, or the diamond in the palm of her hand. She sat in silence for several moments, simply staring at it. Finally, she moved to his side and put it into his hand. He immediately knew what she wanted, and got onto one knee.

"Will you marry me?"

That mischievous glint he'd learned to love so much lit her eyes. Giggling, she held out her hand. And as he slipped it on her finger, she whispered over her shoulder to the kids, "I hope it doesn't turn my finger green."

※

Bob Glasser played with the tackle box, the gift Cabot had given him, for nearly an hour. He put it down only because his wife insisted he could not bring it to the dinner table. He never mentioned that Sue was just as fascinated by the leather-bound copy of *Kidnapped* that Cabot had given her at Elice's suggestion. And he'd never have admitted that he couldn't wait to get home and put their gift to him, a recording of his favorite opera, *Aida,* on the stereo.

Dinner was a festive occasion. Cabot ate ravenously, much to his hostess' pleasure. He'd been nervous about this day, because it was important. . .no, vital, that the Glassers like and accept him. Cabot yearned to be a member of a big, happy family. Bobby's parents were as eager to be accepted as to accept. He couldn't remember a brighter Christmas.

Back at Twin Acres, the children asleep, Cabot and Elice settled in the living room. He loved to sit across the room and peek over the top of the newspaper at her. He watched her sturdy little hands control the knitting needles, and he listened to the quiet clicking as the sweater she was making took form. She'd made the sweater he wore now, a bulky fisherman's knit. He didn't know when she had found the time to make it; had never seen her working on it. But he was quick to point out that it was one of the nicest Christmas gifts he'd ever received.

"How do you feel about two weeks from now?"

His question had cracked the quiet of the night and made her jump. "You made me drop a stitch. Shame on you." Then, smiling, she said, "What's two weeks from now?"

"A week before Father's Night, that's what."

She frowned and put her knitting aside.

"If we get married before Father's Night at school, I'd be more than just a father figure."

Her smile widened, but didn't quite make it to her eyes. "I thought we decided to wait until spring."

Cabot crossed the room in three huge steps and sat beside her on the couch. "I'm not made of stone, Elice."

"Well," she teased, "you can be pretty hard-nosed at times."

He ignored her grin. "Don't make fun of me. I'm serious. You made me promise to keep my distance. Well, I've kept my distance, and my promise. But let me tell you. . .it hasn't been easy."

She stared at her sparkling new engagement ring, but said nothing.

He took her hands in his. "If you love me, marry me!"

Elice withdrew her hands. "It's not that simple."

"It's exactly that simple." He took her in his arms. "It's Christmas," he said. "Forget that stupid promise I made, just for tonight."

She melted against him. "It's only Christmas for ten more minutes. I can bend the rules for that long, I guess."

They sat quietly for a long time, and then she said, "I'm glad you kept your promise."

"Why?"

"Because we appreciate this so much more."

"I've never been the kind of man who takes the good things in life for granted, Elice—"

"Shut up and kiss me," she said. Then, smiling, she added, "And make it a good kiss. It's nearly midnight."

❧

"What do you think I ought to wear?" Cabot asked on the afternoon of Father's Night.

"Your navy blazer and gray slacks, with that wine-colored tie," Elice suggested. "You look very handsome and sophisticated in that outfit."

Half an hour later, he called back. "Maybe I ought to rent a car. The Jeep's pretty beat up."

"No one's going to see it; it'll be in the parking lot."

An hour passed before the phone rang again. "What if someone wants to know why I'm at Father's Night?"

"You'll tell them you're the soon-to-be father of the Glasser group."

He was due to arrive at six o'clock; the phone rang at five thirty. "Are mothers allowed?" he asked.

Chapter 6

L ook, Cabot!" Annie squealed, pointing to a twig. "That tree has a baby!" Leaning over to inspect the new shoot, he said, "Well, so it does." "Where do you spoze it got a baby?"

"Maybe God thought the big tree needed some company."

She nodded her agreement. "God is like that."

As they walked and talked, investigating nature, Cabot knew he learned far more from Annie than he could ever teach her. He recalled the first time she'd seen the pond. It had been a steamy August day. That morning, a thunderstorm had turned the water dark and cloudy. "Yuck," she'd said. "Looks like a giant mud puddle."

"It's murky, all right," Cabot had agreed.

"Murky?"

Chuckling, he explained, "It's another word for 'yucky.' "

"Rivers have names. Lakes and oceans have names. I think your pond ought to have a name, too. I'm going to call it Murk."

Now, as he watched her walk along the frozen bank, Cabot grinned when she said, "It sure would be neat to skate on Murk."

Gently, he squeezed her mittened hand. "No, darlin'. It wouldn't be neat. It looks safe, I know, but it isn't. If you go out there, you'll fall through the ice." The vision of her, struggling in the freezing water, sent chills up his spine. He squatted and met her eyes. "You can never go onto the ice. Not for any reason. It's very deep and very dangerous. You understand what I'm saying?"

She stared into his worried eyes, nodding, one blond curl bobbing from beneath her red stocking cap. "Okay. I won't go out there. I promise."

Cabot stood and lifted her into the air. "That's my good girl. I don't know what I'd do if something happened to you."

While he couldn't say he loved Annie more than the other two, Cabot had to admit he loved her differently. It had been Annie, after all, who'd opened the door to his own personal heaven on earth—Twin Acres. He kissed her cheek.

And she kissed his. "I love you, Cabot."

"Time for me to fix lunch," he said, putting her gently onto the ground. "Stay close to the house, so you can call Emi and Dan for me when it's ready."

She looked up at him, blue eyes overflowing with love. "Okay. I'll play with Cuddles."

He watched her skip toward the barn, where Cuddles the kitten waited for her new, two-legged playmate. Later, after the wedding, the tabby would become a family pet. For now, though, it remained a barnyard cat. At first, it amazed him how quickly Annie bonded with the little thing. Then he remembered how fast he'd fallen in love with Elice and all three kids, and the instant closeness made perfect sense.

He could hear her sweet little voice, jabbering to the kitten about the snow and Danny's treehouse and that she'd save a piece of chicken from her lunch for it. "Don't hide from me, you silly thing," he heard her say, "I love you!"

❧

It had been a mistake, breaking into her house that way, because instead of running from Cabot, as he'd expected, she'd run straight into the big ape's arms.

He'd been on the other side of the road, crouching in the underbrush, when her battered yellow Vega rattled into the driveway. She must have seen it the same moment he had: The open front door. He should have gone out the same way he'd gone in. Why had he been so careless?

Elice was a smart one, all right. Rather than go inside and face possible danger, she calmly and carefully backed the little car out of the driveway and pointed it in the direction of Oakland Road. . .and Foggy Bottom. That had surprised him, because she'd always been so independent, so sure of herself, strong-minded, and opinionated. Those things had been only a few of the reasons he respected and admired her as he did. He didn't know another woman like her and honestly believed no other such woman existed.

He didn't like picking on her. It was the hardest part of his plan. But how else could he teach her, once and for all, that the ex-cop wasn't the man for her?

Apart, they'd been so easy to torment. He'd deliver a well-timed note or place a telephone call, then stand back and watch the excitement. Lights would go on, shadows would race back and forth in front of the windows, agitated voices would rise in pitch and volume. It was wonderful.

Together. . . Well, those few times he'd tried scaring them when they were under the same roof didn't net the expected results. Quite the opposite. It seemed no matter how terrifying his trick, if he struck while they were together, whatever he did only brought them closer. The turmoil and mayhem, rather than blowing them apart like a mental grenade, bonded them. Like that super glue stuff, he thought, grimacing.

What galled him most, though, was the way her eyes glittered when she looked at the big ex-cop. She'd never looked at him that way. Not when he gave her flowers. Not when he invited her to parties. Not even when he brought trinkets for her kids. Sometimes he wondered what he saw in her at all. And then she'd smile that sweet smile, or say something kind, and he remembered.

Now, as he stood in the pines on the other side of the pond, he watched

Cabot and Annie. You'd think they were a real family already, he glowered. It's enough to make a man gag.

It seemed to him that Cabot spent more time with Annie than with the other kids. He seemed to listen more closely to what she said and watch more carefully what she did. He'd heard in town that Cabot's little girl had died in the same car accident that killed his wife. Obviously, in Cabot's heart, Annie had become the daughter he'd lost.

His fingers and toes were growing numb from the near-freezing temperature. Moments ago, he'd considered heading home. But watching them gave him his best plan of attack yet. When he finally did leave, the weather and its accompanying temporary physical discomforts were the last things on his mind.

They would notice his absence if he didn't get back soon. And he couldn't have that. Alibis were all-important to him these days. As he drove the bright red vehicle toward his jobsite, he pictured her: Tiny, warm and kind, beautiful. He blinked away the pleasant image. Can't afford to go soft now, he chided himself. She'd knotted the rope the day she let the dumb cop put that engagement ring on her finger.

A small part of him understood what had motivated the commitment. She'd been scared, and being linked to Cabot by the promise of marriage made her feel safe. But it didn't make their closeness easier to bear.

Still, it had all worked out in his favor in the end. Their oneness had been directly responsible for the false sense of security that surrounded them. He remembered the night when, slinking around the shrubbery beside her dining room windows, he saw the cozy little setting—Cabot at the head of the table, Elice at the other end, passing out slices of cherry pie. When they'd finished eating, the kids happily followed suit as Elice led them in a harmonious rendition of "There'll Be Peace in the Valley." He'd made a decision, right then and there, and had been on a single-minded mission to make it real ever since.

If it were the last thing he ever did, he'd put an end to the peace in their valley. Maybe then he could learn to live without her.

※

"I brought you these, Miz Glasser," said Wally.

"Where did you find such pretty flowers in the middle of winter?"

He blushed, scratched his curly gray head, and said, "I found a five-dollar bill in the parking lot over at Nardi's. I bought 'em at the store."

"You've brightened my day," she said, taking them from his extended hands.

He stood there, twisting his Orioles cap, and grinned. "The lady called them silk flowers."

"Very practical," Elice said, smiling. "They'll never die."

Wally beamed, then asked, "Have you seen Cabot yet today?"

She glanced at the wall clock. "He'll be here any minute."

"Good. He borrowed my typewriter a couple of weeks ago. I need to get it back. I got a card from a friend today. He's in the hospital. I wanna write to him. An' my handwriting is horrible." Wally laughed.

Elice swallowed. "I didn't know you could type, Walter."

He nodded. "Learned in the army. Before they sent me to Korea, I was a clerk for a whole year."

Her heartbeat had doubled, remembering Cabot's original suspicions about Wally. "Where'd you get a typewriter?"

"Found it in Mr. Olson's shed. He told me I could have it."

Elice dialed Cabot's number. Facing the wall allowed her to hide her doubt from Wally. "If he hasn't already left," she said, putting the receiver to her ear, "I'll ask him to bring it right over." *Walter has nothing to do with what's been happening to us,* she told herself as Cabot's phone rang. And by the time he answered, she'd more or less convinced herself she was right.

All the way over to Twin Acres, Cabot thought about her icy tone. He'd talked with her less than an hour earlier; she'd seemed fine then. Cabot supposed she'd connected the fact that he'd borrowed Wally's typewriter with the accusations he'd made that day in her kitchen. He'd never told her that he'd gone over to Wally's and "grilled" him, as she'd put it. And he hadn't mentioned what he'd discovered up there in the big guy's small apartment—that the crooked *e*'s in the notes and the *e* on Wally's typewriter matched, exactly. The moment Wally left with the typewriter, she lit into him.

"All right, Kojak," she said, tapping one foot. "Start explaining."

He didn't leave out one detail about that visit to Wally's. He watched her big eyes grow bigger with shock and disbelief. But before she could defend her friend, Cabot added, "For your information, I agree with you. The better I get to know him, the more I realize he couldn't be responsible for anything that's been going on."

Blinking nervously, she licked her lips. "But then someone used his typewriter to write those notes. . . ."

Cabot hesitated. Elice considered Jack a friend, too. He didn't want to rile her tonight by spelling out what he thought of his old high school chum, because tonight, he intended to persuade her to set a wedding date.

"It must be someone he knows well," she continued, frowning as she paced the length of the kitchen, "because Walter doesn't have much to call his own. If he'd let someone have the typewriter. . . ."

Then she stopped dead in her tracks and stood up straight. Grinning, she said, "If someone had told me all this was happening to them, I'd think they were a little, you know. . . ." Her forefinger drew tiny circles beside her temple.

Chuckling, he agreed.

"I'm glad it's over. These past few weeks have been so wonderful, so calm." Her face brightened and she grabbed his hands. "See? I've been praying for a happy ending. And God answered!"

He held her close, partly because having her there was a comfort, and partly because he didn't want her to see his face. She was so intuitive and intelligent that she'd have known instantly that he didn't think it was over. Far from it. Cabot believed, without a doubt, that it had only just begun.

Gradually, the tranquility of the past few weeks had put the sparkle back into her eyes. She hadn't been this relaxed since. . .since they met.

"Isn't the Lord wonderful?" she said, hugging him tighter. "Look at all He's done for us! I don't think I've ever been happier."

Cabot kissed the top of her head and sighed sadly. At that moment, setting a wedding date was the farthest thing from his mind.

❧

The next morning, stirring sugar and milk into his coffee, Wally smiled. "I like Miz Glasser," he told Cabot. " 'Specially lately."

"Why lately?"

" 'Cause she's always smilin' and laughin'. Just like in the old days. It's good to see her that way again."

"I know what you mean."

"Do you think we'll ever need to put our 'plan' into action?"

Cabot frowned. "I'm not sure. Doesn't seem that way right now, but that may be exactly what he's hoping we'll think, so we'll let our guard down."

Wally took a sip of his coffee and nodded. "Can't be too careful where Miz Glasser and those kids are concerned," he said somberly.

"Maybe we got lucky; maybe having you spend all that time at Twin Acres scared him off."

Wally put the mug onto the table, hard. "I wouldn't ever want to hurt anybody, Cabot. But if somebody tried to hurt her while I was around. . ." The blue eyes narrowed dangerously. "Well, I don't know what I might do."

Cabot liked him. And he trusted him, too. Elice would always be safe in his presence, because Wally was the type of man who'd lay down his life for a friend. "She's lucky to have a friend like you."

He flushed. "I'm the one who's lucky. She's been good to me." Then, after a moment's hesitation, he dug in his pocket and pulled out a large pocket knife. "I found this while I was weeding under her bedroom window yesterday," he said, placing it on the table. "Is that the knife you got stabbed with?"

Cabot pulled out the blade. "Did you wipe it clean?"

Wally shook his head. "Never even opened it."

"Well, there's not a trace of blood. And from what I remember, that knife wasn't the retractable kind." He turned it over and over in his hands. "Maybe this one is Dan's."

Wally shook his head again, harder this time. "No way. Miz Glasser would never let him play with anything sharp. She's a good mother."

Cabot nodded in agreement, then closed the knife and placed it on the table.

The men sat there, staring silently at the thing for a long time. Then Cabot thumped it, sending it spinning in a dizzying circle on the table top. He thought Wally seemed agitated. He'd never seen him looking so distraught. "Did you stop by this morning to show me this, or was there another reason?"

Wally leaned back in the chair. "It gave me the creeps. I wanted to see what you thought."

"Gives me the creeps, too."

"What will you do with it?" Wally asked, watching Cabot open and close the blade again.

He'd clamped his jaws together so tightly they'd begun to ache. Then Cabot relaxed and tried to smile. "I'm not sure. But let's keep this between us, okay? This could be nothing. I wouldn't want to scare Elice for no reason."

Wally stood and headed for the back door. "No, sir. Don't want to see that look on her face again. Not ever."

Cabot watched Wally drive off in the shiny red car. The big guy had changed, somehow, in the months Cabot had known him. He seemed keener, smarter, a little more sophisticated. Chuckling as he climbed into his Jeep, Cabot remembered feeling the same way when he drove the convertible.

❧

Cabot heard Elice's laughter first, then his. And when he walked into the room that evening, his heart nearly stopped at the sight of them, sitting across from each other at her kitchen table, mugs of coffee and a plate of cookies on the table between them.

"Howdy, Cabot," Jack said, tipping an imaginary hat. "How's tricks?"

"Fine," he said, warily. He didn't smile. "You?"

"Same."

She greeted Cabot with a peck on the cheek. "Jack brought us a surprise," she said. "Pie filling."

"I'll admit I had an ulterior motive," Jack said. "Figured if I brought her the fixings, she'd be obliged to whip me up a pie." He winked at her. "She hasn't baked for me in quite a while."

Cabot's left brow rose high on his forehead. "Is that so?" He helped himself to a cup of coffee and sat between them at the table.

Jack leaned back, prepared, it seemed, to stay forever. "Leecie here invited me to supper." He winked at her again. "And this old bachelor has been craving some of her home cookin', let me tell you."

Cabot didn't like the possessive way Jack looked at Elice. The man didn't belong in this house. Something ominous shrouded him. Something that tainted everything around him. He'd liked Jack once upon a time, but right now, Cabot felt anything but friendly toward his former schoolmate, who sat there smugly sipping coffee and making small talk as if he were a frequent and welcomed visitor.

What Cabot had intended as a short visit turned into a long, dreary evening. First supper then dessert then conversation afterward. He'd left a lot of chores undone. But he wasn't about to leave Jack alone with her. He'd stay until next New Year's if that's what it took.

"You were very rude," Elice scolded when Jack finally left.

He didn't respond. It was true—he had been rude.

"He's been bringing us dented cans from the factory since Bobby died," she said, putting the last clean dish into the cabinet. "He's just trying to be helpful, Cabot. He knew it was hard for me at first."

Cabot pocketed his hands and stared at the toes of his boots.

"And Jack knows that you and I are engaged now."

The muscles of his jaw flexed in anger.

She frowned. "He says he's happy for us—"

"I'll just bet he is." The bitter edge to his voice hung heavy in the air.

Elice sighed. "He's a friend, Cabot. That's all he's ever been, and he knows it."

Cabot felt foolish, making such a big deal out of it. But a nagging sense that something horrible was about to happen struck when he saw Jack in her house, and it didn't leave, even after Jack was long gone.

She smiled sweetly. "You have no reason to be jealous. Jack's not my type."

Forcing Jack from his mind, he returned the smile. "Oh, yeah? What's your 'type?'"

Elice pretended to be deep in thought for a moment, then said, "Tall. Strong." She stood beside him. "Handsome," she added, "with curly blond hair and almost-brown eyes. Someone who does a horrible Kojak imitation. That's my type."

He forced a brave, friendly smile, but nothing she said made him feel any better. The little kiss that had punctuated her statement and the tender hug that followed it didn't improve his mood, either. Not even her admission of undying love erased the sense of doom that Jack Wilson had delivered to Twin Acres, disguised as pie filling.

❧

Cabot didn't know how many times the phone had rung before he had heard it. He'd been up half the night, replaying every smart-alecky word Jack had said earlier at Elice's house. When he had finally dozed off, Cabot had slept deeply and soundly.

"Cabot Murray?" asked a gruff voice.

"Yeah."

"Detective Sergeant Murray, of the Chicago Police Department's Homicide Division?"

He read three-fifteen on the alarm clock's dial. "Do you have any idea what time it is!" Cabot growled, propping himself up on one elbow.

"You mean you don't recognize my voice? I'm crushed."

The voice was familiar, but Cabot couldn't put a name or face with it just yet. "Whaddaya want?" he demanded angrily, sitting on the edge of the bed now.

"Just passing through," the familiar voice said, "and since your home town is just a hop, skip, and a jump from Baltimore, I thought it'd be rude not to pay my respects."

The voice was strangely familiar, but Cabot couldn't put a name or face to it, so he decided to try out an old trick: "You're not welcome here, Deitrich."

A pause. Then a brittle snicker filtered through the phone and into Cabot's ear. "So you do remember me. I'm touched."

Cabot wanted to hang up, but didn't dare. A few more minutes of scrutiny and he'd be able to identify that voice.

"I'm headin' south at first light. I only came east to settle up with a fella who owed me."

Cabot ignored the implied threat. "That was pretty stupid, Deitrich, breaking out of prison with only two years left to go."

The crazy snicker again. Then, "Two years is a long time in a place like that."

The guy was crazy, all right, but he wasn't Hawk Deitrich. Deitrich hadn't escaped. He'd been legally released from prison months ago.

"Why not call Judge Bollinger back in Chicago," Cabot said, still testing. "Let him know you're not interested in carrying out those death threats. You never know when you might need a couple of character witnesses."

"Who says I'm not interested?" he said. And without so much as a by-your-leave, he hung up.

Cabot stared at the receiver for a long time before replacing it in its cradle. He went into the dark kitchen and stood at the sink, staring into the yard as he sipped cold milk from the carton.

An hour later, still unable to put a name or face with the voice on the phone, Cabot got dressed and headed for the barn. It was nearly daylight, anyway; an extra hour or so would almost make up for the time he'd lost last evening at Elice's, babysitting Jack Wilson.

The phone call haunted him as he went about his work. He realized that anyone who'd ever watched television cop shows were convinced that cops, responsible for the imprisonment of criminals, received occasional death threats. The caller had been banking on that, hoping to throw Cabot off the trail.

He could have been one of those ex-cons who'd threatened Cabot. Slim possibility, but a possibility nonetheless. But it was definitely not Hawk Deitrich. Because a convict who forgets the name of his sentencing judge was a changed man, indeed.

Besides, Judge Bollinger didn't even exist.

❧

Northern Maryland's heaviest snows accumulate in mid-February. That winter,

Mother Nature took her work especially seriously, six times causing traffic jams and school closings in a two-week period. Like every kid in Freeland, Elice's children took full advantage of the extra play time, molding the fluffy white stuff into snowmen and snowballs and snow forts. When they ran out of building space at Twin Acres, they decided to move the freezing construction activities to Foggy Bottom.

On the first Saturday of the month, Elice got an order to create several signs for a local insurance company. She stayed home to catch up on her work while Cabot and the children headed for the farm.

Too impatient to wait for the others, Annie headed straight for the barn, calling Cuddles' name. Danny shouted that he planned to climb the big forked tree near the pond, where he'd built a treehouse last summer. And Emily announced that she'd rather stay inside and read beside the woodstove.

Cabot looked out the windows occasionally, checking on Annie and Danny. As he watched them scamper through the snow, giggling and squealing with delight, he smiled, pleased to know they enjoyed his place so much. It wouldn't take them any time at all to adjust to living here once he and Elice were married.

He watched Danny inch his way higher into the big tree, then settle himself inside the plywood cube he'd designed and constructed from scraps he'd found in Cabot's shed. Below him, Annie headed for the barn. Satisfied the two were safe and happy, Cabot settled into his easy chair, waiting for the chicken noodle soup Elice had sent over with the kids to heat up. He'd barely cracked the sports page when he heard the terrified screams.

"Cabot!" the voice shrieked. "Hurry! Get out here!"

Not taking time to step into boots or slip into a jacket, Cabot reacted to the panic-stricken cries and bolted outside without even closing the door behind him.

"What's going on?" Emily wanted to know as she ran behind him.

"It's Annie," Danny shouted. "She went toward the man. He had Cuddles. . . ."

Looking in the direction Danny pointed, Cabot saw a gaping hole in the ice, just a few feet from shore. Emily saw it at the same time and immediately began to sob. He headed for the barn, and both children ran alongside him.

"I was up in the tree," the boy explained, crying harder than ever. "I told her to stop. I told her to stay off the ice. But she wouldn't listen. She was too busy listening to the man."

Cabot grabbed a rope from the peg beside the barn door, then headed for the pond. Despite Emily's and Danny's pitiful wails, he'd never heard a more deadly silence. Cabot couldn't take his eyes from the jagged hole in the pond, where a soggy red mitten clung to the ice.

He tied one end of the rope around a tree trunk. "Call 911!" he hollered as he tied the other end around his waist. "Tell them there's been a drowning. That'll get them here fast." Then, with no regard for his own safety, Cabot crashed through the ice.

Fortunately, Annie had fallen into the only shallow spot the pond had to offer. As he splashed around in the frigid water, he prayed with all his might: "Please, Lord, let me find her. Guide my hand to her." When Cabot's nearly frozen fingers felt a solid object, he formed a numb fist, held tightly, and pulled hard. Soon he could see the wet pink material of Annie's parka. He sloshed out of the water, holding her close, trying to warm her with his own body heat.

His heart pounding with fear, he stumbled toward the house, clutching her limp body against him. He hoped he'd reached her in time. It seemed like she'd been under the dark, cold water for hours instead of minutes; seemed like miles from the pond to the house instead of yards. He had to get her inside, where it was warm. His breaths were ragged and his mind confused when finally he reached the back porch.

Tears oozed from the corners of his eyes as he gently lay Annie on the floor near the woodstove. He pinched her tiny nose and began breathing into her mouth. Listening for the sound of his breath to exit her lungs, he prayed harder: "Not Annie, too, Lord," he said. "Not Annie."

He heard the sirens, but continued to force breath into her until the paramedics arrived. Then he and Emily and Danny huddled in the middle of the room.

"Is she going to die?" Danny sobbed.

Cabot hugged them tighter and whispered, "She can't."

🌿

The paramedics hadn't wanted the extra passenger, but they wanted a wrestling match with Cabot even less. He sat on the floor between the two narrow cots, holding her tiny hand, his cold, wet clothes clinging like a second skin. One of the paramedics draped a blanket around his shoulders. Cabot didn't seem to notice.

At the hospital, when he insisted on remaining at Annie's bedside in the emergency room, an orderly threatened to strap him into a chair. "Stand back and let the doctors and nurses do their jobs," he said, then disappeared around the corner. Someone handed Cabot a large styrofoam cup of hot, black coffee. Another kind soul guided him to a hard, white chair. "Put these on," the orderly said, handing him a set of dull green surgical scrubs, "before we have to sign you in as a pneumonia patient."

Mechanically, Cabot obeyed, and changed in the tiny bathroom just outside the E.R. He wondered how Elice would react to the news of the accident, wondered how long it would be before she'd arrive, hoped Annie could hold on until then, and prayed Elice wouldn't hate him.

Seated in the stiff-backed chair once more, he waited and listened and watched as the white-garbed professionals efficiently tended to Annie. An hour slipped by as he sipped the coffee, Danny's words echoing in his head: "She went to the man. She went to the man. She went to the man." *What man?* Cabot demanded of no one.

"Mr. Murray," said a soft voice. "You can see her now."

He jumped up so fast, the coffee splashed on the doctor's garb he'd borrowed. "Is she all right?"

"Still unconscious, I'm afraid," the nurse said, pointing at the second pastel-curtained cubicle in the E.R.

He'd expected it to be bad, but Cabot hadn't been prepared for this. Annie looked like a little robot with all those tubes and needles and hoses connecting her to the beeping, humming monitors. Standing at her bedside, he held her tiny hand and brushed a strand of flaxen hair from her forehead. "Look at you," he said, stifling a sob. "The nurses have put a nightie on you. It's got blue flowers all over it. Blue, Annie. . .your favorite."

No response.

"Your mom's on the way," he added, sniffing. "Wake up, now, so you can show her your pretty pajamas."

She didn't open her eyes or smile or giggle. Not one precocious remark came from the blue-gray lips.

"Hey, darling," he said, hot tears burning his eyes, "sing 'Rock-a-Bye' with me." Cabot swiped at a tear that rolled down his cheek. "C'mon. . .wake up and sing for me."

"She's in a coma, Mr. Murray."

Cabot faced a pair of bespectacled, somber, brown eyes.

"I'm Dr. Cummings," he said, extending his hand.

Cabot ignored it, trying to make sense of the doctor's words.

Dr. Cummings put his hand back into his large white pocket. "It might be brief, or we could be in for the long haul. We have no way of predicting, since we don't know for certain exactly how long she was deprived of oxygen."

Cabot swallowed, then glanced at Annie, pale and lifeless. "But she'll be okay, right? She won't die?"

"I wish I could tell you what you want to hear, Mr. Murray," the doctor said quietly. "But at the moment, I honestly don't know. I'm sorry."

Cabot squared his shoulders. "She's going to be fine," he said. "She's going to wake up and be her old self any minute now."

The doctor sighed. "Well, we can hope."

Cabot felt weak, light-headed. He slumped into the chair beside the bed. His broad shoulders lurched with each sob, and the dry, racking sounds of his misery echoed throughout the small cubicle.

"I'll be on this floor for another half hour or so," the doctor said, backing out of the room. "If she moves, even the slightest, have me paged."

Cabot scooted the chair closer to the bed and sandwiched her tiny hand between his big ones, then began singing Annie's favorite song: "Hush little baby, don't you cry . . . ." His voice trembled, but he forged on. "Daddy's gonna sing you a lullaby. . . ."

He noticed warmth, a slight pressure on his shoulder, and turned to look into Elice's eyes.

"I'm so glad you're with her," she whispered through her tears. "I'm so glad you're here for me." Elice slipped her arms around him and leaned her head atop his. She held him that way for a long time.

❧

They'd been at her bedside more than twenty-four hours, Cabot pacing, Elice praying. But Annie hadn't come to yet. Obviously, it wasn't a day for miracles.

Dr. Cummings made several visits during the night, studying Annie's chart, shining his little light into her eyes, taking her pulse, and reading the printouts from the monitors that clicked and beeped and hummed relentlessly. He spoke no words of hope, showed no sign of encouragement. His manner, while kind and professional, indicated certain doom. "You need to get out of here for a while," he suggested to them. "It's important to keep up your own strength; you'll need it if there's a change."

Cabot looked at Elice closely. She hadn't cried, not since those first harrowing moments after she'd joined him at the hospital. "The doctor is right," he said. Taking her hand, he led her to the cafeteria, where he purchased two sodas and two bologna and cheese sandwiches.

"She's in God's hands now," Elice said when he slid the tray onto their table. "There's nothing we can do but wait and pray."

Her voice had lost its vitality, yet she sat there, composed and calm, fully expecting God to intervene on Annie's behalf. It was a dangerous game she played, Cabot thought. A game he'd played himself years ago. . .and lost. Elice had always been a strong woman, but Cabot knew that the death of a child required much more than emotional strength. He didn't know what, exactly. He only knew he didn't possess that magical, secret character trait, because losing Maggie and Lindy had nearly killed him.

He'd tried hard to fight his disbelief. Everything he'd learned his whole life told him that his doubts were wrong . . .sinful. But in the end, after he'd gone through the motions of pretending to be brave, honesty won out.

Everyone experiences grief differently, his pastor had told him. For some, he'd said, memories of the deceased became a lifeline. Cabot had been a father, a husband. Then suddenly, with no warning, he was a man alone. For him, memories were not helpful, and grief was a bitter heart that blamed the Creator for his solitary lifestyle.

"It'll pass," the pastor had said. "You're angry now, and that's normal. But the Lord will forgive your anger, because He understands. He lost a son, don't forget."

The pastor had been right. Time dulled the raw edge of Cabot's pain. But doubt is a strange, reverberating, haunting thing, for though he knew he'd been forgiven, Cabot couldn't make himself believe again in a Being that allowed such agony to touch the innocent. First He had allowed Maggie and Lindy to suffer a painful death. And now Annie, pure as a newborn, lay just out of reach of Death's cold hand. Cabot wanted to know where God had been when she walked onto the ice. Where He was now that she teetered between life and. . . .

"Danny asked about you when I called home," Elice said.

Her words startled him back to the present. Cabot remembered how upset Danny and Emily had been earlier. "How's he doing?"

"He blames himself."

Cabot met her eyes. "What?"

"He said if he'd been faster. . ." She stopped talking and swallowed the tears that threatened to choke off her words. Elice sipped her coffee, then continued. "I told him if he hadn't been in that tree, Annie wouldn't be alive at all. But he wasn't having any of it."

Her smile, feeble though it was, warmed his heart. "He's a lot like you that way," she said.

Cabot nodded. "I'll talk to him. Set him straight."

She touched his hand. "What would I do without you?"

Cabot grimaced and pulled his hand from beneath hers. *You'd do a lot better*, he thought. *You'd be safe and calm and happy, like you were before I came into your life.*

"I know what you're thinking," she said, waiting for him to meet her eyes before she continued. "You're blaming yourself, just as you've been doing over every little thing that's happened." She took a deep, shaky breath, and squeezed his hands between her own. "It's not your fault. None of it. Especially not this."

He couldn't meet her eyes.

Elice touched his cheek. "You saved her life," she said. Then, the awe she obviously felt echoed in her voice: "You saved her life!"

He stared past the cash register, over the heads of other hospital visitors, beyond the staff members who filled empty food bins and restocked shelves. If Annie didn't make it, what difference did it make that he'd saved her? Unless she woke up, able to enjoy life as she had before, what had he accomplished, really?

Besides, the awful truth gonged too loudly to be denied: The man in the pines, the writer of the notes, the destroyer of their peace was one and the same person, acting out some dark, demented need to avenge something he believed Cabot had done to him. He could handle that, alone, but watching them suffer. . . .

"I love you," he heard her say.

Cabot felt the sting of tears behind his eyelids again. He'd turned her tranquil life into one of torture and torment, and now, on top of it all, he'd become a full-time sniveling weakling. How could she love a man like him?

"Drink your coffee, Cabot. It's getting cold."

He nodded and took a sip. *Get a grip*, he told himself. *She needs your strength right now. She deserves a man she can lean on.* So he blotted his traitorous eyes

84

and blew his nose on a paper napkin and sat up straight. He'd be brave and strong. . .for Elice.

Whatever he did from here on out would be for her.

Because he honestly didn't care what happened to himself any more.

※

Cabot worked on his bravado all the way over to Twin Acres. If he didn't put on a good show, Danny would continue feeling responsible for Annie's accident. He couldn't have that, since every horrible thing that had happened to the Glasser family since he'd returned to Freeland had been his fault.

When the boy greeted him, Cabot noticed his tentative smile and red-rimmed eyes. Hugging him, he said, "How's my boy?"

"Fine." The boy's shoulders slumped from the burden of his grief and guilt, and he refused to meet Cabot's eyes.

Cabot looked across the room at the picture of Annie on the mantle. Her smile, sincere and sweet, beamed out at him, and his heart throbbed. He cleared his throat. "So, what's all this nonsense about you feeling like it's your fault that—"

Danny broke away and flopped onto the couch. "It is my fault."

Cabot sat beside him. "You're a hero, Dan. Why, if you hadn't been up in that tree, Annie would be dead right now."

Dead. Annie would be dead. The words chilled him.

"If anyone is to blame," Cabot continued, "it's me. I should have been out there with you guys. I never should have allowed her to play—"

"You're the hero, Cabot. You're the one who jumped into the pond and saved her."

Cabot forced a grin. "So it's a tie, then. It's not your fault, and it's not my fault," he lied, "and we're both heroes." He hated lies and fibs and half-truths but, at times, he believed, they were necessary. This was one of those times. At least now, the blame had shifted from Danny's little-boy shoulders to some unknown place. In Cabot's mind, though, the lie had been exactly that: He'd carry the guilt and blame for the rest of his life.

※

There were plenty of things he'd done in his past to be sorry for, but this topped them all. He'd sunk mighty low to have used a little girl that way.

He didn't have anything against her. She was a pretty little thing. Every time he'd seen her, she'd reminded him of a storybook princess. Too bad she, like her mother, had swallowed Cabot Murray's lines. So it was more the cop's fault than his. Murray had pushed him into doing it.

The newspapers were having a field day at his expense, calling him a maniac, a madman, a lunatic. If they knew the whole story, the true story, they'd realize he wasn't any of those things. Angry, maybe, but then he had a right to be. Cabot Murray had cost him plenty.

Perhaps he'd send a bouquet of flowers to the hospital. That would show them he wasn't heartless. Maybe he'd buy Annie one of those great big teddy bears he'd seen at the York Mall. Or maybe he'd get both. That would prove he wasn't such a bad guy after all.

He'd show them.

He had feelings, too.

Chapter 7

Look what I brought for you today," Cabot said quietly. The candy bar slid easily from his shirt pocket. "Remember the first time I brought you one of these? It was the day after we met." He sat on the chair beside her hospital bed. "You got chocolate all over your mom's skirt." Chuckling softly, seeing it in his mind, he put the candy into the nightstand drawer with the rest of the gifts he'd been bringing Annie since she fell into the pond.

"How 'bout if I read you a story?"

When he picked up the book of fairy tales, the teddy bear caught his attention. "Where'd this come from?" he asked the silent sleeping child. Cabot lifted the envelope that lay beneath the huge brown bear and opened it. As he scanned the message, his hands shook violently, and his heart began to beat hard. Cabot ran into the hall and headed straight for the nurse's station.

"Who delivered this to Annie Glasser's room?" he demanded, holding the stuffed bear in midair.

"A man delivered it first thing this morning," said the nurse.

"He put it into her room himself?"

She nodded. "Said he was an old family friend."

"Did you get a name?"

She shook her head. "I was on the phone when he came in. Sorry."

Cabot's fear turned to fury. "What did he look like?"

She winked. "Not bad. Not bad at all."

"Describe him," Cabot snapped.

The nurse stood taller and frowned with annoyance at his tone. "He was tall. Very tan. With one of those Marlboro Man mustaches."

"Dark hair? Light hair? What!" Cabot demanded.

"Lots of hair. Curly and dark brown." Her voice was cold and unemotional now.

He'd made her angry with his ceaseless questions and aggravated tone. Cabot tried to sound a little gentler. "Have you ever seen him before?"

She smiled at that and winked again. "I'd remember if I had. He was quite a handsome fellow."

Cabot lifted the receiver of her telephone and put it into her hand. "Call the cops. Tell them to get down here right away. Tell them they're going to need to post a guard outside Annie's door, because that 'handsome fellow' is the guy who tried to kill her."

Back in Annie's room, waiting for the police to arrive, Cabot read and reread the note, typed on that same blue paper, complete with the tilted *e*'s. "Get well fast," it said, "so you can give your new friend a nice name."

His eyes moved to the bed and settled on Annie's pale face. That guy had been here. Right here in this room, looking at her, possibly touching her. What psychotic message is he sending now? Cabot wondered.

He believed Annie could hear him. Believed that comatose patients were aware of everything around them. "Annie, darlin'," he said, "you're gonna get better. I'll see to it if I have to spend every minute right here at your side."

Cabot insisted on a police guard. He'd marched straight into the office of the chief of police and demanded that Annie be protected. In the end, once he learned Cabot had been a cop in Chicago, the chief agreed. Satisfied once the uniformed officer was in place outside her door, Cabot rode the elevator to the hospital's first floor. It took a moment to find the door he'd been searching for. Inside the quiet room, he sensed peace.

Kneeling at the rail, Cabot folded his hands and bowed his head, hoping God wasn't too angry at him to hear his plea. "I know it's been a long time since I've admitted it," he began, "but somewhere deep inside, I still believe You can do anything.

"Maggie and Lindy. . . . That was an accident. It took a while, but I accepted that. What happened to Annie. . . . That was deliberate, and we both know it. I can't accept that."

Cabot hid his face in his hands, then focused on the crude wooden cross that hung on the wall above the altar. "Help me find the guy," he whispered to the Man hanging there. "We can't let him get away with this. We can't let him hurt anybody else."

�֍

For two days and two nights, Cabot stayed at Annie's side, leaving her only long enough to spend a few moments in the chapel. He had no proof that his time there did any of them any good. He only knew that being there gave him hope, and he hadn't had hope in a long time.

He'd seen the guitar at the nurses' station on his way to the first floor earlier. Cabot had read to Annie until he was hoarse. Surely she was as tired of hearing the same old stories as he was of reading them. "Mind if I borrow that for a few minutes?"

The nurse handed him the instrument. "No rock and roll, now," she warned, grinning. "We've got sleeping people up and down these halls, don't forget."

His melody wafted gently around Annie's room, changing the stark, sterile atmosphere into homelike warmth. "Hush little baby, don't you cry," he sang. It was her favorite song, and she'd made him sing it every time he tucked her into bed. "Daddy's gonna sing you a lullaby." After hearing it several times, she'd learned the words and had begun to accompany him. She loved to sing. Once she'd figured out how good she was at it, she sang things that ordinarily would be spoken: "Danny's got his shoes on the co—ouch," she'd tattle. Or "Mommy's got paint on her fin—gers."

"If that diamond ring don't shine," he continued, "Daddy's gonna buy you a silver mine."

"Where's Cuddles?"

His hands froze and the singing stopped. Cabot thought he must be losing his mind, for he could have sworn he heard her speak.

"Did she get lost in Murk?"

Cabot looked at her. At the sleepy, but open, clear blue eyes.

"I don't know how that man got her," Annie said, her voice hoarse from days of silence.

"Don't look so sad," she told him. "It's not your fault Cuddles got dead."

The hazel eyes glistened with tears. "Darlin'," he said, "I'm not sad. I'm the happiest man on earth to see you awake. That was some nap you took!"

Her smile, weak though it was, brightened the entire room. "I'll be right as rain in no time," she said. "You'll see."

He'd taught her that one-liner. It made him grin.

"What's in your pocket today?"

He leaned the guitar against the nightstand and pulled a box of crayons from his shirt pocket. "I know how much you like to color."

A grin curved her pale lips. "I'm going to color you a beautiful guitar."

Hugging her tenderly, Cabot chuckled.

"Know what I wish?"

"What do you wish, darlin'?"

"That I could climb into your pocket."

He laughed and sat back, and looked into her sweet face. "Now, why would you want to do that?"

"Because. . .it's always so full of love."

❧

Annie spent another week in the hospital. Keeping her in bed those first few days at home had been hard work for Elice, Emily, and Danny, for she wanted to run and play as if nothing had happened.

Cabot watched her closely, looking for signs that the underwater experience had permanently damaged her. Gratefully, he acknowledged that she'd been spared even the slightest scar.

It was Elice who worried him most. She'd never been a heavyweight but, since the pond incident, she'd lost a good ten pounds. She blamed her dark circles on Annie's recuperation, saying she'd been sleeping with one eye opened, listening all night in case the child might need her.

But Cabot knew better.

While they were doing the dishes together one evening after supper, he asked Emily, "How's your mom these days?"

She shrugged. "She's okay, I guess."

"She looks tired," he said.

Emily sighed. "She cries a lot in the night. But I know she sleeps some, because she has bad dreams."

Cabot took her hand and led her to the table. Seating her on his lap, he tucked a lock of hair behind her ear. "Tell me about them."

"Well, I think she dreams about the man who had Cuddles that day. She hollers at him. And she hollers at Cuddles. She won't let any of us out of her sight for a minute. She must think he'll come back. That he'll try to hurt one of us." She paused. "Do you think so, Cabot? Do you think he'll come back and hurt one of us?"

Cabot closed his eyes, unable to face Emily's scrutiny. "Of course not," he said. If they gave an award for telling convincing lies, he was sure to win it. But he summoned even more conviction into his voice, just in case. "Definitely not."

Emily got up from his lap and headed for the door. "Maybe you ought to tell Mom that."

He didn't know where the thought came from, but St. John the Baptist, the church where he'd worshipped as a child, came to mind. The place was miles away, but when he left Elice's that evening, he headed for the quaint little chapel.

Seated in the last pew, his eyes fixed on the large, stained-glass window behind the altar. In colorful gleaming shapes, Jesus stood in the Garden of Gethsemane, arms and eyes raised to heaven, beseeching the Father to hear His last prayer. Cabot got up, walked slowly to the front of the church, and fell to his knees.

He had a lot to be thankful for. Annie hadn't merely survived. . .she was her old self again. Danny and Emily had accepted him as a permanent part of their lives. And Elice loved him, still, despite the pain his past had brought her.

Yet he felt lost, alone.

Worse, he felt guilty.

The Sacred Heart beamed down from another stained glass window, a symbol of suffering and love. Mary smiled gently upon him. Joseph's understanding eyes met his. The crucifix edified Christianity.

And he thought of Elice, who hadn't been sleeping.

Of Emily, who worried about her mother.

About Danny, who tried so hard to be a man, long before his time.

And Annie, who'd nearly died because of him.

He stood there in the church of his youth, knowing full well what he must do.

"When the police catch the guy who's been terrorizing them," he said to his found-again Friend, "I'll pack up and move on. I'll get out of this place before anyone else is hurt."

Cabot waited and listened for a silent blessing. A sign from God that he'd made the right decision. Getting no visible or audible clue from the Creator,

Cabot stood. He left the church, convinced that his decision had been blessed by the Almighty.

He wasn't the first human to make the mistake of second-guessing God.

※

Every day Wally spent hours at Twin Acres, weeding, mowing grass, running errands. At the end of a long, spring afternoon, he stopped at Foggy Bottom on his way home. "Miz Glasser isn't happy any more," he confided to Cabot. "I think she misses you."

Cabot had been avoiding her since making his decision. "You're good to go over there and help her out," he said.

"Jack's been helping, too," Wally said. "If he's not on the phone, he's stopping by."

The news made every muscle in his body tense, though Cabot couldn't explain the reaction. It was no secret that Jack liked her. Everyone in town knew he'd set his cap for her long before Cabot returned to Freeland. But Jack had more or less kept his distance since that night at the carnival—until now.

"What do they talk about?" Cabot asked.

Wally snickered. "You oughta visit more, Cabot. Then you'd hear for yourself." Twisting his baseball cap, he added, "Mostly, she talks about you."

"Me? She talks to Jack. . .about me?"

Wally nodded. "She tells him she can't understand why you stopped coming around. Yesterday Miz Glasser told him she never loved anyone more. Said she didn't know what she'd done to offend you."

He hadn't meant to cause her pain. In fact, Cabot had given it a lot of thought. Short and sweet and to the point, he'd decided, would be the least painful way to end it. "Next time my name comes up, just tell her I'm busy."

"Tell her yourself," Wally said, grinning as he imitated Cabot's straightforward mannerisms and voice.

Cabot couldn't help smiling. "Maybe I'll just do that," he said.

※

It was like the proverbial snake! Cabot felt lucky not to have two fang prints as a result of overlooking the obvious. If only he had some proof.

"Hey, old buddy," he said into the phone, "how's life?"

Jack didn't speak for a long time. When he did, he said, "What do you want?"

"Well, it's like this, Jack. . . . I got a letter from my insurance company today. Seems they want to raise my rates. And I'm going to dash off a hot letter, and let them know I won't stand for it. But I want it to look professional, so they'll know I mean business. Trouble is, I don't have a typewriter. Maybe I could borrow yours?"

"I don't have a typewriter."

"Strange. I could have sworn I heard Wally say you'd mailed a typed letter to the *Baltimore Sun*. A letter to the editor, I think he said it was."

"Oh, that." Jack remained silent for a moment, then added, "I borrow Wally's machine when I want to type something. It's not much, but it's better than nothing."

Cabot felt the heat of adrenaline race through his heart the moment Jack stopped talking. "Well, thanks for the tip, pal. You take care, now, y'hear?"

He sat there, rubbing his chin for a minute or two, wondering if his call had elicited the expected reaction. Right this minute, he hoped, Jack was planning retaliation. He'd have to be an idiot not to know that Cabot suspected him.

When three uneventful days passed, Cabot began to think maybe he'd given Jack too much credit. Maybe he'd been such a good actor that Jack hadn't seen through his ruse. He remembered the day he paid Wally a visit.

"I need to have a look at your typewriter," he said the moment Wally opened his apartment door.

"Sorry. Jack stopped by this morning and took it home."

Cabot's fists clenched and his jaw tensed.

"What's wrong? You look strange."

He looked at Wally. "Can I trust you with some very important information?"

"Sure!" Wally closed the door and pulled out a chair for Cabot. "I'm good at keeping secrets. You know that."

Cabot took a seat at the kitchen table. "I know who tried to kill Annie."

The blue eyes widened. "Who?"

"You can't tell a soul. If any of this got back to the wrong person, it would be very dangerous for Elice and the kids."

Wally made the Boy Scout salute. "I swear. It'll be our secret."

Cabot took a deep breath. He was taking a big chance, telling Wally everything, but he had no choice. If he hoped to prove his suspicions, he couldn't do it alone. With Wally's help, Cabot could get the information—and the evidence—that would ensure a long prison term for Jack Wilson.

"Ever notice that your typewriter has a crooked *e*?"

Wally shook his head.

"Well, the *e*'s on notes Elice and I received are exactly like the ones on your machine."

"I didn't do it!" Wally sounded as wounded as he looked.

"I know that. Someone who borrowed your typewriter did."

His brow furrowed. "Mr. Olson," he said, holding up one finger. "You," he added as another finger popped up. "And. . . ."

The blue eyes brightened and he inhaled deeply.

"And Jack," Cabot finished.

Wally's frown deepened. "But why would he want to hurt Annie? Jack told me once he loved Miz Glasser. That he'd marry her if only she'd let him. Why would he do something like that to her if he loves her?"

Cabot sighed, shrugged. "I haven't a clue, Wally, but we have to stop him before he does any more damage. We might not be so lucky next time."

The blue eyes darted to the place where the typewriter usually sat. "He even borrowed my paper." He looked angry now. "Do you think he wanted her to blame me?"

Cabot followed Wally's gaze to the stack of blue paper on the tiny table beneath the window. He nodded. "And we're going to let him go right on thinking you're responsible. That'll keep him off guard. His next mistake will cost him his freedom."

※

Wally came running into the barn at Foggy Bottom. "He was over at the Glassers'," he said, trying to catch his breath. "I saw him. I saw what he did."

"Calm down, Wally." Cabot draped an arm around his shoulders. "Let's go inside. You can tell me all about it."

"It was a long time ago," Wally began as they walked toward the house. "It was in the summer. I was having supper with the Glassers. I didn't want to go home, so I sat under the kitchen window afterwards. I went around to the living room then, and sat in the bushes over there."

Cabot only nodded.

"I fell asleep, and a noise woke me up. I saw somebody running away from the house. Running across her back yard. The next day, she found that note."

Inside the house, Cabot poured Wally a tall glass of cold water and gestured toward a chair. As the big guy gulped the water, Cabot thought of the calculations he'd made before Wally showed up.

"I could see something shiny in the dark," Wally began. "I saw him running, then he stopped and stood beside the shed for a long time. He had on a cowboy hat, so I couldn't see his face. But there was enough moonlight that I could see his belt buckle. It was silver. And big. And it had a red stone in the middle of it."

Cabot sat across from him, leaning forward, testing his patience so Wally could tell his story without interruption.

Wally ran his hands through his hair and moaned. "I wish I wasn't so dumb. If I had remembered this before, maybe Annie wouldn't have been hurt. Maybe none of that stuff would have happened."

"Remembered what, Wally?"

He looked deep into Cabot's eyes. "I see that belt buckle all the time. Nearly every day, lately. I didn't realize it until he brought back the typewriter. It was Jack's belt buckle."

It wasn't much. But it was all they had.

※

It was sketchy at best, the D.A. told Cabot. And with Wally's mental condition and reputation in town, it wasn't likely his testimony would be weighed with much seriousness. Cabot had never been more frustrated. He knew that no matter how long the arm of the law grew, it couldn't reach all the dark and ugly corners of a mind like Jack Wilson's.

Well, he would come up with more proof. He'd find another piece of evidence that would prove, without a doubt, that Jack was not only unstable and dangerous, but capable of committing every act of aggression that had tormented the Glasser family.

Wally kept his word and didn't tell a soul that Jack was Cabot's prime suspect. He made one mistake, though, perhaps a fatal one.

Elice had sent him to Nardi's for milk and eggs. While he stood at the cashier's counter, Marge asked how Annie was these days.

"She's fine," he said. "And I know who hurt her. I can't tell you his name, but I know who he is."

"You do?" Marge gasped. "How would you know a thing like that!"

"Me and Cabot figured it out. And we're gonna fix him good, too. When we catch him, I'll go to court and tell the judge what I saw that night." He stuck the baseball cap back on his head. "He's gonna spend a long time in jail for what he did, that's for sure."

Marge shook her head and handed Wally the bag of groceries. "Be careful with that," she said, grinning. "Elice doesn't want scrambled eggs this late in the day."

Wally laughed. "I'll be careful."

His confidence had grown considerably since he'd been helping Cabot. He took greater pains with his appearance and paid more attention to his grammar, too. Everyone had begun to notice the new Wally—including the shadowy figure that came out from the bread aisle after the big guy drove away.

"Will that be all today?" Marge asked.

"Yup. Just the bread."

"Haven't seen much of you these days, Jack. You find yourself a pretty lady to chase?"

He made himself return her smile. "I've been busy," he said, handing her a five-dollar bill, "that's all."

"Well, don't be such a stranger," she said. "I miss seeing that handsome face of yours."

He grinned crookedly, picked up his bag, and pocketed the change. As he headed out the door, he sent her a flirty wink over his shoulder. And, as he revved up the motor of his shiny red truck and shifted into reverse, he decided the simple-minded fool would never testify against him. Because he wouldn't live long enough to take the stand.

❧

It had been difficult to dial her number. Difficult to make small talk with Danny before the boy ran off to find his mom. She'd behaved as though they'd talked an hour ago, rather than nearly a month ago. Cabot knew her well enough to understand why: She'd done some heavy-duty praying, and God had no doubt informed her that because of all he'd gone through with Maggie and Lindy, he needed some time to put his life in order. And because she loved him, Elice was giving him that time.

"Maybe you and the kids can come for dinner after church on Sunday," he said, trying to sound jovial.

She'd responded immediately with a friendly, "We'd love to." Then, after a moment, she added, "We've missed you, Cabot."

He'd missed them, too. But that wouldn't change what he had to do. "Stop by at about two o'clock," he told her. "I'll whip up one of my specialties."

"Can I bring dessert?"

"Sure." He heard the pain and uncertainty in her voice. It broke his heart. "I'll see you Sunday, then," he said, and hung up.

He hated the awkwardness that existed between them now. Knowing that he'd single-handedly caused it didn't help matters. What they had would soon be a thing of the past, so he wanted this meal to be special. Something they could all remember with fondness. They deserved one pleasant memory of their time with him, he decided.

He planned the menu carefully, shopped thoughtfully. Once he'd put the groceries away, he started cleaning. He wanted the meal and the house to be perfect. That's what Elice was, after all.

She deserved perfection on their last day together.

❦

He was pleased, when she arrived, to see that she'd lost that tired, withered look. Silently, Cabot thanked God. He knew he'd never be able to carry out his plan if she had continued to go downhill physically.

Elice wore a sweater, exactly like the fisherman's knit she'd crocheted him for Christmas, with crisply pressed jeans. Her chestnut curls framed her face like a halo. She was the best thing that had happened to him since he'd lost Maggie and Lindy. Cabot prayed he'd have the courage to carry out his plan.

All through dinner, she looked at him with that giving, loving expression. Years from now, he knew, when he closed his eyes, it would be that look he'd see.

How he managed to keep the conversation going as they ate was a mystery to him. Mostly, he admitted, he had the children to thank for that, with their nonstop chatter and never-ending questions. He was glad he'd invited Wally, too. The big guy loved family gatherings. Elice had been right, after Annie came home from the hospital, when she'd said that Wally was blossoming in their family atmosphere.

"I'm going out to pet the horses," Wally announced after dinner. The children grabbed their jackets and followed him into the crisp, spring sunshine.

For a moment, he lost himself in the past, thinking of the meals and laughter and happiness they'd shared in months past. Then he remembered the reason he'd arranged this meal, and the memory destroyed his blissful daydream.

She seemed to sense that something bad was about to happen and jumped up to start collecting the dirty dishes. "Why don't you put your feet up and read the Sunday paper," she suggested, "while I wash up these dishes."

He stood beside her and took her wrists. "We need to talk," he said gently.

Her eyes, wide and frightened, reminded him of the terrified little fawn he'd caught in his headlights several nights ago. Cabot coaxed her back into the chair, then refilled her coffee cup.

"Things have been pretty peaceful lately, haven't they?"

Elice nodded.

"Do you know why?"

She shook her head.

"Because I haven't been around, that's why. I've been very selfish," he said, his voice softer now, "exposing you to all that misery, simply because I couldn't stand to live a day without you."

Her mouth formed a thin, angry line. "Are we back to this again?" She took a deep breath, then let it out slowly. "You scared me for a minute there. I thought it was something serious."

He thought she was beautiful when she smiled like that. But Cabot wouldn't—couldn't—be dissuaded. "You're right. . .we've had this conversation before. But this time will be the last time. I've made up my mind."

She rolled her eyes and clucked her tongue. "Honestly, Cabot, I don't know what I'm going to do with you."

Cabot decided not to respond to her teasing. Rather, he stuck to his carefully rehearsed speech: "You're going to say good-bye. And then you're going to load the kids into the car, and go home, where it's safe and peaceful."

Elice's smile vanished like smoke, and the frightened doe-eyed expression returned. "What about you? What will you do?"

"Wally will run the farm for me. I'm heading for the mountains."

She began stacking plates again. "I realize that everything that's been going on. . .it's been hardest on you, Cabot. I think you deserve a vacation. How long will you be gone?"

He'd practiced this speech over and over. So why couldn't he just say it? "I won't be back," he said quietly, staring at the floor.

Elice didn't say a word. She seemed to be waiting for him to take back what he'd said. When he didn't speak, she slumped into a dining room chair and said, "I never blamed you for anything that happened."

She sat there, hands folded primly in her lap, her jaw set, her shoulders back. It was her "hold the tears back" stance, he knew, and he felt even worse knowing he'd pushed her this far. He held his head in his hands and prayed for the strength to do what must be done.

"I love you," she said softly. "You can't hide from that. No matter how far away you go."

Cabot sprang to his feet and stomped around the dining room. "I'm not hiding, Elice. I'm. . .I'm trying to guarantee your safety."

She stood, too, and carried a pile of dirty dishes to the kitchen sink. "By leaving me? You're ridiculous." Elice put the stack of plates onto the kitchen counter with a clatter.

"Maybe so," he admitted, "but I'm also dangerous."

Elice followed him, then stood in front of him and faced him head-on, hands on her hips, eyes blazing. "I never met anyone so full of himself in all my life! You're just a man, Cabot, with flaws and limitations, just like the rest of us. And here's a news flash for you—you're pretty easy to love, in spite of them!"

He tucked in one corner of his mouth. This wasn't going according to plan at all.

"You know that I love you, don't you?" she asked.

He nodded. He knew it like he knew his name. Like he knew the sun would rise in the morning and set at night, though he didn't deserve an ounce of it.

"Do you still love me?" she asked.

The question shocked him so badly that he answered without thinking. "Of course I do."

"Then I don't understand why you're running away."

"I told you; I'm not running away, I'm—"

". . .leaving because you're 'dangerous,'" she paraphrased, her voice thick with sarcasm. And then she laughed. "The man who sings children to sleep and comforts them during thunderstorms and cries at Disney movies. Dangerous, indeed."

Cabot frowned. "I'm leaving tomorrow. I've already packed. My mind's made up."

"Well, I'm glad to see you're sure about something."

He couldn't talk to her when she was like this. She looked exactly as she had on the day he'd met her—self-confident and secure. She'd be fine. In a few weeks, she'd be back on track, getting on with her life. He didn't have to worry about her. Elice was the strongest woman he'd ever met.

"What will you tell the kids?" he asked.

"You needn't worry about them. They'll be just fine."

She'd implied, with her words and her tone, that the four of them were accustomed to being loved and left. He'd never live this mistake down. Not if he lived to be a thousand.

"But—"

"But nothing," she snapped. "If you really feel this strongly, well, then go already. I hope you find what you're looking for."

Suddenly, his decision no longer made quite so much sense. He knew he was the biggest fool on earth to even be considering walking away from a woman like this. "I'm not looking for anything—"

Elice moved closer to him and said, "Promise me something."

He couldn't have denied her anything, especially now.

"Write me from time to time, so I'll know you're all right."

Several moments passed before he could answer her. He'd have given anything to put his arms around her, hold her close, and whisper into her thick, soft hair that he'd never leave her. But he remembered that day at St. John's, when he'd presumed the Lord's silence was a blessing upon his decision to leave.

"I'll keep in touch."

"One more thing," she said, wiggling her forefinger.

Puzzled, he leaned closer.

She wrapped her arms around his neck and held him tight, then kissed him long and hard. "You'll get another just like it when you come home," she said, and shoved him onto the porch. "Enjoy your fresh air!" she said and slammed the door.

Cabot stood there for a long moment, shocked silent by her outburst, amazed by her strength and determination. He couldn't help but grin—a woman as tiny as Elice had put him out of his own kitchen. Before his feet even hit the lawn, he knew he wasn't going anywhere, except maybe to buy a marriage license.

The long walk around the pond cleared his head. He'd go inside and apologize, and promise never to be so stupid again. He'd make her set a wedding date, and they'd put this whole sorry business behind them. And if anything more happened, at least he'd be there to protect her. The decision felt good, felt right. Much righter than the one he'd made in the chapel. So much better, in fact, that he realized he'd misread God's signals.

Heading back to the house, Cabot heard a ruckus in the barn. Wally's voice, undoubtedly in pain, cried out above the sounds of frightened farm animals. "You can't get away with this," he shouted. "Cabot knows about you and—"

Wally's words ended so abruptly that Cabot's blood ran cold. He sneaked up to the window and looked inside. What he saw took his breath away. Jack had pinned Wally to the floor and was rubbing his face into the straw. "You're not going to tell anybody anything," he said through clenched teeth.

Cabot walked quietly around to the back of the barn where double, smaller doors overlooked the fields. Slowly, he lifted the wooden slat that held them closed. Silently, he opened one slightly and slipped through the small opening. Luckily, the stalls blocked him from Jack's view.

The metallic sound of a releasing pistol hammer echoed in the huge space. He'd been wearing the .32 ever since Annie got out of the hospital. Jack was a severely disturbed man, and Cabot felt he needed to be prepared for anything. He was glad now that he'd broken the promise he'd made to himself upon returning to Freeland. It had been silly, anyway, to vow that he'd never touch a firearm again. Guns and violence had been a part of his life for so long that Cabot should have realized he couldn't hide from it.

Cabot felt dampness between his palm and the pistol grip. He was ready for whatever lay ahead.

Jack's constant mumbling drowned out the sound of Cabot's cautious footsteps as he crossed the barn's floorboards. With only a wall of plywood between him and them, Cabot couldn't afford even one misstep. One mistake could cost Wally his life.

Easing nearer the edge of the wall, Cabot stood behind the big black mare. Jack's back was to him, his right arm arched high above Wally's head, a crowbar in his hand.

"Get into that stall," Jack hissed. "Hurry up! Before I use this on you!"

Wally's eyes seemed fixed on the weapon. He sat up and crab-walked away from Jack. It was as he stood that Wally noticed Cabot, standing beside the mare in the stall behind Jack.

Cabot pressed a forefinger over his lips and prayed the big guy would have the good sense to look away, before Jack could follow his gaze. Otherwise, he wouldn't be able to get around the horse and over the stall quickly enough to prevent Jack from hurting Wally further, and he'd be forced to use the .32.

His prayer was answered. Wally walked backwards, inching away from the stall. There was a vicious cut above his right eyebrow, and another on his lower lip. A huge bruise glowed on his left cheekbone, and both blue eyes were nearly swollen shut.

"I said get in there!" Jack demanded. He laughed then, and added, "It'll look like you scared the horse, and she stomped you. Let's see you sit in a witness box after she gets through with you."

Wally moved slowly, very slowly. "Why did you do it, Jack? Why did you try to hurt them? I thought you loved them."

The questions stopped him. Jack lowered the crowbar slightly. "He's taken things from me for as long as I can remember. My dad used to say 'Why can't you be more like Cabot Murray? Why did George get a son like that. . .and I got you?'"

Jack nearly let the iron slip from his hand. His massive shoulders slumped forward. "Job. Cars. Girls. Everything I ever wanted, he took from me. Even Elice."

Cabot used the moment well and leaped over the gate. "Put down the crowbar, Jack," he said in low, even tones.

Jack spun around, but didn't seem at all surprised to see Cabot standing there, gun in hand, facing him. "Well, hello there, old buddy. When did you get here?"

"Put down the crowbar," Cabot repeated. "You don't need it any more."

In an instant, Jack whirled around and grabbed Wally, throwing the big man off balance. Jack got him in a headlock and held the crowbar's angry teeth inches from his temple. "I don't think I want to put it down, Cabot. But you might want to put the gun down."

Cabot felt a bead of sweat slide down his spine. "You're already in enough trouble, Jack. Don't make things any worse for yourself."

The crowbar pressed into the soft skin beside Wally's eyebrow. "I'm not one of your Chicago crooks," Jack spat. "Show a little respect when you talk to me."

Cabot knew it wouldn't take much pressure to drive the crowbar into Wally's temple. He could squeeze off a shot, no doubt, and take Jack down. But Jack's reflex could kill Wally.

"You're caught and you know it," Cabot said. "Put down the crowbar."

Jack's dark eyes blazed with fury. "Not this time. This time, I win." With that, he began listing his grievances: "You and me were up for halfback in high school, remember? And the same job down at the quarry. We both wanted that convertible."

Cabot stood, quietly waiting for him to make a wrong move.

"Because of you, I didn't make the football team. Because of you, I didn't get the job at the quarry. You bought the car with money you earned on that job."

Jack tightened his grip on Wally's throat.

"But then you took Maggie, Cabot. She was my girl. But you came back in that pretty blue uniform and swept her off her feet. You killed her, you know. If she'd stayed here, with me, she'd still be alive."

The words, though Jack had whispered them through gritted teeth, plowed into Cabot's brain like a locomotive.

"But that wasn't enough, was it, Cabot?" In his anger, he'd increased the pressure of the crowbar, and didn't seem to notice the trickle of blood on Wally's temple. "It wasn't enough to have everything else I ever wanted. You had to come back to Freeland and take Elice, too."

Cabot had heard enough. "Put the crowbar down. You nearly killed Annie. You going for broke this time?"

Jack looked at Wally. The sight of the big man's blood seemed to frighten him for a moment, but his expression soon returned to a mask of dark vengeance.

Cabot watched the muscles in Jack's forearm tense. Cabot didn't have time to dwell on possibilities. He only knew that he had to save his friend. He took aim at Jack's right shoulder. The harsh crack of the gunshot reverberated in the barn, and the scent of gunpowder momentarily overpowered the sweet smell of hay.

Jack blinked, and the crowbar hit the hay-strewn floor with a thud. "You shot me. I can't believe you shot me." He slumped to the floor, moaning in pain.

Cabot didn't move, didn't breathe. He stood there, gun arm hanging limp at his side, the pistol dangling from his fingertips. "Are you all right, Wally?"

"Yeah. I'm fine." Wally wiped his temple. "It's not too deep."

Only then did Cabot notice her in the doorway. How long had she been there? How much had she seen?

The moment he met her eyes he knew: She'd seen it all.

He'd stared revenge in the eye more times than he cared to remember. The hateful glare haunted his dreams. But the fear and disappointment on her face was far more difficult to look at. He ached inside, knowing she wasn't afraid because of what she'd seen. Elice was afraid of him.

Maybe it was best that she'd seen him in action; seen the real Cabot Murray. Now she'd agree it was for all their good that he leave Freeland. She was on her knees, tending to Jack's shoulder wound when he realized it wouldn't be difficult now to convince her he didn't belong in her world.

Chapter 8

Elice had been kneeling beside Jack, dabbing his shoulder with the kitchen towel she'd carried into the barn. "He needs medical attention," she said, "and he needs it now. You must have hit an artery; he's bleeding like crazy."

It was her subtle yet polite way of telling him to leave. It wouldn't have surprised him if she'd spoken only after asking the Lord exactly how she ought to dismiss him. . .in the kindest, most Christian way possible, of course. Telling him to go inside and get help, he decided, had been God's answer.

But he refused to leave her alone out there. Even with a .32 caliber bullet in his shoulder, Cabot didn't trust Jack Wilson. "You call the ambulance," he told her. He hadn't budged since he'd fired the shot. "And call the police while you're at it."

She looked at her blood-soaked hands, then met his eyes. "You could have killed him." Her voice trembled, and her eyes, wide and bright with tears, blinked nervously. "Where did you get that gun?" she wanted to know.

Jack took her hand, nudged the diamond engagement ring on her finger. "He's evil, Elice. Evil and violent. He's not good enough for you."

"Nobody's good enough for her," Cabot snapped. "Not me, and certainly not the likes of you."

Jack closed his eyes. "Maybe you're right for once," he rasped.

Elice stood, held her bloody hands in front of her, then at her sides, in front of her again, as though the vital fluid that had flowed from Jack onto them was a deadly concoction of some kind. She looked at Jack's shoulder, at the gun in Cabot's hand, at Wally's battered face, at her bloodstained hands again. Taking a deep breath, she closed her hands into tight fists, as if the action might hide the awful, sticky mess. When she saw that it didn't, she met Cabot's eyes. "You have to keep pressure on that wound," she said, "or he's going to bleed to death." Then, without another word, Elice fled from the barn.

She hadn't closed the door behind her, and Cabot stared at the huge, empty opening. Sighing heavily, he shook his head. It was over now, once and for all. He could, with a clear conscience, leave Freeland. That day in the cemetery, standing between the twin headstones that marked the graves of his wife and daughter, he thought he'd never live a harder day. He'd been wrong. Leaving Elice would be just as hard—harder, maybe.

"I'm going inside and see if Miz Glasser needs any help," Wally said.

102

The big man's voice reminded him where he was. . .and why. "Good idea," Cabot said. "Make sure the kids don't come out here. They don't need to see this." Using the gun as a pointer, he indicated Jack.

Once Wally was gone, Cabot looked at the gun. Clicking the safety into place, he tossed it aside. It landed with a quiet thump in the hay.

"What do you think will happen to me?" Jack asked.

Cabot walked over and crouched beside him, found the last clean spot on the towel, and pressed it against the bullet hole. "I don't know," he said truthfully.

Pale now from loss of blood, Jack winced in pain. "How many years do you think I'll get?"

Cabot shook his head. As always, Jack was concerned only with himself. That he'd caused Elice and her kids many months of terror never occurred to him. That he'd nearly caused Annie's death never crossed his mind. Certainly that he'd taken Cabot's last chance for happiness didn't enter his head. "Shut up," Cabot said, disgust ringing in his voice.

"I'll never make it if they put me in jail," Jack said, opening his eyes. He was having trouble focusing and squinted hard, trying to look Cabot in the eye. "Don't do this to me, Cabot." He leaned forward, bent one knee, and planted a booted foot on the floor, seeking the leverage to stand. "I'll be okay. It's just a flesh wound; you've seen injuries like this before. . .this one's no big deal, right? I can leave. I'll go to Mexico. To Alaska, maybe. Don't turn me over to the cops. Don't let them put me away."

Cabot grimaced. "I put a .32 slug into you, Jack, and it blew your shoulder apart. You're bleeding like a stuck pig. You wouldn't make it to the Pennsylvania border."

Jack grinned a little. "But. . .Pennsylvania is only three houses up the road."

"Exactly. You'd be dead before you left Maryland."

He thought about that for a moment before asking, "Think she called the cops yet?"

Nodding, he said, "Elice is your friend, you fool. In spite of everything, she wouldn't want you to suffer."

Jack relaxed again and closed his eyes. "You're not a bad shot, considering you're a little out of practice."

That made Cabot grin a little. "Coming from you, I guess that's pretty high praise."

The men's eyes locked in silent battle for several moments. "I don't suppose I'll be welcome at the wedding. . . ."

Being reminded that it was over between him and Elice wiped the grin from his face. "There isn't going to be any wedding."

Jack inhaled. "I guess it's true what they say, then."

Confused, Cabot's brows furrowed. "What do you mean?"

"Every cloud has a silver lining," he said and passed out.

The cops took Cabot's gun and the one spent shell they'd found on the barn floor, and the paramedics took an unconscious Jack. Cabot carefully inspected Wally's injuries and, satisfied he'd suffered no permanent damage, advised the big guy to go home and get some rest. Once Wally was gone, he climbed into his Jeep.

"Wait, Cabot!" Elice yelled.

If he didn't waste time, he could start the motor and be gone before she reached the vehicle. Cabot didn't know what he'd say to her; he surely didn't want to hear anything she had to tell him right now. "You could have killed him," she'd said in the barn. He believed he'd see that horrified look on her face for a long, long time.

"Where do you think you're going?" she asked, her hands resting on the track of the open window.

Cabot stared at the steering wheel. "To hitch up the trailer, and head on out," he said quietly.

She was silent for a long time, and then she said, "I distinctly heard that policeman say you should make yourself available." Though he wasn't looking at her, Cabot knew her well enough to hear the smile in her voice when she added, "He sounded like a sheriff in an old western, telling the bad guy, 'Don't leave town.' "

So, she'd finally accepted the facts, he thought. She'd opened her eyes and looked long and hard, and seen him for what he really was—the bad guy.

"They know where to find me if they need me."

"But. . .what if I need you?"

He looked at her then. Standing there beside the Jeep, she seemed smaller and more fragile than ever. "Jack was right," he said. "I'm not good enough for you."

She looked off in the distance, up into the sky towards her house. It startled him when she grabbed his collar, and Cabot jerked back slightly. "If you say so. But remember this: I've always thrived on a good challenge." She pulled him close and kissed him, long and hard, before releasing his shirt and taking a step back.

Cabot sat there, stunned, blinking in confusion.

"Well, what are you waiting for?" she asked, hands on her hips. The inner turmoil made him dizzy: Half of him was relieved that she'd finally seen the wisdom of his decision to leave. The other half grieved that she'd stopped trying to talk him out of it.

"Go on," she said, waving him away.

Couldn't she see his heart was breaking?

"Because the sooner you leave," she added, "the sooner you'll be back."

The place looked horrible, and putting it into some semblance of order filled the lonely hours of that first empty day. He wondered how long it had been since he'd been up there. Ten years? Fifteen?

Cabot poked the logs in the tiny woodstove, the cabin's only source of heat, and squinted at the hot, glowing coals. The radio's morning weather report predicted warm, sunny weather for Baltimore and vicinity, but up here in the mountains, they'd be lucky to see sixty-five degrees. And that early in the day, temperatures rarely climbed past forty-five.

Standing in front of the wide picture window, Cabot surveyed the grassy knoll below him. He and his father had built this dwelling, board by board. They'd started construction just before Cabot's tenth birthday and drove the last nail shortly after he turned thirteen. The place had seen plenty of good times, having been the gathering place for several generations of Murrays. Until yesterday, the only tears shed inside the little building had been cried by small cousins and nieces and nephews, inspired by bee stings and snake sightings and fish that got away.

On the other side of the window, Ragged Mountain soared heavenward, the cloudless blue sky surrounding it like mother love. His dad had often said he didn't understand how anyone could say they didn't believe in God, especially after they'd witnessed the awesome beauty of the vast mountain landscape.

Cabot turned from the view. It wasn't that he didn't believe; his deep, abiding faith had been the root of all his doubts. He'd been raised to believe that no matter what stumblingblock life put in his path, the Lord would show him a way around, over, or through it. He'd never questioned that. He had accepted life's disappointments as easily as its rewards, because he understood that God knew what was best for him.

But when Maggie and Lindy had died, Cabot had felt as though his whole world had stopped spinning. He had held onto police work like a drowning man clings to a life preserver. The constant, daily reminders that the earth was overpopulated by willful, evil beings had only underscored the doubts that had begun chipping away at his faith on the day he had lost them.

With his "Nothing ventured, nothing lost" motto set firmly in his mind, he had left Chicago, determined to live out his life alone. It had been a difficult decision, and it had been a big heartache that caused him to make it. After nearly five years as a solitary man, all it had taken to make him see how wrong the decision had been was a five-foot, hundred-pound bundle of energy called Elice.

The Lord knew what He was doing, all right. It seemed no matter what Cabot did, or where he was when doing it, he thought of Elice. Only one activity could blot her from his mind—prayer. Cabot had been praying a lot since arriving at the cabin. He had his solitary life back, and he had his God. What more did he need?

Coffee mug in hand, he stepped onto the narrow porch. A gentle rain had begun to fall, pattering on the leaves above and splashing quietly into the little stream that ran alongside the cabin. He took a deep, cleansing breath, then sipped the strong, hot brew. Smiling sadly, he remembered their parting scene. By now, surely she'd accepted how wrong he was for her. One painful fact echoed in his heart and mind: As wrong as he was for her, she was exactly right for him.

Cabot sighed and put his mug on the flat, wooden railing, and stared across the expanse of mossy grass at the wild rosebushes that grew on the hillside beyond the cabin. Elice would love them, he thought, picturing her flower-studded yard. She'd love the huge, majestic trees and the sparkling stream and the narrow, winding path that led deep into the thick forest. She'd love the deer that feasted on wild berry bushes, the toads that hopped beside the pond, the locusts and crickets that sang day and night. But mostly, she'd love the serenity that shrouded this place. Pity, he thought, that she'd never see it.

He noticed a rotting tree across the way, damaged, he presumed, in a recent thunderstorm. He'd cut it down today and, by nightfall, he'd have half a cord of wood stacked, aging, and ready to warm him from next winter's chill.

❧

It had taken most of the day to accomplish the task and when he was through, Cabot's bones and muscles were tense with the satisfying ache that hard work brings. He allowed himself a moment to admire the neat woodpile, then lifted the big chainsaw and returned it to the tiny shed behind the cabin. He hadn't eaten since breakfast, and his stomach grumbled angrily. Cabot could almost taste the chicken, left over from the bird he'd roasted yesterday.

An eagle soared overhead, shrieking its triumph at having snared a rabbit for its supper. It swooped low enough that Cabot had a clear view of its bright eyes. "We've both had a productive day," it seemed to say as it disappeared into the dusky sky.

After a refreshing shower, he dined by the light of a single lamp that sat on the kitchen table, then rinsed his plate and fork, and flopped into the black leather recliner that still bore the indentations of his father's muscular frame. He clicked on the lamp beside the chair and picked up yesterday's copy of the *Baltimore Sun*. Old news, he decided, turning to the "Style" section, was better than no news. Tomorrow, there would no doubt be a report about the shooting. Perhaps it would detail everything that had happened, right from the beginning. Tomorrow, he wouldn't read the paper.

He had no idea how long he'd been asleep and blamed the crick in his neck for waking him. The newspaper had slipped from his lap and lay in a sloppy heap at his feet. Cabot stacked it neatly and put it near the woodstove. In the morning, he'd use it to stoke the fire. Right now, he yearned for the comfort of his bed.

He hadn't had the dream last night and, as he climbed between the cool white sheets, he hoped it wouldn't return tonight, either. He had plenty of reminders that his life had ended the moment he had backed out of her driveway. He certainly didn't need the nightmare to confirm it. Punching his pillow, Cabot said the words he'd been saying every night of his life. "Keep it plain and simple; just talk to the Lord as though He's your friend, his mother had taught him, because that's exactly what He is."

"Lord, thank You for this day. I'll talk to You tomorrow. . . ."

He'd been saying it so long, it had become a habit. Cabot sat up in bed and tossed the covers aside, realizing he'd never really abandoned his faith. Smiling, he got up and paced around the room. He'd strayed from the straight and narrow, maybe, but he'd never actually fallen off the path. The knowledge filled him with a sense of peace and joy, and he laughed out loud.

"Lord," he said into the darkness, grinning from ear to ear, "I'm back!" He would make it. He knew that now.

❧

Elice promised herself as he drove away that she'd give him a week. If he hadn't returned by then, she'd bring him back—by the hair of his head, if necessary.

It had taken nearly three days to get hold of the police officer who'd taken the information from Cabot. In the ten days since she'd last seen him, Elice had made a few decisions.

First, she'd make him see, once and for all, that he hadn't been responsible for anything that had happened. If it took the rest of her life, she'd convince him of that.

Second, she'd force him to admit that his belief in God had never faltered, not really. She'd point out all his wonderful qualities, and prove to him that it had been his faith that had made him such a decent, caring man.

Third, she'd get him to agree to a June wedding. Elice had always wanted to be a June bride.

The Glassers had taken the kids to Williamsburg for the weekend. They'd loaned her their second vehicle, a blue, long-bed pickup that Bob Glasser used to haul wood and groceries and supplies for his dollhouse-building hobby. It took a while to grow accustomed to maneuvering the big truck but, after an hour on Route 70, she'd started to enjoy the high driver's perch and the power of the engine so much that she decided to trade in the Vega for one just like it.

The officer had been very helpful, drawing her a detailed map. He could get her as far as Route 68, he told her; after that, she was on her own. So Elice stopped at the Hancock Park 'n' Dine, ate a hearty meal, and asked the restaurant patrons who shared the lunch counter with her if they had any idea where Artemas, Pennsylvania might be. Advice came from all sides. Everybody up there, it seemed, knew George Murray. And everybody had a different way to find his mountain cabin.

Elice sat in the truck cab for a good fifteen minutes, sifting through the stack of paper napkins, each of which bore contrasting routes and different maps drawn with the waitress's blue ballpoint pen. The common denominator, she decided, was the intersection of Old Cumberland and Mount Hope Roads. If she made it that far, the old man in the coveralls had told her, she'd be able to see the peak of the Murray cabin roof. She took a deep breath and pointed the truck north. "Be my navigator, Lord," she prayed as she shifted into first gear.

❧

Cabot stood back and surveyed his well-stocked pantry. He could easily tough out a long, hard winter up here now. Never mind that it had taken two-hundred-fifty dollars and fifteen bags of groceries. And never mind that he'd cleared nearly every shelf at Helmick's Corner Store in nearby Flintstone, Maryland to do it. His goal in stuffing the Jeep with all that food was to drive down the mountain into town as seldom as possible. He'd never been much of a milk drinker, but when the mood did strike, he'd mix up a batch of the powdered stuff. Poured over ice, a man could almost make himself believe it was really milk. He'd jammed the freezer with beef and poultry parts. The ready supply of goodies made the place feel a little more like home.

He'd just closed the door on his supplies when he heard the unmistakable sound of tires, crunching over gravel. So few people drove this far up the mountain that he was always inspired to run to the window each time he heard it, just to ensure himself the driver wouldn't be pulling into the narrow, uphill drive that led to his hideaway. This time, in place of the relief that washed over him as a vehicle shot on by, a sense of doom invaded him, for a shiny blue pickup headed his way.

For an instant, he considered drawing all the blinds, turning down the radio, pretending no one was home. But the smoke, billowing from the stovepipe, was a dead giveaway that someone, recently, had been here. He'd just have to hope that this unwanted, uninvited visitor was lost. He'd give the misguided fellow directions and send him on his way.

He turned down the flame beneath the coffeepot and stepped out onto the porch, waiting for the driver to exit the pickup and tramp across the grass toward the cabin's only entrance. "Well, what do you know," he said to himself, instantly recognizing the dark curls that surrounded her lovely face.

She waved and smiled, and ran toward him. Cabot thought of that ancient butter commercial, where the lady and the man ran in slow motion across a sunlit field of wildflowers, arms outstretched, grinning like hyenas, until they met at last, and he lifted her off her dainty feet and twirled her, causing her dress to float on the breeze. He didn't know how it had happened, but suddenly Cabot found his arms full of her. She felt good, too good. He hadn't realized how much he'd missed her.

He looked into her face, unable to hide his joy. "What are you doing up here? How on earth did you ever find this place?"

She smiled. "Heavenly navigation," she explained.

The smile faded somewhat. "Are you okay?" she asked, taking a step back. "You look terrific, I'll say that much for you."

And he did, too. It hadn't even been two weeks since she'd seen him last. But the dark circles under his eyes and the lines around his mouth had disappeared. He was wearing faded, work-worn jeans and that denim shirt she liked so well, its sleeves rolled up past his elbows, revealing his muscled, tanned forearms.

"You didn't answer my question," he said. "What are you doing here?"

She glanced at the cabin. "Aren't you going to show me around?"

He followed her gaze, then shrugged. "There's not much to see."

Elice frowned. "You don't seem very happy to see me. Maybe I should have called first."

Cabot grinned at that. "Wouldn't have done much good. I don't have a phone up here."

She nodded, her frown intensifying. "I'm not surprised. What would a hermit want with a communications device?"

He ignored her sarcastic remark. "There's a pot of coffee on the stove. Can I interest you in a cup?"

Again she glanced at the cabin. In her moment of hesitation, she seemed to be debating whether or not to stay; seemed to be trying to determine whether or not she was welcome. Without a word, she headed for the porch.

Her tiny gasp echoed throughout the cabin's interior when she stepped inside and visually inventoried the paneled walls, the braided rugs, the comfy, overstuffed furnishings, and the wide, uncovered windows. "Oh, Cabot," she said, "what a wonderful place!"

He filled two mugs with hot coffee and put them on the kitchen table. "Have a seat," he said, pulling out an old wooden chair.

But she ignored him and wandered around, mesmerized by the place. "It's like a little bit of heaven," she said, looking out the big window. "What I wouldn't give for a view like that!" After a long moment, she turned from the scene and began inspecting the inside of the cabin, opening and closing doors and drawers, peeking into every nook and cranny. When she saw the huge food supply, she faced him. "How long do you plan to stay up here?"

"Permanently." He sat at the table.

She didn't even try to hide the disappointment his answer inspired. Elice sat across from him. "Well, I can hardly blame you. It's positively beautiful here."

He leaned back in the chair. "You still haven't answered my question."

The silence, thicker than the trees in the woods across the way, separated them. She broke it when she said, her voice a near whisper, "It's time for you to come home, Cabot."

"I am home."

The bluntness of his response rocked her. He knew because her beautiful brown eyes widened momentarily, then focused on her hands, which she'd folded primly on the table top.

She took a deep breath. "I called the detention center before I left," she said. "The duty officer said Jack's shoulder is healing nicely. He was in the hospital for three days, you know, with a policeman posted outside his door, before they carted him off to jail."

Cabot shrugged. Did she expect him to be relieved? Was she waiting for him to say he regretted shooting the maniac? He'd done what he'd had to do, plain and simple. She'd have to wait a long time before he'd admit anything else.

"His trial is scheduled for next week. The officer who gave me directions to this place told me Jack probably wouldn't get more than a couple of years. His attorney entered an insanity plea."

He grunted. "Now there's a news flash for you."

Elice's brows came together above her dark eyes. Then, as though he hadn't spoken, she said, "I don't think I'll ever forget that scene. All that blood. You could have killed him."

Cabot winced. How many times was she going to beat the fact into him?

"But you didn't. You only did what you had to do to keep him from hurting Walter."

He stared into her eyes. He'd been trying to convince himself of that ever since he had got here. Could it be she didn't view him as the bad guy, after all?

"I was just about to make myself a sandwich." Standing, he added, "Can I make you one for the road?"

"Aren't you the master of subtlety!" she said.

He ignored her sarcasm.

Elice was on her feet in an instant. "I'm not leaving here without you. You may as well get that through your thick skull, Cabot Murray."

Facing her, his brows rose, and he grinned in spite of himself. "How do you propose to get me out of here? Toss me over your shoulder? Drag me by my heels?"

"I'm prepared to do whatever it takes."

He could see by the set of her jaw that she meant it. At least, she meant to try.

And then she began outlining the decisions that had inspired this trip. "Number one," she said, holding up one forefinger, "you will admit you are not responsible for anything bad that happened in Freeland." Another finger popped up. "Number two, you are a God-fearing Christian, with a mountain of faith living in your heart. If you weren't, I could never have fallen so helplessly head over heels in love with you." The finger that still wore his diamond joined the other two. "And you will meet me at the altar on June tenth, because I'm changing my last name to Murray on that date, and I'd look pretty silly standing up there without you."

He couldn't move. Couldn't speak.

"So here's the deal," she continued. "We'll have a light lunch, and then you'll show me around the place. I think it's a good idea for me to know my way around, since we'll likely be spending a lot of weekends up here once we're married. And then I'm going to follow you down that mountain road, back to Freeland. Back home, Cabot," she said, shaking her finger under his nose, "where you belong."

He grabbed her finger, and his hazel eyes drilled into her dark ones. "Ever since I got here, I've been praying for a sign of some sort. Something that would tell me whether or not I'd done the right thing by leaving." His arms went around her. "How does it feel to be a messenger of the Lord?"

POCKETFUL OF
PROMISES

Prologue

Elice smiled, picturing in her mind the way Cabot had stomped around the kitchen, his big hands clasped at the small of his back and him shaking his head as he insisted he wouldn't go to Chicago at all if she couldn't join him there for his best friend's wedding. "I'm honored he asked me to be his best man, but I can't get through a whole week without you near!" He'd gathered her close then and kissed her forehead.

She giggled to herself, remembering how like a young boy he'd looked and sounded when he'd asked, "Could you spend a week without me?"

A week without a daily dose of his big manly arms around her? One hundred and sixty-eight hours without being able to look into his bright hazel eyes? Seven whole days without hearing his deep masculine voice? Elice crinkled her brow and widened her dark eyes. "How can you even ask such a question?" she asked, tucking in one corner of her mouth.

He shrugged his broad shoulders and grinned, pulling her closer. "I was hoping you'd say that."

Of course she couldn't leave her former in-laws just now. Mrs. Glasser had just been released from the hospital, and Mr. Glasser's back prohibited him from helping her get around. And she certainly couldn't leave her three energetic children with the two of them while she traipsed off to his former partner's wedding in Illinois!

But just as certainly, she couldn't let Cabot miss the wedding. He and Joe had been partners in Chicago's homicide division for ten years before Cabot had returned to Freeland. It had taken nearly an hour to convince him to go without her. . .to touch base with old pals. . .to drive through his old neighborhood. . .to visit the graves of his wife and little girl, both of whom had died in a fiery car wreck three years ago.

Although she wouldn't be taking him to the airport until morning, she missed him already. And the nightmare she'd had last night wasn't helping matters, either. Elice blocked the awful images from her mind. "Then thou scarest me with dreams, and terrifiest me through visions." She grinned, quoting Job 7:14.

She refused to believe it had been a warning from on high. It had been a dream—admittedly a terrifying dream—but just a dream, nonetheless. Nothing bad would happen to Cabot while he was in Chicago.

"It was just a dream," she insisted aloud.

Elice closed her eyes and folded her hands beneath her chin. "Please, Lord," she prayed, "show me a sign that it was nothing more than a dream."

Chapter 1

Like an old West cowboy, Cabot Murray had faced leather-jacketed thugs in dark alleys, his 9mm Smith & Wesson drawn and at the ready. He'd kicked in doors of dimly lit, rat-infested tenements in Chicago's grimy Thirty-fourth District and chased drug-crazed thieves down rain-slicked, littered city streets. He'd been shot, beaten, kidnapped, choked, and had faced death a time or two in his heydays as a Chicago homicide detective. But none of it scared him half as much as being a passenger on an airplane.

He drew in a deep breath and tried to enjoy the landscape below. The aircraft's birdlike shadow grew smaller above the patchwork of farmers' fields and housing developments as the 747 climbed higher in the late March sky. What could be more appropriate, he asked himself, than to be heading to Chicago, the Windy City, in March, the windy month? The two proved a turbulent combination as the big jet took a sudden dip in the sky. Neither the beautiful blue surrounding the plane nor the picturesque landscape below could distract him from his hammering heartbeat. Holding his breath, he waited for the aircraft to rise again. More to have something to do than anything else, he pulled down the window shade, shutting out the view.

The airliner lurched again, first up, then down. He swallowed hard, hoping his stomach would soon settle back down where it belonged instead of hovering near his Adam's apple. *Lord,* he prayed, *get me to Chicago in one piece and I'll agree to coach the Little League team for the church. I promise.* Something told him his heavenly Father wouldn't approve of such blatant deal making, but at least he could be sure that God had heard his prayer because, Cabot acknowledged, stifling a chuckle, he was floating around in the Lord's world now.

The high-pitched whine of jet engines and the low din of passenger conversation calmed him, but not much. Cabot tried to focus on the flight attendants, standing at attention in the aisles, holding up mock seat belts. Cabot grinned sardonically because if anyone aboard this plane thought for an instant that he'd unbuckle his belt before landing at O'Hare, they were just plain loco!

A short time later, the hiss and crackle of the overhead speaker told one and all that the pilot was about to speak. "Ladies and gentlemen," began the controlled, deejaylike voice, "we have reached our cruising altitude of thirty-two thousand feet. Please remain seated until the flight attendants have turned off the FASTEN YOUR SEAT BELTS signs."

Cabot didn't hear a word after "thirty-two thousand." His sweaty palms gripped the armrests so tightly that his knuckles whitened. He closed his eyes. Think of something pleasant, he told himself. Something safe and happy and. . .

Immediately, Elice Glasser came to mind. Elice, who had saved him from the haunting memories of the accident that had killed his wife and daughter. Elice, who loved him despite his stubborn refusal to be loved. Elice, who'd taught him that even he was worthy of God's love.

The very thought of his pretty bride-to-be put a gentle smile on Cabot's rugged face as he remembered the way she'd said good-bye at the gate, hugging him with a fierce strength that belied her diminutive size. "You'd better not let anything happen to you out there in the Windy City," she'd admonished, pressing a sweet kiss to his lips, "or I might just have to rough you up!"

It hurt a great deal to leave her standing alone at the Baltimore/Washington International Airport, but when Cabot's former partner, Joe Clancy, had asked him to be best man at his wedding, how could he refuse? In all honesty, the moment Cabot had learned that Elice couldn't accompany him, he had refused.

But Elice wouldn't hear of it. "Clancy is your best friend. He'll be devastated if you don't go," she'd insisted, her fists planted on her curvy hips. "Besides," she had added, wagging a maternal digit under his nose, "it'll be a good chance to catch up on all the gossip at the old station house."

That now-familiar mischievous glint had brightened her dark eyes when she'd said it. In fact, she had looked so cute, her left brow cocked high on her forehead and her long brown hair curling round her delicate pixieish face, that he'd wanted to scoop her up and kiss her for all he was worth.

So he had done exactly that.

Cabot shifted his bulk in the too-narrow coach seat, remembering the way she had sighed and snuggled closer in response to his kiss. Remembering how she'd gotten him to admit that he was looking forward to this trip a little bit, for all the reasons she'd outlined, and then some. Remembering how she'd put her hard-working forefinger to the calendar page and pointed out that, soon after he returned from Chicago, they'd be having a wedding of their very own.

"Where are we?" asked the little boy in the seat beside Cabot's.

"Halfway over Ohio," answered his mother.

The conversation woke him from his pleasant daydreams. Cabot glanced at the Timex belted to his wrist—three fifty-five. The plane would touch down in just over an hour. If he knew Clancy, the big burly Irishman was already fuming at the rush-hour traffic while driving toward Chicago's busy O'Hare Airport.

Cabot pushed up the window shade. It had been a long time since he'd viewed midwestern states from heavenly heights. But he wouldn't see them today, at least not through the billowy white clouds that surrounded the aircraft like mountains of marshmallow cream. He didn't like looking at the distant earth from God's eye view but, being unable to see through the blinding cloud cover unnerved him even more. Again, he pulled down the shade.

Rubbing his throbbing temples, Cabot sat back and closed his eyes, glad he'd remembered to pack the doctor-prescribed pain killers, and hoped that this was just an ordinary headache.

If someone had told him he would doze, in a too-small seat, thirty-two thousand feet up in the sky, he would have laughed out loud. But the drone of the engines and the soft murmuring of his fellow passengers lulled him to sleep.

In his dream state, he wore a uniform so blue it appeared black. Gold buttons gleamed on the cuffs, and his shirt glowed snow white. When he boarded the aircraft, he aimed a jaunty salute at the stewardess at the door and tucked his military-style, black-billed hat under his arm. "Coffee ready?" he asked her.

Smiling, she nodded. "I'll get you a cup."

"Thanks." With a wink and a smile, he disappeared into the cockpit. "Good mornin'," he said to his copilot.

The man grinned. "How's things?"

"Headache," Cabot said, pointing to his temple.

"Great," the copilot said, rolling his eyes. "So I have to actually work today?"

Cabot returned his grin. " 'Fraid so."

He guided the big bird to the end of the runway, building up steam as he went, then aimed the plane's nose at God's eye. Up, up they went. "All's well that ends well," said the copilot.

Cabot would have agreed, if the flames hadn't distracted him.

Fire shot from the left engine and the 747 began a lazy pirouette as it headed back toward the airport, leaving a trail of billowing black smoke in its wake.

Fearful cries and shouts mingled with the screams of the remaining engine as it strained to do the work of two. Cabot heard the copilot signal the control tower; he heard flight attendants trying to calm the passengers. He also heard the loud whooshing of his blood, pulsing as it raced through his veins.

He would save these people. . .or die trying.

It seemed the earth had been catapulted skyward, flying toward the plane like a giant silver bullet. The pale yellow guidelines of the landing strip came into view and grew, and grew, as the earth and the plane came closer to a jolting meeting.

Then, in the distance, he spied a little red car. Inside it, arms flailing helplessly amid the smoke and flames, were his wife and child.

He would save these people. . .or die trying.

The engine fire spread, engulfing the cockpit now. Incredible, scorching heat seared his skin, singed his brows and lashes, and burned the hand that jerked back on the stick. "Pull up!" shrieked the copilot. "Pull up!"

Cabot shifted in the seat, throwing all of his weight into it, but the stick was hot, so hot that he couldn't hold on. He snatched back his hand and shrugged out of his jacket, thinking to use it as a hotpad.

116

He would save these people. . .or die trying.

And then the plane exploded.

Cabot bolted upright. Suddenly, mercifully, he was awake, perspiring, breathing like he'd just run a marathon, and his head ached.

This was no ordinary headache, he admitted dismally.

"Are you all right, sir?"

The stewardess sounded so much like Elice that, for an instant, he thought he might still be dreaming. He looked into her worried eyes—pale blue eyes, not velvet brown like Elice's—and sighed with relief; to have Elice see him in this weakened, trembling condition would have been mortifying. "Headache," he whispered, his voice hoarse.

"Let me get you some aspirins," said the stewardess, "and a cold glass of water."

"Thanks," Cabot said as she headed for the back of the plane.

But aspirins wouldn't put a dent in this headache, he knew that much from experience. Only the little white pills, prescribed by the doctor, would dull the pain.

His first brutal, wracking headache had happened in the hospital nearly three years earlier, in direct response, the doctors had told him, to the shock of learning that his wife and daughter had been killed. For weeks after that, the migraines returned with relentless regularity. . .and so did the dreams.

The peaceful respite that slumber provides most of God's creatures was, for Cabot, a long, terrifying descent into a haunting, horrifying chamber that echoed with the blood-chilling screams of his wife and little girl. A hollow, harrowing chamber, where he experienced, time and again, sensations of uselessness and powerlessness as he tried. . .and failed. . .to put out the flames, to get them out of the car. Each torturous climb back to consciousness came at a heavy price: the mauling grip of migraine pain. . .

As time passed, the pain lessened, as did the frequency of the nightmares. Moving to Freeland had been just what the doctor had ordered, it seemed; he'd had just two migraines since quitting the police force and none since leaving Chicago.

Cabot pushed up the window shade beside his coach seat and peered into the vastness of space. Sunlight sliced through the pale blue sky and slanted downward in brilliant golden shards, like a many-beaconed lighthouse pointing the way from heaven to earth. *God's world*, he repeated. *Take it easy ol' boy, 'cause you're in God's hands.*

The Lord had seen him through the miserable aftermath of the tragedy that had taken Maggie and Lindy from his life. And the Lord had seen him through those harrowing days as Elice's youngest had lain in a coma.

He pressed his fingertips against his forehead. He'd be in Chicago in a few minutes, surrounded by old friends and familiar terrain. He had no reason to suspect anything was awry.

But old dreams and new gonged loud in his memory, bullying their way into his mind like unwelcomed ghosts, awakening sensations of dread and doom and dismay. He'd been a cop too long to ignore the feelings that coiled in his gut like ready-to-strike rattlesnakes. Still, Cabot tried to convince himself that the uneasy churning in his stomach was the result of turbulence, rather than a warning of an oncoming brain-busting headache.

Because, if the migraines were back, it could mean only one thing. . . .

Chapter 2

A white-haired drunk, wrapped in a wrinkled raincoat, snored in the chair that had once been Cabot's as a gum-popping blond in a red leather miniskirt perched on the corner of his old desk. Across the aisle, a tattooed giant in biker boots, shredded jeans, and a denim vest awaited interrogation. Joe Clancy's phone shrilled as the light above his desk winked annoyingly. Could it possibly be the same defective bulb that drove Cabot to distraction when he called Chicago's Thirty-fourth District home?

Cabot, with his overcoat slung over his one arm and his hands tucked into the pockets of his pants, stood in the doorway, smiling a bit as he took it all in. *The more things change. . . ,* he silently repeated the age-old cliché.

His quiet surveillance was disturbed by a hearty slap to his back. "Well, look what the dog done drug in," said a familiar, gravelly voice. Joe Clancy clamped Cabot's hand in his own and pumped his arm up and down so hard that Cabot half expected to see water trickle from his fingertips. "Hey, you guys!" Clancy shouted. "Cabot's back!"

As the detectives drew near, Cabot winked and said from the side of his mouth, "Still a big blowhard, I see."

Chuckling, Cabot's ex-partner gave him another good-natured thump on the back. "And you're still as ugly as my grandma's bulldog."

Andy Flynn joined them. "Only thing ugly as your grandma's bulldog is you, Joe Clancy." With that, Andy gave his former co-worker a brotherly handshake. "Good to have you back, bud."

"Amazing what being around sane people can do for a man," said the blond in the red leather mini. "You look great. Ten years younger, even. Country living agrees with you."

Cabot returned her warm hug. "Good to see you, too, Gail," he said, then quickly added, "but I gotta tell you, I really like the new uniform." Cabot held her at arm's length and surveyed her outfit. "Will spike heels and leather skirts be standard issue for policewomen from now on?" he asked, his brows wiggling above widened eyes.

Gail playfully swatted his shoulder. "I'm undercover, you big lummox!"

❧

The next hour flew by as the homicide detectives sipped strong coffee and devoured the thickly iced welcome-back-Cabot cake that Gail had baked for him. Pictures of his former co-workers' children and spouses were shoved into Cabot's hands as he passed photos of Elice and her children around. He pretended his head wasn't pounding and acknowledged each heartfelt compliment regarding his soon-to-be family.

A time or two, he caught his grizzled ex-partner watching him closely. Was the headache that obvious? Cabot wondered. He got his answer when Clancy drew him aside and said, "You look like something I scraped off the bottom of my shoe." Grabbing their coats from the rack, Clancy led Cabot toward the door. "Let's get you on over to my place so you can catch a little shuteye."

They were in the hallway when Clancy stuck his curly red head back into the office and whistled to get the attention of the detectives, who, balancing foam coffee cups and plates of cake, had already returned to their respective work spaces. "You kiddies are welcome to come over and play with Cabot any time after six," he sarcastically sing-songed through the open door, "but don't forget to bring notes from your mommies, telling me you finished all your veggies, or there'll be no milk and cookies."

Cabot and Clancy artfully dodged laughter, bawdy remarks, and paper wads that sailed in their direction in response to the taunt. Outside, Clancy's jangling key ring was the only sound to disturb the dark and chilly Chicago evening. Quite a contrast, Cabot thought, to the warmth and brightness of the bustling squad room. Clancy pulled up the brown corduroy collar of his weathered green overcoat, reminding Cabot of Joseph's coat of many colors, reminding Cabot that although he'd spent more than a decade in this city, he was a stranger there now.

"You still toodlin' around in this old heap?" Cabot asked, chucking his suitcase into the back seat of Clancy's '68 Mustang convertible. "When're you gonna grow up and get a real car?"

"'Bout the same time you quit askin' stupid questions." Clancy patted the dashboard affectionately. "You know I can't get rid of Bessie. She's family."

"What's she got on her now?" Cabot asked as he settled into the passenger seat. "Hundred forty, hundred fifty thousand miles?"

Clancy snickered wickedly. "Two-oh-two," he announced proudly. "And I'll wager she'll go another hunnert." His big foot pumped the gas pedal and the Mustang roared into action at the first turn of the key. "Atta girl," he crooned, "sing for Daddy."

Ordinarily, Clancy's shenanigans would have inspired laughter. . .a smile, at least. The best Cabot could do on that dark March night was shake his head and grin. . .and hope the Anacin he'd washed down with the bitter station house coffee would soon kick in. He didn't dare swallow any of the prescribed medication just yet. . .not if he wanted to stay alert.

Cabot had retired from the force a little more than two years ago. During the ten years he'd worked the tough streets of this district, gut instinct had saved his life a time or two. He had to wonder if the eerie sensation churning in the pit of his stomach was a warning that something horrible was about to happen, or merely the precursor to a humdinger of a migraine.

"All right. Out with it. What's bugging you?" demanded Clancy.

Cabot glanced over at Clancy. "Nothing. I'm right as—"

"Don't hand me that 'right as rain' garbage, you flatfoot," Clancy interrupted. "You're talking to the man who pounded the beat with you every day for ten long years. Now come clean or I'll—"

"I'm fine," Cabot said. He guessed it would take about five seconds before Clancy started telling him what he believed was wrong. Mentally, Cabot began counting backwards. Five, four, three. . . .

"You told me on the telephone last week that you haven't had a migraine since you left Chicago."

Cabot couldn't suppress a grin, despite the headache. "Yeah. And it was true."

"Was true?" Clancy repeated. "They've started up again?"

"No, no," he said, waving the notion away. "At least, I don't think so."

"Have you seen a doctor lately?"

Cabot shook his head. "What's the point? All he'd say is to take two aspirins and call him in the morning. By then, the worst of it would be over. Besides, it's one headache. Who's to say it's a migraine?"

"Does Elice know about the others?"

"No, and I don't want her to know," Cabot warned. "She's been through enough without—"

"So she doesn't know about the blackouts, either?"

Silence was Cabot's answer. He hadn't told anyone but Clancy about the times he'd completely lost hours, sometimes days, to a migraine attack.

"Whaddaya mean when you say 'she's been through enough'?"

Slowly, Cabot filled Clancy in on the details of Elice's life to date: At twenty-three, she'd married Bobby Glasser, who'd long dreamed of being a race car driver. After ten years of striving to eke by on his meager wages, Bobby left her—with two small kids and a third on the way—to fulfill his dream. He died a year later, when his race car exploded. Elice struggled for years to keep the kids in food and shoes and mittens, Cabot told his former partner, until she put her artistic talents to use. Opening Twin Acres Signs had saved them, financially and emotionally.

Cabot told Clancy it was because of her little business that he'd met Elice, and how, on the day he'd commissioned her to create a sign for his farm, Foggy Bottom, her youngest child, Annie, had practically forced him to stay for dinner. Thanks to Annie, he'd immediately felt part of the loving little family.

He explained how Elice had stood by him through the whole Jack Wilson fiasco, from slashed tires on her battered old Vega to threatening notes placed on her kitchen table. She'd stood by him even when Jack nearly drowned her little girl in Cabot's pond at Foggy Bottom. Once he was sure that Annie would be her old self again, he told Clancy, Cabot moved into his father's cabin in the mountains, thinking it the best and only way to protect Elice from any further danger associated with his past. But, he added, she followed him up there in a borrowed pickup, though she'd never driven a stick shift in her life, to insist they would get married as planned—or else!

"Sounds like just the kind of woman to keep you on the straight and narrow," Clancy said, laughing.

Cabot sighed again. "I've never met anyone like her," he admitted. "She deserves nothing but peace and happiness for the rest of her life. And I aim to try and give it to her. God knows I've already brought her enough misery and pain."

"You're a pigheaded, ornery buzzard, you know that? Elice doesn't sound like the kind of gal who'd hold you responsible for any of what happened."

Clancy made any pigheaded, ornery buzzard seem like an easy mark, Cabot knew. His old partner, who was gearing up to try to convince him to tell Elice about the migraines, could be doggedly determined when he had a mind to. Cabot's voice was dangerously low when he said, "I don't want her to know about the headaches, Clancy. Not this one, not the ones I used to get, not any that might happen. Period. That's my final word."

Clancy held up a hand in mock surrender. "Okay. Okay. Whatever you say. But I think you're nuts 'cause those headaches of yours aren't like anything I've ever seen."

He ignored Cabot's deep sigh. "Could be there's nothin' to worry about. You can ask my sweet li'l Sarah when you meet her tonight. Her mama used to get migraines. Doc gave the old lady some kind of miracle powders. . . ."

Try as he might, Cabot couldn't pay attention as Clancy's voice droned on and on. The headache's hard hammering drowned out his ex-partner's words. But the pounding in his head didn't concern him nearly as much as the growing feeling of unease rumbling around in his gut.

❦

As Cabot stood under the soothing spray of the Shower Massage in Clancy's black-and-white bathroom, he thought of his morning and relaxed slightly.

It was an hour's drive from Freeland to the Baltimore/Washington International Airport, and they'd been on the road forty-five minutes, his big hand resting lightly on her thigh. "You're awfully quiet," Elice had said, patting it.

Cabot had forced a frown. "Maybe I'm coming down with something?"

"That's a lame excuse, and you know it," she'd teased, meeting his eyes. "And you won't be in Chicago for hours, so save your mean-cop face for after you land at O'Hare."

Before Elice had come into his life, he'd never really understood the old cliché, but the truth was she could read him like a book. "Much as I love looking into your big brown eyes, keep 'em on the road, would ya? I already have nightmares about dying in a plane crash; don't add 'road kills' to my list of neuroses."

She had feigned a menacing look of her own before turning her attention back to Baltimore's 695 Beltway traffic. "Hey, I'll have you know I took driving lessons from Mario Andretti. You couldn't be in more capable hands. . .unless God Himself were behind the wheel."

Cabot leaned across the minuscule space that separated them in the front seat of her rattling Vega and planted a soft kiss on her cheek. "Sorry, Mrs. Soon-to-be-Murray," he'd said, "didn't mean to imply you're not a good driver. It's just. . ." Settling back in his own bucket seat, Cabot had drawn a deep breath. "It's just that I haven't talked to anybody but Clancy since I came back to Freeland. Haven't seen most of the guys since—"

Cabot had stopped speaking so suddenly, it was as though someone had wrapped a powerful hand around his throat, because the painful truth was that he hadn't seen most of his police buddies since the day his wife and little girl had died in the fiery car crash.

From the corner of his eye, he had seen her fingers tighten around the steering wheel. "Don't worry, pretty lady. I'm fine. Honest."

He'd never confessed his fib. Once he got on the plane, he'd down a couple of aspirins and pray with earnestness that the headache would vanish. And till it did, he'd try to forget those first terrible bouts with head pain. Back then, during those lonely months after the double funeral, he'd half-hoped that a tumor was at the root of the unrelenting brain throbs. That maybe God had decided to call him home, to join his wife and child.

As it turned out, Cabot didn't have a tumor. The doctor had diagnosed migraine headaches and suggested a diet free of red meats, sugary foods, and caffeine. He had given Cabot a handful of free samples and promised to prescribe a stronger headache zapper if the migraines increased in intensity or frequency. Cutting out chocolate bars and hamburgers hadn't done a bit of good, but going home to Freeland, Cabot discovered, had been exactly the right medicine. He hadn't had a single headache since leaving Chicago.

Without taking her eyes from the road, Elice had affectionately squeezed his hand. That, too, had been good medicine. Sometimes, all it took was a gentle touch from her powerful little hands to soothe away the tensions of a long day's work or the worries of a sleepless night.

She had sighed resignedly. "If Mom and Pop didn't need me. . ."

"You're doing the right thing," he had confirmed. Then, sending a wink her way, he'd chuckled and said, "Proves you won't leave me stranded and helpless when I'm old and gray." And it was true, too, because if her dead husband's mother hadn't needed her, Elice would have come with him to Chicago. But, she was a caretaker to the core. Elice wouldn't hear of a convalescent center or a nurse-for-hire after Mrs. Glasser's surgery. And she certainly didn't want her former father-in-law throwing his back out again, lifting his wife from her bed to her wheelchair. Instead, Elice had moved into the Glassers' house, kids and all, and declared that she'd stay until Mrs. Glasser was well again. It was exactly that kind of loving loyalty that inspired her to take Cabot into her house, where several times an hour she fluffed feather pillows under his head and adjusted his crocheted coverlet, and several times a day spoon-fed him homemade soup and tempted his appetite with home-baked bread while he recovered from Jack Wilson's brutal knife attack.

Just because he hadn't had a headache in two years was no reason for alarm, Cabot told himself. It was certainly no reason to worry Elice. Besides, he knew that if he'd told her how he felt, she would have barged onto the plane and tucked one of those little pillows behind his head. She would have climbed onto some unsuspecting passenger's seat and reached into the overhead compartment so she could cover him with one of the airline's nubby white blankets.

So he had stood in the doorway that led down the long, mazelike tube connecting the terminal to the aircraft and let her hug the stuffings out of him, and pretended his head didn't hurt at all. It's just nerves, anyway, he had told himself. Excitement. Fear of flying. Looking forward to seeing Clancy and the guys again. Not until the flight attendant had buttoned up all the overhead bins and double-checked each passenger's seat belt did Cabot allow himself to admit this was no ordinary headache.

Now, he lay back on the narrow twin bed in Clancy's spare room and tucked his hands under his head, waiting for the drug to take effect. Typically, it took half an hour for the medication to work its magic. Tonight though, upon arriving at Clancy's apartment, he'd downed two capsules and the pain still beat mercilessly into his brain.

And so did the feeling that something awful was about to happen.

Chapter 3

When Cabot had phoned from Chicago, he hadn't said a single thing to make Elice think that something was wrong. So why couldn't she shake the uneasy feeling that he faced uncertain danger?

Elice sat, her open Bible in her lap, waiting for Emily's ride to bring her home from the Christian youth group meeting. Elice's older daughter had become more involved in school and church activities since Cabot had come into their lives.

A loving smile flickered across Elice's delicate features as she remembered the night he'd gathered all three of her children close and told them how, as a boy, his Scout troop cleaned up an old graveyard. "It wasn't just the satisfaction of seeing the results of our hard work," he'd said in his usual, fun-loving way. "It was the grateful looks on the faces of the people who had family members buried there." Cabot had paused, kissed each child on the forehead, and added, "There's no greater reward than that."

Right then and there, Elice had seen the light of eager anticipation glowing in Emily's clear blue eyes. But she couldn't have known just how big an impact Cabot's story would have on her young daughter's life. Thanks to her association with the youth group, the once-shy twelve-year-old began volunteering to head up all sorts of projects. Her most recent effort was the weekend-long White Elephant sale, whose proceeds sent Jimmy Bartell to Disney World, his fondest dream since learning that leukemia would soon end his young life.

"Doing good deeds" spread like honey through the Glasser house. Before Elice knew it, Danny had roped several of his pals into helping him whip Mr. Harrison's yard into shape. Crippling arthritis had prevented the old guy from tending his roses as he'd been doing for as long as the ten-year-old could remember. "I bet he misses sitting on his porch, smelling and looking at those pretty flowers," the dark-eyed boy had said one night over supper. Next morning, he'd ridden his dirt bike to the public library, checked out six books on the care of roses, and studied each one carefully. Convinced he now possessed the knowledge required to revive Mr. Harrison's neglected plants, he got straight to work. While they were at it, Danny decided, he and his friends would edge the walkways, prune the trees, and trim the hedges. "No point doin' a job halfway!" he had announced, quoting Cabot verbatim.

Six-year-old Annie got into the act, too, when she talked her first grade teacher into letting the class clear debris from the schoolyard. The little tykes, following Emily's example, held a massive bake sale and used the money to purchase bulbs and annuals that would flank the main doors of Prettyboy Elementary. Marigolds surrounded the big flagpole, petunias cascaded from hanging baskets at the entrance, and daisies bloomed at the feet of the marble-faced Abe Lincoln.

Listening to their grandchildren's squeals of joyful satisfaction had inspired the Glassers to organize a food-and-clothing drive for the homeless.

Cabot had made quite an impression on the little family, indeed, but none bigger than he'd made on the woman who, until his love touched every corner of her well-sheltered heart, believed she'd spend the rest of her days alone.

Unable to concentrate on her evening devotions, Elice closed the Bible and returned it to a shelf in the entertainment center. She glanced at the mantle clock across the room and thought again of Cabot's call. It had been hours since he'd assured her that he was fine, just fine. Why couldn't she just take him at his word? And when would this nagging sensation of approaching doom dissipate?

For the hundredth time that evening, Elice replayed his call in her mind. After a series of "I love yous" and "I can't wait to get homes," Cabot had told her about the raucous welcome he'd received upon arriving at his old stomping grounds. He'd chuckled as he described Clancy's nervous fidgeting at any mention of his own upcoming nuptials. He had told her he'd met Sarah, Clancy's fiancée. Why, he'd even gone so far as to compliment the meager lunch served on the plane!

Elice determined it wasn't so much what Cabot had said that so disturbed and frightened her. Rather, it was what he hadn't said that sent tremors of unrelenting dread coiling up her spine. The ominous feeling reminded her of those bleak harrowing days, when, side-by-side at Annie's hospital bed, she and Cabot had waited for the child to regain consciousness. Elice hadn't known what was eating at him then, either. Gently, she'd quizzed him, hoping he'd open up. But it was not until she had followed him to the mountains, where he'd gone because he believed himself a danger to her and the children, that he confessed his feelings of unworthiness.

And earlier, halfway through their long-distance conversation, when she'd pressed him about his careful word choices being an attempt to sound jovial, did he say, in his matter-of-fact way, that all was well.

But it wasn't.

Everything, from the tone of his voice to the way he'd hesitated a second or two before answering, told her that something was wrong. . .very wrong.

Elice closed her eyes and quoted Psalm Twenty-seven: " 'The Lord is my light and my salvation; whom shall I fear?' " Immediately, she focused on the mantle and the photograph she'd taken of Cabot and the children on Father's Night last December. In the enlarged, framed snapshot, Cabot grinned with paternal pride as he wrapped her three bundles of energy in his brawny arms. A lock of tawny hair fell across his forehead, giving his handsome face a boyish quality. Her heart fluttered slightly as she looked at his warm, hazel eyes. Eyes that, even in a photograph, shimmered with love for her and her children. And oh, she loved him, too!

Cabot had warmed every cold place in her heart. He'd brought genuine fatherly love to her children. He'd welcomed Bobby's parents into his life as easily and readily as he'd welcomed Wally, the slow-witted, big-hearted man who'd been friend and family to Elice and the children since Bobby's death.

All it took to remind her of Cabot's uncharacteristically dour mood was a quick glance in the direction of the kitchen wall phone. He deserved happiness, not sadness; peace, not stress. But he was in Chicago, and she in Freeland, Maryland. Not even the breadth and width of the huge love in her heart for this wonderful man could reach across the hundreds of miles between them and comfort him.

Only God could comfort him now.

Elice lowered her head, clasped her hands in front of her, and prayed silently a verse she'd memorized long ago from Psalms. *I will trust in the mercy of God forever and ever.*

The sound of a slamming car door caught her attention, and Elice returned the picture to its place on the mantle. Emily, intuitive and intelligent beyond her years, would notice immediately if something were amiss. Elice couldn't allow the concerns for Cabot coursing through her to worry her daughter. So she threw back her shoulders, faced forward, and plastered a warm, welcome-home smile on her face. "Dear Lord," she whispered as Emily's blond head appeared in the front door's oval window. "Please keep him safe from harm."

❧

"So what's Clancy got planned for you this morning?" Elice asked.

"I thought maybe I'd just tag along with him and Gardner. See if the kid's as good as I was," Cabot replied.

In the background, Elice heard the laughter and good-natured complaints of Joe Clancy and Cabot's replacement, Mark Gardner. But she also heard that same tone in Cabot's voice that had worried her so last night. It wasn't like him to sound downcast and forlorn, to sound so. . .sad. "You'll be careful out there, won't you?"

"Of course I will. I'll call you this evening. Kiss the kids for me, and tell 'em I love 'em."

"They send their love, too."

After a long, silent pause, he said, "Can't seem to make myself hang up." Cabot took a deep breath. "I haven't been gone twenty-four hours, yet I miss you like crazy."

"I miss you more," she said, playing their I-love-you, I-love-you-more game.

But she wasn't smiling when she said it because, despite herself, Elice couldn't shake the ungrounded notion that something was very much awry. "We went all through this before you left," she said, deliberately summoning her mom-knows-best voice. "You needed a break. This trip will be good for you. Besides, it'll give you a chance to spend some time with Maggie's folks."

Cabot's dead wife's parents lived in the town the newlyweds had called home. Her dad still bought and traded postage stamps from his little shop in a nearby strip center, and her mom sold handicrafts in a quaint Main Street store. Since their only child and granddaughter were now buried in Glen Ellyn, they'd made the Chicago suburb their permanent home. Surely Cabot would want to join them for a visit to Maggie's and Lindy's graves.

"You'd better enjoy these next few weeks," Elice advised, "because once you get home, it's business as usual."

His sigh filtered through the earpiece. "I suppose you're right."

"Absence makes the heart grow fonder, you know."

"Impossible," he said. Then, "Well, they're signaling me it's time to leave. Talk to you tonight, pretty lady."

The sudden appearance of hot tears surprised her. Quickly, she swallowed and blinked them back. "Enough of this mush!" Elice scolded playfully. "Now go have some fun, for cryin' out loud, or I'm gonna wallop you a good one when you get home!"

The last thing she heard before hanging up was Cabot's rough-edged voice whispering "I love you."

Sweet Jesus, she prayed silently, *watch over him.*

❧

Clancy, Gardner, and Cabot had interviewed the neighbors of a homicide victim and were on their way to talk to the dead man's coworkers when the three cops pulled into the drive-through lane at McDonald's.

"And these guys think they can get away with murder," Gardner was saying over the hiss and crackle of the voice on the loudspeaker. "We round 'em up," the lanky young cop continued, "and the bleedin' heart judges put 'em right back out on the streets."

"Faster'n we can say Rumpelstiltskin," Clancy added.

"Aw, sing a new tune once in a while," Cabot clowned.

"When something is worth saying," Gardner defended, crumpling his youthful brow, "it's worth repeating."

"Six hundred and fifty million times?" Clancy drove the four-doored black sedan around to the side of the building.

From the back seat, Cabot said "This trip is supposed to send me back to Baltimore saying, 'Why can't they have cops like that in Maryland?' So what do I find? A bunch of blubberin' babies!"

"Put a lid on it, Murray," Clancy injected. "You got no right to complain."

He faked a scowl at Cabot in the rearview mirror. "Left me high and dry, with this greenhorn to train, yet. Y'oughta be ashamed of yourself, that's what!"

Cabot's laughter was short lived, for each chuckle increased his discomfort. He'd more or less accepted the fact that this was no ordinary headache boiling in his head like a cauldron of witch's brew. At least he'd managed to hide it from Elice. He sent a silent prayer of thanks heavenward that God had seen fit to bless him with a moment's worth of acting talent. Because the long and short of it was, if Elice had so much as suspected Cabot was in pain, she would have demanded that he catch the next flight home so she could nurse him back to health, just as she'd done when Jack had shoved the hunting blade deep into his side. Covering his face with both hands, Cabot summoned her image.

"I think we oughta bump 'em off, one at a time," Gardner was saying. "Don't give any of 'em a chance to take another victim. That's what I think."

Clancy pocketed the change from the cashier and handed Gardner the sack of food. "Fortunately for the citizens of Chicago, you're not getting paid to think. Ain't that right, Cabot?"

Cabot came out from behind his hands long enough to meet Clancy's concerned eyes in the rearview mirror. "Huh?"

Clancy glanced at Gardner and shook his head. "Give him his Big Mac before he keels over." To Cabot he said, "I told you what would happen if you skipped breakfast. It's the—"

"I know, I know. It's the most important meal of the day," Gardner and Cabot said in unison.

Clancy nodded. "Yeah, well, it's true."

For a block or two, they rode in companionable silence, wolfing down their burgers and gulping their giant sodas. Gardner was first to speak. "About what I was saying earlier," he said around a mouthful of cheeseburger, "I'll bet Cabot agrees with me." He turned sideways in the seat and met Cabot's eyes. "Especially after what happened to your wife and kid."

The guttural sound that popped from Clancy's mouth made Cabot wonder if his pal might be choking on a pickle. "Shaddap and eat, ya big-mouthed brat," Clancy said, punching Gardner's shoulder.

Cabot stopped chewing and frowned, unable to connect Clancy's sudden fury, the accident, and Gardner's anger at the system.

The young cop ignored his partner. "I mean, I'll bet you wanted to strangle that bomber with your bare hands."

For an instant, even the headache stopped. Cabot neither heard nor saw anything but Gardner's wide, innocent brown eyes blinking back at him. *What bomber?* he wondered as Clancy gave Gardner's bicep another hit.

"Didn't your mama teach you never to talk with your mouth full?" Clancy growled. Then, meeting Cabot's eyes in the rearview mirror, he shrugged. "See what you left me with? You oughta be shot, I tell ya. Now, don't you feel guilty?"

Cabot knew that look. . .had seen it hundreds of times during the ten years he and Clancy rode together. His ex-partner was trying to disguise the situation with jokes. But what situation? Cabot wondered.

Gardner rubbed his shoulder. "Hey, Clance, what gives? I was just—"

Clancy's hard stare silenced the good-looking young cop. "What do you say we ride on over to the Twenty-first, Cabot?"

Despite their back-and-forth banter, Cabot hadn't moved, hadn't spoken, hadn't breathed. He took a short swallow of air and tried to ignore the quick exchange between Clancy and Gardner; the older partner's glare clearly warned the younger one to button his lip.

But why?

Cabot searched his memory and silently repeated Gardner's last comment: *I'll bet you wanted to strangle that bomber with your bare hands.* "A bomber had nothing to do with what happened to Maggie and Lindy," he said at last. "They died in a car accident." He looked into the rearview mirror, hoping to find a sign of confirmation in Clancy's pale blue eyes. "On the Dan Ryan Expressway," he added when the burly Irishman refused to meet his gaze. "Tell him, Clance."

"Yup."

Cabot had worked with Clancy long enough to recognize a stall tactic when he heard one. No doubt, the hesitating, one-syllable response had been uttered because Clancy knew him well, too, and knew he wouldn't be satisfied with no answer at all. He opened his mouth to say just that when Clancy blurted out, "I told the guys over at the Twenty-first you'd be in town, and they said to bring you on by. Everybody's looking forward to seeing you again," the freckle-faced fellow said, ignoring Cabot's question. "Cabot and I started out there together," he explained to Gardner.

The young cop rolled his eyes. "Like I haven't heard that ten thousand times."

An uncomfortable silence sputtered in the sedan's interior, as though someone had loosened a live wire, then sprayed water over it. Cabot scooted forward and leaned over the front seat and, gripping Gardner's shoulder with one powerful hand, said in low, even tones, "What bomber?"

Gardner shrugged, despite the weight of the big hand. "Uh, I. . ." He looked to Clancy for guidance.

Clancy signaled a left turn, floored the big sedan, and pulled it into a metered space at the entrance to Ryan Woods. He threw the car into PARK and turned off the engine. The big vehicle bounced slightly when Clancy got out and slammed the door. "So you're gonna be a stubborn mule, eh?"

Cabot only stared at him.

"I know that look," Clancy said. "Well, all right then, since you're so all-fired determined to hear this," he growled, opening the back door for Cabot, "the least I can do is tell you myself, face to face."

Cabot and Gardner got out of the car at the same time, their doors closing in one unified thud. They stood for a long moment, staring at the toes of their highly polished black shoes.

Clancy was first to break the silence. Clearing his throat, he cast an angry glance at Gardner, who looked from his partner to Cabot and back again. Lifting his shoulders in a gesture of humility, Gardner said softly, "I figured he knew."

Cabot had had about all of this he could take. His head hurt worse than ever, and his stomach had tied itself into a tight knot. "Knew what?"

Gardner blanched and stuck his upturned palms into his coat pockets. "I'll wait for you guys in the car," he mumbled as Clancy dropped heavily onto a park bench.

"Have a seat, Cabot," he said, a beefy forefinger indicating the empty space beside him. At Cabot's hesitation, he added, "Trust me, ole buddy, this is one story you'll want to hear sitting down."

Chapter 4

Evidence supporting the district attorney's contention that Maggie's car had exploded minutes before crashing into the other vehicle that rainy afternoon on the Dan Ryan Expressway was sketchy, at best. So the decision to keep the whole truth from Cabot, Clancy explained, had been a unanimous one. No one at the old Thirty-fourth wanted to be the one to break it to him. Nothing would be gained and a lot could be lost, Cabot's fellow officers determined, by inundating him with a truckload of innuendo and supposition. Without tangibles to back up the bomb theory, his comrades were rightly concerned that such news would drive him right over the edge, particularly on the heels of burying his wife and only child. They had nothing concrete to go on, no fingerprints, no telltale M.O., no proof of any kind that could lead to an arrest, let alone a conviction.

Still, it was a lot to hear, all at once like that, and a lot to absorb in one brief telling. Because, hard as it had been to learn to live without Maggie and Lindy due to what he believed had been an accident, it would be harder yet to find the strength to live with the fact that, in all likelihood, it was someone he'd once arrested and jailed who had wreaked his vengeance by killing them. Elice and her children had also paid a hefty price for his past, what with Jack Wilson's threats and tricks. In fact, Annie had nearly paid with her very life.

Now he realized that Maggie and Lindy had paid with theirs.

He got up from that park bench and shuffled woodenly over to the black cop car, slumped into the back seat, and didn't even bother to close the door. Cabot didn't speak, didn't cry, didn't think he could do either even if he tried. Maybe, if he were lucky, Clancy wouldn't close the door. Maybe, he'd drive away from the park and, as he turned onto the highway and accelerated, Cabot would tumble into the oncoming traffic.

Of course Clancy slammed the door and insisted on driving Cabot to his apartment. Insisted, too, that Cabot take a long shower and a short nap before dinner.

Cabot took a hot shower. A shower so hot, in fact, that when Clancy saw the billows of steam erupting from under the bathroom door, he burst in and bellowed "You're gonna scald yourself, you big dumb lummox!" Indeed, when he toweled himself dry, Cabot's skin did prickle, like a bad sunburn. It took nearly fifteen minutes of arguing to convince his ex-partner that he hadn't taken his headache pills before getting into the shower. The news didn't comfort Clancy. "The man's so distracted he nearly boils himself alive," he mumbled under his breath as he headed for the door. "Can't go to dinner with Sarah tonight and leave you here alone in this condition," he added in a considerably louder, and angrier, voice.

It took another fifteen minutes for Cabot to talk Clancy into having dinner with Sarah—alone. And once the big guy had left to pick up his fiancée, Cabot tried to nap. But he felt he was coming apart at the seams. One thought sounded in his mind like an ancient oriental gong: *You killed them. You killed them. You killed them.*

Without bothering to undress, he lay atop the covers on the twin bed in Clancy's spare bedroom. But he didn't sleep, didn't dare. For if he did, he might have the awful dream again. He'd been free of its brutal grip far too long to allow it a new foothold in his life.

Cabot got up and dug around in his suitcase for the prescription vial, then swallowed two capsules, gulping greedily at the cool tap water in Clancy's immaculate kitchen. He'd get good and involved in a spirited game of basketball on Clancy's wide-screen TV, that's what he'd do. Maybe that would get his mind off the horrifying revelation that Maggie and Lindy had been murdered.

Settling into his ex-partner's broad leather recliner, he pressed the remote's ON button. Michael Jordan dribbled across the polished wooden floor, his high-topped sneakers making little squeaks in direct contrast to the power and strength of his moves. He'd recently rejoined the Chicago Bulls after a stint as a "boy of summer," but the drawn-out strike had made Michael's baseball dream impossible.

Cabot thought he understood how Jordan felt, because he'd wanted a few things he had dreamed of, too. From the moment he had set eyes on her, he wanted nothing more than a simple life with his loving wife and a passel of giggling kids. It seemed, after Maggie and Lindy were torn from him that day on the Dan Ryan, that the picture-perfect lifestyle was nothing more than an impossible dream. As he was placing the twin bouquets of roses at their grave markers, he'd stopped believing in love, at least in his lifetime, in the possibility of a family, and in God.

Time, though, performed its magic on his battered heart, and Cabot came to realize that he had never really stopped believing in them. Instead, he simply wished he could have stopped believing, because loving that much had left him exposed, susceptible to loneliness, and unprotected from the anguish that shrouded him when they were snatched away in a fiery flash. Certain that he no longer possessed the strength, the courage, the ability to trust—whatever character trait that would allow him to put his heart on the line again—Cabot avoided intimacy at any level.

And then, along came Elice, who made him believe there was love left in him, after all. Enough love, in fact, to grab hold of all those things he'd dreamed about, and then some. Her unfailing, unconditional acceptance of who and what he was had given him hope, had given a newer, righter purpose to his life. Cabot thanked God each and every day for that. Thanked Him for Elice's huge capacity for faith and trust, for it had been contagious.

Praying soothed him somewhat, but not enough to block the pain in his brain. Light, even the dim, flickering beams radiating from the TV screen, made his head ache more than ever. He depressed the OFF button and sat in Clancy's darkened, hushed living room, listening to the steady thrumming of his heart, each and every beat a throbbing reminder that the migraine was in full control.

The migraine nagged like an aged fishwife. His only escape, he knew, was sleep. But slumber scared the daylights out of him, so he fought it. At first, the quiet clicks as his upper eyelids met the lower ones came in quick succession. Gradually, though, the sound slowed, then stopped as he allowed his burning eyes to close. Long, ragged breaths scraped from him like sandpaper on rough-hewn wood, and he knew that sleep—and respite from the migraine's gnawing grip—would soon descend. *Don't let me have the dream*, he prayed, *just don't let me have the dream.*

Those first moments of restful repose were short lived. Like freeze-framing the most grisly scenes in a horror movie, the pictures in his mind pummelled him.

He heard the call on his police radio and immediately recognized the dispatcher's staccato listing of license plate numbers. It amazed him that his heart could beat so fast, despite the fact that he was holding his breath. Cabot was both thankful and surprised that his car could actually travel the hundred and twenty miles an hour promised by the speedometer. "Dear God," he prayed aloud as he sped through the crowded city streets, "let it be a mistake. Don't let it be Maggie and Lindy."

Two fire trucks, three ambulances, and dozens of squad cars blocked his path, and Cabot was forced to park nearly a block away. He ran the entire distance full out, and when he broke through the front line in the crowd of curious onlookers, he spotted Maggie's little red sedan, engulfed in flames. Inside, he saw his wife and daughter. He heard them, calling his name. He sensed them, trying to reach for him from behind the smoke-filled windows.

As Cabot headed for the car, several uniformed officers grabbed him. "Get back, buddy," they ordered. "You'll be toast. . . ."

Precious seconds ticked by. If he didn't go in, Maggie and Lindy would be. . . . Cabot wrestled free from the officers and headed straight for the car. In the seconds it took to go the distance, and as the firefighters rushed to uncoil their hoses, his cop-quick mind assessed the scene.

The blaze had all but devoured the back seat, and was hungrily licking at the front seat now. When Maggie's car and the black sedan collided, the electrical system shorted out, freezing the power windows in the closed position. He had to act fast, or lose them to the fire's voracious appetite.

Ignoring the searing heat that singed his eyebrows and lashes, Cabot pounded on the front passenger window, hoping to shatter it and give the smoke somewhere to go. When that proved useless, he stepped back and slammed the sole of his shoe into the glass.

But the window refused to break.

On the other side of it, Maggie, crying and coughing, slapped furiously at the flames gnawing at Lindy's hair. Somehow, she'd managed to unlatch the lock, and frantically pointed at it between smacks.

"Thank you, Lord!" he shouted, grabbing the door handle.

Instinct, though, made him snatch back his hand as hot metal scorched his palm. Immediately, he began unbuttoning his suit coat, planning to use it as a hot pad. *Help me get them out of there,* he prayed silently as he shrugged out of the jacket.

He smiled at them then, to share his belief that any minute now they'd be safe and sound. And just as his fingers touched the handle, the car exploded. The huge fireball propelled him backward, rendering him unconscious.

When Cabot awoke in the hospital, he saw his partner asleep in the chair beside his bed. Cabot ached all over, but his head hurt worst of all. He gave himself a quick once-over. His right arm was in a sling, his left hand bandaged. But nothing made sense. Why was he here? Had he been wounded in the line of duty?

"Hey," he whispered, sticking a bare foot out from under the covers to nudge Clancy's knee. "Hey, Joe. . . ."

The red-haired man came to and sat up.

"I'm gonna report this to the captain," Cabot said, grinning as much as his swollen, bruised jaw would allow. "Napping on the job is against regulations."

The solemn expression on Clancy's face scared Cabot. "What's going on, Joe? What am I doin' here?"

"There was an accident," Clancy began softly. "On the expressway."

It came back in an agonizing flash, almost as blinding as the fire itself: Red car. Red flames. Maggie's red hair. Lindy's little red mouth screaming "Daddy. . . help us. . .Daddy. . . !"

Cabot sat up, grimacing with pain. "Where are they?" he demanded, swinging his legs over the side of the bed. "In pediatrics? In the Emergency Room?" He grabbed a fistful of Clancy's shirt, ignoring the pain it caused his burned palm. "Where are they? Tell me where they right now, Clance, or I'm gonna deck you!"

Gently, Clancy pushed Cabot back onto the mattress. "They're gone, Cabot."

He blinked up at his partner. "Gone? To Shock Trauma, you mean?" Cabot tried to stand and swayed woozily.

"Get back into bed," Clancy insisted. "They've shot you full of painkillers. You're swayin' like a drunk."

Cabot sat on the edge of the bed, boring hotly into Clancy's eyes. "Go get the car, I tell you, or I'll get it myself."

Clancy only shook his head and said sadly, "Cabot, listen to me." Placing a warm hand on his friend's shoulder, he repeated, "Maggie and Lindy are gone."

Gone? he thought. *As in DEAD? Naw. . .they can't be. I prayed like crazy all the way from the station to the accident. Every word out of my mouth was aimed straight at God's ear. Surely He wouldn't let them. . . ?*

"What do you mean. . .they're gone?" he managed to get out after a moment.

Clancy sighed heavily. "Why me?" the big man whispered to the ceiling. "I mean gone, Cabot. G-O-N-E."

A deep furrow formed in his brow as he tried to fight back the tears. "You're lying. He wouldn't do this to us. To me. All my life, I've believed. He wouldn't do it. Couldn't do it. . . ."

"Who?" Clancy wanted to know. "Who wouldn't do what?"

Clancy never got an answer to his question, for Cabot lay back against the cool, crisp pillowcase and covered his face with the bandaged hand. Nurses, doctors, paramedics—everyone in the E.R.—stared when the mournful wailing began. Then, as though embarrassed to have intruded on his grief, each looked away and pretended to be engrossed in work.

The dream stopped there every time. Just as surely as "The End" would scroll up at the conclusion of an old black-and-white movie, Cabot would wake from the dream, groggy and perspiring, his heart beating fast and tears streaming down his face.

But not this time. This time the dream droned on.

Cabot saw himself, standing at their bedroom window, as he often did when sleep eluded him. It comforted and calmed him, somehow, to peer into the peaceful darkness that blanketed their tidy yard, where the blossoms that Maggie had planted shimmered like pearls in the bright moonlight. From somewhere beneath the tangle of covers on the bed behind him, Maggie sighed sweetly, reminding him that her love, like a reassuring embrace, surrounded him, as steady and as sure as her soft, sleeping breaths.

A slight movement near the curb caught his attention, and Cabot bent closer to the glass to focus on the dark-clothed figure that crept up the driveway. It scurried, ratlike, from shadow to shadow, a small bundle tucked under its right arm. Then, crouching low, the silhouette rolled onto its back and crawled in a crablike fashion under Maggie's car. When it slipped out again, it's hands were empty.

When or how it happened, Cabot didn't know. But somehow, as he stood watching the secretive somebody dart to and fro in his yard, he'd been hog-tied. Bound and gagged, he couldn't warn her; couldn't stop this terrible tragedy from happening.

The scene he'd just witnessed replayed in his mind faster than the landscape whizzing past him when, as a boy, he would speed downhill on his Schwinn racing bike.

The bundle was a bomb.

The bomb would explode.

The explosion would kill them.

And Cabot was powerless to prevent it.

There, in Clancy's recliner, Cabot moaned in his sleep as surely and loudly as he'd moaned that afternoon in the Emergency Room. His long legs moved slowly across the thick pile carpeting as his head thrashed left and right and left. But did he cry out from the pain of the migraine, or from the pain of what his dreaming mind saw?

I'll bet you wanted to strangle that bomber with your bare hands, Gardner had said. . .*wanted to strangle that bomber with your bare hands.*

Cabot's tightly clenched fists pounded the chair's leather arms once before he leapt to his feet and, with a murderous glaze in his hazel eyes, he stormed out the door.

Cabot stood, ashen-faced and alone, truly alone, for at that moment, he was without God in his heart. There on the corner of 103rd and Halsted, he stared across the street and read the Fernwood Park sign. A jetliner, on its way to Midway Airport, whined above him. Its engines caused none of the anticipated agony, for the migraine had, thankfully, released its brutal grip.

How he'd ended up here was as big a mystery as the condition in which he seemed to be. Cabot glanced down at the scuffed toes of his oxblood loafers and noticed that his shirttail had come untucked. One side of his white collar poked out from beneath the navy sweater that Elice had crocheted for him for his birthday. The Windsor knot of his silk tie had come undone and hung sloppily out of the sweater. Haphazardly, Cabot shoved it inside, where it belonged.

He ran a trembling hand through his touseled blond waves and winced with pain. Holding both hands out in front of him, Cabot inspected his injuries. Six of his eight big knuckles were bloodied and bruised; three of his fingernails were torn and jagged.

One quick glance at his reflection in the wide window of the Halsted Diner was more than enough to confirm the obvious—the migraine had caused another blackout.

Cabot took ten wooden steps, then sagged onto the brightly painted bus stop bench. Leaning his elbows on his knees, he held his head in his hands. *Lord God*, he prayed, *don't let me have done anything I'll regret.*

A white-uniformed nurse sat beside him and clutched her huge purse tightly to her bosom. She cast a sideways look in Cabot's direction and grimaced, as if disgusted by the very sight of the disheveled bum who shared her space. She stole a quick glance at her watch and sighed deeply, her very demeanor clearly stating she hoped the Number Seven would be on time, especially this morning.

Cabot leaned weakly against the red-and-white Coca-Cola ad plastered across the bench back and closed his eyes. When he opened them, the first thing he saw was the bright blue newspaper box on the corner, and in it were the words: EXPLOSIVES ASSAILANT FOUND NEAR DEATH.

It wasn't the lead story, yet it screamed for his attention. Cabot dug in his pocket and withdrew a quarter, then walked to the box and retracted the morning edition of the *Chicago Sun Times*. Back on the bench again, he read silently: John James Johnson, 34, of the 300 block of Cicero, was found near death last night in an alley near Fernwood Park, a police department spokesman said.

Cabot blinked several times and swallowed hard. Hadn't he arrested a guy named Johnson several years ago? For the contract murder of a pal's cheating wife, if memory served him. And the choice of weapon, if he recalled right, was a bomb.

His heart beat faster as he scanned the rest of the article. Johnson. . .arrested last week on charges of attempted murder. . .self-made bomb. . .attached to his ex-fiancée's car. . .released due to illegally secured evidence. . .connected to other bombings, including one of revenge against a Chicago homicide detective.

Cabot stopped reading and wadded the paper in his hands. The nurse gasped at the sudden crinkling sound and leapt from the bench. Muttering under her breath, she glared at Cabot and stood a careful distance away.

But he paid her no mind. He was far too engrossed in trying to connect his unaccounted-for hours and his rumpled appearance with the newspaper story. Had Gardner's innocent comment planted a seed of an idea in his pain-racked mind? Had the power of suggestion been enough to encourage Cabot to seek out the demolitions expert. . .seek vigilante vengeance for the crime he believed the man had committed against his wife and daughter? In one heartbeat, he shrugged. *So what if you did? He deserved to die if he killed your wife and daughter.*

In another heartbeat, he shook off the evil thought. He'd already lost his family, and he had devoted himself to upholding the law. If he permitted the animal known as John James Johnson to take that, too, from him, he would be a hollow shell of a man, indeed, with nothing left to give his beloved Elice. He refused to give Johnson that kind of victory.

But he was familiar with the sophisticated computers at the station, after all. And recognizable enough to waltz right in and request any information he wanted. . .and get it.

His tongue studied the swollen, bloodied cut on his bottom lip. With aching hands, he rubbed his stubbled chin and found it sore, too. *How'd you get in this shape, Murray?* he asked himself. *And how'd you get so far from Clancy's apartment?* But as he stared at his battered hands, he thought he knew the answer.

The huge city bus rolled to a squealing stop at the corner, and the frazzled nurse climbed aboard. From the safety of her seat, she shot Cabot a haughty look through the window, tossed her head, and stared straight ahead. The doors closed with a hiss, and the lumbering vehicle lurched forward, taking the angry nurse and her fellow passengers far from the place where Cabot Murray sat. . .far from the place where someone had nearly beat John James Johnson to death.

Again, Cabot glanced at his abraded knuckles. Suddenly, one particular line from the *Sun*'s article reverberated in his head. Opening the paper to the front page, he searched for it. Because of insufficient evidence, Johnson, who was arrested in connection with a similar bombing several years ago, was not charged with any crime. Could the reporter have been referring to the explosion that killed Maggie and Lindy? Fury whirled through him like a cyclone, starting in his head and roiling to his fingertips. He clenched his fists. Had he clenched them similarly last night. . .around the throat of John James Johnson?

Cabot glanced at his watch. The blackout had lasted nearly nine hours. Plenty of time, he admitted, to have committed assault and battery. Assault nothin', he chided himself. Attempted murder is more like it!

He hailed a cab and stepped nearer the curb when the yellow vehicle stopped. "You know where the Thirty-fourth Police Station is?" he hollered through the closed window.

"You betcha."

Cabot got in and slammed the back door.

"Hey. Go easy on this old tub," the cabby said. "Damages come outta my pay, don't ya know."

But Cabot, trying to reconstruct where he'd been all night, never heard the warning.

Ten minutes later, the duty officer confirmed that Cabot had, indeed, visited the Thirty-fourth late last night and had asked to see the logbook for the date of Maggie and Lindy's accident. Cabot's heart pounded and his ears grew hot as the officer handed him a small, spiral tablet. "You left without it," the uniformed cop said.

In a glance, Cabot read the names and addresses, scribbled in his heavy hand. Marcus Donnelley. Booker Lee Dayton. George Allen. John James Johnson. Mitchell Joseph Cruden.

John James Johnson?

It was looking more and more like Cabot had been Johnson's attacker, and Cabot didn't quite know what to make of that. If he'd found himself in the same predicament in those painful days immediately following the double funeral, he would have thrown back his head and laughed aloud that the vermin who had murdered Maggie and Lindy had paid for his vile crime. But time had softened the hard edge of the hate that had burrowed into his soul. Time and Elice, who had shown him the way back to God. United with his Maker once more, Cabot no longer felt compelled to seek an eye for an eye.

At least, that's what he had believed until this morning. Somewhere deep inside him, in a place his mind seldom visited, hatred had been doing a slow burn. How else could he explain the evidence that was so quickly stacking up against him? The migraine. The blackout. His disheveled condition. The fact that he'd used his position as a former detective to secure information about Johnson.

Cabot pocketed the tablet, then began the two-mile walk from the Thirty-fourth to Clancy's apartment. He hoped that by the time he got there, Clancy would have left for the station house, giving him the privacy to call Elice.

Cabot prayed she'd be home, prayed that she would have time to talk with him. He prayed that he would have the strength of conviction to protect her from this latest bout with his sorry, violent past because, before he told her anything, he needed to find out what part, if any, he had played in the near-fatal attack on John James Johnson.

For now, Cabot wanted to hear her sweet voice, whispering assurances of undying love into his ears.

Chapter 5

Elice stared through the wide, curtained window above the Glassers' kitchen sink, unaware that she had been scrubbing the same pot for nearly ten minutes, unaware of anything, really, other than Cabot.

From the moment he had made the decision to go to Chicago, his mood had turned from warm to cool, his behavior from up-close to distant. And in every phone call since he'd arrived at Joe Clancy's apartment, she'd heard the tension in his voice, though he tried hard to disguise it with well-timed jokes and sweet talk. His serious tone during his most recent call, just moments earlier, added weight to her suspicions that something more than blustery spring winds had chilled him in the Windy City.

"They're letting me tag along with them," Cabot had said, chuckling. "I whip out my notepad and pencil and pretend to take notes, just like in the old days."

"Are they feeding you well?" Elice had asked.

The familiar resonant tones of his masculine laughter had tickled her ears. "If it were up to you, I'd be too fat to fit into the barn back at Foggy Bottom. Yes, they're feeding me well, pretty lady."

So why, then, she had asked herself, did he sound so weary? So forlorn? "When was the last time you had a decent, balanced meal?"

When he had sighed, she had pictured him, eyes closed and one corner of his mouth turned up in that way that was decidedly, uniquely Cabot.

His answer, quick and simple, had caused her heart to skip a beat. "Almost a week ago," he'd said, "at your kitchen table. Juicy ham and sweet potatoes, green beans, and—"

"A steady diet of burgers and fries and pizzas will clog your arteries. Make you listless and. . ." And sad? she had almost added. But she had stopped herself, because a brand new sensation—doubt—had started bubbling in her mind. Did he love her as much as he said he did? Or was this trip to his old stomping grounds the beginning of the end of them? Would being back on familiar turf, surrounded by friends and comrades, make Cabot regret his move to Freeland? Had being in the place where he'd lived and shared. . .and lost. . .Maggie and Lindy, made him yearn to return. . .and stay. . .near memories of his first and only love? Much as she wanted to comfort him, doubt kept her silent. *What a selfish woman you are,* she had scolded herself, *to be having such self-centered thoughts!*

And so she said, "You need some healthy food inside you. If that's all they're feeding you, it's no wonder you sound. . ."

She had squared her shoulders and raised her chin in stubborn defiance of the new emotion. *I will not ask him to tell me what's wrong!* she had told herself. But no amount of standing tall and no degree of teeth clenching could erase the feelings lurking so near the surface of her heart.

"No wonder I sound what?"

Elice had bitten her bottom lip and prayed for God's guidance. Could she be honest with him without spoiling his trip?

"Are you talkin' to Cabot?" Annie had asked, tugging Elice's apron. "I wanna talk to Cabot. Can I talk to Cabot, Mommy. Can I? Huh?"

"Put that little angel on the line," he had said, "so I can send some sugar from Illinois to Maryland!"

Once she'd handed the phone to her youngest child, Elice had looked toward the ceiling. *Thank You, Lord,* she had prayed, for this little respite. Now, if the Lord would only give her back her determination to be strong.

"We miss you. When are you coming home?"

Elice had watched her child smile and nod in response to Cabot's words. "And I love you, too, all the way to Pluto even!" she had squealed happily. "Danny? He's right in the next room."

A fraction of a second had ticked by before Elice had been forced to protect her eardrums by clamping both hands over her ears.

"Da-a-a-an-ne-e-e-e-e!" Annie had hollered. "Cabot's on the phone!"

A moment of silence had followed, then the thundering sounds of the boy's approach. "Hey, Cabot," he had said, breathless from his run. "How's everything?"

Like Annie, Danny had grinned as Cabot spoke. "Uh-huh. And we won! Eleven to seven! If you hadn't taught me how to pitch a zinger. . ." And then, "Nope. She's at Youth Group. They're getting ready for the annual spring festival, y'know."

Again, the nodding boy had listened as his dad-to-be had talked. "Sure, I'll tell her. Um-hmm, she's standing right here." Beaming, Danny had handed Elice the phone. "He says he's playin' cops and robbers for a couple more days, and that he'll be home real soon."

In the early days of their relationship, Elice's heart would throb mercilessly whenever one of her children announced that Cabot was on the phone. Now, though many months had passed and she'd promised to become his bride, it still pounded just as hard.

"Hello," she had said. "And how are you?" It was what she would always say, no matter how brief the break in their conversation.

And, as always, Cabot had laughed. "I'm exactly as fine as I was five minutes ago. How're you?"

Giggling like a girl, Elice had turned away from the children to hide her blush. "I'm fine," she had said. "Just fine."

"You can say that again."

No doubt he was wiggling his blond brows as he said it, she had admitted, grinning.

"Now, why don't you tell me how much you miss me so you can get back to whatever you were doing when I interrupted."

"I was washing dishes," she had said. "You can interrupt that anytime." The delicious tones of his laughter had warmed her, and she had said what she'd been thinking since answering the phone: "Oh, Cabot, I love you so much, I think I might burst!"

"Ick," Danny had said, faking a scowl. "I'm gettin' out of here before the mush gets any thicker."

"What's mush?" Annie had asked, following her brother toward the living room.

"It's that goofy talk that's comin' outta Mom's mouth right now." But as he was turning the corner, he had faced his mother, winked, and sent the okay sign her way.

"I love you, too," Cabot had said. "But I'd better let you go."

"I don't want you to go. I miss your handsome face. I miss seeing you in that big old chair in my living room. I miss your call every single day with 'G'mornin', sweetie.'" Hot tears had stung her eyes, but she had fought the urge to cry. "I miss you more than I thought it possible to miss anyone." His quiet chuckle had warmed her heart. Maybe she had imagined the sadness in his voice. . .because she was missing him so much.

"Well, good, because I miss you, too." A silent moment had passed before he added, "I wish you were here."

So she hadn't imagined it after all. Elice had tried to identify the edge in his voice. Was it grief or sadness or pain? "I wish I were there, too," she had admitted. "Are you sure you're all right, Cabot?"

One second, then two had ticked silently by before he had answered. "I'm fine. Nothing to worry about. Got a little headache is all."

She remembered seeing him suffer with what he referred to as "a little headache." In the hospital, while waiting for Annie to wake from her coma, Cabot had blamed himself for the accident, saying that if Jack Wilson hadn't had a bone to pick with him, none of the horrible things they'd endured during those bleak, dark months would have happened. He'd been in the hospital chapel, holding his head in his hands, when she had slipped quietly into a pew several rows behind him. Even from that far back, she had been able see the veins throbbing in his temples. "Migraine," he'd whispered once she sat beside him and took him in her arms. "I get them from time to time, when things get. . .crazy."

Later, with Annie home again, safe and sound and healthy, he had sloughed the migraine off with a wave and a shrug. "They started when Maggie and Lindy died. But the docs gave me some pills, and they worked like magic."

Elice hoped that what he suffered now was, as he'd said, nothing more than "a little headache." But, just to be safe, she had said, "Take a dose of that magic medicine the doctors gave you and get some sleep."

Her worried frown intensified as she realized he wouldn't have bothered to pack the prescription unless he suspected things might get. . .crazy.

"I love you, Cabot. You're always in my prayers, you know."

The second hand on the kitchen clock had slid from the two to the three before he had whispered, "Please don't ever stop."

Did he mean don't ever stop loving him, or don't stop praying? she had wondered, gripping the phone more tightly.

Thoughts of his call stopped short when Emily rested her hand on Elice's forearm. "Hey, Mom," the girl said, "you're going to wear a hole in the bottom of Grandma's spaghetti pot if you keep that up." She pressed a gentle kiss to her mother's cheek. "Is everything okay?"

Elice met Emily's clear blue eyes and smiled reassuringly. "I'm a little worried about Cabot. When he called earlier, I got the idea he's a little. . ." She searched for an appropriate word. "I think he's homesick."

Emily pulled her mother's hands from the sudsy water and blotted them on a thick dish towel. "I'm going to put on the kettle and brew us a cup of blackberry tea. And while I'm doing it, you're going to sit in Grandma's recliner and read the evening paper."

Elice hung the red-and-white striped towel on the hook beside the window, then placed a hand on either side of her daughter's face. "You're a honeypot," she said, "and I love you like crazy!"

"I love you, too," she admitted, her hands atop her mother's. "Now get in there, put your feet up, and relax for a change!"

Elice allowed herself to be led into the Glassers' well-appointed living room, where Emily all but forced her into an overstuffed blue chair. She would sit, but only to please Emily. And she'd turn the pages of the *Baltimore Sun* the girl had handed her, but she wouldn't read. Most of all, she would not relax. How could she, when Cabot's last words were still ringing loud in her ears?

"Please don't ever stop," he'd said when she assured him of her prayers. "Please don't ever stop."

Elice closed her eyes tightly and hid behind her hands. *Dear Lord, my God,* she prayed, *You brought this man into my life, and he taught me to love again. Touch him now with Your loving grace.*

There, alone in the quiet room, Elice reflected on Christ's love. His life had been one of quiet and humble grace. Always, He put others before Himself, without complaint and with gentle strength. And others drew strength from Him, from His words, from His healing touch. "Sweet Savior," Elice whispered into the darkness behind her hands, "Your final words were of love and forgiveness." She took a deep breath. "As You entrusted Yourself to Your Father's care on that holiest of days, I entrust Cabot into Your care."

The teapot whistled merrily from the other room, interrupting Elice's heartfelt plea. Now that she had put Cabot in God's capable hands, she should have felt comfort, should have felt peace in the knowledge that the Master would watch over her beloved.

Instead, she felt shame, because she had no reason to doubt her Lord. Hadn't He always been there for her? Hadn't He always provided shelter and comfort and every worldly need? What earthly reason did she have to doubt Him now!

"Please don't ever stop," Cabot had said in a voice wracked with pain and grief. "Please don't ever stop."

Elice's heart swelled with love for him, and her mind raced with concern as she considered all the possibilities that might have caused that hard, weary edge in his voice. She folded her hands more tightly and tried again.

"You carried my cross and died in my place. You live in my heart, my Savior, my Friend, my Lord.

"You opened my eyes to joy when I was blind to it, and banished my every fear with a simple promise: Everlasting Life.

"As in Matthew 28:20, You said, 'And, lo, I am with you alway, even unto the end of the world.' Shower Cabot with that belief, Lord, so he'll believe, as I do, that You're there for him, always."

This nagging suspicion that God had not heard and might not answer her prayer was almost too much for Elice to bear. She fled to the powder room and locked the door. Surrounded by Mrs. Glasser's happy, sunflower-papered walls and brightly colored fixtures, she stood alone, and wept softly.

❧

Alone in Clancy's apartment, Cabot replayed the conversation in his mind, over and over again. He should have summoned more strength before dialing that number. Why, even in his own ears, he'd sounded like a sniveling weakling. *No wonder Elice asked, time and again, if you were all right.* He'd brought her enough suffering and pain already; from now on, he affirmed, he wouldn't call unless he could send positive messages and attitudes her way.

Well, he would have more than enough time for self-recrimination this night; Joe and Sarah wouldn't be home from dinner at her mother's for hours, yet. Sarah's mother had invited Cabot to join them, but he had begged off. Now he jammed his hands into the pockets of his pants and winced at the pain that caused his bruised, swollen knuckles.

The agony reminded him that when he returned from his nocturnal wanderings early that morning, it hadn't been easy to explain his physical condition to Clancy. "Tripped and slid down an embankment," he had said, laughing to hide the ugly truth that, in all likelihood, he'd nearly murdered a man with his bare hands. True, that man had, in all likelihood, killed Maggie and Lindy. But that

145

gave him no right, as a man who claimed to live his life by the book, to hold himself up as judge and executioner.

Still, could Gardner's innocent outlaying of information have been like an evil seed planted in his tormented mind? Could Cabot actually have sought out Johnson and nearly beat him to death during his migraine-induced blackout?

Sighing, he lay on Clancy's sleek modern sofa, his hands tucked under his head, as he waited for the prescription pain medication to take effect. Closing his eyes, Cabot summoned Elice's image. Immediately, her petite form, topped off by that mop of dark curly hair, appeared before him. He saw her long-lashed brown eyes, glittering and glowing with unabashed love for him. Saw too, the wide and easy smile that proved her joy at the very sight of him.

Usually, the pills took effect slowly. Tonight, thankfully, their numbing powers made him feel groggy and heavy within moments. Cabot yawned deeply and stretched. He was tired, so very tired. But, afraid of the dreams, afraid of the aftermath of unendurable physical and emotional pain that followed the dreams, he had been avoiding slumber. Maybe this time, he would slip into an easy rest, because this time, his drowsy mind focused on the melodious tones of her sweet voice. She could rouse him from a sour mood, it seemed, with nothing more than her tinkling laughter, and the memory of a long harrowing day could be blotted clean away by the simple caress of her reassuring words.

"Are they feeding you well?" she had asked him in a voice that rang loud and clear with love, pure as it comes.

It made him grin, remembering how young and innocent she'd sounded when she proclaimed, "Oh, Cabot, I love you so much, I think I might burst!"

Elice had never been big on physical demonstrations of affection, at least not in public. And she'd never been one for billing and cooing verbally, either, at least not in public. Cabot knew that for her to blurt out such a thing, with her children nearby and, quite possibly, Mr. and Mrs. Glasser as well, had been an incredible admission. She couldn't have said it, wouldn't have said it, unless she loved him all the way down to her toes.

The thought turned the grin into a slight smile. Cabot floated toward sleep, as though blanketed and pillowed by the soft, comforting cloud of her love. Surrounded by the pure completeness of it, he felt safe, sure, protected from bad dreams and pain of any kind.

The smile grew slightly as he admitted a huge truth: Much as he loved his old pal, Joe Clancy, and much as he wanted to see the big guy happily married, Cabot had no desire to be here in Chicago. He wanted to be in Freeland, in Elice's humble kitchen, watching the movements and hearing the sounds and inhaling the scents that were more proof of her love for him.

Oh, he'd go through the motions required of a best man, from the dreaded bachelor party to the boring rehearsal dinner to the toast at the reception. And then he'd hustle himself back to Baltimore as fast as any 747 could carry him.

Once he got there and had picked her out from the crowd that would be waiting at the gate for loved ones to deplane, he'd throw down his beatup old suitcase, scoop her up in his arms, hug the living daylights out of her, and plant a big juicy kiss on her full, waiting lips!

Smiling for all he was worth now, Cabot slept. For the moment, at least, car crashes and deadly bombs and vengeful thoughts had no place in his mind, because, for the moment at least, his mind swirled contentedly with thoughts of his beloved, his Elice.

Chapter 6

The painful crick in Cabot's neck woke him and he opened one eye, wondering when, during the night, Joe's comfortable couch had started feeling hard as a rock. Only then did he realize it felt as though he'd been sleeping on concrete because he had been sleeping on concrete.

Slowly, he sat up and surveyed his surroundings.

The constant thundering traffic overhead told him he'd settled, after his latest nocturnal wandering, beneath the Chicago Skyway. This time, he was miles from Joe's place. Cabot shook his head, amazed at the distance he'd covered on foot, amazed at the pain medication's powerful drugging effects.

As he'd done on the previous night, after having taken the prescribed dose of the painkillers, he tried to sleep off the mind-banging effects of the migraine. And, like the night before, he'd wandered from the safety of Joe's apartment.

Well, the headache was gone and with it, his peace of mind, because, like the night before, he'd gone walking in his bleary mental state.

Cabot could only pray he hadn't done any damage this time.

Slowly, he got onto his knees, then to his feet, and assessed his physical condition. The elbows of his suit jacket were frayed and torn and so were the knees of his pants. Cabot pinched the bridge of his nose and squinted, trying hard to remember when he'd put his jacket and tie back on. He could have sworn he'd taken them off the minute he entered Joe's apartment, and tossed them on the bed in the spare room.

The bruises and knicks on his hands and knuckles hadn't yet healed from his previous night's meanderings; he counted six more scrapes and two new bruises. And his right thumb had swelled to twice its normal size; if it wasn't broken, it was badly sprained.

Somehow, he'd lost a shoe. Not an easy undertaking when a man double-ties his size twelve wing tips to keep the narrow, rounded laces from loosening themselves.

Both shirt cuffs had lost their buttons and the blood on the left one was the same sickly shade of brown as the bloody stain on the shirttail that hung, wrinkled and ragged, over his belt.

A wave of nausea rolled over him, sending him reeling toward the hard dusty earth. Leaning against the concrete abutment behind him, Cabot slid wearily to the ground. "What have you gone and done this time?" he asked himself. "Oh,

Lord in Heaven, why me?" Leaning his elbows on his knees, he hid his face in his hands then ran his fingers through his hair. Quickly he dug his knuckles into his teary eyes.

Almost immediately, he pulled himself together. He had no time for self-pity or self-loathing. Not if he wanted to find out what dirty deed he'd done last night. He had to find Joe and ask him whether or not he had heard something, had seen him leave, or could offer some scrap of information that would help Cabot piece together the events of last night.

He tried to ignore his hammering heart and sweaty palms and got back onto his feet. Snippets of Matthew 11:28–29, one of Elice's favorites, came to mind: Come unto me, all ye that. . .are heavy laden. . .and ye shall find rest unto your souls.

Using one battered hand to shield his tired eyes from the bright morning light, Cabot stepped out from under the highway. Another verse, Psalm 57:1, emboldened him as he limped like Deedle-Deedle Dumplin, one shoe off and one shoe on, up the embankment: In the shadow of thy wings I will make my refuge, until these calamities be overpast.

"I'm in Your hands, Lord," he whispered, tucking his shirt into his trousers. Then, shoving the bloodied shirt cuffs under his jacket's sleeves, he added, "Hold on tight, Lord, and don't let go."

Joe's apartment was empty when Cabot locked the door behind him. Joe had already left for the station house, said the note on the kitchen table. "You're sure kickin' up your heels big time, buddy," said the heavy scrawl. "Well, you'd better make hay while the sun shines, 'cause soon, we'll both be shackled men!" Grinning, Cabot read Joe's instructions to call him at the station the minute he got home.

But first, Cabot would shower and a shave. Much as he needed to speak to Joe, he needed to get his head clear before subjecting himself to another of Joe's intense grillings.

He flipped on the big-screen TV in the living room, turned up the volume, and listened to the morning news anchor recite the events of the previous night. As he adjusted the shower's water temperature, his hands froze above the knobs when he heard, ". . .was found strangled beneath the Chicago Skyway early this morning."

Cabot belted the thick bath towel around his middle and ran into the living room without even thinking to close the shower doors. "Al Winters," the reporter said, "is believed to have been involved in numerous car bombings, as evidenced by the explosives paraphernalia found by police in his North Chicago apartment."

Suddenly, his usually strong legs grew rubbery. Breathing heavily, Cabot steadied himself, grasping the pillowy headrest of Clancy's recliner. The sounds of running water reminded him he'd left the shower doors open. Splashing through puddles on the tile floor, he cranked both knobs to stop the water's flow, then blotted up the mess with towels he'd pulled from the shelf. There, on his hands and knees, everything stopped cold as the horror of what he'd probably done last night gripped him.

Cabot hung his head in misery and shame.

He'd been an honorable man his whole life. Admittedly, he'd stepped from the righteous path, but only a time or two, and only for short periods. And yes, he'd had one bout with spiritual faithlessness, but eventually, even he had admitted that the distance he'd put between himself and the Lord had been a normal, natural reaction to a such a tragic loss.

When confronted with temptation—and as a cop in Chicago's meanest district that had been a daily battle—he'd always chosen the right path. When confronted with the choice to throttle a wife beater or kick the stuffings out of a dope peddler or beat a little old lady's mugger senseless, he did his job by the book. Even when his own life had been on the line, "shoot to kill" hadn't been his style. And when judges and juries put the bad guys back onto the streets before his paperwork had been typed up and turned in, he hadn't sought back-street vengeance, because, well, because he actually believed that "vengeance is mine, sayeth the Lord."

But maybe Gardner's innocent slip of the tongue, informing him that Maggie and Lindy had been deliberately and calculatedly killed by one of the vicious criminals he'd arrested, had planted a seed of hatred in his heart and mind. Maybe those thoughts of vengeance that he'd so carefully controlled all those years on the force had burst like an aneurism and were slowly leaking venom whenever he thought that his family had paid with their lives for his dogged determination to do things by the book. Or maybe that seed of evil had grown large and thorny, twining through his aching head like a giant poisonous vine, spewing messages of "get even" throughout his being.

"I'll bet you wanted to strangle that bomber," Gardner had said.

"Truth was," Cabot now admitted to himself, "I wanted to do far more than strangle the lousy, worthless. . ." The moment understanding dawned, and he'd reckoned with the ugly truth of what had really happened to his wife and little girl. . .

Had that been the mind-set that propelled him into Chicago's dark night world? Had it prompted him to seek out—with the intent to destroy—anyone who might have been Maggie and Lindy's killer?

Unwittingly, Cabot squeezed the towels. Water bubbled quietly between his fingers before being quickly reabsorbed into the thick, wet terry. Blinking, he tried to place the strange sound echoing in the tiled bathroom, a sound remarkably like one he'd heard, years earlier, in a crowded hospital emergency room. Not until hot tears slid down his cheeks and splashed softly, silently on the backs of his already damp hands, not until he became conscious of his heaving chest and lurching shoulders did he realize that the horrible, hacking sounds were sobs, coming from deep inside him.

Eye for eye, tooth for tooth, hand for hand, foot for foot, Cabot recited Exodus 21 mentally. But there was more to the Old Testament verse. Much more, if he remembered correctly. Sitting back upon his heels, his disjointed, confused mind struggled to remember the rest of it: *If men strive, and hurt a woman with child. . . he shall be surely punished, according as the woman's husband. . .shall pay as the judges determine. . .shalt give life for life.*

But hadn't Christ been born, hadn't He lived and died to change all that? Wasn't it spelled out clearly in Matthew?

Cabot rose slowly and strode purposefully to the bookshelves lining Clancy's living room wall. He'd seen the Holy Bible there, on a shelf beside the fireplace. Balancing the leather-bound volume on one open palm, he paged through the book until he found Matthew 5:38-39 and 44 and recited what he'd been looking for: " 'Ye have heard that it hath been said, An eye for an eye, and a tooth for a tooth: But I say unto you, That ye resist not evil: but whosoever shall smite thee on thy right cheek, turn to him the other also. . .But I say unto you, Love your enemies, bless them that curse you, do good to them that hate you, and pray for them which despitefully use you and persecute you.' "

Tears dampened the pages of God's accumulated Word as Cabot murmured: " 'Love your enemies. . .do good to them that hate you. . .pray for them which. . . persecute you.' "

Pray for the filth who murdered my wife and child? Love them? Cabot slammed the Holy Book and jammed it back onto the shelf. Like a caged, enraged tiger, he paced back and forth in Clancy's living room, his right fist slamming into his left palm, over and over and over.

Turn the other cheek? *God, most of all, should understand how I feel,* Cabot told himself. His only Son died a cruel, horrible death. . .was deliberately murdered!

Cabot knew he would never forget those desperate last seconds of their lives, just before the huge fireball propelled him into unconsciousness. He'd never forget the fright in their eyes or the pain on their sooty faces. That dastardly deed had robbed him of more than Maggie and Lindy. It had also robbed him of their memory, for his every thought of them was now tainted by their torturous and terrible deaths.

But he thought he'd forgiven. Thought he'd put the worst of it behind him, when he'd met Elice and her children, when he'd accepted the lessons learned in her warm and cozy little house about God's greatest gift to mankind—His only Son. The fury boiling inside him grew hotter with every step, with every remembered moment of that awful day alongside the Dan Ryan Expressway.

If he'd forgiven, truly forgiven as he believed he had, he couldn't have succumbed, not even when half-mad with rage, to the temptation to avenge the vile and violent deaths of his wife and little girl. If he'd forgiven, truly forgiven, not even the ferocity of his hot-blooded wrath could have propelled him into the city streets, to find and mete out the Old Testament's "eye for an eye" judgment.

Cabot stopped his angry pacing and stood at Clancy's wide, uncurtained window. Below, the sounds of hissing, distant traffic were punctuated by the occasional wail of a siren, the random blare of a car horn, just as it had on that life-altering day. His arms, which had been so taut with tension that large blue veins snaked from wrist to elbow, now hung limp at his sides, and his fists, which had been flexing with every beat of his heart, finally relaxed. He looked beyond the busy highway, beyond the picturesque Chicago skyline, beyond the cloudless expanse of blue morning sky. Somewhere up there, where his 747 had so recently floated in that same summery space, God dwelled. Somewhere up there, He watched and listened. . .and understood.

Cabot felt God's love around him as surely as he'd felt Elice's before falling asleep the night before, and his heartbeat quickened in response to the awe of it. "You were with me through shadowed valleys," Cabot whispered, his deep, powerful voice quaking with emotion. "You took up my cares and fears and burdens, and showed me the way through the darkness, to a place where I found proof of Your promises." Lowering his head, Cabot fell to his knees and wept openly, quietly, humbly. *I will not drown, even in these troubled waters,* he prayed silently, *if I hold fast to You, my rock, my anchor.*

He had no ready explanation for where he'd gone or what he'd done these past two nights, but Cabot couldn't believe the Lord would allow him to sin against His commandments. Couldn't believe his God would stand idly by as His servant committed two cold-blooded murders.

Strength renewed, Cabot got to his feet and headed for the bathroom, where he took that much-needed shower. And as he shaved his whiskered face, he met the eyes of the man in the mirror.

Eyes that Elice called almost brown. Eyes, she often said in her whispery, lilting voice, that were more golden than green. Eyes, she told him, that looked at her like no man ever had, making her feel more womanly than she ever had.

They were eyes that had seen unconditional love in the faces of his wife and child, and when he believed he'd never see that kind of love again, remarkably, miraculously, he saw it on the faces of Elice and her children.

But just as they'd overflowed with joy when the nurse lay his darling baby daughter into his waiting arms, they'd also poured with grief and misery as they lowered her little white coffin into the unwelcoming, cold brown earth. And on the day Gardner told him the whole ugly truth about what had caused her death, those same eyes blazed with hate. Hatred hotter and whiter than any he'd ever seen aimed at him from the backseats of squad cars, more, even, than he'd seen looking out at him from behind prison bars.

He'd wanted, exactly as Gardner had suggested, to strangle the breath from the man who had murdered them. But the mean mood had passed, because the eyes that had turned from the Lord had, thanks to Elice's loving patience, turned back again. He had forgiven, he told himself.

Hadn't he?

It had been remarkably easy to get into the second-floor apartment. *My buddies don't call me Spider-Man for nothin'!* he told himself. Inside, with only the dim beam of a key chain Bic lighter lighting his way, he'd scurried, ratlike, from room to room. Knowing that neither cop, snoring in the bedrooms on either side of the long dark hallway, had any idea that he was there, sent tremors of excitement up and down his spine as he searched the kitchen counters and the bathroom cabinet for Cabot Murray's headache medication. Excitement turned to frustration as he poked and prodded and continued to come up empty-handed. Until, right there on the night stand beside Murray's bed, he spied the familiar brown plastic vial that contained the cop's only escape from pain. He knew more about Murray than Clancy, probably, because he'd done his homework well. They didn't call him Sherlock for nothing!

He walked softly toward the night stand, stepping cautiously, stopping when the cop's breathing pattern changed and he turned, moaning, in the bed. He held his own breath until Murray's resumed a restful, regular pace. Only then did he venture forward, toward the bottle that held the key to making a success of his plan. Wrapping his black-gloved hand around it, he carefully brought it to him as if it might explode, so that the pills inside would not rattle against their container. Then, tiptoeing into the kitchen, he opened the container and dumped its contents into his pocket, and then replaced the prescribed medication with white pills of the same size and shape. It made him lurch a bit when the lid went back on with a quiet snap. He froze, waiting, listening, hoping the sound hadn't roused one of the slumbering detectives. One minute, two minutes later, assured that it hadn't, he made his way back to the room where Cabot Murray slept, and put the bottle back where he'd found it.

He should have left then, should have scurried right back down the hallway, out through the patio doorway, over the balcony railing, and down the brick wall.

Instead, he stood there, hovering like a living, breathing shadow, above the cop's bed. It would be easy, so easy, to slide the big hunting knife lashed to his thigh from its sheath, and draw it across the sleeping man's throat. He would be dead before he even knew what hit him.

But he didn't want him to die a quick, painless death. No. He wanted this cop, this detective, to die as his father had, day by day, rotting in a prison cell for something his son was sure he hadn't done.

He had been sixteen when Murray had arrested his dad on charges of armed robbery. Positive identifications and strong witness testimony, said the newspapers on the day the verdict was handed down, had proven the police case against him. His dad had been loading the dishwasher when another inmate had stabbed him; he died three months before he would have been released on parole.

Cabot Murray had been the one most responsible for his father's conviction. He and the crummy public defender appointed by the state. Who knew how long it would take the dimwits in City Hall to find that lawyer's body? One thing for sure, they'd never connect the murder to him. They didn't call him Einstein for nothing!

Murray, like a bloodhound, had sniffed out all sorts of so-called evidence of his father's guilt. If it hadn't been for that cop, his dad would be alive today. At first, back then—it seemed like a lifetime had passed these two short years—he wanted to shoot him on sight. But after the funeral, after a few weeks had dimmed his bloodlust, he decided that slow torture would be a more suitable punishment.

So he bought plastic explosives from John James Johnson then bought a detonator from Al Winters and a timing mechanism from Dave Hoffman. The explosion went off without a hitch, killing Murray's wife and kid instantly, almost killing Murray, too. That hadn't been part of the plan. He wanted to watch Murray suffer a while before making him pay the final price.

He couldn't have been more surprised when the cop quit the force. Try as he might, he couldn't get any of his informants to tell him where Murray had gone when he left Chicago. At first, it infuriated him. But then, he realized, he was young and that he had a lifetime to track down the man responsible for his father's death.

Lady Luck smiled on him three times last week. Her first visit was when Winters and Johnson and Hoffman had met him after work, roughed him up a bit, and promised to go to the cops and spill their guts about the bomb he'd put under Maggie Murray's car. They'd do a couple years, maybe, under a roof and eating three squares at the state's expense, but he'd get the gas chamber. They had demanded ten thousand bucks apiece for their silence.

But he knew their type. When the money was gone, they'd be back, bigger than ever, demanding even more. There was only one way to shut them up, once and for all.

Lady Luck's second grin in his direction allowed him to tie everything up in one tidy package: Cabot Murray came back to Chicago to be best man at his ex-partner's wedding. He couldn't have ordered a more perfect scenario from Sears Roebuck and Company!

The Lady's third smile was prettiest of all, simply because she had the good grace to put him in the right place at the right time. Standing there, outside the Thirty-fourth District station house, he had overheard a couple of suited cops lamenting that their old pal was in bad, bad shape.

"Horrible headaches," one had said.

"Not just headaches," the other had said, "but migraines."

"Has to take special pills," the first one had continued.

"Hates 'em," the second one had replied, " 'cause they dope him up too much. . .cloud his mind."

It would be so easy, with that knowledge in hand, to kill four birds with one stone. He'd also frame Murray for the murders of his blackmailers. But why kill him now, when he could do it slowly, a day at a time?

He stood there a moment longer, his smile growing as he made his way through the darkened rooms, onto the patio, and down the brick wall, where he was swallowed up by the thick black night.

Chapter 7

C hanging the dressing on Mrs. Glasser's incision twice a day, keeping her former in-laws' house and yard in tip-top shape, then heading back to Twin Acres to paint and deliver signs to her customers, should have kept Elice far too busy to give more than a cursory thought to Cabot's well-being. Yet every time the telephone rang, Elice lurched for it, always hoping it would be him, always disappointed when it wasn't.

Elice thought about him as she helped the children with their homework. She thought about him while dropping the children off for softball practice or picking them up from piano lessons. Why, she even thought about him during her morning and evening devotions.

Would he have been on her mind to this degree if he hadn't sounded so blue the last time he phoned, three long, lonely days ago? Elice sighed resignedly, knowing full well that he would.

Earlier that day, while peeling potatoes for the stewpot, she'd made a decision: If he didn't call by morning, she'd call him.

The night sounds echoed louder than normal as she tossed and turned in the elegant, feminine room at the top of the Glassers' spiral mahogany staircase. She stared at the crocheted canopy above the cherry four-poster bed. The she fluffed thick down pillows and neatly folded then refolded the lace-trimmed sheets over the white satin comforter.

A mug of warm milk didn't calm her. Listening to soft gospel music didn't soothe her jangled nerves. Not even a warm bubble bath provided the slightest tranquility. As the inky black of night gave way to the deep purple of early dawn, she admitted the obvious: Nothing but the sound of his voice would restore her serenity.

Elice paced the big house all night and continued to prowl as the dark sky brightened with streaks of orange and gold. She had watched the sun set the night before and thought it only appropriate that she watch it come up again that morning. Even as a child, Elice loved to rise before dawn, holding her breath as she waited for the sounds of that first robin's trills as he sought to rouse birds of every feather from their nests.

She heard the unmistakable patter of her younger daughter's tiny bare feet as they made their way down the long staircase. Annie, Elice decided, was a lot like that first robin, determined to wake everyone else in her nest.

"I'm sleepy, Mommy," said the child, hoisting the Good Book to make room for herself in her mother's lap.

Elice held her tightly and laughed softly. "Then why did you get out of bed so early, my sweet silly girl?"

Annie snuggled closer. " 'Cause I had a bad dream. I dreamed Cabot got in a fight. A bad man hurt him." Rubbing her sleepy eyes, she looked up at Elice. "I want Cabot to come home, Mommy. When is he coming home?"

There was absolutely no reason to pay any attention to the girl's childish dream, yet Elice's heart thundered. "He'll be home as soon as he can." She hoped Annie hadn't heard the tremor in her voice. "As soon as Mr. Clancy's wedding is over, he'll be back with us, where he belongs." Elice didn't know who—Annie or herself—took more reassurance from her words.

She glanced at the polished brass face of the grandfather clock across the room. Only six o'clock, five o'clock, Chicago time. Would he be fast asleep, dreaming sweet dreams? Or was he awake, fighting with some nameless, faceless bad man?

Elice sighed and gathered Annie into her arms and stood. "Let's get breakfast started. You can make the toast."

Annie rested her head on her mother's shoulder. "Goody," she said around a yawn. "I love making toast." With that, she was asleep.

Grinning, Elice kissed her pudgy cheek and slowly climbed the stairs. She stood between the twin beds where Emily and Annie had been sleeping since their grandmother was released from the hospital, and searched her daughters' angelic faces for a clue as to how she, herself, might recapture a moment of that innocent peace. A cold, clammy feeling wrapped around her as the ugly reality presented itself: Innocence, as she'd known it, was long gone. As for peace. . .

Elice sighed, suddenly weary, and headed back to the room at the top of the stairs. Huddling beneath the luxurious bedclothes, she buried her face in the pillow and cried softly. Cabot was in some kind of danger out there in the Windy City. She knew it like she knew her own name. Yet he hadn't felt he could trust her enough to tell her what kind of danger.

What was it that the Lord said to Abram? Elice searched her memory of Genesis 15:1. " 'Fear not, Abram: I am thy shield, and thy exceeding great reward,' " Elice whispered. *Fear not, for I am your shield.* Surely, with God as his shield, Cabot would be safe.

She tried to forget that every day the horrible truths of wars in third world countries, deadly diseases, and weather-related tragedies pummeled her from the radio, the TV, the newspaper. But the horrors struck close to home, too. Just last week, Annie Crandall had been hit by a car while she was crossing the street near the movie theater. Shortly before that, Pearl McKenzie's happy, healthy brother took ill and died.

Truth was, she didn't have to set foot outside of the house to look horror right in the eye. It seemed like only yesterday that Bobby, Elice's first love, left her, pregnant with two small children to take care of, to make a name for himself in the auto racing world. She'd prayed Genesis 15:1 then, too, hoping God would protect her from angry bill collectors and unscrupulous salesmen until Bobby came to his senses and returned to his family. Bobby had come home, all right—in a plain pine box.

And what about all the atrocities doled out by way of her so-called friend, Jack Wilson? Believing he had some sort of grudge to settle with Cabot, he'd spent months threatening her and the children, and threatening Cabot, too. Jack had flattened tires, left mysterious notes in her house. Who knows what he might have done if Cabot hadn't seen him, lurking beneath her bedroom window. Cabot had paid dearly for his heroics that night, with a near-fatal knife wound in his side. Jack's maniacal need to balance his imaginary scales of justice had pushed him so far that he'd nearly caused Annie's death. It had been Cabot, not God, who'd shielded her little girl that awful day.

Where was God as innocent children were hit by cars? When wars took innocent lives in faraway places; when a madman had the power to claim her daughter's life, right here at home?

Elice had been a little girl when her mother died, and she lost her father during her senior year in high school. Yes, Bobby had left her penniless. Then he died, adding his funeral expenses to her debts. But her faith in God had seen her through it all. The Lord had blessed her with strength and patience and a will to survive.

And she had survived!

So why, oh why, Elice wondered, was she questioning Him now? Shame burned brightly on her cheeks. She had no right to doubt her Savior. He'd been there for her, like a brother, like a friend, to guide her past all the debris that life had strewn into her path. How dare she even think He'd abandon Cabot!

Elice wanted to believe that God would watch over her husband-to-be. Wanted to believe He'd protect this man, who had taught her so much about love and acceptance. Wanted to believe that, as He had for Abram, God would be Cabot's shield, too.

Of course He would! She'd asked it, hadn't she? And didn't He promise, "Ask and ye shall receive?" Disgusted with herself for doubting the One Who had given her so much, Elice bolted upright and threw back the covers. It surprised her, when she brushed her hair from her face, to feel the damp proof that she'd been crying. Angrily, she dried her eyes with the backs of her hands, put both feet firmly onto the floor, and marched purposefully to the kitchen. She started breakfast. . .and counted the minutes before she could call Chicago.

Finally, at nine o'clock, she dialed long distance information. "I'd like the number for the Thirty-fourth District Police Station," she told the operator.

Minutes later, the friendly, gravelly voice of Joe Clancy grated into her ear.

"What can I do for you, Miz Glasser?"

"Please, call me Elice."

"Okay. And you can call me Joe."

Joe had been Cabot's best friend, partner, and confidant for ten long years; Elice didn't even try to hide her concern from him. "Joe, I haven't heard from Cabot in days. I'm sure he's fine, and that you fellas have just been keeping him busy, but—"

"Elice," Clancy interrupted, "I can't tell you how glad I am you've called." He lowered his voice in tone and volume. "I don't want to worry you, but, well, frankly, Cabot hasn't been himself since he got here."

Her hand flew to her mouth. *Tell me everything!* she wanted to say, swallowing a gasp. *Don't protect me from the truth.*

"He's been having those headaches again. You know the ones, where he sees little stars and can't hold down a meal to save his soul."

She was chewing her fingertips now. He hadn't had a migraine in so long. What, Elice wondered, had happened to awaken the sleeping monster?

"He'd have my hide if he knew I was telling you this, but I really think he needs you here! If he wants to knock my block off for that, so be it."

When she'd loaded the dishwasher moments earlier, Elice had opened the window above the sink. As she listened to the urgency in Joe's voice, a gentle westerly breeze lifted the wispy white curtains and gently mussed her hair, the way Cabot's big hands often did. It was as though Cabot were whispering his need to her on that breeze from the Windy City. She made the decision in a heartbeat.

"I'm going to hang up now and book the next flight to Chicago."

"Gimme a call when you land, little lady, and I'll meet you at O'Hare."

Blinking back stinging tears, she licked her lips. "Thanks, Joe."

"No thanks necessary. We gotta look out for our boy."

All Elice knew was that Joe would be parked outside the baggage claim area at O'Hare. She had never met Joe Clancy, had never even seen a snapshot of the big Irishman. Yet the moment she stepped into the sunshine, she recognized him. He gave her a huge, welcoming hug, grabbed her suitcase, and stuffed it into the back seat of the big black sedan. Then, draping an arm over her shoulders as though they'd been friends for years, he walked her around to the passenger side of the car.

"You'll be staying with Sarah, my fiancée. She insisted, and nobody argues with Sarah Miller!"

Once Clancy had maneuvered the undercover cop car onto the highway, he patted her shoulder. "Don't look so worried, Elice. Whatever's eatin' at Cabot ain't terminal."

She bit her lip, then grinned sheepishly. "I know it seems silly for me to be so concerned, but—"

"Not silly at all," he interrupted. "Somethin's got him by the throat. Even a big dumb guy like me can see that!" he added, laughing long and hard. He grew quiet and somber. "Maybe seeing you will snap him out of it." Again, he patted her shoulder and, just as suddenly, he was grinning again. "We gotta cheer him up before we put that monkey suit on him. I don't want his foul mood gettin' folks down in the mouth and blubberin' all over the place; it'll make the tiles slippery, and I can't afford a personal injury lawsuit." Laughing, he slapped his thigh.

As they headed down Manheim Road and away from the airport, he talked nonstop, about the traffic, about inconsiderate drivers, about potholes. He wondered aloud what the weather would do. And he told her all about his lovely fiancée, Sarah Miller. When at last they arrived at the station house, Clancy pulled into a "No Parking" zone out front. "Don't worry," he said in response to her raised brows, "if we get a ticket, I can get it fixed." Winking, he added, "I've got friends in high places."

She tried to enjoy his little joke.

Lifting her chin on a bent forefinger, Clancy said, "Smile, little lady, 'cause I have a feeling somebody up there likes you." Using his thumb as a pointer, he gestured toward the old three-storied brick building. Elice nodded feebly and summoned her courage. Clancy's hand felt warm and reassuring on the small of her back as it guided her up the flagstone steps.

"Hey, everybody," he announced once they were inside, "look who's here."

Most of the detectives recognized her from the photos Cabot had shown them and, within moments, Elice was surrounded. They shook her hands, kissed her cheeks, embraced her as if she were a long-lost relative. A pretty blond in a skimpy black dress hugged her. "He's gonna be so happy to see you!" she squealed. "Cabot talks about you constantly!"

"Murray musta gone to charm school to win you," said one cop.

"Charm school," laughed a second. "Why, he'd be expelled before the tardy bell rang!"

"How'd the big galoot get so lucky?" a third wanted to know.

"I've asked myself that a hundred times."

She would have known that voice anywhere.

A thrill shot through her as she whirled around, and the moment she set eyes on him, tears of joy welled in her eyes. She'd worried all through the flight that he might not be pleased to see her or that he might resent her intrusion here, in this place where he'd lived a completely different life from the one he'd been living in Freeland. But the warm welcoming light in his eyes told her what she wanted to know. Ignoring more introductory handshakes that were coming her way, she burst through the circle of detectives and hurled herself into his waiting, extended arms.

"What're you doing here?" he asked, lifting her off her feet in a hearty hug.

She placed a hand on either side of his face and kissed him soundly. "Do I really need a reason? Because if I do—"

"Plead the Fifth, Elice," hollered somebody from behind them.

"You don't need a reason to kiss me like that," yelled someone else.

Gently, Cabot set her down and, holding her to him with one strong arm, he shook his other fist at the mob of detectives. "Hey," he said, grinning, "give a guy a little privacy, why don't you?"

Clancy led them to an interrogation room just off the main hall. "G'wan in there," he whispered, shoving them inside. "It's soundproof. And the miniblinds actually work," he said to Cabot, winking. "Ain't we fancy?" With that, he closed the door behind him.

Cabot lifted his arms in a helpless gesture. "I can't believe you're here." He shook his head, as if to prove his disbelief. "So. . . How's Mrs. Glasser?"

She pretended not to have heard the note of discomfort in his voice as he pocketed both hands. "She's getting around real well. Mr. Glasser hired a private nurse to take care of her, and he's going to mind the children while I'm away." Elice pulled his hands from his pockets and wrapped his arms around her waist. "They all send their love, by the way."

The waving, winking taunts of the detectives on the other side of the window caught his attention. "Hold that thought," he said, crossing the room. With a grin and a flourish, he snapped the blinds shut.

"You're like a breath of fresh air in this stale old place," he said, gathering her near to him once more. Closing his eyes, he inhaled deeply, then held her at arm's length and smiled. "To tell you the truth, I don't care why you're here. All I can say is, thank God!"

He managed to laugh softly, but hadn't quite managed to mask the strange, distant note in his voice. Clancy was right; something was most definitely eating at Cabot. "Whatever it is," Clancy had said, "it ain't terminal."

❧

Elice had chattered endlessly all through dinner. Danny's Little League team uniforms had arrived, she told him. Emily's youth group would use the surplus funds that they had raised through the White Elephant sale to go and see Phantom at the local dinner theater. Annie, Elice informed him, had taken over one of the flower beds for her herb garden. And Wally had painted Cabot's barn at Foggy Bottom. Though Cabot had nodded politely through it all, he didn't seem to have heard a word she'd said. Elice reached across the table and laid her hand atop his.

"You've barely touched your spaghetti."

The broad shoulders lifted, then fell. "I had a big lunch."

"Cabot," she said, gently squeezing his hand, "look at me. Please?"

The reflected candle flame danced in the dark centers of his golden eyes. One side of his mouth drew back in a feeble attempt at a smile. "You're beautiful tonight."

Elice rolled her eyes. "Thank you. . .for the tenth time." She took a deep breath, then sipped her water.

"There's something I have to tell you," he said, drawing figure eights with his breadstick in the marinara sauce on his plate.

Again she squeezed his hand. "Well, it's about time."

He met her eyes and frowned, then pointed at her plate. "You finished?"

The only other time she had seen him looking so forlorn was at Annie's bedside, as they waited and worried that she would never wake from the coma. "Yes, I'm finished. And you?"

Cabot nodded, then signaled for the waitress to bring the check.

Elice glanced around the restaurant, at the wood-trimmed archways above each tiny alcove that, like their own, glowed warmly, thanks to the egg-shaped red candle on each table. But none of that warmth was reflected in Cabot's tired eyes. Elice couldn't imagine what ominous news he intended to deliver.

Had he changed his mind about marrying her, now that he'd had a taste of Chicago life again? Had being back in the town where his wife and daughter were buried rekindled his longing for them. . .and doused his ardor for her? Had following Clancy and his new partner through the city streets made him yearn for the days when he, too, was a detective? The fear churning inside her reminded her of the day she woke and found Bobby's note on the pillow beside her head. *Going to Virginia,* he had written, *to see if I can make a name for myself. I'll send money when I can.* She had never felt more alone or abandoned. . .until now.

She hadn't shown anyone her fear the day Bobby left her. And she wouldn't let Cabot see it now, either. Smiling brightly, she stood and told him she needed to use the ladies' room before they left. There, leaning her forehead on the cool metal of the coral-colored door, she closed her eyes and prayed for strength. She would need that and then some if what Cabot was about to tell her meant he wouldn't be coming back to Maryland.

Right from the start, Elice had seemed able to zero in on Cabot's feelings, no matter how carefully they were hidden. Sometimes, it took no more than a glance at his face for her to know, instinctively, that all was not well. He should have realized that she would hear something in his telephone voice that signaled trouble.

He had been so wrapped up in his own misery that he almost hadn't seen hers. But he had seen it just then, as she headed for the bathroom. Oh, she had tried to disguise it, as usual, with her brave smile and cheery conversation. But in that fleeting instant, as she rose from her chair in that graceful, feminine way of hers, Elice's big dark eyes had clouded with a painful combination of worry and fear.

She had left her children to come to him. She hadn't come to that decision easily. Cabot had never seen a mother more fiercely protective than Elice. Only once before had she been without her youngsters and that was when her former in-laws took them to Ocean City. The only reason Elice agreed to that separation was to protect them from Jack Wilson's threats. Jack wouldn't have been a threat if he hadn't believed he had some mysterious score to settle with Cabot. Cabot knew he alone had been responsible for that separation and that he had been responsible for this one, too.

The waitress had left four cellophane-wrapped mints on the tiny rectangular tray where Cabot had left her tip. He unwrapped one and popped it into his mouth. With each inhalation, he felt the powerfully invigorating sensation of peppermint on his tastebuds. All that from something no bigger than a nickel.

He had never been much of a poet, and he had to grin slightly at the comparison forming in his head. Elice was a lot like that mint—cleansing. . .refreshing. . . sweet. All that from a woman whose head barely reached his shoulder.

The grin faded as reality returned: All too soon, the mint would dissolve and, when it did, its refreshing components would vanish like smoke. Would Elice disappear, too, once she knew the truth about him?

Chapter 8

As Cabot waited for Elice to return from the ladies' room, he sat in the quaint Italian restaurant, rearranging the salt and pepper shakers, sliding around the thin white vase that held a single rosebud, moving the candle from here to there on the small round table.

His eyes were drawn to the flickering flame. Its hot, blue-green center mesmerized him. Flashes of memory sparked in his mind—searing heat. . .frightened eyes. . .terrified screams . . .a thundering explosion.

Blinking rapidly, he tried to shake off the memory and focused instead on the rose—red, like Maggie's car; red, like Maggie's hair; red, like the flames that hungrily, greedily devoured them; red, like Lindy's little mouth, yelling, "Daddy, help us!"

Cabot's heartbeat doubled and his regular breaths became gasps. He could never be sure when a flashback would attack, when something as simple as a quiet candle might trigger memories of that dark day. But why did the nightmare have to return this night, of all nights, when he needed every ounce of his self-control and strength to tell Elice what she must be told?

The Lord is my rock and my salvation.

Just that quickly, the frightening pictures in his mind dimmed. He remembered well how the accident that snatched Maggie and Lindy from him had created a vast chasm between himself and the Lord. If it hadn't been for Elice, with her unerring faith, he honestly didn't know when he might have found his way back. . .if ever he found his way back.

Cabot searched his mind for words, one word, even, that would appropriately define his gratitude to God for blessing him with the greatest gift he'd ever received—Elice. *I thank Thee that Thou hast heard me,* Cabot decided, would do just fine. If he remembered correctly, John, chapter eleven, went on to explain Lazarus's sisters' grief at their brother's death. *Didn't I tell you that if you believed strongly enough, your prayers would be answered?* Cabot paraphrased Christ's words. And sure enough, when Mary and Martha truly believed, Lazarus rose. Cabot took a deep satisfying breath, remembering that he hadn't needed to believe, yet God, in His infinite wisdom and loving mercy, heard Cabot's unspoken plea, and answered his prayers anyway by sending him an angel in the form of a woman named Elice.

She was strong, determined, loyal. She was all those things by dint of her own drive and determination, but she gave credit to the Lord for what she called her "finer qualities." If she indeed exhibited any of those qualities, she insisted, it was God Who'd made them part of who she was. But Cabot had a feeling that long before Elice had matured enough to boldly admit her need for a Christ-centered life and invite Him to be her Lord and Savoir, she was still a woman like no other.

He, on the other hand, had survived those lonely years following the accident because God had stubbornly, lovingly pushed him through. It was a minor miracle, he believed, that, in his weakness, God could do His marvelous work in him. Yes, he had blindly stumbled through life, unaware that the hand leading him had been the hand of God. It had taken Elice, bright as a heavenly star, to make him see who had been his guiding light. She had been his heavenly beacon. As the North Star guides a wayward mariner to a sheltering harbor, he'd made it through the storms of Jack Wilson's dastardly deeds, because she had shown him his way back to God.

And God had steeled him.

Now, though the headaches and blackouts had weakened him, had tormented him physically and emotionally, they had no power over his spirit, because, as in Psalm twenty-three, God would see him through this trial, too. *Yea, though I walk through the valley of the shadow of death, I will fear no evil: for thou art with me.*

Cabot glanced at his wristwatch and wondered what was taking Elice so long in the ladies' room. Knowing her, she probably had spoken a word of kindness to some woman there, and the word led to two. . .and three. . . .

Truthfully, he was in no hurry to leave the restaurant, because once they arrived at Joe's apartment, he'd have to spell it all out for her—the headaches, the blackouts, the murders.

Help me choose words that won't hurt her, Lord, he prayed silently. Then, somewhere deep in his subconscious, he prayed a second, more important prayer: *Help me accept it if she decides there's no place in her life for a man who could take the life of another.*

He couldn't help but think of Job, who had suffered far greater losses than Cabot had. Yet Job came through it all with little more than faith to hold him up. Yes, Job had had many moments of doubt but, at the end of it all, he'd been rewarded very well for his faithfulness. Cabot pressed his fingertips into his eyes and shook his head. He didn't want thousands of head of sheep or oxen. Didn't want twice what he had before. Didn't want to live to be one hundred and forty years old. He only wanted to spend the rest of his days with Elice and her children. With a heavy sigh, he remembered more of Psalm twenty-three: *Thy rod and thy staff they comfort me.*

The minute Elice returned to the table, Cabot could see that she had been crying. But, true to course, she plastered a brave smile on her pretty face and gave him her best I'm-ready-when-you-are invitation to leave the restaurant. He couldn't imagine what had inspired her tears. . .unless Joe had told her more than he should have.

They had arrived at the restaurant in her rented black sedan; Cabot had insisted on driving. Now, as he took the keys from his pocket and unlocked the passenger door, he hesitated. Silhouetted by the parking lamps, Elice appeared to glow. The shimmering white-bright outline of her dark hair, her pixieish face, her narrow shoulders, made her appear tinier, younger, more vulnerable.

As he stood there, looking at her, the love he felt for her flooded over him. Gently, his knuckles grazed her cheek. "I'll love you 'til the day I die," he admitted, his voice a raspy whisper.

She smiled and then tilted her head, trapping his hand between her cheek and shoulder as her brow furrowed, smoothed, then furrowed again.

Cabot wondered what was going on in that pretty head of hers. Wondered what he had ever done in his miserable life to earn the love of a woman like this. His list of her attributes would take hours to recite aloud here in this darkened parking lot. Still, he wanted to tell her how much she meant to him. How undeniably lucky he felt to have been blessed with her love. How unbelievably lovely she looked, wearing that tailored ivory dress and matching heels as her rich brown mane softly rustled with the sweet spring breeze. And oh, he wanted to shout, how he loved her open, expressive face! Illuminated by the soft halogen bulbs, she appeared simultaneously angelic and womanly.

But when Cabot opened his mouth to tell her all he felt, he found himself unable to get out a single word. His ears had grown hot, and his stomach knotted. Tears burned behind his eyelids, and his throat ached from repressing the sob that had formed in his chest.

Elice took his hand in both of hers and blinked up at him, love shining from those chocolate brown eyes like warm radiant beams. "You'd better love me 'til the day you die," she said softly, kissing his palm, "because I'd hate to have to hurt you."

She punctuated her statement with a flirty wink, obliterating his urge to cry as surely as a single, foaming wave can obliterate a sand castle on the beach. Cabot gathered her closely and kissed the top of her head. And though he knew no one stronger—man or woman—she felt small and fragile against his big muscular body. Elice needed his protection less than just about anybody he could name, yet that's exactly what he wanted to do: Protect her from all life's tragedies; shield her from all harm; spare her from all pain.

"Cabot. . ."

Only when he heard her muffled voice did Cabot realize he had been holding her so tightly he had all but mashed her lips against his lapel. He loosened his hold and held her at arm's length.

Elice grinned, gently puffing lapel lint from her lips as she took a huge gulp of air. Laughing, she said, "You give a whole new meaning to the cliché, 'I love ya to death.'"

He hadn't realized how much he missed the sound of her laugh. Light and melodious, she could chase away blue moods and fears and anxieties, just by letting a few of those lilting, lyrical notes bubble happily from her throat.

At that precise moment, it dawned on him that what he had to tell her would snuff that musical sound just as surely as the sight of a skulking cat could rob the robin of its song. Cabot forced himself to step away from Elice; he unlocked the car door. Right then and there, he made a decision: For the forty minutes it would take to drive to Joe's apartment, he would see to it that she enjoyed every second of their time together. Fear thundered inside him as he added the gruesome qualifier: *because it might well be our last happy time together.* Summoning his courage, he bowed low. "Your carriage awaits, m'lady."

As she slid her dainty body into the passenger seat, he heard it again, the delicious giggle that soothed his eardrums and lifted his heavy heart. *Lord,* he prayed, *walking around to the driver's side of the car, wrap Your loving arms around her; shield her from the pain my words will cause.*

How thorough a detective could Murray have been, not to have noticed that the Fiorinal had been replaced with Percocet? True, the white tablets the cop had been swallowing to dull his migraines were nearly the same size and shape as those with which he had replaced them.

Still, every time he'd watched Murray wash down the promise of pain relief, he tensed, wondering if the big guy would notice that the Percocet's imprint was different from the Fiornal's; small difference to the average guy's eye, but a trained detective's eye should have picked up that tiny detail right off.

He chose to focus on brighter, more satisfying thoughts. Like the fact that, even without that ingenious switch, he certainly would have been able to permanently silence two of the thugs who had tried to extort money from him. Silence them, yes, but he wouldn't have been able to blame the murders on Cabot Murray.

He laughed right out loud at that one as he put his Gillette back onto the shelf beside the shaving cream. Two down and one to go.

Smiling, he grabbed the Old Spice, shook four drops into his right palm, and put the bottle back where it belonged, right beside the razor. Rubbing his palms together, he lifted his chin and slapped his cheeks, wincing slightly as the cold cologne stung his freshly shaved skin. Two down and one to go, he repeated. *One more, and I'll be a man without a worry in the world.*

Well, that wasn't exactly true. He wouldn't be totally carefree until Murray had been tried and convicted of all three murders. Tried, convicted, and sentenced to three life terms in Joliet Prison, where the inmates—each and every one who had a grudge against some cop somewhere—would make what was left of the ex-cop's life as miserable as his father's had been before a cell mate drove a handmade knife between his ribs.

He forced the ugly memory from his mind and made himself think about what a pleasant and unexpected surprise it had been when Murray's fiancée showed up in town. Now he'd be able to mete out a little more of his own kind of justice before taking the cop out, once and for all. He hadn't been privy to Murray's pain and suffering when the explosive device he'd planted killed the detective's old lady and kid. But this time, this time, he'd could actually watch the big buffoon's torment—from a careful distance, of course.

The pièce de résistance, he thought, smugly satisfied that he still remembered a phrase or two from his high school French course, would come as they hauled Murray off in handcuffs for all the neighbors to see, put him on trial, and sentenced him to do time for crimes he had never committed. Would Murray realize at any point in time how closely his own fate resembled that of a man he'd arrested years ago?

Watching his reflection in the mirror, he knotted a blue silk tie at his throat and fastened the pearly buttons of his starched white shirt, marveling at how much he looked like his dad, now that he'd reached full maturity. The similarity was so startling, in fact, that he was genuinely surprised Murray hadn't seen it, too.

Because it had been Murray's cuffs that bound his father's wrists that day, Murray's testimony that sent an innocent man to prison. Never mind all the so-called evidence that Murray had dug up. Never mind all those witnesses who had backed up the cop's courtroom testimony. Circumstantial, all of it, he thought bitterly; it had all been part of an intricate plot to frame his dad.

At the time he had wondered why Murray had gone to such trouble to make his innocent father look guilty. Then he had read the lead story in the *Chicago Sun Times*, and he knew: Murray got a promotion and a raise for his trouble. Got a handshake from the mayor and a plaque from the chief of police, to boot. There's justice for you, he thought glumly. They called Murray a hero and called Dad a killer.

His grin became a snarl as he slipped initialed gold cuff links through satin-trimmed holes of the shirt's French cuffs. Yes, Murray would pay for his father's death. Even the Bible said "an eye for an eye." Murray was to blame for his father's death as surely as if it had been his homemade knife that had pierced his father's heart, and he would pay for it. He could see the headline now: FORMER COP GUILTY OF TRIPLE MURDERS.

Surely some bleeding-heart types would say Murray's so-called crimes had been justified. He had killed only to avenge the deaths of his wife and daughter and beloved bride-to-be, they would say. But it wouldn't matter what they said. Because Murray would be behind bars, trembling with fear each time he heard a noise, each time he saw a shadow, wondering when someone would slip up behind him and. . .

He wanted to yell from the rooftops that, single-handedly, he had plotted and planned Murray's downfall. Now it was time to execute that downfall. And the beauty of it was, no one in their right mind would suspect him of such a devious plot. Good-looking, well-educated, fun-loving, he was Mom and apple pie all that "American Boy" jazz rolled into one. *Why,* he added, laughing aloud again, *I even drive a Chevrolet!*

Maybe, when it was all over and done with, he would actually start living the clean-cut life he had been pretending all this time.

He turned out the bathroom light, leaving nothing but the hollow echo of his evil laughter behind. "Now, what would my old pals down at the pool hall say to that!" he wondered aloud.

Cabot had arranged the early dinner knowing full well that Joe wouldn't be back until after midnight. He yearned for the privacy promised by the bachelor's apartment, because telling Elice what he'd been up to since arriving in Chicago would be hard enough without a larger audience.

He insisted that she find a soothing station on the radio while he put on a kettle of hot water. Cabot's search of Joe's cupboards proved successful when he found a box of herbal tea behind a box of saltines. His attempt at putting cups and saucers on the tray that Joe kept behind the toaster on the counter wasn't quite as productive.

"What's all the racket?" she asked, rushing into the kitchen in response to the clatter of shattering glass.

"Butter fingers," Cabot said through clenched teeth. "Go back and sit down. I made the mess; I'll clean this up."

But even before he finished the sentence, Elice was already on her hands and knees, picking up the bright red and blue remnants of the mugs. "Where does Joe keep his broom and dustpan?" She sat back on her heels, balancing colorful ceramic bits on one palm. "Is that a broom closet?" Elice asked, pointing to the door behind him.

Cabot shrugged. "I dunno. I never opened it."

She grinned. "It's okay to snoop. . .if there's a really good reason," she said, winking.

The way she sat in the middle of the black-and-white tiled floor, her head tilted to one side, made his heart swell with love. He wanted to stomp over there, scoop her up in his arms, and run as far from this place—and its miserable memories—as his long legs would carry them. Instead, he smiled sadly and walked toward the pantry.

Inside, with canned goods, potato chips, and cookies, stood an ironing board, two pairs of boots, and a half-dozen empty milk jugs. Cabot grabbed the broom and dustpan and sent a silent prayer heavenward for this momentary reprieve from telling the truth.

All too soon, they sat side by side on the deep leather couch in Joe's living room, Cabot's arm around Elice's waist, her head on his shoulder. For quite a while they seemed content with their quiet togetherness but then she wriggled and snuggled closer. Draping an arm across his chest, she looked into his eyes. "When are you going to tell me what's bothering you?"

For a moment, lost in the depths of her eyes, he could only blink and silently stare back at her. But the look of earnestness on her face roused him to reality. "What makes you think something's bothering me?"

Tucking in one corner of her mouth, she shook her head. "Really, Cabot. It doesn't take a rocket scientist to know you haven't been yourself, not for one moment, since I got here. Now spit it out. . .or do I have to beat it out of you?" Playfully, she shook a tiny fist under his nose.

The threat, her veiled attempt at humor, fell short of its mark. Cabot wrapped her little fist in his big hands and squeezed gently. Then, placing soft kisses on her knuckles, he sighed. "How is it you know me so well?"

She wriggled one hand free of his hold and used it to turn his face toward hers. "Sometimes," she said, reminding him of another place, another time, "I don't think I know you at all." She kissed his chin, the tip of his nose, his lips. "Tell me, Cabot. What's wrong?"

He lurched forward and got to his feet. For a while, it seemed he might be frozen to one spot in front of Joe's wide window. But then Cabot folded his hands behind his back and began walking. Back and forth he went, like a caged zoo animal, looking at the carpeted floor as though on it were a map that led from wall to wall and back again.

"I don't rightly know where to begin," he said, running a hand through his hair.

She tucked her legs up under her. "Why not start with the headaches, Cabot."

That stopped him dead in his tracks. He met her eyes, dark and knowing and overflowing with love, and drew in a deep breath. The air in the room seemed too thin to provide him with the oxygen required to fully inflate his lungs, so he took another gulp of it. "How'd you know?" But he knew. Cabot hung his head and whispered, "Joe."

She patted the empty cushion beside her, ignoring his implication that Joe had spilled the beans. "I haven't seen you in ages. Come sit with me."

He took one faltering step, then halted.

"Please? I don't like you being so far away."

Though she tried hard to mask it, tension had etched her lovely face with worry lines and sadness. Slump-shouldered, he joined her on the couch. *Well, here goes. Lord, be with me.*

"The migraine started on the flight out here," he admitted, leaning against the sofa back. "I never sleep on airplanes, but I did this time, and I had a terrible nightmare. Thought I was the pilot. The plane was falling out of the sky. I saw

Maggie's car on the runway, right where we'd crash. Woke up seeing double."

Elice's cool-tipped fingers tenderly stroked his cheeks, smoothed wayward locks of hair from his forehead, massaged his temples. From time to time, her lips pressed softly against his closed eyes. This was her silent, soothing language of love.

"I found out that Maggie and Lindy didn't die accidently."

Her hands froze. "It wasn't an accident? What do you mean?" She found the answer, it seemed, in her question. In one swift movement, she wrapped him in a warm and understanding hug, and held him as he told her the rest.

"They were killed. Deliberately. Murdered, no doubt by somebody I arrested and testified against." He turned slightly to face her. "When Jack nearly killed Annie, I told you I was dangerous." Shrugging, he added, "How much more proof do you need?"

She placed a sweet kiss on the tip of his nose. "Need I remind you what I said the last time you told me that?"

They'd been celebrating Annie's recuperation, and he'd decided to leave Freeland for good and live at the Murray family cabin in the Maryland mountains. Elice had accused him of running away, and he'd argued, saying he wasn't doing any such thing. "I'm leaving," he had told her, "because I'm trying to guarantee your safety."

"The man who sings children to sleep and comforts them during thunderstorms and cries at animated movies. . .dangerous, indeed." She had laughed.

Cabot chuckled softly, remembering the scene. But his quiet laughter was short-lived as the truth reared its ugly head: He was, in all likelihood, a cold-blooded murderer. All the signs pointed to his guilt.

Cabot looked away, and a deep furrow formed between his brows. He took a deep breath, then plunged in with, "I think . . .I think I might've killed someone, Elice." *There. I've said it. The truth is out in the open. Now let the chips fall where they may.*

He wouldn't have been the least bit surprised if she'd run crying from the apartment after hearing such a thing. Instead, as on the night he had told her he'd be moving to the mountains, Elice giggled softly. "Killed someone! Why, I've never heard anything more ridiculous in my—"

He could tell by the look in her huge dark eyes that, the moment she caught sight of the serious glint in his, she wasn't at all sure of his innocence. But, in her typical Elice way, she squared her shoulders and lifted her chin in stubborn defiance. "All right, mister. Let's hear it." She kicked off her heels and sat facing him, cross-legged on the big brown couch, arms folded across her chest. "The whole story. And don't you dare leave out a single detail."

Slowly, he ground it out, step by bloody step. Cabot was exhausted when he finished telling it. Covering his face with both hands, he closed his eyes and waited for the inevitable.

And waited.

Finally, he came out of hiding and copied her position on the couch, cross-legged, arms over chest. "Well," he started, "say something. Do something. Kick me. Punch my lights out."

Elice reached out and pressed her palms to his cheeks. "Cabot, sweetie, you couldn't have murdered anyone. Not even to balance the scales of justice for what they did to Maggie and Lindy."

He wanted so much to believe her. He shook his head. "How can you be so sure?"

She tweaked his nose. "Because you're fixated on details. Even in a migraine-induced stupor, you'd need proof. You'd dig up evidence. Even if you were the kind of man who could take another's life—and you are most assuredly not—you'd make sure you got the right bad guy. Why, with that big heart in your chest, it's a wonder there's room for your lungs! Nothing will convince me you went on midnight rampages, like some bloodthirsty vampire, killing all of Chicago's mad bombers in the hopes that one of them was the one who—"

She froze. Sitting there like that, so quiet and still, she looked for all the world like a beautiful manikin.

"Go ahead," he said. "You can say it. 'The one who murdered Maggie and Lindy.' I've been saying it over and over for days. It's the one thing that makes me think maybe I could have."

"I won't hear another word about it!" she snapped, snatching back her hands. "You didn't kill anyone, Cabot. You couldn't have!"

It was his turn to cradle her face in his hands. "Why, pretty lady? Because you've opened your heart to me. . .shared your family with me. . .agreed to spend the rest of your days beside me?" He slid his hands to her shoulders and squeezed them gently. "Scares you, doesn't it, to think maybe you've promised to marry a nut. A basket case. A tootie-frootie."

Her lips narrowed and so did her eyes. Above them, the delicate well-arched brows drew together in a serious frown. "If I believed for an instant that you were a nut, would I do this?" she demanded, then kissed him full on the mouth. "If you were crazy, would I do this?" she asked, wrapping him in a fierce hug. "Would I be wearing this for a basket case?" she concluded, holding up her hand, so that the diamond he had given her gleamed before his eyes. "May I remind you, Cabot Murray, that on June tenth, I intend to stand before God and man, and promise to love you in sickness and health. . .forever. Now, I'll grant you that maybe these headaches of yours have you blanking out and meandering through the night. But if I were a betting woman, I'd wager you didn't even harm a fly during your. . .wanderings."

She was genuinely angry with him for even considering the possibility that he might be responsible for the murders. "If I'm so innocent, Elice, why haven't I gone to the police? Why haven't I told them what I think might be happening? If

I'm so all-fired good, why would I allow another night to pass, knowing I could very well go out there and—"

Her kiss silenced him. Even lip to lip, he could see love glittering from her eyes, like stars in the night sky. Purposefully, he placed his hands on her shoulders and drew away from her. "Thank you, darlin', for believing in me. You'll never know how much it means. But, until I can be as sure as you are. . ."

Chapter 9

For the first time since Cabot had arrived in Chicago, he didn't have a headache.

"You're lookin' mighty chipper this morning," Joe said as he maneuvered the Mustang through rush-hour traffic.

Cabot grinned. "I'm feeling chipper. Good night's sleep. . ."

Joe laughed. "Dinner with a beautiful woman, sweet dreams. . ." He glanced at his ex-partner. "She's a knockout, buddy. How'd an ornery old guy like you win the heart of an angel, that's what I want to know."

"I could ask you the same question. Sarah is one terrific lady."

The smile that replaced the smart-alecky grin looked out of place on the big Irishman's ruddy face. "Yeah. She's a looker, all right. And good as gold, too." He focused on the highway. "Three days and I'll be a married man." Whistling, Joe shook his head.

Cabot shook his head, too. "Hard to believe. I thought you were a confirmed bachelor. Tell me, what made you give up the single man's life?"

Shrugging his broad shoulders, Joe sighed. "I wouldn't tell another living soul this, Cabot, but you an' me, we go way back. I know you won't poke fun when I say I went head over heels the minute I laid eyes on her."

"Your secret's safe with me, pal. Far as everybody else is concerned, you're the greediest, meanest, nastiest, most ornery old. . ."

Joe snickered. "I knew I could count on you to protect my tough-guy reputation." He slowed the car in front of Mark Gardner's apartment building. "I'll sure be glad when the snot-nosed kid gets his car out of the shop. This running around town, chauffeuring him, is getting real old, real quick."

As if on cue, Gardner stepped up to the old Mustang. "Good morning!" he sang, grinning merrily. "Are we ready to face a brand new day?"

"Aw, button yer lip and get in the car," Joe said, faking an angry sneer. "Save all that sunshine and light for somebody who might appreciate it."

"Don't pay any attention to Oscar the Grouch," Cabot joked as he stepped out of the car and climbed into the back. "He's three days from the altar and scared out of his trousers."

"Speaking of somebody who might appreciate my sunny personality," Gardner wisecracked, wiggling his brows at Cabot, "what do you suppose my chances are with a gal like Gail?"

Joe rolled his eyes and sang the first line of the old Everly Brothers hit: "Dre-e-e-am, dream, dream, dream. . ." He shook his head then, and said, "Now shut the door and buckle up. We've got a heavy schedule today."

Gardner frowned. "New case?"

"Naw. Somethin' new on an old case. Remember the Eisensee murder?"

Nodding, Gardner put his arm over the back of the seat. "Wife beating, as I recall. Did one of Laura Eisensee's neighbors decide to testify against the husband after all?"

"Uh-huh. Seems the woman next door has her very own personal abuser. She called me just as I was on my way out last night. Said she didn't want to become a statistic like poor Missus Eisensee. Said she talked a couple of her lady friends into testifying, too. To hear her tell it, old Bill liked it when the rest of the fellas in the building could hear how strong and powerful he could be. He liked an audience, she said."

Gardner shook his head. "My dad didn't have very many rules for me when I was a boy, but. . . ."

"Whaddaya mean, 'when you were a boy'? You're still wet behind the ears!" Joe interrupted.

The young cop snickered good-naturedly. "Like I was saying," he continued, "I didn't have many rules growing up, but my dad told me if I ever hit a girl—for any reason—he'd tan my hide." He was quiet a moment, then added, "Laura Eisensee had three kids, didn't she?"

"Two," Joe corrected. "A boy and a girl. Not even in school yet, as I recall." Then, almost as an afterthought, he said, "Hitting a girl is like hitting a squirrel. Only a nut would do such a thing."

Gardner chuckled. "Maybe Eisensee's retreated into his shell by now. . .ready to crack!"

Laughing softly, Cabot listened to the exchange between partners, remembering a time when he and Joe had similar conversations. It was common knowledge that the bond between partners could be stronger, more durable, even, than the bond between man and wife.

"So their mama's dead and their daddy's goin' to jail. Who's gonna take care of those kids?" the young cop asked no one in particular. Grimacing, he added, "I hope they gas the—"

"Now, now, Mark my boy," Joe injected, "don't make me get that bar of Ivory out of the glove box. . . "

Cabot was happy that Joe had found a partner with whom he could be himself. Joe liked to kid around, because it took the hard edge off the tough cases. Not everyone could make light of the heavy circumstances surrounding murder. What would Joe and Mark say if they knew he might be a murderer? Would they hope the state of Illinois would sentence him to death, too?

Cabot said nothing as the partners continued to taunt one another with good-humored one-liners. Said nothing as Joe parked the Mustang behind the old brick station house. Said nothing as they climbed into the four-doored black sedan and headed for the stucco apartment building where Laura Eisensee's neighbors gave the detectives the information they needed to arrest her husband. Said nothing as they drove toward Chicago's lakefront docks, where Bill Eisensee worked as a warehouse foreman.

He watched as Joe led the wife beater to the waiting black-and-white. Watched as Gardner's big left hand moved awkwardly across the pages of his pocket tablet to note the details of the arrest.

Behind the warehouse, black clouds billowed from a cigar-shaped smokestack that stood four stories tall. The dark fog told one and all that a new shipment was being fired in the huge kilns. Beside the factory, railroad cars stood waiting to unload the red Georgia clay used to make industrial refractory bricks. Years ago, Cabot had investigated a murder down here, had interviewed the employees of the brickyard. The heat near those ovens could be intense; he'd been forced to remove his sports coat and cuff his shirt sleeves. Sweat had poured from his face as he quizzed the man who monitored the ovens. He remembered lurching with fright when the fellow pulled back on a long handle to vent the oven and allow the gasses to escape through the smokestack. Inside, the roar was deafening, like the belch of a giant monster. Outside, the man explained, a ball of fire exploded from the chimney's opening. The man's description made Cabot picture the World War II film footage of the bombing of Hiroshima.

He focused on that smokestack, wondering if he would see in person the fiery red mushroom cloud puff from its mouth. Cabot should have been prepared for the rumbling explosion. Instead, he backpedaled until the undercover police car stopped him. He stared at the fireball that blotted out the sun. And where the sun had been, Cabot saw a tiny red car. Inside it, a woman and a child reached out to him.

Trembling, he closed his eyes, hoping to block the vision before it formed fully in his mind. It was no use. Though he stood half an acre from the spitting, spewing chimney, Cabot imagined that he felt the heat from its furnace. But it wasn't the fire of the brick factory he felt on his face and hands; it was the fire, caused by a well-placed explosives device, that seared his skin.

Quickly, he turned his face away from the fire's glare, leaned on the roof of the police sedan, and buried his face in his hands. *You're losing your mind, Murray. You're prowling at night, and now you're seeing. . .feeling things.*

A heavy hand on his shoulder roused him from his thoughts. "Hey, Cabot, you okay?"

It was Gardner. "Yeah. I'm fine," he lied. "Just had a memory lapse, is all."

Gardner gave his shoulder a friendly shake. "C'mon. Let's take a walk. Get away from here for a minute. Joe's got things under control," he said, gesturing toward his partner, standing in the center of a crowd of uniformed cops who listened carefully to whatever the big cop was saying.

"You wanna talk about it?" Gardner asked as they headed for the water's edge. "Or you want me to butt out?"

Cabot pocketed his hands. "It was nothing. It's just. . .every now and then, I get a flashback to that day. . . . Always throws me when it happens."

"You mean that day when your wife and daughter were killed?"

Cabot nodded.

Gardner gave him a brotherly, sideways hug. "Must have been tough. I don't know what to say, except I'm sorry."

"Thanks." He felt like an idiot. A weak, spineless, whimpering fool. Why couldn't he get control of himself? Why couldn't he put that day behind him, once and for all?

"There's a lunch cart over there," Gardner said, pointing at the silver cart across the parking lot. "How 'bout I buy you a stiff one?"

He knew that Joe Clancy would teach this young cop how to be a great detective. He also suspected that, once trained, this young cop would be a trustworthy cohort. "Joe's a lucky man," Cabot said as they waited for the lunch cart matron to pour their coffee, "to have you for a partner."

Gardner's handsome face flushed. "Coming from you, that's high praise." He stirred sugar into the foam cup, sloshing the black liquid onto his right hand. "Yeeow, that's hot!" he bellowed, then said to the cart owner, "Y'oughta post a sign. Some old woman might file a lawsuit against you for a million bucks!"

She cackled. "My last name isn't McDonald," she said. "Besides, you can't squeeze blood from a turnip."

The episode lightened the mood. "What say we bring a cup to Clancy?" Gardner suggested. "Let's put milk and sugar in it."

Cabot laughed heartily. "He'll have your head on a plate. You know how he hates sweetened coffee."

"Yeah, but did you ever know him to turn down anything free?"

Cabot grinned. "Make that a large coffee," he said to the matron, handing her a dollar bill.

"Extra large," Gardner insisted.

They laughed all the way back to the parking lot.

❧

Elice had never been one for coffee klatches and telephone gossip, so arranging to meet Sarah Miller hadn't been easy for her. But the moment the tall blond walked into the diner across from the station house, Elice knew she'd like her.

"Just look at you," Sarah said, gathering her in a warm embrace. "You're like a Munchkin, you're so tiny!"

They ordered tea and bagels with cream cheese. Like herself, Sarah didn't waste any time on idle chitchat. "So what did you call me away from my very important secretarial work to talk about, Mrs. Soon-to-be-Murray?" she teased.

"Flower arrangements? Wedding gowns? Invitations? Ask me anything. I'm a regular marital encyclopedia!"

Elice could tell by the wizened look on Sarah's face that she knew very well that this meeting had nothing to do with wedding trimmings. Without a moment's hesitation, she launched into her explanation. "It's Cabot. I'm worried sick about him. Has Joe said anything to you about his—"

"About his weird behavior? I should say so!" Sarah said. Leaning forward, she whispered conspiratorially. "You're not to breathe a word of this to Cabot—he'd slug my sweetie if he knew that Joe told me—but it seems Cabot's migraines are back."

Elice sighed and stirred an ice cube into her tea. "I know. But that isn't all. There's more."

Sarah placed a warm hand over Elice's. "My word! You're cold as ice, girl. C'mon. Tell Sarah all about it. I think you know you can trust me."

Elice looked across the table into eyes as blue as cornflowers and sensed that yes, she could trust this woman. "I'd tell Joe myself, but I don't know when I'd find the time to get him alone."

"You'd better not let me catch you alone with him!" Sarah injected, laughing as she squeezed Elice's hand affectionately. "Pretty little thing like you? Why, he might up and cancel the wedding on me. And then what would I do with all those big white bows I'm gonna hang on the pews at Harvester Baptist?"

Elice smiled despite herself. She liked this woman, liked her a lot. "Last night Cabot told me that he's been. . .wandering in the middle of the night."

Sarah folded her hands primly on the table. "Because of the headaches, you mean?"

Elice nodded. "He sort of. . .blacks out. And while he's out, he. . ."

"Look, sweetie, all kidding aside, here, you look like you've met up with the wicked witch of the West. Out with it, now, before it eats you alive. Whatever it is, I'm sure you'll feel better once you've told someone about it." She paused, smiled, then squeezed Elice's hand again. "Besides, knowing that big-hearted fiancé of yours, how bad can it be?"

It can be bad, Elice thought. Very bad. She took a deep breath and slid the newspaper clippings from her purse. "Have you been following this story?" Elice asked, laying them on the red-speckled Formica table.

Sarah pulled them nearer and read the headlines. "Sure. Who hasn't?" Drawing her well-arched blond brows together, she frowned. "But what's this got to do with Cabot?"

"He thinks he's responsible."

Sarah's pale-lashed eyes widened. "You don't mean. . ."

"For the murders," she concluded. "He thinks that, during the night, while the migraine is in control of his mind, he's been hunting down bad guys."

"But why?" Sarah wanted to know. "What reason would he have for killing"—

she pointed at the headline on top—"for killing explosives experts?"

Elice told her the story of how Cabot's wife and daughter had been killed in an accident on the Dan Ryan Expressway and how, when arriving in Chicago, he had learned that it hadn't been an accident at all, but a pay-back for his having put some bad guy in prison.

Sarah listened, mouth agape, as Elice told her how Cabot had gone to the police station and secured a list of known bombers from the computer. Two of the six men on the list were now dead, Elice emphasized, finished with her story.

Slowly, Sarah sipped her tea. Wrinkling her brow, she rested her chin on a doubled-up fist. "You don't believe any of that, do you?"

"No. Not for a minute. But Cabot believes it. And if I don't do something. . . and fast. . .he's going to turn himself in. It'll be all over the papers in no time, and whoever is responsible for the murders may just sit back and let Cabot take the blame. I won't let that happen."

"We won't let that happen," Sarah corrected. "I'll tell Joe about it. We'll put our li'l pumpkin heads together and come up with something that'll work. I'm sure of it."

Elice smiled at her new friend. "I already have an idea. Maybe you can run it past Joe and see if he agrees it'll work."

Sarah's blue eyes glittered with excited anticipation. "Well, don't be a mummouth," she insisted. "I'm all ears, so spit it out!"

Looking left, then right, Elice leaned forward and lowered her voice. "It's quite simple, really. All we have to do is. . ."

❧

"It'll sorta be like guard duty, back in my Army days," Joe said. Sarah would take the nine-to-midnight shift, Joe the midnight-to-three shift, and Elice the three-to-six a.m. shift. They'd sit in the dark parking lot across the street from Joe's building, eyes fixed on the front door, and wait. And when Cabot went wandering, he'd be accompanied by a very determined shadow.

In the morning, the red-eyed friends compared notes. Since Cabot never left the apartment once during the night, they had had no one to follow. "We can't give up yet," Joe insisted. "We'll keep it up until he makes a break. We'll dog his heels. We'll prove he isn't responsible for the killings."

"I have a better idea," Cabot interrupted, causing Elice, Sarah, and Joe to lurch with surprise. "No need to babysit me." He held up his hand to silence their objections. "Don't think I haven't been aware that I've had a sidekick every minute of the day." Smiling, he added, "Look, I appreciate your concern, but there's no sense any of you losing sleep over this. Why not just stick me in lockup overnight?" he said to Joe. "If I'm behind bars and some bomber takes a hit, we'll know it isn't me doing the dirty deeds."

And if nothing happened while Cabot sat on a lumpy jail cell mattress, was the unspoken concern of all four, they'd have a harder time proving Cabot wasn't the killer.

That night, through some subtle but strategic string pulling, Joe convinced the duty officer to put Cabot into a cell, telling the cop Cabot had lost a bet. "Don't make me back down," he whined. "You know how hard it is to get cash from a cop."

And so, when the lights went out at the old Thirty-fourth, Cabot got on his knees. It was a fine line he walked that night, for he truly didn't want another bomber to die, no matter how much he believed the criminal's violent acts deserved dire consequences. *But if someone, some godless person was so all-fired resolved to balance the scales of justice, let it happen while I'm locked up,* Cabot prayed. And then he prayed for forgiveness for his selfish prayer of self-preservation.

When the sun rose, washing the gritty city streets with amber light, Joe unlocked the cell door. Cabot knew the moment he set eyes on his old friend that nothing had happened as he counted the minutes of the long, bleak night. He breathed a sigh of relief, because he honestly didn't know what he would have done if another bomber had been murdered as he paced the sticky concrete floor of the cell. He couldn't very well have celebrated another man's death, even one who'd senselessly killed others, just to secure his own peace of mind. . .could he?

Chapter 10

To determine who would take the first watch, Elice, Joe, and Sarah played Scissors, Paper, Rock. Elice believed that in childhood, Joe and Sarah must have played it a whole lot oftener than she had, for she lost miserably. Ever the big-hearted Irishman, Joe agreed to play the best two out of three, and still she lost. She'd wanted to win the first watch so she could enjoy Cabot's company during waking hours, rather than as he slept. Fortunately for her, Joe was also an incurable romantic and, understanding her disappointment and the reasons behind it, he traded shifts with her.

"We've got a last-minute meeting with the photographer," he told Cabot, "uh. . .to. . .to discuss what he's supposed to do at the reception."

Cabot only nodded, his slightly raised left brow and thin-lipped grin telling Elice he wasn't buying Joe's alibi. Much to her surprise, Joe recognized the suspicious look, too.

"You can just wipe that I-don't-believe-a-word-of-it look off your face, Murray," Joe barked, wearing a pretend scowl of his own. "I'm old enough to stay out past midnight without your permission."

Holding up his hands in mock surrender, Cabot's grin grew. "Hey. You want to stay out all night, smooching with your sweetie, it's no skin off my nose." He assumed that paternal pose that Elice had seen him use on her kids. . .arms folded over his broad chest, head turned slightly to the left, chin up just a mite.

"Need I remind you that you're the one who has an eight o'clock meeting with the chief."

Joe held out his hands pleadingly to Sarah. "Are you absolutely sure that was my dad we buried two years ago? 'Cause this guy," he said, giving Cabot a playful punch to the bicep, "sounds exactly like him."

Sarah shrugged into her trench coat. "The two of you remind me of my squabbling brothers. You don't want to know how I put a stop to their bickering," she warned, one hand on her ample hip. "Let's make tracks," she said to Joe, opening the door.

Beaming, Joe said, "Now that's some woman!" Grabbing his overcoat, he gave his fiancée a peck on the cheek. "See you guys later." And with that, they were gone.

"She's got him wrapped around her little finger," Cabot said, smiling. "But then, if you were my height and weight, I guess I'd do as I was told, too."

Elice sidled up to him and narrowed her eyes. "If I were the kind of woman who gave orders. . .and I most definitely am not," she said, raising her own left brow now, "I wouldn't need to be your height and weight to get my way. I'd use. . .strategy."

"So I'd think I was doing what I wanted to do all along, eh?"

"Exactly!"

He threw back his head and laughed long and hard. "Well, all I can say is. . . good thing for me you're the old-fashioned, demure type."

Elice snuggled closer.

"And obedient, too. 'Wives, submit yourselves unto your own husbands, as unto the Lord,'" he quoted from Ephesians 5, "'For the husband is the head of the wife. . .so let the wives be to their own husbands in every thing.'"

She placed her fingertips over his lips to silence him. "All right. All right. I get the picture." Kissing his chin, she added, "Good thing for you I'm a church-goin' Christian girl."

They spent the next hour fine-tuning their own wedding plans. He wouldn't have been the least bit surprised if Elice had wanted a huge celebration, a fancy dress, flowers everywhere and a parade of attendants, because had Elice told him she'd made her first wedding dress from the damask tablecloth her mother had left her and had made her bouquet with blooms of the wild rose shrub in her front yard. There had been no reception, no honeymoon. The moment she and Bobby returned from the five-minute ceremony in Pastor Donneley's office, he'd changed into coveralls and started tinkering with his jalopy while she unpacked the boxes that contained all his worldly possessions and found places for them in the house she'd inherited from her father.

The ceremony that joined her to Cabot on June tenth would indeed be an elaborate affair. . .and all their closest friends and family members could show up in blue jeans and cowboy boots, if they had a mind to. Her next door neighbor, Sue Pue, would bake the cake, and Liz Beck, who lived behind Sue, would shoot and develop ten rolls of film. The Glassers volunteered to provide chicken, hot dogs, and hamburger meat, and other assorted invitees would bring breads, condiments, salads, baked beans, or pie to the backyard barbecue/reception. These contributions, Elice insisted, would be their wedding gifts.

She glanced at her watch. "Oh no!" Elice said, leaping up from the couch. "I promised the kids I'd call them tonight."

"Call from here," Cabot pleaded, reaching for her hand.

"Can't," she insisted, slipping into her jacket. "I made a promise to Sarah, too. . .to stuff a hundred and twenty-five little mesh bags with birdseed for their guests to shower them with as they leave the church. It'll probably take me all night."

Cabot rose and headed for the hall tree to get his coat. "I'll come with you. I can help."

Elice stood on tiptoe and kissed him. "Thanks, but no thanks. With those big loving eyes of yours distracting me from across the table, I'd be lucky to get ten bags filled." She hugged him tightly. "Besides, haven't you ever heard that 'absence makes the heart grow fonder?'"

"Sure I have. I lived it until you got here."

She kissed his chin. "You need some sleep a lot more than you need to be with me. Why not take a couple of those magic pills the doctor gave you and climb into bed? And tomorrow, you can take me to see Chicago's famous Loop."

"Why? 'Cause you're loopy for me?"

"No," she teased, "because it's windy down there and it reminds me of you, ya big blowhard!"

He threw his head back and laughed out loud.

"Now get some sleep!"

Cabot tightened his hold on her. "Maybe you're right. Joe and Sarah are getting married in two days. I don't want to look like a ghoul up there on the altar."

"So you do have a headache, don't you?"

He nodded.

"Why didn't you say something earlier?"

"'Cause when you're with me, it doesn't hurt so much." He held her face in his hands and kissed her soundly.

"Much as I enjoy your sweet kisses," she said, taking his hand, "they're not helping me get those little bags filled."

Hand in hand, they walked to the door.

"See you first thing in the morning," he said.

"Bright and early," she agreed. "Maybe I'll bring breakfast in a bag!"

Chuckling, he drew her close once more. "Sleep tight, pretty lady. I'll miss you."

"And I'll dream of you." With that, she left him in Joe's apartment, alone.

❧

Moments later, in the rental car, Elice hurriedly slid jeans and a long-sleeved black tee shirt over her blouse and black jeans. Sarah had loaned her a navy blue knapsack and, as she had the last time she kept watch outside Joe's apartment, waiting for Cabot to leave for another nocturnal wandering, Elice had stuffed a flashlight, a water bottle, a spiral notebook, and a pen inside it. She tested the two-way radio Joe had given her. If she needed him for anything, Joe had promised, he'd be monitoring channel nine. Ready for anything, she told herself as she hunkered down behind a bushy rhododendren.

The first hour passed slowly. She wished she had brought a magazine to flip through. She could have balanced her checkbook, if she'd thought to bring it. Or written postcards to the children. She wondered how people who did this kind of thing for a living survived, because Elice honestly couldn't remember her heart beating this hard or her blood racing this fast through her veins.

Deliberately, to get her mind off her trembling, traitorous body, she focused on her children. They'd sounded happy and healthy when she'd talked with them earlier, telling her about all the projects their grandparents had planned for them. School, they'd said, was fine. . .except for the fact that the teachers had been doling out far too much homework.

"When are you coming home, Mommy?" Annie had asked when it was her turn to talk.

"In a few more days, sweetie," she'd answered. *When the wedding is over and I'm sure Cabot isn't out killing people in the middle of the night,* she'd added, mentally.

"It's okay if you stay a long time," her younger daughter had said, giggling, " 'cause Grandmom doesn't make us do dishes and we don't have to make our beds, either."

"But you're brushing your teeth and flossing twice a day, right?"

"Um-hmm. Granddad says if we don't, all our teeth will fall out and we'll have to wear plastic ones that go click, click, click, like his."

Just thinking about the long-distance conversation made Elice smile. It would certainly be good to get back home and wrap those dear ones in a huge hug. It was also good to know they were in good hands. Her former in-laws couldn't love her children more if they'd been born to them.

Elice was trying to think of a special gift that would show them how much she appreciated their help, when movement across the street caught her attention. She held her breath as she got onto her knees to watch the shadowy figure dart from behind a tree trunk to a nearby telephone pole, then silently scuttle across the pavement like a two-legged rat. She couldn't be sure from this distance, but the broad shoulders and long strides told her it was a man.

Good thing she had decided not to sit in the car to observe Joe's building; from this vantage point, on a grassy knoll in the little park across the way, she could clearly see the comings and goings from behind the leafy shrub. Tensing, she crouched to peer through the parted branches of the budding plant. She glanced at her wristwatch, pressed the tiny button that lit the dial—one forty-two and four seconds.

In one artful leap, he leapt up and grabbed the railing surrounding Joe's second-floor balcony, then began a slow swinging motion with his long legs, building up the steam required to fling them over the railing. Once there, he crouched low and moved smoothly toward the sliding glass doors. He looked right, then left, and in seconds, it seemed, he disappeared into the darkness of Joe's living room.

Not even Joe had anticipated anything like this. Like Elice, Joe had expected Cabot to exit the building—alone. And the one on watch would follow at a safe distance to find out what, if anything, he'd been doing in the middle of the night. Not Joe or Sarah or Elice considered the possibility that someone might have accompanied him on his late-night travels.

What if the man in black was nothing but a burglar? What if, when he got inside and started snooping around for something worthwhile to steal, he discovered Cabot asleep in the extra bedroom? What if he felt it necessary to harm Cabot—or worse—to keep himself from being jailed for breaking and entering?

She took another peek at her watch—one forty-two and ten seconds.

Everything in her told her to run screaming across the street, bang loudly on the door to apartment 4C, and alert Cabot. But Joe had warned her she'd experience that urge. "Don't give in to it," he'd instructed. "Keep your mind on the project and never leave your post, no matter what."

Would that have been his advice under these circumstances? she wondered. This was no Halloween costume party. She'd donned the spylike getup to help Cabot, not hurt him. Would giving in to the urge to interrupt the burglar, or whatever he was, cause more harm than good?

She dug around in the knapsack and pulled out the walkie-talkie, flicked the switch on, and whispered into the speaker. "Joe! Joe, are you there? Come in, Joe." Her watch dial now said one forty-three and one second.

The radio crackled, hissed, but Joe's familiar voice didn't follow.

"Joe! It's me, Elice. Something's going on over here. You've got to tell me what to do."

Silence.

One forty-three and six seconds.

If storming the building was a mistake, so be it. Elice couldn't just sit there while some guy in black harmed her husband-to-be. Joe's warning ricocheted through her mind. "Don't leave your post. No matter what."

Elice decided to give the radio one more try. "Joe! Come in, Joe."

Now it was one forty-three and fifteen seconds.

❧

"I would have bet my last nickel that Elice would be calling every fifteen minutes," Sarah said, handing Joe a cola as she sat beside him on her couch.

He yawned, stretched, then took a gulp of the fizzing drink. "Elice may be tiny, but she's tough. She'll use the radio if she needs us, not before."

Sarah leaned against his side. "Maybe. But if it were me out there in the dark, I'd be making contact just to remind myself I wasn't alone." Sarah leaned forward and picked up the walkie-talkie, turned it over, wrinkled her brow as she inspected it. "You checked the batteries?"

Joe nodded. "Twice."

"And tested it?"

He shot her an impatient glare. "I wouldn't send her out there without backup."

Sarah shook the radio again. "Then why isn't it making any noise? Isn't it supposed to gurgle and gargle and stuff, like in the movies?"

With a patronizing sigh, he held out his arms. "C'mere and give us a hug."

Smiling, she let him wrap her in a hug. "You cops are all alike. Calm in a storm and all that."

"What's to get excited about? If she needs us, she'll call."

"I suppose you're right," she agreed, leaning her head on his shoulder. "I just wish this feeling that something is wrong would go away."

"Hey. Cops are the guys with gut instincts." He poked his soft belly. "When it rumbles, then you can worry."

She giggled. "If that were true, I'd be worried nonstop."

Joe sat up straight and took the radio, scowling. "You and your feelings," he muttered, holding it under the beam of the table lamp, "are giving me the heebie-jeebies." He flipped the walkie-talkie over, loosened the case, and jiggled the battery.

In an instant, he was on his feet. "The terminal wire's come loose!" he thundered.

Just as quickly, she leaped up and stood beside him. "What's that mean?" Sarah asked, frowning at the radio's exposed innards.

"There's no connection, that's what it means."

Sarah gasped. "So she's out there alone. . . ."

"With no backup." Joe's ruddy face paled. "Get your coat! We're goin' over there!"

❧

Elice shoved the walkie-talkie back into the bag. Something was wrong, very wrong. Much as she would have liked to get Joe's advice, she had no way to contact him. Surely he hadn't intended her to sit idly by while something terrible happened to Cabot. If she cowered there in the shrubbery, heart beating like a frightened rabbit's, the man in black might. . .

The possibilities were too horrible to imagine. She'd make a huge racket and wake all the neighbors. The noise, she surmised, would frighten the would-be burglar, or whatever he was, out of the apartment. True, they may never know who he was or what he'd wanted, but the important thing now was Cabot and his safety.

Just as she was about to step out from behind the bush, the door to Joe's building swung open. Cabot, hands tied behind his back, leaned heavily on the shadowy man. He stumbled and staggered alongside his captor like a man who'd left the pub after one too many beers.

The full bulk of his captive's weight was a lot to bear, and she heard the proof of it in the captor's grunts and groans as he led Cabot away from the building.

What could be going on? she asked herself.

But she had no time for questions. . .she had time only for action.

If she walked fast and silently, she could slip up behind the shadowy man and bop him on the bean with the big black flashlight Joe had loaned her. Elice rummaged in the bag for it. It took mere seconds to pull it out and flip the ON switch—just enough time for the captor to shove Cabot into the passenger seat of the black sedan that was parked, motor running, near the curb.

Had the car been there all along, motor running? Why hadn't she noticed it? Why hadn't she heard it? Guilt raged inside her. Guilt and fear that she may never see Cabot again if she didn't do something, and do it now.

Elice ran full speed toward the car, fully prepared to use the big flashlight like a club. But she was too late, for just as she'd made it to the other side of the street, the captor slammed the driver's door shut and steered the car away.

She stood in the middle of the road, holding the light high above her head, listening to the hideous sounds of the accelerating motor, the squealing of tires, and she watched as the black sedan disappeared from view.

Her hand went limp, and the light clattered to the pavement before rolling beneath another parked car. She'd felt this helpless, this useless, on only one other occasion in her life. . .when Annie lay in a coma at the hospital.

Lord, God, she prayed, *help me.*

A voice whispered in her subconscious. "C-Y-N-2-2-4," it whispered.

"C-Y-N-2-2-4," she repeated aloud.

She stood, awash in the glow of headlights, as Sarah's blue Camaro screeched to a stop behind her. "C-Y-N-2-2-4," she said, pointing in the direction the black sedan had gone. "C-Y-N-2-2-4."

With that, she melted to the blacktop and began to cry.

❧

"Stop blaming yourself," Joe insisted, patting Elice's back as he looked helplessly over her shoulder at Sarah. "It was all my fault. I could kick myself; I should have checked my radio one more time."

"But I could have done something. I could've tried to clobber him," Elice cried into his shoulder. "I should have. . . ."

Sarah joined the hug. "Honey, if that had happened on my watch, I'd have fainted dead away, and we wouldn't have a license number or anything else to go on."

"Which reminds me," Joe said, breaking away from the teary eyed women. "That was Smitty on the phone a few minutes ago. The car is registered to the city of Chicago."

Elice and Sarah exchanged puzzled glances. "You mean. . .the man in black. . .is a cop?" Elice asked.

Joe grimaced. "I doubt it. Could be a stolen car. Happens all the time in the city. Either way, we'll know within the hour. Smitty's checking on it right now."

As if on cue, the telephone rang, startling all three. Joe lifted the receiver. "Yeah? Right. Izzat so? Well, whaddaya know." When he hung up, he scratched his head. "It wasn't on the list of stolen vehicles. That means it's an operational vehicle. Smitty's running it through now to see who the car is assigned to."

Elice stood at the window, arms across her chest as if fending off a frigid wind. "Where do you suppose he is right now? What do you suppose that. . . ? What do you suppose he's doing to Cabot?"

Sarah put her hands on Elice's shoulders. "Cabot's a strong, determined man. I wouldn't want to be that guy. Not for all the tea in China."

"You didn't see him. He'd been drugged." Elice allowed her new friend to offer a comforting embrace. "If anything happens to him, I'll never forgive myself for not trying to do something when I had the chance. If anything happens to him. . ." A sob choked off the rest of her sentence.

The nagging doubt that had been eating at her since Cabot's very first call from Chicago to Freeland raised its ugly head and the questions that had been plaguing her rang loud once again. *Why did God allow Cabot to be taken from me?* she wondered. *How could He let this happen to such a good man?*

She left the comfort of Sarah's arms and slumped onto the supple leather seat of Joe's couch, hugged her knees to her chest, rested her chin on her knees, and mentally recited Matthew 21:21. *Verily I say unto you, If ye have faith, and doubt not. . .ye shall say unto this mountain, Be thou removed, and. . .it shall be done.* Christ's promise in the next verse was even more powerful than His promise in the first. *Whatsoever ye shall ask in prayer, believing, ye shall receive.*

When had she stopped believing? Tears squeezed from the corners of her tightly closed eyes. She yearned to be faithful again, to ask something of God and know, with absolute certainty, that He heard and would answer. *Ask, believing, and you'll receive,* she reminded herself. She could ask a thousand times over, but until she believed, truly believed, she couldn't be certain she'd receive.

Under the circumstances, she didn't believe she deserved to be heard.

Chapter 11

The last thing Cabot recalled was gulping a tumbler of water to wash down his Fiorinal and climbing into bed. He'd had many strange dreams in the past as the medication took effect, but this one most assuredly topped the list.

The ticking Baby Ben alarm and the soft whir of the furnace echoed, as though he'd entered the hushed and hallowed sanctuary of a cathedral. When Cabot opened his eyes, he wasn't at all surprised to see a man, dressed all in black, standing beside the bed. A priest, no doubt, his dreaming mind explained. Strange, Cabot noted, that the preacher wore no notched white collar around his neck.

"Get up," whispered the minister, nudging Cabot's shoulder, "and put on your pants."

Cabot's thoughts were coming in ragged fragments, and he frowned to help deepen his concentration. Pants? Not wearing pants? In church? He didn't understand, but the preacher seemed so patient, so paternal, that Cabot tried to follow his instructions. It didn't take long to realize that he had neither the energy nor the coordination to perform a task as routine as stepping into his trousers.

Chuckling softly, the preacher gently pulled Cabot into a sitting position and slid one leg of the pants on over a bare foot. "This is getting to be a habit." *Habit?* Cabot repeated. *I've. . .church. . .without pants. . .before?* It was a wonder the minister didn't scold him soundly, for hadn't it been only yesterday that the black-suited man had to help him in a similar way?

Fully dressed now and on his feet, Cabot swayed drunkenly. "Wazzit?" he mumbled, fumbling with his belt buckle. "Wazz gonon?"

"Never mind what's going on," the minister said reassuringly. "I'll do that."

Unable to question the man further, Cabot stood beside the bed, like an obedient child. In moments, the preacher guided Cabot from the spare bedroom, into the long narrow hallway that led onto the porch of Joe's building. The moon and stars beamed brightly, and he wondered when they had started holding church services in the observatory.

"This way," the preacher sighed, "just a few more steps. . . . Stand still now, while I open the door for you."

Leaning against the car's right rear fender, he listened to the steady purr of

189

the motor. Hands tied, he thought, trying to scratch an itch beside his nose. He tugged, pulled, wriggled left and right to loosen them, and lost his balance. Was this his punishment for coming to church improperly dressed?

"Careful now," the minister's quiet voice admonished, "or you'll fall."

"Sorry. . . ."

"Nothing to be sorry about. Just get in."

"In a car?"

"Yes," he soothed. "In the car." Then, more to himself than to Cabot, he said, "How many of the Percocets did you swallow, anyway?"

As the preacher closed the passenger door, Cabot tried to repeat the word. "Perco. . .Per. . ." But it was no use. His drug-dulled mind simply couldn't remember what the priest had said.

Suddenly he became aware that the car was in motion. He listened as its tires hummed over the blacktop. "Wh're we goin'?"

"Never mind where we're going. Just lie back and enjoy the ride."

"Shhhh," Cabot whispered, his head lolling. "Shhhh."

The preacher drove for hours, it seemed, as Cabot's mind grasped at police sirens and honking horns, the deejay saying, "It's one forty-five in the morning." One forty-five? He'd gone to bed at one o'clock, right after Elice left Joe's apartment.

When the car came to a stop, Cabot's head bobbed forward, then bounced off the headrest. "Wha. . . ?"

"Shhh," the preacher soothed. Then, in a voice like a hypnotist's, he added, "Close your eyes. Go to sleep. I'll be back."

"Shhh. . . ."

His bleary eyes opened slightly and, to his muddled mind, it seemed the man in black walked for hours, instead of moments. And when he disappeared through the rusting metal doors of the warehouse, Cabot blinked. Almost immediately, he heard voices. Men's voices, echoing from inside the aluminum building, then angry shouts, breaking glass. . .and one long, ear-piercing scream.

Cabot's brow furrowed as he listened to the sounds of violence emanating from the warehouse. He tried, unsuccessfully, to hold open his eyes, then he struggled to sit up so that he could look through those doors. But his eyes and arms, heavy from the effects of the Percocet, refused to cooperate. Cabot moaned softly, his forehead pressed to the cool window, right up until the door swung open.

He toppled to the ground with a muffled ooomph and sprawled beside the car like a marionette whose puppeteer had suddenly let go of the strings. He lay cheek-to-blacktop as shiny black wing tips shuffled past. It was the priest, Cabot thought, relieved, come to help him to his feet. But instead of the familiar friendly voice, Cabot heard a grating demanding order: "Turn over."

His mind was clearing slightly. Enough, at least, that he knew it should have hurt when the priest's fist connected with his jaw, causing him to bite his own lip. But the dulling effects of the narcotic blocked the pain. Slowly, Cabot ran his tongue along the lip and tasted blood. Why had the priest hit him? Cabot wondered.

Somehow, he found the strength to open his eyes. To keep them open long enough to look directly into the shadowy face of the preacher. Where had he seen that face before? Somewhere on the fringes of his frazzled memory, Cabot knew he'd seen it. Several nights ago? And at least once, during daylight hours, too. He squinted in a concerted effort to focus on the blurry face before him. Then he concentrated, trying to put a name to that face.

The image floated there between full consciousness and the last effects of the drug: Navy double-breasted suit. Blue tie. Black wing tips. He lifted his hand to point at the man who leaned on one knee and stared down at him.

"You're no priest," Cabot slurred. "You're. . .you're—"

The second blow to his jaw knocked him out cold.

✼

All the way home, he flexed his left hand and cursed Cabot Murray's sharp incisors. *I'll be lucky not to get an infection,* he complained. He'd read once, long ago, that more germs lived in the human mouth than practically anywhere else. What had gone wrong to make Murray rouse sooner than expected?

On the previous nights, when he'd led the staggering detective from Clancy's apartment into the dark Chicago streets, he hadn't needed to resort to unnecessary violence. The cop responded well to his quiet directives. And when the time was right, a few well-placed punches had been more than enough to give Murray the look of a man who'd been involved in a fight. Yes, the Percocet had been doing its job well. . .until tonight.

Tonight, the drug's effects didn't seem to have the hold on Murray's mind that it had had on the two other nights, when he had dragged the cop to prearranged meeting places to discuss extortion, first with J. J. Johnson, then with then Al Winters. Blinded by a narcotic daze, Murray hadn't seen or heard a thing either night.

With a vicious snap, he pulled the black turtleneck over his head, rolled it into a ball, and aimed, then chuckled when his neat rim shot sunk into the hamper.

Actually, he thought, stepping out of his black jeans, he knew full well that Murray had seen and heard everything on both nights. But the Percocet he had exchanged for the cop's Fiorinal had made a sleepwalker out of him. Cabot had been aware of his surroundings, but was too drugged to react. . .or recall.

Too drugged, he surmised while adding his jeans to the dirty clothes pile, to remember anything. Not the loud arguments that had ensued when Al Winters and J.J. Johnson had learned that he wouldn't exchange ten thousand dollars for their silence. Not their muffled cries for help as his viselike grip encircled their throats. Not the sounds of their bodies crumpling onto the ground of the grimy alleyways. Afterward, when he had dumped Murray nearby, the cop's rheumy eyes had made a filmy sort of contact with his. Tonight, the cop had stared right at him, and had been nearly wide awake at the time.

Remembering the look of near-recognition on Murray's face, he shuddered. One more instant, he knew, and the detective would have recognized him.

He couldn't let that happen.

And that's why he had slugged Murray, rendering him unconscious. He wasn't taking any chances. Why else would he have spoken softly, gently, to a man he despised? He had studied somnambulism, and he knew what to do—and what to avoid—so as not to rouse Murray from his drug-induced near-sleep. Careful not to ask questions, so Murray wouldn't need to reach a higher level of wakefulness to answer. Careful to unscrew the bottle of wine and drizzle it into the mouth of the unconscious ex-cop.

Not careful enough, he reprimanded himself.

Still, it had gone well, all things considered. Three down and one to go, he told himself, his mouth widening with a satisfied grin. And tomorrow, when he finished laying the groundwork for Murray's demise, he'd get to work on the cop's perky little fiancée.

❧

Cabot woke with a start. . .and a shooting pain in his left side.

"Get up!" a man shouted. "Come on, get on your feet, you bum."

Cabot opened his eyes and held a hand between them and the bright sunlight that silhouetted the loud-mouthed man. Raising onto one elbow, he grimaced with pain.

"Gimme a hand here, Bobby. This one's nearly out cold." The loud man's hands folded around one bicep. "Why don't they go to the shelters to sleep off their Thunderbird? I'm a cop, not a garbage collector."

His buddy snickered. "Trash men make twice what we earn a year and don't have to get their hands dirty with vermin like this one," he said, grabbing Cabot's other arm.

Suddenly, Cabot was on his feet.

"Get his wallet," said the first man. "Find out who we're gonna write up for vagrancy."

In a flash he saw the glint of brass against dark blue. These guys were police officers, Cabot realized. The loud one's name tag read Trevera. His partner's pin said Otto.

"Name's Murray," he explained, holding his pounding head. "Cabot Murray. I was with the Thirty-fourth. . .Homicide Division."

"Yeah?" said Trevera, sliding Cabot's driver's license from the billfold, "and I'm Danny Rostenkowski. That's my government surplus furniture store over there," he sneered sarcastically, pointing to the rusting warehouse. He handed the license to his partner without even looking at it.

Otto studied it as Trevera looked through the wallet.

"Whoa," Trevera said, pulling a business card from the money pocket. "He really is who he claims to be." To Cabot, he said, "How long since you retired, pal?"

Cabot rubbed his aching jaw. "Three years, almost."

"This is a Maryland license."

Cabot nodded and repocketed his wallet.

"Say!" Otto exclaimed, "I know who you are! You're the guy whose old lady and kid were—"

Trevera's glare silenced his partner.

Cabot sighed, then shrugged. "It's okay. I'm getting used to it." He gave the second cop a sad half-smile. "I'm the guy whose wife and daughter were blown up on the Dan Ryan." The words ached inside him every bit as much as the effects of his night hurt his body.

"Sorry," the officers said in unison. "Tough break."

"Yeah. Tough." He tucked in his shirttail and adjusted his jacket. "You guys through with me yet?"

"I guess. What're you doin' down here, anyway?" Otto wanted to know.

Cabot blanched. How could he tell them he didn't know what he was doing down here. . .where was here, anyway? "I. . .uh. . .guess I had one too many last night." And it was true, after all. The Fiorinals were helping dull the migraine, but they were dulling everything else, too. Right then and there, he vowed never to take another. No matter how badly his head hurt.

"You need a ride someplace?" Trevera asked. "We're headed for Cicero. . . ."

Cabot ran a hand through his hair then worked his sore jaw back and forth. "Naw. I think I'd better walk this off. Thanks, though."

With that, the officers left. "You take it easy, hear?" Otto said over his shoulder.

Cabot sent him a weak salute. "Thanks. I'll do that."

"Breaks your heart, don't it?" he overheard Trevera say.

"Yeah," Otto responded. "Sometimes I hate this job."

"If my wife and kid had been murdered. . ." Trevera didn't finish the sentence.

"Guess he's got a right to go a little bananas."

A little bananas. Is that what I am? Cabot looked around to get a fix on his whereabouts. Somehow, he'd ended up in the industrial district this time, more than four miles from Joe's apartment.

He had a long, lonely walk ahead of him.

❧

"Hey, T. J.," hollered Clancy, "you missed a spot."

"Shut up," T. J. muttered, pushing his mop toward the tile that Clancy had indicated. "You think 'cause you got me this job I gotta take this offa you?"

Joe laughed heartily and slapped his meaty thigh. "That's exactly what I think. You'd still be makin' license plates if it weren't for me, and don't you forget it."

T. J. shook his left fist under Clancy's nose. "As if you'd let me forget it." He leaned his chin on the broom handle. "Where's my coffee, you big ugly jerk?"

"Right where it always is, you stupid creep."

They stood, toe to toe, glaring at one another.

"Aw, why don't you guys pay somebody to write you a new script?" Gail wanted to know. "I'm sick and tired of hearing the same old argument every morning of my life."

Grinning, Clancy stood and dropped a brotherly hand on T. J.'s shoulder. "She has a point. Maybe tomorrow, I'll deck you, just for a change of routine."

T. J. smiled right back. "Yeah? I'd like to see you try."

"I could take you, blindfolded!"

"Fat chance. You start something, Joe Clancy, and they'll have to put me away again. For good, this time."

Laughing, Clancy handed T. J. his coffee. "Where'd you get the boo-boo, buddy boy?" he asked, pointing at the bandage that hid his knuckles.

"Cut myself shaving," T. J. said.

"I'm not surprised. Must take you hours to shave, you hairy gorilla." Then, lightly slapping the man's tanned cheek, he said, "Be careful drinking that coffee, now, 'cause it's very, very hot. Wouldn't want you to burn that filthy mouth of yours."

T. J. slapped Clancy's hand away. "You ought write yourself a ticket," he said, grimacing at the foam cup, "using these sewer cloggers as coffee cups." He raised his voice and said, to everyone in general, "Y'all oughta be ashamed of yourselves." Then, almost as an afterthought, he faced Clancy and, in a friendly, little-boy voice, asked, "Did you put in two sugars?"

"Uh-huh. And two milks, too."

The innocent grin turned upside down. "You know I take only one."

Clancy shrugged and shot him a sneer. "Why do ya think I did it?"

T. J. shook his fist as he headed toward the door. "One of these days. . . ," he said, doing his best Jackie Gleason imitation.

"Pow, right in the kisser!" Clancy finished, laughing. "Now get to work before I call your P. O. and report you for insubordination."

T. J. ambled away, his powerful left hand dragging the big mop.

"One of these days, he's gonna snap," Gail cautioned, perching on the corner of Clancy's desk, "and he'll bop you with that mop. And big as he is, you won't have to go to L. A. to see stars. They'll be twinkling all around your stubborn Irish head."

Clancy waved her warning away. "Yeah, yeah, yeah. And I'm gonna be the next mayor of Chicago."

She stood and tugged at the hem of her tight red miniskirt. "I'm not kidding,

Clance. The guy served ten years for first-degree murder."

"Yeah, yeah. 'Killed a guy with his bare hands.'"

"You can laugh it off if you want," Gail said, heading for the door. Then, suddenly, she turned on her stiletto heels and faced him. "Mark my words," she said, wagging a daggerlike red fingernail at him, "you can't rehabilitate a guy like that."

Clancy spun his wheeled chair around to grimace at the pretty cop. "He's been walking the straight and narrow for nearly a year. Give the guy a break, why don't you?"

She fluffed her blond curls and squinted her heavily mascaraed blue eyes at him before marching off in a huff. "Whatever you say, smart guy." Over her shoulder, she added, "Don't come crying to me if he wrings your neck some day."

Clancy only shook his head, then wheeled around to face the mountain of paperwork on his desk. "Women," he muttered. "They're all alike."

"I heard that, Joseph Patrick Clancy," Gail hollered from the doorway. "And I also heard you tell Sarah there wasn't another woman like her in the entire world." Her hand formed a gun, and she aimed it at Clancy. "If there isn't a Danish on my desk when I get back, with a sweet apology from you right beside it, I'm gonna tell her what you said!"

Gripping his throat, he feigned exaggerated fear. "You wouldn't. You couldn't," he whimpered. "I thought we were friends, Gail."

Laughing, she tossed her long blond mane. "Danish. Apology." She tapped her gaudy faux-jeweled watch. "By three. Or else." With that, she was gone.

Grinning, Clancy could only sigh and shake his head. When he faced his desk once more, he caught sight of T. J., leaning on his mop handle, watching him from the hallway. For a moment, as he stared into the ex-con's dark eyes, the fear he'd pretended for Gail became real. Just as quickly, he shook it off. "What're you lookin' at, Bozo!" he snarled.

"That's what I'm trying to figure out," T. J. said, grinning menacingly.

When T. J. disappeared around the corner, Clancy had a strange urge to follow him, to make sure that bandaged hand was safely wrapped around that mop handle of his.

Chapter 12

I'm sorry to hear your sister can't make it, Sarah, but I'd love to be your matron of honor." Elice had put as much excitement into her voice as she could muster, because she couldn't get her mind off Cabot. Her heart thundered and her palms grew damp as she recounted all the frightening things that might have happened to him since he'd been carted off by a man dressed like a cat burglar.

She recalled a verse from Genesis. *Have no fear, the Lord said to Abram, for I am thy shield.* Elice bit her bottom lip and folded her hands tightly on the table top. Would God protect Cabot, wherever he was? Would He shield him from pain? Did she dare ask such a thing of Him, knowing how unfaithful her heart had been these past few days?

At first, it seemed as if Sarah's voice came from far away in some distant, hollow tube. Elice blinked and tried to focus on what her friend was saying.

"I don't mind telling you, I'm scared to death. What if he's made a mistake? What if he wakes up sometime in the middle of the night and says to himself, 'Clance, what are you doing here with her?' "

Elice would have plenty of time later to browbeat herself for doubting God and to worry about what might have happened to Cabot. Right now, Sarah seemed to need her. Elice laid her hand atop her friend's. "Stop talking nonsense," she scolded. "Joe loves you to pieces!"

Sarah's eyes lit up for an instant. "Do you think so? Do you really think so?"

Smiling, she said softly, "It's written all over his face."

Sarah picked up the paper napkin beside her plate and began shredding it into long, thin strands. "I know what I am, Elice. I'm a secretary, with nothing but a high school education. I'm head and shoulders taller than most men. I'm not demure and dainty, like. . ." Tears shimmered in her blue eyes when she looked up. "He deserves someone smart and successful. Someone sweet and dainty. Someone—"

"Someone who loves him," Elice interrupted. "What he deserves," she said, emphasizing the last word, "is a woman who'll love him, no matter what. Someone who will dote on him until he feels he's the most important man on earth. Who'll be there for him when he's standing tall and proud. . .and when the weight of this job wears him down."

And this job, she thought, could certainly weigh a man down, seeing, day in and day out, the evil that people can do. She pictured Cabot as she last saw him, staggering and confused as the stranger in black led him to the waiting police car. For all she knew, as Sarah and she chatted comfortably about love and weddings, her beloved sat someplace, right this minute, beaten, bound, gagged. . . .

"Joe doesn't care that you're a little taller than he is," she said, forcing the worry from her mind. "You make him believe he's more beautiful than Michaelangelo's David. He's got a partner he can depend on at the police station; he deserves a life partner he can depend on, through thick and thin, forever. You love him, Sarah," she finished, squeezing the woman's hand, "and that's what he deserves."

The women sat in silence for a moment, Sarah's face brightening as she admitted the rightness of her companion's words, Elice's eyes brimming with unshed tears as she considered the possibility that she might never see Cabot alive again.

"She's right, you know."

They lurched at the sound of the deep masculine voice.

"Cabot," Elice whispered, relief and joy flooding over her. She wanted to leap up and wrap him in a fierce hug, wanted to dot kisses all over his weary, whiskered face. "Cabot," she sighed again, knowing that his standing there, looking almost good as new, was a miracle. . .an answered prayer.

But she could see by the lines that creased his forehead that her trembling lips and teary eyes caused him concern. Even in his condition, he thought first of her! she realized. Elice took a deep breath, squared her shoulders, and smiled. "You scared me half to death, popping out of nowhere like that!"

"And you scared me the other half," Sarah injected, quickly picking up Elice's cue to avoid drawing the attention of other diners in the crowded restaurant.

He gave Sarah's shoulder an affectionate squeeze. "I'll tell you this much, Sarah," Cabot said, never taking his eyes from Elice's, "if Joe loves you one iota as much as I love. . ."

Gently, he brushed his fingers through her hair, telling her, with the simple gesture, that he, too, believed they had experienced a miracle.

She'd been up all night, crying, pacing, praying for his safe return, but felt none of the exhaustion that normally followed hours of worry and fear, because her concern for him far outweighed the physical after affects of a sleepless night. He seemed slightly dazed, though he smiled warmly as he gazed into her eyes; he seemed surprisingly vulnerable, as though whatever had happened during the harrowing night weighed heavily on his six-foot-two-inch, two-hundred-pound frame.

A new bruise pulsed on his jaw, and his lower lip had swelled up around a cut that hadn't been there yesterday. He reeked of alcohol and, she noticed, as he tried unsuccessfully to slide his hand into the torn pocket of his sports coat, his knuckles were bleeding and scraped. At the moment, she didn't care to know how he'd gotten into this shape.

She only yearned to comfort him, to whisper words of assurance into his ears, to promise, right then and there, that she'd stand beside him, no matter what. But there was time for all that. . .later.

Elice reached out and gently touched his wounded hand. When he winced, she wanted to wrap him in her arms and kiss away his every ache and pain. Instead, she slowly withdrew her hand, knowing all too well how Cabot felt about public displays of affection: "It's like they're trying to prove to us what they don't believe themselves," he had said at last summer's county fair, when a young couple kissed passionately near the Ferris wheel. "If you're in love," he'd scolded loud enough for the newlyweds to hear, "it shows in your eyes." No, she wouldn't offer him any physical comfort here, in the crowded diner, but later, when they were alone, she'd all but smother him with motherly care and compassion. She'd bandage his chin and. . . .

As though he could read her mind, Cabot pressed his own fingertip to the cut. "It's nothing," he assured her.

"I'm just thankful you're all right," she admitted, her relief sighing from her in a whisper. Thank God. . .

They stayed that way for a long moment, Cabot standing, eyes held fast by an invisible thread of loving intimacy.

"Oh, for cryin' out loud," Sarah said, rolling her eyes. "Sit down, Cabot, before you fall down."

Chuckling, his cheeks flushed as he slid onto the bench beside Elice and wrapped his arm around her waist. "You're a sight for sore eyes," he said, kissing her cheek.

She frowned, trying to determine whether the dark circles around his eyes were the result of his terrifying night. . .or someone's fists.

Sarah seemed to be having the same thought. Winking at Elice, she said, "You look like somebody who got hold of the dummy end of the binoculars trick, Cabot."

It hadn't been what either of them expected to hear, and they sent her a bewildered look.

"Don't tell me you didn't play that trick as kids?"

Cabot's brow furrowed as he took a sip of Elice's coffee.

"You know," Sarah continued, laughing nervously, "where you put shoe polish around the eye holes, so the next guy who uses 'em. . ."

"Gets black eyes," Elice finished, grinning as her eyes widened in amazement. "Sarah, I'm surprised at you!"

Feigning innocence, she held out her hands, palms up. "I grew up with three big brothers. I always believed that survival of the fittest was a rule written just for us."

"No wonder Joe loves you so much," Cabot said, laughing.

He was trying hard to put on a "tough guy" show, Elice knew. But the proof that he had serious matters on his mind was the fact that his smile never quite reached his eyes.

"You're two of a kind," he told Sarah, laughing again. At her quizzical expression, Cabot added, "Practical jokers, the pair of you."

Despite the attempt at levity, Elice couldn't take her eyes off Cabot. Even smiling, he looked like a man who. . .who had been kidnapped and. . . . Elice shook the terrifying possibilities from her head. "You're exhausted. Let's get you to a doctor." She faced her friend. "Sarah, can you recommend someone?"

"A doctor? I don't need any doctor." And in response to her look of disapproval, he countered, "I'm fine. Got myself a humdinger of a headache, but otherwise I'm okay."

Was the ragged tone in his voice anger or leftover confusion from his maddening night? Elice wondered. "You're not fine!" she countered, frustration mounting in her voice.

"Uh-oh, that's my cue to leave you lovebirds alone," Sarah said, rising. "I'll see you back at my place later, Elice." She gave Cabot a peck on his forehead. "Don't be so stubborn. Go and see a doctor, then get some rest." She mussed his already disheveled hair. "Cause you look like something the cat dragged in, you big lug."

He sent her a half-hearted grin. "You sure know how to turn a fella's head."

" 'I sez what I means and I means what I sez.' " And before waiting to see what either of them thought of her Popeye imitation, Sarah had gathered her things and was halfway to the door.

Forgetting his public affections rule, Cabot held her tightly, then kissed her soundly. "Can we go someplace where we can be alone?" The loving light in his eyes dimmed when he added, "We need to talk."

He had always been strong, calm in a storm, fiercely determined to make the best of even the worst situation. Now, he seemed distracted and even distant, even though he sat pressed up against her. He also seemed to be sad. So incredibly sad and the telltale signs of stress and strain were evident all over his face. It frightened her a little, seeing him this way, because she felt helpless, powerless to do anything that would make things better. "Joe is still at the station. . . ."

Cabot glanced at his watch, tapped the crystal. "Well, would ya look at that. It's busted." He shook his wrist then put the timepiece to his ear. "Stopped dead," he said.

Dead. The word rang loudly in her ears. She held a hand over her heart, hoping to still its hammering beat.

Then, staring at the dial, Cabot said, "Stopped at one forty-four." He took a deep breath and grimaced. "What time is it now?"

Elice pointed to the huge schoolhouse clock on the wall behind the diner's horseshoe counter. Nine oh-five, it said.

He ran a battered, quaking hand through his hair. "That makes nine hours unaccounted for this time."

This time. . . . Elice started to tell him what she'd seen last night, to ease his tortured mind, to beg his forgiveness for not doing something, anything to stop it, when Cabot stood, gasping heavily.

"I've got to get out of here," he said, his terrified eyes darting around the diner's interior. "I can barely catch my breath."

Hurriedly, Elice withdrew a five-dollar bill from her purse and laid it on the table beside her half-filled coffee mug and uneaten bagel. Silently, quickly, he took her hand and led her from the diner.

Since Cabot had flatly refused medical care, Elice insisted that they head straight back to Joe's apartment. The moment they arrived, Cabot gathered fresh clothes from his suitcase. "I'm gonna take a long, hot shower," he told her as he headed for the bathroom. "Maybe I can wash some of this. . .confusion down the drain."

Cupping her elbows, Elice paced the length of Joe's living room, remembering how Joe had called the station when they had returned from the miserable failure of a stakeout and reported Cabot missing. She made a pot of coffee and put the mugs from last night's caffeine-fest into the dishwasher. Then she grabbed the phone and dialed Joe's work number, knowing he'd be as relieved as she to know that Cabot had come home.

"I'll cancel the APB right away," he said. "You okay?"

"I'm fine. Any word on the car?" she asked, slumping onto the sofa.

"Not yet; Smitty's still looking into it." He hesitated. "Can you talk, or is he standing there breathing down your neck?"

Elice allowed herself a tiny giggle. "It's okay. . .he's in the shower."

"Good," Joe said. "So tell me. . .how's he doin'?"

She sighed. "He looks pretty rough around the edges, but he's alive, at least."

"Has he told you what happened?"

"No, and I'm not sure he knows what happened."

She could almost picture Joe, sitting at his desk, nodding his head. "That's pretty much what happened the other nights he disappeared." He drew a deep breath. "I've talked to the police shrink, and she says the migraines were the direct result of shock."

"Of learning the truth about what happened to Maggie and Lindy, you mean?"

"Uh-huh. And she thinks the sleepwalking. . .I don't know if I'd call it that. . .is aftershock."

She hadn't known Joe long, but she knew him well enough to hear the tension in his voice. "What would you call it, Joe?"

Again he sighed. "I honestly don't know what to think, Elice. Maybe there's a nut case loose, and he's kidnapping cops and taking them for long walks."

"But how could he have known that Cabot wouldn't be himself? That he'd be. . .dulled by the effects of the pain medication?"

"You got me by the feet. The only explanation, as I see it, is that whoever he was, your 'shadow man' knows Cabot. Probably knew him back when—"

Just then Cabot, wearing a navy sweatsuit, padded into the room in bare feet. "Who's that?" he asked, soaking up the water in his ear with a towel-covered pinky.

She couldn't have him think they'd been talking about him; Cabot had enough on his mind. Joe would understand, and if he didn't, she'd just have to explain later. "Wrong number," she said directly into the mouthpiece before hanging up.

Cabot headed for the couch, towel-drying his hair as he came. "We have to talk, Elice," he said, draping the towel around his shoulders.

The way he sat there, smiling beneath his damp, tousled hair, it wasn't much of a stretch to imagine how he might have looked as a boy, before grownup torments erased the innocence of his youth. "We'll talk," she said, brushing stray locks of hair from his forehead, "after you get some sleep."

Cabot lifted one corner of his mouth and raised both brows. "I look that bad, huh, even after a shower?"

Leaning forward, she pressed a tiny kiss against his cheek. "You always look wonderful to me. But you're exhausted." She pursed her lips. "When was the last time you had a decent meal?"

He leaned against the sofa's back cushion. "I have no idea. Sometime yesterday, I guess." He shot her a weary grin. "If you call that junk in Joe's kitchen 'food,' that is."

Elice stood and strode toward the kitchen. After a moment, she called out, "We have canned spaghetti in the pantry and fish sticks in the freezer. Choose your poison."

Laughing softly, he opted for the canned pasta. "Joe's entire digestive system is gonna go into shock once Sarah starts cooking real food for him on a regular basis." Then, "Can I help?"

"Absolutely not!" she insisted. "You just lie there and rest. I'll bring it to you when it's ready."

It took little more than ten minutes to heat up the pasta, so it surprised her, when she carried the lunch-laden tray into the living room, to find him sound asleep, snoring softly.

Quietly, she placed the tray on Joe's glass-and-brass coffee table, and tiptoed to the bedroom to pull the quilt from Cabot's bed. Once she'd eased it over his sleeping body, Elice sat on the floor beside him. She yearned to run her fingers through his curly golden hair. To smooth her fingertips over his thickly lashed eyes and trace the contours of his slightly parted lips.

His breaths puffed out softly, steadily. Despite the dark circles beneath his eyes, he seemed more at peace than she'd seen him since dropping him off at the Baltimore/Washington Airport, days ago. Could this big, sweet-looking guy be responsible for three deliberate, cold-blooded murders?

Certainly, all the evidence pointed in that direction. Cabot hadn't been able to explain where he'd gone those nights. Hadn't been able to explain the cuts and bruises that proved he'd been involved in a physical confrontation. And why, each time, had he come out of his drug-induced stupors within blocks of where the mangled, strangled bodies had been discovered. . .bodies of men who, through their long and checkered pasts, had tinkered with explosives. . .explosives like the one that had killed Cabot's wife and little girl.

Cabot groaned in his sleep, then rolled over onto his side, facing her. Instinctively, it seemed, he reached for her hand, resting on the couch cushion, and wrapped it in his. The furrow in his brow, no doubt induced by some memory of what he'd witnessed last night and the nights before that, smoothed as a slight grin tugged at the corners of his mouth.

Elice knew how much he needed this sleep. Knew that to touch him might disturb that rest. But, unable to help herself, she lightly pressed her free hand against his cheek and smiled lovingly as the day's growth of whiskers tickled her palm.

Could this gentle, thoughtful man, who'd brought so much love into her life, have taken the lives of those men? Could he, who had taught her children to trust again, have killed? Could those hands, hands that had tended to Annie as she lay helpless in a coma, have squeezed the life from others? If he could, it would mean that those golden, warmly glowing eyes of his had bored coldly into the eyes of his victims before.

Elice shook her head. She refused to believe Cabot had had any part in the vicious acts.

Lead me to a rock that is higher than I, she quoted Psalm 61:2–3. *For thou hast been a shelter for me, and a strong tower from the enemy.*

But who, exactly, was the enemy? Certainly not this gentle, sleeping giant. She shuddered as doubt took hold.

I am troubled; I am bowed down greatly; I go mourning all the day long, she prayed, *but my groaning is not hid from thee . . .in thee, O LORD, do I hope. . .forsake me not, Oh LORD, my God; be not far from me.*

He stirred slightly and rolled onto his back once more. He chewed a bite of imaginary food, then swallowed it. Elice almost laughed out loud at the sight. Perhaps he smelled the ham sandwich she'd placed beside the steaming bowl of pasta.

Tears formed in her eyes, and his sweet, sleeping face blurred before her. How could she have thought him capable of murder—not one, but three! Everything in her made her yearn to wrap her arms around him, protect him from the memories of what had happened that day on the Dan Ryan, shield him from thoughts that he might have killed to settle the score.

In thee, O LORD, do I put my trust. . .be thou an house of defence to save me. For thou art my rock and my fortress.

If Cabot had killed those men, it wasn't because he, like they, delighted in evil, but rather because the pain of his grief had driven him to it. He'd been there for her through the whole Jack Wilson fiasco, assuming complete blame for the acts of a madman.

Again, she looked at his handsome face, at the long golden lashes that dusted his rugged cheeks, at the strong broad nose above lips that had kissed her tenderly, lovingly.

Cabot's big hands rested on his gently heaving chest, and Elice focused on the jagged cuts across the big knuckles, on the gash in his jaw. How he had acquired the injuries suddenly seemed unimportant. Supporting Cabot, that was all that mattered now.

She watched as his peaceful, sleeping face contorted in an expression of agony. Was he seeing those monsters that had interrupted her dreams after Bobby died? Those ugly, snarling beasts that clawed at her heart and nipped at her heels, reminding her that a life had been stupidly wasted? Was Cabot seeing monsters of his own, monsters that forced him to look, time and again, at the fiery scene on the highway, when his wife and child had been senselessly killed by a man so demented he believed that only their deaths could balance his cockeyed scale of justice?

A sense of purpose swelled within her and it came, she knew, straight from God, in answer to her prayer.

The Lord had not abandoned her and she would not abandon Cabot. . .even if he had taken too literally Exodus 21:24.

Chapter 13

"Y ou got a problem?" T. J. seemed surprised by Clancy's harsh expression. "Yeah, I got a problem," Clancy steamed. "Park it, right there in that chair."

T. J.'s face reddened, but whether it was due to anger or embarrassment, Clancy didn't know. What he did know, however, was that the man's eyes had narrowed dangerously. Suddenly, it didn't seem difficult at all to picture those powerful hands wrapped around a man's neck, choking the life right out of him.

"Where were you last night?"

T. J. scratched his bristled chin. "What time?"

"Between midnight and four."

"I was home. Like always. Where else would I be?"

Clancy ignored the question. "Can you prove you were home?

The big man folded his arms across his chest. "Why should I?"

Clancy measured his words carefully. " 'Cause we found a friend of yours last night."

T. J. interrupted with, "Who?"

"Al Winters. Your old roommate at Joliet."

He shrugged. "Yeah?"

"We found him three blocks from your apartment."

The cocky attitude heightened. "So what?"

"He's dead, T. J. That's so what."

The janitor sat up straighter in the hard wooden chair beside Clancy's desk.

"From what I hear, you an' Al didn't win any congeniality awards. . . ."

He leaned both elbows on his knees. "I ain't seen Winters since I got out. Ain't seen none of them guys," he growled. "My parole officer told me to keep away from 'em if. . ."

Clancy lifted his chin and focused on something behind T. J.'s back. "Your P. O. said a lot of things you didn't pay attention to."

He looked up at Clancy. "Like what?"

"Like that gun in your belt. It's illegal for ex-cons to pack heat. You know that."

T. J. leaned back hard, as if to disprove Clancy's theory he was carrying an illegal handgun. "You can maybe prove there was no love lost between me an' Al Winters, but you can't hang his murder on me. I was home, just like I said I was."

"Can anybody back that up?"

The stocky body slumped. "No." The defeat in his voice said clearly what his words needn't have. "Ain't nobody can back it up." He sat in silence for a moment, then said, tears glistening in his dark eyes, "I didn't do it, Clance. I swear I didn't. Why would I do somethin' that would send be back to that place? I hated it in there."

Clancy balanced a foot on the seat of his chair and leaned an elbow on his bent knee. "I like you, T. J. That's why I got you this job. I thought you deserved a break." Pausing, he shook his head. "You believe that?"

T. J. nodded. "Yeah. You been real good to me, Clance."

"I want to believe you. So start talkin'. Give me a reason to be on your side."

❧

"Remember that afternoon in the hospital, when I came to after the stabbing and thought you were an angel?" Cabot asked.

Elice nodded, smiling. "How could I forget?"

Cabot squeezed her hand. "I had the same feeling just now, when the first thing I saw when I opened my eyes was your beautiful face."

She giggled. "Careful, now, or you'll give me a big head."

Up on one elbow, he lifted her chin on a bent forefinger. "Not a chance in the world of that happening." He paused and stroked her cheek with his thumb. "Do you have any idea how much I love you?"

Reminding herself of the promise she had made to stand by him, no matter what, Elice sighed. Yes, perhaps she knew how much her love meant to him, if only because she had compared it, dozens of times, to what his love meant to her. She leaned forward and pressed a kiss on his cheek, then got to her feet. "I'm going to reheat your SpaghettiOs," she said. "Why don't you get started on that sandwich while I'm in the kitchen?"

Cabot sat up. "I happen to know there are two things in Joe's freezer: fish sticks and an orange ice pop." He patted his thigh. "Since neither appeals to me as an after-lunch treat, how about you giving me my dessert now?"

Elice climbed onto his lap and wrapped her arms around his neck. "You know what Danny would be saying if he could see this?"

Cabot laughed. " 'Ick. Mush. Right in my own house!' " he mimicked the boy. "That kid of yours sounds more and more like a broken record every day." Suddenly, he grew silent and serious. "I'm the luckiest man on the planet." He gave her a little squeeze. "I could be luckier."

"How?" she asked, squeezing him right back.

"By changing your last name." His gaze grew distant for a moment, and then he said, "What would you think about me adopting the kids after we're married? Change their last names to Murray, too."

Fear coursed through her hot and fast, and Elice tensed in response to its sudden appearance. She'd made a decision to be there for Cabot through this ordeal, no matter what. How could she have done such a thing without considering how it would affect her innocent children. She had never made a move without first determining how Emily, Danny, and Annie would react to it.

She knew that they couldn't love Cabot more even if he had been their natural father. He'd been patient and loving, kind and understanding, and right there when they'd needed him most.

But they had already suffered parental abandonment twice in their young lives. First when Bobby left them to race stock cars and then when he died in the attempt. How would they fare after having so willingly handed their hearts and their trust over to Cabot only to live with the possibility that he could spend years in prison—for murder!

"You're stiff as a board."

Her silent hesitation had hurt him. She could see the proof of it in his sad eyes. Elice tried to smile. "I most certainly am not."

He looked away, at some distant unknown spot across the room. "Not that I blame you. It's not every day a murderer wraps his arms around you."

Elice had kept the fear in check fairly well, until now. She summoned the strength to protect him from her uncertainty just a little longer. He had come back to her, safe and sound, and she had thanked God for the miracle. Another miracle could happen, couldn't it?

He sat there, slumped and stooped, like an old, old man who bore the weight of the world on his shoulders. "Let's go someplace where we can talk," he had told her in the diner. "There's something I have to tell you," he had said. Something told her that Cabot planned to say he had killed those men. The other night, as the man in black hustled him into the waiting sedan, she had sat there, frozen with indecisive helplessness. But she would not, could not sit here now and add to his already heavy burden.

She took his face in her hands. "Look at me, Cabot," she insisted. "You remember all the Jack Wilson nonsense?"

He nodded. "How could I forget? He nearly killed Annie."

"Yes. And he's sitting alone in a prison cell right now, paying for his crime."

Cabot opened his mouth, no doubt to repeat his part in all of it, she surmised. Gently, ever aware of his bruised and battered lip, she lay her fingers over his lips to silence him. "You had nothing to do with all of that," she said in the sternest voice she could muster. "And very soon now, we're going to have proof that you had nothing to do with those murders."

His brows quivered for just an instant before he buried his face in the crook of her neck. If she'd blinked, Elice might never have seen the tears glistening in his clear-eyed, golden gaze. His pain sliced through her heart like a dagger. *Lord,* she prayed, *give me the strength to help him through this.*

She held him tightly. "I love you, Cabot Murray." And she did. With every fiber in her being.

"Thank you," he whispered against her throat. "If I didn't have that. . ." He choked back a sob. "If I didn't have that, I'd have nothing."

She could hear in his voice that he meant it. . .with every fiber in his being. Again, Elice thought of her children. God would heal them from any hurt they would experience, not just in the days ahead, but every day, for the rest of their lives.

She had to believe that, because, hard as it was to admit, Elice couldn't. . . wouldn't abandon Cabot now, not even for her children.

❧

While waiting for Joe Clancy to return he sat at the desk, snickering under his breath, sure that he had covered his tracks so well, that no one, not even a detective with as many convictions as this one, could produce enough evidence to pin him with the murders. He wondered if, at the end of the long life he intended to live, he would meet up with his father, wherever he was, and if his old man would appreciate what he had done to avenge his death.

His dark eyes focused on his bandaged hand. He'd almost lost his composure for a minute when Clancy had asked how he had hurt himself. But, true to his nature, self-control won out over fear, and his answer seemed to satisfy the big Irishman just fine.

Rather like the time when, as a boy, his dad had peered over his shoulder as he hovered in the backyard and had asked, "What're ya hidin' there, boy?"

Even at ten, he stood almost as tall as the man who had fathered him. He stood and met the man's eyes. "It's Grandma's canary," he had said, pointing at the tiny yellow bird.

"Well, what did you do to it?" the parent had asked, stepping back as he grimaced at the bird's bloodied body.

"I wanted to see what made it sing, Pa," he'd answered.

At first, he recalled, his dad had scowled at the sight of the dead pet. Soon, though, the frown had become a grin. "Did ya find out?"

The boy had nodded.

"Grandma ain't gonna be too happy with you, boy."

"I didn't mean to kill him, Pa."

He could have sworn his father had sent him a proud smile before saying, "We'll buy Grandma a new canary. As forgetful as she's been these days, I doubt she'll even notice the difference."

Once or twice, though, his grandmother had commented that Sugarlips wasn't singing the way he once had. Together, he and his dad had pulled one over on the old woman, just as surely as he'd pulled one over on every cop in the Thirty-fourth.

Every cop but Gail, that is. It seemed she had taken a dislike to him from the moment she set eyes on him. His jovial personality won over every cop in the station, but had absolutely no effect on good old Gail.

What did the opinion of a woman like that matter to him, anyway? She'd volunteered for an undercover assignment that forced her to wear spiked heels and short skirts and enough makeup to choke a Vegas showgirl. And for what? To find out who'd been killing hookers downtown? Why, they were hardly worth the time, let alone the city's money.

Several times he had voiced his opinion on the case but to no avail. Folks didn't pay much attention to him, but frankly, he didn't care. What he'd planned, and successfully accomplished thus far, proved to him that he had more smarts than all of them combined!

As he sat there, quietly sipping the coffee that Clancy had fetched for him, he watched her strut back and forth, her high heels clicking on the worn green linoleum like tiny hammer blows. If she hadn't been so pretty, he wouldn't have wasted his attentions on her. So far, he'd done a good job of hiding the effect her rejections had had on him. She'd shot down every friendly advance he'd made, and some of her matter-of-fact put-downs, he recalled bitterly, had been as cold as steel.

She stopped at the water cooler, where several of the detectives had gathered, and joined the conversation. In moments, she had the men howling at her reminiscence of her evening at the beauty parlor.

" 'What did you do to your head?' my hairdresser wanted to know."

Gail struck a little-girl pose, folded her hands beneath her chin, and ground the toe of her right foot into the floor. "'I used an over-the-counter hair product. Can you forgive me?' I said."

"Did she forgive you?" Clancy asked, barely able to contain his laughter as Gail reenacted the scene.

"I should say not! 'What did you use?' she wanted to know. 'Blond Like Me,' I said. 'Blond Like Me!' she said. 'Why there's peroxide in that stuff!' "

He sat there in the chair beside Clancy's desk, watching as the burly, suited men howled with laughter at her silly salon story.

"And then what?" Flynn wanted to know.

Gail grabbed a handful of hair on each side of her head, looking for all the world like a blond Pippi Longstocking. "She clipped my hair up, like this, and said 'You're gonna sit here that way as an example, so everybody will think twice before they buy an over-the-counter product!' "

Everybody loved Gail, all right. She had worked hard to climb the ranks and earn the title of detective, and she'd done it without the usual self-pitying feminist whimpering. She'd earned the respect and admiration of her fellow detectives, male and female, all of whom agreed on the subject of her outer beauty. She carried her head high on that slender, shapely neck of hers. And why wouldn't she? Surely she knew, too, there wasn't a woman in ten half as gorgeous. . . .except maybe Cabot Murray's lady.

He smiled a smug, self-assured grin. A glance at his watch told him that things were ticking along, right on schedule. Maybe, just maybe, once he'd finished with Cabot Murray and his pretty little bride-to-be, he'd give himself an extra treat. He could almost feel his hands, snug around Gail's long white neck. He deserved a bonus, didn't he?

Clancy would pitch a fit if he walked by right now and saw black wing tips propped on his desk alongside a small mountain of file folders and a sloppy stack of pink while-you-were-out messages. No doubt the hot-tempered Irishman would slap his feet with a heated warning to keep his shoe leather on the floor, where it belonged. Of course, the warning would be issued with the same good-natured grin Clancy had always reserved for him; he'd worked hard this past year to earn the big guy's respect. And the warning would be accepted in the same high-humored attitude with which it had been delivered. They'd shuffle around between the desks, playfully dodging one another's air punches and, after a couple minutes of roughhousing, both he and Clancy would settle in for their long day's work, the big guy never suspecting that the guy he'd been hunting for killing the bombers was right there, within arm's reach.

He leaned against the hard wooden chairback and clasped his hands behind his head, laughing softly to himself. Yes, his dad would be quite proud of him, all right.

✼

"It's as plain as the nose on your face," Gail said, her elbow playfully nudging his rib cage, "and that's pretty plain!" The seriousness of the situation registered on her face when she added, "What are you going to do about it, Clance?"

He slumped into his chair and sighed heavily. "I don't know, Gail." Shaking his head, he said, more to himself than to her, "I honestly don't know."

"I'll tell you what I'd like to do. I'd like to beat him within an inch of his life, then drag him downstairs and book him."

"Can't," Clancy said. "We haven't got any proof yet."

"What do you call that!" she snapped, slapping the log book. "That's his name there in big black letters, isn't it? He signed that car out every single time a bomber was killed. He was so sure of himself, he didn't even bother to use his own car. Of all the arrogant. . ."

Clancy shook his head. "It's not enough proof, Gail." Lifting his phone's receiver, he said, "I'm gonna put a tail on him. If he did it, we'll catch. . ." He angrily bit off whatever he was about to say.

"Whaddaya mean if he did it? He's as guilty as sin, and you know it." She paced back and forth in the small space between her desk and Clancy's. "I never liked that guy. Right from the start, I knew he was bad news."

"So maybe you ought to hang up a shingle," Clancy spouted, his voice taking on a deejaylike quality. " 'Mama Gail, Premonitions and Presentiments. Palmistry and. . .' "

Playfully, she smacked the back of his head. "You'd better practice pretending

209

you feel some respect for women's intuition; you'll be a married man soon. And I have a feeling. . . ," she said, winking.

Then, perching on the corner of his desk, her grin disappeared. "Why'd he do it, Clance?"

He raised his brows in feigned shock. "Ya mean ya don't know?"

Gail smacked him again.

Clancy grew serious when he slid the computer-generated report from beneath the log book. "According to this, Cabot arrested his father several years back." He squinted at the faint, dot-matrix lettering. "Seems the department racked up a whole slew of evidence against the old man. Put him away for three years." Clancy threw the report onto his desk, then pointed at the last paragraph. "He had three months of his sentence left when a fellow inmate shoved a knife between his ribs."

"Killed him?" Gail sighed. "Wow! So this whole thing. . . from the explosion that killed Maggie and Lindy. . .to every one of these murders," Gail said, thinking out loud, "has been his way of getting even."

Clancy stood and pocketed his hands. "It's times like these that makes me wish I hadn't given up smoking. I sure could use a cigarette right now."

"Let me get you some coffee instead," she offered. "It's not much healthier, but. . ."

He held up a hand. "Thanks, but I've had enough coffee." Clancy dropped heavily into his chair again, oppressed, it seemed, by the tiresome string of events that lay ahead, and getting a judge's permission to have the maniac watched, round the clock, would be only the beginning. "Whew," he said, wiping imaginary perspiration from his brow. "Why does life have to be so hard?"Gail massaged his tense shoulders. "I don't know, Clance. I honestly don't know."

Chapter 14

I didn't come all the way out here to play cops and robbers," Cabot had said when Sarah and Elice arrived at the station house to join their men for breakfast.

Elice's private explanation to Sarah moments later was far more to the point. "He'd never forgive himself if what's been happening to him made you cancel the wedding." She nudged her friend's elbow. "Besides, he has to pay for that tuxedo he rented whether he wears it or not."

Sarah sighed and looked across the room to where Cabot and Joe stood in the crowd of serious-faced detectives. "I suppose you're right. He looks awful, if you don't mind my saying so."

Elice stared at Cabot, in the center of the group, and sighed. He stood taller than the others, despite the distress that had slumped those massive shoulders, nodding and shaking his head. Each blond curl and wave on his head was accented by shadows, cast by the light of the fluorescent fixtures overhead. His brow furrowed as he concentrated and the muscles of his powerful jaw tensed, then relaxed, in reaction to whatever Clancy was saying over there. Thirty feet, and as many desks and chairs, she guessed, separated her from him, yet she could clearly see the pale gold of his eyes, outlined by that dense fringe of lashes.

And even with the dark circles beneath those beautiful eyes, even with the worry lines that creased his face, even with sadness turning down the corners of his masculine mouth, looking at him just standing there caused Elice's heart to beat in double-time. Oh, how she loved that man!

As she studied her man, Sarah rattled on nonstop about the rehearsal dinner and the flower arrangements. Elice smiled and nodded politely, not wanting her new friend to know she hadn't been paying attention. No, she didn't mind Sarah saying that he didn't look very well, because she couldn't deny her part in his bearing, his carriage, his appearance. If she'd put his needs ahead of hers. . .

"So when are you going to have your dress altered?"

If Sarah hadn't placed a hand on her forearm, Elice might not have heard the question at all. "Sometime this afternoon," she said distractedly, her eyes still on the tall handsome man across the room.

"Well, good," said Sarah, "because I think it's high time you shaved your head."

Elice looked at her friend and frowned. "What?"

Sarah laughed and squeezed Elice's hand affectionately. "Just testing," she said, "to see if you were paying attention."

Her cheeks flushed. "I'm sorry. I don't mean to be so self-centered. It's just that—"

"Self-centered! Why, you're the most other-centered person I've ever met! How many women. . .no, make that people. . .how many people do you know would leave their business, their kids, and hop a plane to a strange city at the drop of a hat because someone needed them? How many, Elice? Answer me that."

Elice had to smile slightly, for Sarah's tone, decibel for decibel, matched what Emily, Danny, and Annie called Elice's "scolding voice." Why, Sarah had even rested a fist on her hip. But the smile faded when she said, "I had to come, Sarah. He sounded so. . ."

Sarah gathered her in a motherly hug. "I know, I know. My point," she said, holding Elice at arm's length, "is that if you'd given a thought to yourself, you wouldn't even be here."

She leaned on the edge of the nearest desk. "He thinks I don't believe in him."

Sarah frowned. "That's ridiculous. How could—"

"He asked me if he could adopt the children. I didn't answer right away. The children. . ." Elice sighed. "I remember what it was like for them, after Bobby left us. . .after we found out he'd died." Staring at her hands, she shook her head. "It took us so long to put the pieces back together."

Sarah folded her arms over her chest. "Elice, don't do this to yourself."

Again she shook her head. "It crossed my mind, just for an instant there, that if he's found guilty and goes to prison. . ." Expelling a breath, she looked at the ceiling. "I wondered how they'd get through those years."

"They'd be fine," Sarah injected, "because they have a strong, determined mommy."

She smiled sadly. "I know that. But in that couple of seconds before I could answer Cabot, I admitted that God had pulled us through some pretty tough times, and He'd get us through this one, too." Elice met Sarah's eyes. "Cabot saw the doubt, Sarah. It lasted that long." She snapped her fingers. "But he saw it, and it cut him to the quick."

Sarah draped an arm around Elice's shoulders and gave her a rough, sideways hug. "He understands." She pointed at the men across the way. "Look at him over there. Standing tall. . .jaw set. . .feet apart. Why, he looks ready to do battle."

"He shouldn't have to battle me. He deserves to know I believe in him."

"But you do," Sarah insisted, standing.

Elice glanced in the direction of the detectives, then stared at a flattened cigarette on the floor between her shoes. "Yes. But he doesn't know it."

Sarah placed both her hands on Elice's shoulders and looked her squarely in the eyes. "I will say this only once." She stepped back and said, "I took a fiction writing class ages ago, and one thing the teacher said stayed with me all these years. 'Show, don't tell,' she said."

Elice stood and grinned; Sarah grinned, too.

Elice began to walk back and forth in the narrow aisle, a crooked forefinger under her chin as she considered the importance of Sarah's advice. She stopped dead in her tracks. "You're absolutely right. Words are useless now, anyway. So I'll show Cabot that I believe in him!"

"Speaking of tuxedos," the good-looking young detective said, joining them, "I've got a fitting at two o'clock."

"Have you been eavesdropping, Mark Gardner?"

His tanned cheeks flushed slightly. "Yeah, I guess I have, Sarah." He flashed her a wide friendly smile. "But only 'cause I'm worried about Cabot, too." He glanced toward his coworkers, his smile becoming a mischievous smirk. Stepping in between them, he draped an arm over the women's shoulders. "Besides," he whispered, "your conversation was so much more interesting. . .that detective stuff gets real boring sometimes."

That inspired a laugh from all three.

"So you're having a tux fitting at two?" Sarah asked.

Gardner nodded. "Trouble is, my car's in the shop. I don't have any way to get there."

"I have a fitting this afternoon, too," Elice injected, "and I've got a snazzy rental car. Why not come with me?"

He stepped away from the women, then faced them. "Thanks, Elice. I've got a few loose ends to tie up before I leave, though. Whatsay I meet you out front in ten minutes. I'll buy you lunch, to thank you for taxiing me around town." He glanced at Sarah. "You'll join us, of course."

"I'd love to," she said, shrugging into her trench coat, "but I can't." Pulling a roll of adding machine tape from her pocket, she continued, "I've got places to go, people to see, things to do." And to emphasize just how busy she'd be, Sarah unrolled the coil.

"Wow!" Elice gasped. "That list is—"

"Long as my rap sheet," T. J. injected. Smirking, he said, "Don't mind me, ladies, I'm just here to clean up." He dumped the contents of the metal trash can into a huge plastic bag, then returned it to its place under the desk with a loud and unceremonious clank. He was there and gone before anyone could respond with so much as a polite "hello."

Sarah pretended to shiver. "I know I'm supposed to be open-minded about these things, but that guy gives me the creeps." She looked at Gardner. "Why was he in prison?"

He wiggled his brows and sneered. "Killed a man," he said, spreading his fingers. Then, making claw shapes with his huge hands, he punctuated the answer with an evil laugh. "With his bare hands!"

Smiling, Elice waved him away. "You know who you remind me of?"

Gardner repeated the monstrous laugh. "Frankenstein?" he asked, a hopeful, boyish grin on his face.

"Hardly," she said, giggling. "You remind me of my little boy. Danny's always trying to scare the daylights out of me, too."

"No reason to let this youngster scare you, Elice Glasser," T. J. said from across the aisle. "He's so wet behind the ears, I'm surprised he doesn't have a rash back there." He left the area then, dragging the huge trash bag behind him. "But just 'cause he's young don't mean he's harmless," he flung the bag over his shoulder. "I sure wouldn't want to get into that pretty black rental car of yours alone with him. Who knows if you'd live to see your three li'l young'uns again."

When she was sure T. J. was out of earshot, Sarah whispered, "How'd he know your name? And how'd he know what kind of car you'd rented?"

She opened her mouth to admit she didn't know, when Gardner, walking backward toward the door, said, "It's hard to get any privacy around here. I'll bet he overheard something when Cabot was showing everybody those pictures a couple of days ago."

She looked from the janitor's retreating form to Gardner's face, and remembered again her son, whose eyes had glowed in that same dark way when she caught him eating fudge-nut brownies the day after his tonsillectomy. She missed that boy, missed his sisters, too.

But her children were quickly forgotten as her heart hammered and her palms grew damp. Why had the big ex-con overtly pointed out that he knew so much about her? And what thoughts were flitting around in Mark Gardner's head to paint such a guilty look on his face? Mark had very obviously practiced that winning smile of his, but he could have used a few more hours' practice, Elice thought, because the smile never warmed his cold, dark eyes.

❦

The detectives agreed that they had a solid case against the man and that he'd serve three years minimum in the state penitentiary. Listening to the story of how Eisensee had beaten his wife to death, Cabot lingered about twice as long as he could stand his headache. The migraine hadn't returned full force yet, but it was threatening to do so. As he walked, head down, through the empty hallway, he never noticed Elice on the stairs.

He had managed to hide his rumpled shirt by buttoning up the brown herringbone sports coat. But, as he moved through the dimly lit hallway, he'd unconsciously unbuttoned the jacket and tucked his hands into his pants pockets, exposing the shirt front as effectively as the big brass hooks holding back the faded green draperies at the chief's office window.

He shouldered his way into the mens' room, the heels of his oxblood loafers clack, clack, clacking as he crossed the white tiled floor, then he leaned toward the mirror, his palms on the cool, white enamel sink.

Cabot almost didn't recognize the man in the mirror anymore. Whiskered, weary, and worried, he believed his face told the story his heart was too cowardly to tell: He had lost it. . .that razor-thin edge that separated decent men from killers.

Everything seemed dark and bleak, from the circles beneath his eyes to the. . .

He shook his head to clear the slowly forming mental picture of a man, dressed all in black, and a sedan that shimmered like coal under the street light.

Cabot twisted the cold water knob, unaware that the heavy spray was splashing from the bowl onto his trousers. Bending at the waist, he cupped his hands and filled them with the cool, clear liquid, splashed it onto his hot face, held his hands there until the water warmed, then dipped into the stream for another helping of the refreshing stuff. "Get hold of yourself, Murray," he muttered, blotting his face with a brown paper towel.

But despite his desperate attempt to blot the vision from his mind, it returned. He gripped the sink tightly with both hands and hung his head and, though he'd shut his eyes, he saw again the ebony shirt. . .a jet black car. . .and through the inky sky floated the hollow echo of angry voices.

His brow furrowed as he tried to reason out why it all reminded him of the dream. Not the nightmarish reliving of the explosion that killed Maggie and Lindy, but the eerie addendum to it that starred a shadowy figure, scuttling around in the yard with its package, like a rodent taking a stolen treasure back to its rathole. That secretive somebody had clothed himself in black, too.

Gardner's voice echoed in the deep recesses of his memory. "I'll bet you wanted to strangle that bomber with your bare hands."

Hands, big hands. . .

Cabot punched the sink and listened to the dull ring that reverberated through the hollow bowl. The hazy picture hovered somewhere just beyond the edges of his memory.

Hands had slapped him, shoved him this way and that. He remembered seeing a left hand double up into a fist and pull back beside the shadowy figure's head. Then, like a slow-motion cartoon, the fist moved forward, growing bigger and bigger until, looking as large as a cantaloupe, it blurred before his eyes. He felt rather than saw its impact with his face, causing streaks of silvery light to crisscross through the dark sky, exploding into tiny starbursts of bright yellow and red. The fist drew back and then, in the instant before the veil of black unconsciousness draped over him, he saw red. . .blood red droplets across the knuckles of the fist.

Instinctively, Cabot's right hand went to his jaw, worked it back and forth. In the mirror, he saw the cut that had scabbed over on his lower lip. *Your teeth cut the guy's hand*, he told himself, if there was a guy. . . .

His mind conjured up the image of the janitor, lazily pushing his broom through the squad room with his big left hand. With his big bandaged hand! He remembered hearing Clancy ask T. J. how he had hurt himself. "Cut myself shaving," had been the janitor's joking answer. Moments later, Cabot had seen Gardner pour himself a cup of coffee. As the young cop stirred powdered milk into the mug, he realized Clancy's new partner was left-handed. Cabot might never have noticed, except for the bandage that called attention to his knuckles. . . . But what did either of those things have to do with his own unaccounted-for hours? With his waking up, blocks from the bodies of three dead men, sporting cuts and bruises that indicated he'd been involved in life-and-death struggles.

As Cabot turned off the water and dried his hands on the same brown paper towel he'd used on his face, Genesis 41:15–16 came to mind: *And Pharaoh said unto Joseph, I have dreamed a dream, and there is none that can interpret it: . . . And Joseph answered Pharaoh, saying, It is not in me: God shall give Pharaoh an answer of peace.*

God will give you the answer, he thought. "I'm ready when you are, Lord," he said, tossing the towel into the trash can before he left the mens' room.

※

True to his word, Gardner was waiting when Elice pulled up in front of the Thirty-fourth. "Want me to drive?" he asked through the closed passenger window. "It might be easier, since I know my way around."

Elice gave his offer a moment of thought, then unbuckled her seat belt. Nodding her concurrence, she slid across the seat as Gardner walked around the rental car. "I love the smell of a new car," he said, sniffing the air as he slammed the driver's door. "My old jalopy never smelled this good."

"You bought it used?" she surmised.

He signaled, then made a tidy left turn. "Uh-huh. Couldn't afford a new car on my paltry cops' salary."

"How long have you been on the force?"

Adjusting the rearview mirror, he said, "Little over three years now."

Her raised brows echoed how impressed she was. "And you made detective? Already? You must have worked round the clock."

Gardner shrugged. "Naw. But I did work hard."

She couldn't help noticing that he'd clenched his jaw when he said it. "We're all driven to succeed when we're young."

"Have a lot to prove, you mean?"

"Stepping into adulthood, it's all about proving ourselves, isn't it?"

His fingers whitened as he tightened them around the steering wheel. "I had things to prove, all right, but my drive, as you so aptly put it, had nothing to do with my age."

Elice didn't know why, exactly, but his tone of voice frightened her. She had a feeling, and a strong one, that it wouldn't be very smart to let him see her fear, so she looked into the side mirror. Just then, she caught sight of a white van. Almost immediately, it slipped from view, hidden behind a delivery truck.

She recognized its rusting hood and dented grill, because it had been parked beside her at the Thirty-fourth.

"What're you in the mood for? Italian? Chinese? French? This part of town is chock-full of good restaurants."

She glanced at her watch. "You know, I'm not the least bit hungry, so there's really no point in wasting time," she said, forcing herself to sound calm and cheerful. "Why don't we just head straight over to the bridal shop?"

At the next intersection he braked for the red light then faced her. "What's the matter? Did what T. J. say get to you?"

Peeking into the mirror, Elice spied the white van again. She laughed nervously. "Of course not. It's just that I know how busy you must be. Taking time from your schedule to entertain me is—"

"A pleasure," he finished for her. "Honest."

She remembered a line from an old black-and-white western: "Git, whilst the gittin's good!" It seemed like very good advice right about now. "Well, if you're sure," she conceded against her better judgment. She noticed immediately that his satisfied smile never quite reached his dark eyes, and she shivered in response.

"Aw," he said, sounding truly sympathetic. "You're cold. Want me to turn up the heat?"

Elice waved the offer away. "No. I'm fine. Cabot says I have reptilian blood, because I'm always cold."

He chuckled and steered the car toward the curb. "Mama Ilusio's is famous for its gnocchi."

"Knock—eee?"

Just as Gardner threw her rental car into PARK, the white van pulled into the parking lot. The driver wore blue striped coveralls, open at the throat. . .like T. J.'s!

Gardner, walking around the front of the car, distracted her from the van and its driver. "Not knock—eee," he said, laughing good-naturedly as he opened her door, "but nyawk—eee. They're potato dumplings that melt in your mouth. Trust me," he said, taking her hand to help her out of the car, "you're gonna love 'em."

As they walked side by side, Elice thought, *I might love 'em, all right, but I sure don't trust you!*

The moment they were inside, he signaled the hostess. "Say, would you mind taking my lady friend here to that table in the corner?" Gardner pointed to the booth at the far end of the restaurant. "I forgot something in the car." Patting the big side pocket of his overcoat, he told Elice, "I'll be back in a flash."

Funny, she didn't remember that pocket looking so overstuffed earlier. Didn't remember Gardner having anything with him when he got into the car, either, and couldn't imagine what he might have forgotten.

As Elice sat alone at the table, she stared through the filmy white curtains that covered the window. Her heart lurched at the sight of the van, its driver silhouetted by the bright sunlight that streamed through his back windows. He seemed to be wiping his aviator sunglasses on a white handkerchief. Elice leaned forward slightly, waiting, watching for the man to finish his polishing and exit the vehicle, because she wanted to get a good look at him when he entered the restaurant.

A minute ticked by, yet the driver made no move to get out of the van. He appeared to be fumbling with the top buttons of his coveralls. Her trembling hand reached for the water-filled goblet beside the neatly folded maroon napkin. Condensation sparkled like morning dew on its bowl, causing her fingers to slide to the stem, sloshing cold water onto her hand. It took no longer than a blink to look from the parking lot to get a careful grip on the glass. But it was long enough, she realized when she looked back, for the driver to disappear.

Her eyes darted around the restaurant, searching each face for a newcomer. For a man in coveralls and pilot-style dark glasses. But no one fit her mind's eye description of T. J.

If it had been the janitor, why had he followed her and Gardner? She giggled nervously under her breath, thinking that perhaps he had a secret addiction to gnocchi.

"Git whilst the gittin's good," she whispered as Gardner headed for the table. Alice in Wonderland's Cheshire cat crossed her mind, too, as Gardner took a seat across from her.

Chapter 15

I've been looking everywhere for you," Clancy said when Cabot stepped into the hallway. He flapped an official-looking document under his former partner's nose. "Know what this is?"

Cabot squinted at the paper. "Looks like a warrant. Who's under arrest?"

"Nobody. . .yet."

The men walked away from the hum of voices that filtered from the squad room.

"Is it for me?" Cabot asked, his voice barely audible.

Clancy laughed. "No. It ain't for you."

Cabot ran a hand through his hair then leaned against the sickly green wall in the hallway. "I'd just as soon get it over with. This waiting is driving me crazy."

"Waiting for what? You don't seriously think anybody suspects you of strangling those bombers, do you?"

He inhaled deeply, picturing the sad, frightened look in Elice's eyes when he had asked to adopt her kids. "Why wouldn't you suspect me? I suspect me."

"Well, then you're not the cop I thought you were." He led Cabot into an interrogation room. "Shut those blinds," he ordered, locking the door behind them, "and park it."

Cabot took a seat in one of the red plastic chairs and folded his hands beside the reel-to-reel recorder. Clancy sat across from him and slid a manila folder across the battered wooden table top. "Take a gander at that, pal. Careful now; your eyes are liable to pop clean out of their sockets."

Inside the folder, Cabot found two computer readouts. He scanned the shortest one first. After a moment, he pinched his nose between thumb and forefinger, as if unable to believe what he'd read.

"He's been on you from day one," Clancy said, his beefy finger tapping the report. "I had the lab check out your migraine pills. He must have switched 'em, 'cause it says 'Fiorinal' on the label, but it's Percocet in the bottle."

"Percocet?" Cabot repeated, a dim memory ringing in his ears. He rubbed his eyes. Percocet. Where had he heard it before?

And then he knew. The man in black had asked him how many of those pills he'd taken. "It was real," he whispered. "It wasn't a dream."

But Cabot didn't even notice Clancy's quizzical expression. "Once the

Percocet had doped me up good, he could waltz right in and lead me around like a boot-lickin' pup."

"Yup. Stuffed you in the car and took you along with him on his missions."

Cabot leaned back and then ran both hands through his hair. "But how'd he get the car? He doesn't have the authority to sign off on it."

"He does if he says I okayed it." Shaking his head, Clancy leaned back in his chair, too. "He had me fooled, I don't mind telling you."

Cabot frowned. "But I don't get it. What's he got against me?"

Clancy thumped the file. "It's all in there, buddy boy. Read it and weep."

Slowly, Cabot leafed through the second report. And then, as understanding dawned, his brow smoothed. He had arrested Sam years ago for armed robbery and murder in the first degree. But it had been one of those cases with so much proof that the perp slid through the system like a well-greased pig. Cases like Sam's were quickly, thankfully forgotten. It was the tough ones, those that took months of heavy investigation and miles of legwork to prove, that Cabot remembered best.

He should have remembered Gardner's son, because the boy had been front and center every day of the trial, glaring at him and every witness who testified against his dad. He wasn't as tall or muscular then, but the dark angry eyes hadn't changed. And he looked amazingly like Sam.

Cabot's blood began to boil. He'd almost turned himself in for the murders, telling himself it was the right thing to do. If he had, this nut would have gotten away with murder, and Cabot would have paid for it. He slammed his fist on the table top and muttered under his breath. "If I ever get my hands on him. . ."

"Looks like the kid grew up and walked in his daddy's footsteps," Clancy said.

Cabot snorted, cracking his knuckles. "Yeah." He nodded toward the file. "I guess I can see why he thought he had a score to settle with me, but what did he have against the guys he killed?"

Clancy shrugged. "Since when do nut cases need reasons for the crazy stuff they do?"

"I know it's not exactly 'by the book,' Clance, but I want to be there when you bring him in."

"Shouldn't be a problem."

The feeling of relief churning inside Cabot was so overwhelming that he didn't know what to say, let alone what to do. He wanted to hug Clancy, to jump up and shout for joy, to get on his knees and praise the Lord. But he only sat there, grinning, and tipped his chair back on two legs and said, "I can't tell you how good it feels, knowing I didn't—"

Cabot stood so suddenly that his chair clattered to the floor. "Where's Elice? I've got to tell her."

"Easy, boy," Clancy said, chuckling. "You think the department's made of money? These old tables and chairs have gotta last us till the turn of the century." Then, "Last I saw of her, she was with Sarah." He nodded beyond the curtained window. "Right out there."

Cabot neatly stacked and restacked the file's contents, then closed the folder.

His ex-partner expelled a huge breath. "Hand me that phone over there so I can call the little woman before you drive me nuts with your fidgeting."

Cabot did as he was told. Had it really been just a week since he'd left the quiet peacefulness of Freeland? It seemed like months since he'd last had a decent night's sleep. He glanced at the folder that allowed him to breathe easy again.

He heard the beeping tones of the number Clancy dialed, followed by the unmistakable sound of a phone, ringing on the other end of the line. Then Sarah's voice, bright and cheerful as always. He righted the chair as Clancy spoke to his fiancée. In the past, when he watched his old pal talking to his girlfriend, those blue eyes would light up and the ruddy cheeks would redden with boyish exuberance. Cabot stiffened at the marked difference this call was having on his friend.

"I love you, too," Clancy said into the mouthpiece before hanging up.

"What?" Cabot demanded. "What?"

Just as he opened his mouth to answer, Gail hollered through the locked door. "Clancy! T. J. is missing. You want me to call his parole officer?"

He jumped to his feet and jerked open the door. "What's he trying to do, get himself thrown back into Joliet?"

He blew past Gail, who grinned as she pressed her back to the wall. "I take it you're gonna call the P. O. yourself?" she asked as he sped by.

Only then did it seem that Clancy realized he still hadn't answered Cabot's question. "C'mere," he said, waving Cabot into the hallway.

Instantly, Cabot recognized the signs of tension in his friend. A thin sheen of perspiration glistened on Clancy's forehead and upper lip as his right fist slammed into his left palm. His red-blond brows drew together in a serious scowl.

Cabot grabbed a handful of Clancy's shirt. "Tell me where she is, Clance! Where's Elice?"

Grinning patiently, Clancy rolled his eyes. "You're not gonna make a habit of this, are ya, pal?"

He focused on the bundle of white material bunched in his fist and remembered how he'd done precisely the same thing in the hospital, when Clancy told him that Maggie and Lindy had been killed on the Dan Ryan Expressway. The fright he'd experienced that day had been exactly what he'd felt, moments ago, when the signs of fear showed up on Clancy's usually calm face. Because if the Irishman was about to tell him that something had happened to Elice. . .

Cabot released his friend and stepped back, his cheeks reddening with shame. "Sorry, Clance. I don't know what got into me."

"No need for apologies," he said, "because I know exactly what got into you." He gave Cabot a brotherly punch on the arm. "Relax, okay? She's all right for now, at least."

Cabot wanted to tell her he was innocent. Innocent! Wanted to wrap her in a bear hug, lift her off those tiny feet of hers, and kiss the daylights out of her. "Where is she?"

"Don't get your trousers in a knot," Clancy said. "Sarah told me Elice had a fitting. . . . You heard Elice is takin' over for Sarah's ailing sister, didn't you?"

Cabot nodded.

"Well, it's got something or other to do with that matron of honor dress."

Cabot grit his teeth. *Okay*, he wanted to shout, *get to the point, will you, Clance!*

"Gardner had an appointment to have his tux fitting this afternoon, too. And since his car is in the shop, he asked Elice to drive him over. He's buying her lunch to thank her for chauffeuring him around."

Cabot's jaw clenched as his fists flexed. *She's all right. . .for now, at least,* Clancy had said. He would hold onto that thought, but he wouldn't relax. . .not until she was safe in his arms.

❧

There had been so much foot traffic on the sidewalk that he was afraid he wouldn't be able to plant the bomb. But his patience, as always, paid off handsomely and, within minutes, he had managed to slip into the front seat of the rental car and attach the device to the underside of the dashboard. There was enough plastique jammed up there behind the steering column to blow her sky-high and back again.

He had discovered, too late, that he hadn't used enough of the soft gray, claylike stuff on the little red car that Murray had bought for his wife. It had been sheer luck that he'd stuck the bomb to the car's undercarriage, a mere foot from the gas tank. When he had depressed the detonator, the bomb had gone off all right, but it hadn't packed enough power to do more than cause an annoying little fire under the vehicle. And, if he hadn't also unscrewed all the lock buttons from the doors, they would have escaped.

This time, he couldn't afford any mistakes.

If she had had a mind to, Elice could have been a cop, he admitted, grinning, a good one. He'd seen proof of her natural gut instinct there in the squad room, when those gentle doe eyes darkened, first with suspicion, then with fear.

And she was smart. That was evident in her big brown eyes, too. She'd known, somehow, just by looking at him, that he was up to something. He flexed his fists and ground his molars together. Eventually, she'd puzzle it out, and then where would he be? His whole masterful plan would unravel.

Even if she hadn't already been part of his plan to squash Cabot Murray, he would have to kill her, simply for seeing in him what he had so carefully tried to hide all this time.

He had never met Murray's wife and daughter. So when he had watched from his perch on the bridge above the expressway, it hadn't bothered him a bit to see them futilely beating against the windows. Hadn't tweaked a nerve to hear their voices, muffled by the car's insulation, calling out for help. Still, it had been a relief when the explosion finally ended their pitiful pleas.

Watching Elice die a slow, agonizing death, he knew, wouldn't be so easy. He'd heard enough station house scuttlebutt to know she was a scrappy little thing who'd faced down some fierce opponents, and won. She hadn't used her feminine wiles, the grapevine said, to get some man to buy her bangles and baubles. Instead, she'd put her God-given talents to use and built a thriving business from a one-time hobby, and supported herself and three little kids on the money she'd earned! She'd suffered enough, in his opinion, so he'd added an extra dollop of plastique to ensure a quick end. She'd be dead long before the sound of the explosion registered in her brain.

He slammed the passenger door and walked away from the rental car. Patting his breast pocket where he'd tucked the detonator, disguised as a ball point pen, he chuckled under his breath. She's a devout Christian, he'd heard Gail say to Flynn. One click of his pen and she'd meet her Maker.

He searched his memory for the Bible verse he'd learned as a boy. His memory amazed him. He'd been a lad of nine when old Mrs. Simmons had made him memorize that verse from 1 Corinthians: "In a moment, in the twinkling of an eye, at the last. . .trumpet shall sound. . .and we shall be changed."

Well, it wouldn't be a trumpet she'd hear at the end, but Elice most assuredly would be changed.

❧

The search warrant gave them permission to break into the apartment, and Cabot watched with unbearable anticipation as two burly uniformed cops slammed the battering ram into the door. Bits of the wooden frame scattered in all directions, causing the cops who had gathered in the third floor hallway to shield their eyes with their hands and forearms.

One by one, they stepped over the steel door that lay in the foyer. And one by one, they searched each of the tidy rooms, looking for clues that would tell them where he might be at this precise moment; looking for evidence to back up their assessment that he had killed all three bombers.

"Hey, you guys." The voice came from the spare bedroom. "You've gotta see this. He's got enough stuff in here to blow the whole city off the map."

The bright flash of the photographer's bulb blinded them all for a moment.

"Get a shot of the closet, too," said Flynn, the lead investigator.

Cabot opened and closed desk drawers, rifled through cabinets, poked his head into every cupboard, every nook, every cranny. A leather-bound book beside the wide-screen TV caught his attention, mainly because it had been stuffed in among worn paperbacks and tattered magazines. He slid it from the shelf and opened the cover. "If the camera guys and the bomb squad team don't get enough to bust this guy but good," Cabot said to Clancy, "this oughta do it." Cabot handed Clancy the journal. "It's in there. All of it." Shaking his head, he added, "I gave him too much credit. I called him brilliant, the way he set me up to take the fall. But he signed his own death warrant, putting it all in writing."

"It ain't gonna be easy for his lawyer to keep that lethal injection needle away from him, that's for sure," Clancy agreed, leafing through the book. "He's got names, dates, places. . . . The D. A. is gonna dance a jig when he sees this!"

Cabot couldn't fully appreciate justice at work, because his mind was on Elice. "Where do you suppose Gardner took her? You're his partner. Did he ever mention any favorite restaurants to you?"

"I've already taken care of it," Clancy said. "Sent a black-and-white to Mama Ilusio's."

Cabot blanched and headed toward his ex-partner.

Clancy slapped both hands over his chest in a protective gesture. "Keep your big mitts to yourself," he warned, narrowing one eye. "Don't make me deck you, now," he added when Cabot kept advancing.

"Mama Ilusio's?" He socked the journal. "Says in there he's gonna plant a bomb at Mama Ilusio's. You don't think. . . ?"

Clancy grabbed a handful of Cabot's jacket. "I do think so." Then, smoothing the material, he shot his pal a crooked grin. "Sorry 'bout that." Hitching up his trousers as he headed for the bedroom, he said over his shoulder, "Don't know what got into me."

Cabot laughed despite the tension of the moment, and followed Clancy into the bedroom.

"Gather your things, boys. There's been a change in plans."

"What are you babblin' about, Clance?" Flynn asked. "We've got an hour of work to do, minimum, before—"

"Not you," Cabot interrupted. "The bomb boys here." Focusing on Greene, their leader, he explained: "This guy's busy fillin' his gullet with gnocchi down at Mama Ilusio's. If we hotfoot it over there, we can catch him before he gets to the dessert course."

"Gelato," Barboni corrected.

Cabot faced the uniformed rookie. "Gela–what?"

"Gelato." The young cop flushed. "It's Italian for ice cream."

Clancy grabbed Barboni by the elbow. "You're comin' with us, boy."

Grim-faced, Cabot agreed. "Who knows? We might just need us a translator."

※

They hovered together in the dark interior of the van, huddling around the recorder that would tape every word out of his mouth.

"Man, it's hot in here," Barboni said, tugging at his navy blue tie.

"Not as hot as it's gonna get," Cabot told him. "Once that thing starts rolling," he said, pointing to the reel-to-reel, "that's when you're gonna sweat."

"And speaking of sweat," Clancy said, "you're not even gonna think about breaking one."

Cabot stared in disbelief at his friend. "But you said—"

"I said you could be here," Clancy interrupted. "I didn't say you could do anything. We do this by the book, or we lose him. You want us to lose him?"

Cabot scowled. He had no authority to participate in the bust, and he knew it. He was lucky, actually, that Clancy had allowed him to be this close to the action. He sighed heavily. "All right," he conceded. "What do you want me to do?"

"Get out. Now."

He met Clancy's blue eyes. "But Clance, it's pouring rain—"

"You ain't made of sugar; you won't melt." Then, in a softer tone, he added, "You don't carry a badge anymore, Cabot. You could botch things, just by being here." He gave his pal a friendly shove. "Now beat it."

Cabot took a final glance at the restaurant. From inside the van, they had a clear view of the wide, curtained window. He could see Elice, smiling and chatting with Gardner, as if she'd known him for years instead of days. But earlier, he'd looked through the powerful binoculars and had known in a glance that Elice was putting on a show, and a mighty good one, for Gardner's benefit. She couldn't have known that the good-looking young cop was dangerous, or that he meant to harm her. She'd guessed it, somehow, and Cabot sent a silent prayer of thanks heavenward then sent another prayer up right behind it that the bomb squad had disarmed the device that Gardner had attached to her rental car.

So far, their plan was working like magic. First, three undercover cops created a distraction, a fight, outside the restaurant's side window. As expected, restaurant patrons, Elice and Gardner included, huddled in the window to see what the fuss and bother was all about. The fight in the street continued while Davis, one of the Thirty-fourth's best, slid under the car.

He'd only been under there ten, maybe fifteen seconds when he slid back out again and shook his head to tell the rest of them he hadn't located the bomb yet. Kneeling beside Elice's rental car, he fiddled with the lock until the door opened. He was inside and out in minutes, carrying a cylinder the size of a one-pound coffee can. Davis gave them the okay sign then disappeared from view.

Then it was Cooper's turn at the car. In less time than it had taken Davis to remove the bomb, Cooper had removed the car's fuse panel and rigged all four door locks to a radio-controlled device. Cooper's high salute was the signal for Barboni to break up the undercover cops' fake fight.

They had nothing to do now but wait.

Just as Cabot turned to exit the van's back doors, he whirled around and pointed to the restaurant. "They're on their way out. I can't leave now; he'll spot me."

Clancy moaned softly and slapped his forehead in a gesture of futility. "All right, but don't do anything, hear?"

Cabot nodded. He wanted this guy a whole lot more than the rest of them did. He worked his way to the front of the van, to get out of the way of the team. "You guys better not mess up, that's all I can say," he growled, facing the back of the van, "or you're gonna have to answer to me."

Each of the five men in the van nodded.

"Don't worry, Cabot," the guy up front said. "They won't let you down."

Until now, he hadn't heard a peep from the driver. Cabot faced front. "T. J., what're you doin' here?"

Grinning, the janitor winked. "Gardner knows all the police vehicles. This is my brother-in-law's van. It's got Wisconsin plates. No way he'd make it for a stake car."

Cabot could only shake his head. "How long has he been in on this?"

"Since Gardner left with Elice."

"You knew it was Gardner all along?"

Clancy shook his head. "Not until that last report came in." He nodded toward the driver's seat. "It was his idea to follow them, too."

"So that argument in the station. . . ?"

Clancy grinned. "All for the benefit of those who might tell tales out of school."

Cabot might have hugged them both if Gardner hadn't chosen that moment to open the restaurant door. The team in the van watched him reach into the breast pocket of his sports coat and retrieve a very ordinary looking ball point pen.

"What's the pen for?" T. J. wanted to know.

"That's the detonator," Davis explained. "When he clicked it just now, he thought he'd started the timer."

"How long do we have?" T. J. asked.

Davis held up the diffused bomb. "Long as we need," he said, wiggling his hairy black brows.

They had also recruited Marty, a retired cop from DuPage County. Fully miked, Marty, who was standing under the awning when Gardner made his exit, made it possible for the cops in the van to hear everything that went on within ten feet of Gardner.

"I've got a couple of errands to run," the cops heard Gardner tell Elice. "The bridal shop is straight ahead, on your right. You can't miss it," he said. "I'll meet you in five minutes. I promise."

Marty pretended to lose his balance and fell onto Elice, knocking her over. He whispered, inches from her ear, "Cabot says to tell you to play along."

Flat on her back, she nodded.

"Aw, lady," Marty said, clamoring to his feet. "I'm sorry. Honest I am," he added, helping her up. "Are you okay? Did I hurt you?"

Elice didn't have to work very hard to look confused and frightened. "I'm fine. A little shaken up, that's all."

"Aw, lady, " Marty repeated, clumsily dusting her coat. "Would ya look at that?" He held out his hand. "And now it's rainin'. What more could go wrong for you today, huh?"

He turned to Gardner. "You her date, mister?"

Gardner scowled. "Yeah, you clumsy old fool. I guess you could say that."

"You parked nearby?"

Gardner pointed at the rental car, parked near the curb.

"Look at him sweat," said Davis, watching through the van's blackened side window.

"He's gonna start droolin' any minute," Cooper agreed, laughing.

"You got an umbrella in there?" they heard Marty ask, " 'cause this pretty li'l thing oughtn't have to get wet. Not after takin' a nasty spill like that."

Gardner looked to Elice for advice.

"There's an umbrella on the back seat," she said, adjusting her clothing. "I have a feeling we'll all get on our way a lot faster if you get it for me."

"Aw, g'wan, mister. Get it for the lady, why don't ya? Can't ya see she's all shook up?" He grabbed Elice's hands. "Aw, lady," he said for the third time. "I'm really sorry."

Gardner glanced at his wristwatch.

"He's wondering if he has time." Davis slapped his thigh, laughing now, too.

Unaware of his audience, Gardner walked from beneath the restaurant's curved green awning and stomped to the car. He left the passenger door open as he poked around inside, looking for the umbrella. When he spotted it, on the floor behind the driver's seat, he climbed in.

And when he did, Barboni slammed the door behind him.

And when Barboni slammed the door, Cooper, from his watch post inside the white van, flipped the switch that locked all four doors.

"Hey, what's goin' on?" Gardner hollered, tugging at the locks. He sat on the back seat and pounded on the windows. "Hey! Lemme outta here!"

"Cabot, get over there and tell Marty to get closer to the car. We need to make sure we get this on tape," he barked.

"Yessir," Cabot said, saluting. He was out of the van and across the street in a heartbeat. Cabot walked up to Marty. "You're not close enough," he whispered.

Nodding, Marty fell into stride beside Cabot.

When they reached the car, Gardner was lying on the back seat, trying to kick out the rear passenger window. "It's gonna blow!" he shrieked at Marty. "Get help! You've gotta get me out of here!"

Cabot couldn't help himself. He sauntered up to the car, right beside Marty. "What's all the ruckus, Markie, my boy?"

Gardner's face drew back in a desperate, maniacal grin. "Cabot," he said.

"Am I ever glad to see you! You've gotta get me out of here. Right now!"

Chuckling, Cabot said, "You're acting like the car's gonna explode. Take it easy, Gardner. You're as safe as a babe in its mama's arms. Besides, it's raining. At least in there, you're warm and dry."

"You don't understand!" Gardner shrieked. "There really is a bomb. We've got only a couple of minutes before—"

Clancy shouldered his way past Marty and Cabot. "I thought I told you not to do anything, pal," he barked. "Now, step aside."

Cabot refused to budge.

"I mean it, Murray. We do this by the book," Clancy reminded him, "or we'll lose him."

Cabot was clenching his jaw so hard it ached. Trembling with rage, he punched the hood of the car. He wanted to blast his bare hands through the glass and yank Gardner out of that car by the scruff of his neck. He wanted to slam him to the concrete and beat him senseless for what he had done to Maggie and Lindy. . .for what he had almost done to Elice.

"Cabot."

Immediately, at the sound of her soft soothing voice, Cabot forgot all about Gardner. He turned to face her. Her big dark eyes were wide with fright, but she was all right. She was all right!

"Elice," he whispered, scooping her up in his arms and carrying her out of the rain to the shelter of Mama Ilusio's big green awning. "Thank God you're all right," he said, and then, oblivious to the gathering crowd, he kissed her rain-slicked cheeks. "Thank God."

Epilogue

C abot stood at the front of the crowded little church and tugged nervously at the cuffs of his suit. On one side of him, Danny shuffled from foot to foot.

"When's it gonna start, Cabot. . .I mean, Dad?"

"Any minute now, Son," he said, a hand on the boy's shoulder. "Any minute."

On Cabot's other side, Clancy fidgeted with his tie. "I thought this was gonna be a casual affair. Blue jeans and plaid shirts and sneakers. . ."

"That's just for the reception," Cabot whispered. "You didn't expect Elice to get married in a cowgirl getup, did you? Besides, did I complain when you stuck me in that penguin suit?"

Clancy sighed and stared at the toes of his shiny black rented shoes. "All right. I'll shut up."

As if that were her cue to begin, the organist began her medley of wedding tunes. Cabot stiffened. Any minute now, Elice would walk down that aisle to him.

Cabot adjusted the white rosebud on his lapel, then patted the pocket that held the children's notes. *I'll love you forever, Daddy, I promise!* Annie had printed in red crayon. *I promise that when you're my dad, I'll love you till you pop,* said Emily's dainty script. *When you're my dad, you don't have to call me Dan ever again. I promise.* Danny had handed him all three notes as the "guys" changed into their suits in the tiny room behind the altar.

For their vicious and vile crimes, Jack Wilson and Mark Gardner were behind bars. And Gail, back in Chicago, would be Clancy's partner when he returned to Chicago. God had cleared the slate, just as Elice had told him as they waited in the crowded O'Hare Airport for the two o'clock plane that would bring them home.

Friends and family present and accounted for, Cabot told himself as the organist began the first thrilling notes of the Wedding March.

Annie appeared first in the double doorway at the rear of the church, and sprinkled rose petals as she walked slowly up the white-clothed aisle. Behind her, Emily strutted purposefully forward. Following Emily was Sarah, who glowed with the knowledge that in seven short months, she and Joe would have a child of their own. Then Wally's tall thin frame stepped into the doorway; he didn't look at all simple-minded as he proudly crooked his left arm for Elice to take.

And then came the bride, beautiful in a simple ivory suit. Even behind the

229

veil of her hat, Cabot could see those big dark eyes of hers, staring straight at him. Smiling, he stood taller, and when he did, the notes in his breast pocket crinkled again. He would always treasure the sweet messages written by the children. But the note he would cherish most was the one that Clancy had handed him as he had snapped his cummerbund into place:

Cabot,

Until you, living was just one more thing I had to do. (Are you there, or am I only conjuring up what could be true?) I'm no child. . .visions of sugarplums faded from view long ago. I've seen tides well up and surge, and crest and foam, and ripple with images that sink in the loam.

With you, I am that tide. Without you, living would be just one more thing required. . .like dinner at six or a plane from Chicago at two.

I will love you always. . .I promise.

Elice

Finally, Elice stood beside Cabot.

Life was grand, Cabot surmised.

But then, why wouldn't it be? He had a pocketful of promises!

THE WEDDING WISH

Dedication

To all those who have suffered the loss of a loved one,
and to those awaiting that loss.
Your courage and steadfastness has earned God's promise:

*And it shall come to pass in the day that the LORD
shall give thee rest from thy sorrow, and from thy fear,
and from the hard bondage wherein thou wast made to serve.*
ISAIAH 14:3

Prologue

January 5, 1998

I n his decade as an oncologist, Ron Peterson had given patients bad news before, but it never got any easier.

Something told him it never would.

"Are you sure?" Leah asked, her voice a scratchy whisper.

He met her eyes—not an easy feat considering what he'd just told her. "You can go the holistic route, as we discussed a while back—"

"Been there, done that," she said flatly. Then, nodding, Leah took a deep, shuddering breath. For a moment, she sat still as a sculpture. "Well, then," she said, getting to her feet, "I guess I'd better be on my way." And more to herself than to the doctor, "I have a lot to do."

Experience had taught him that words could be woefully inadequate at a time like this. And so Peterson laid a hand on her shoulder as that oh-so-familiar feeling of helplessness surged through him.

She sent him a trembly half-smile, blue eyes glistening with unshed tears as she gave his hand a comforting pat. "Aw, don't look so sad, Doc. It isn't your fault."

Then whose fault is it? he demanded silently. Someone needs to accept responsibility for ending a young mother's life! Teeth clenched in grim acceptance, he slid a business card from the brass holder on his desk, scribbled a number on the back. "If you need anything, anything at all," he said, handing her the card, "this is my private line."

She dropped it into her purse with barely a glance. "Thanks, Doc. You're a peach."

He had a dozen or so patients who, like her, demanded straightforward answers to their questions. Peterson admired them all, but none more than Leah. She'd put her life in God's hands—her words, not his—and no matter how negative the news or how painful the procedure, she wore that "grin and bear it" demeanor like a protective cloak—not around herself, but around her little girl. Even now, she faced the ugliest of truths with dignity and grace. Amazing grace, he thought, because it was amazing that she insisted in the possibility of a

233

miracle. "And you're a piece of work, Leah Jordan."

He walked her to the door. She had no parents, no siblings, no husband—just a two-year-old beauty named Fiona. "So how's that little angel of yours?"

A loving, maternal smile lit up her face. "I'm afraid she's entered the 'mixing stage.'"

A furrow of confusion lined his brow.

"At lunch today, she stirred ham and peas and mashed potatoes into her fruit punch—and ate it!"

Chuckling, Peterson feigned an upset stomach. "And to think that just this morning, I was complaining about not having any kids." He shrugged, opened his office door. "Go figure."

"Yeah," she sighed, a wan and wistful smile tugging at the corners of her mouth. "Go figure."

He watched her walk down the hall toward the reception room, nod politely at the nurse, and wave good-bye to the receptionist. You'd never know she just received a death sentence, Peterson thought. Her tenacity reminded him of his mother, whose courageous battle against breast cancer had been the reason he'd become an oncologist in the first place. At least he'd had eighteen wonderful years with her before she lost the war; Leah's daughter was only two.

"How do you prepare a toddler for the death of her only parent?"

His nurse looked up from her clipboard. "I'm sorry," she said distractedly, "did you say something, Doctor?"

Shaking his head, Peterson frowned, realizing he'd unintentionally spoken the question aloud. Then, gesturing toward the examination rooms, added, "How many more?"

"Three."

Heaving a sigh, he nodded. Eyes still on Leah Jordan's retreating form, he said, "Give me five minutes."

Closing his office door softly behind him, Ronald Peterson—medical doctor—slumped into his chair. And head in his hands, Ron Peterson—ordinary man—wept.

❧

It was hard to believe a month had passed since the prognosis.

Just as Dr. Peterson predicted, it was happening fast, very fast. Leah had, at best, a year; at worst. . .

She chose not to waste time thinking about that. She had no idea when the cancer would completely deplete her energy to the point that she could no longer care for Fiona, and couldn't afford one moment of self-pity.

Far better to dwell on the many things she could be grateful for. Like the motorized wheelchair donated by fellow parishioners that helped conserve her waning strength. Hot, nourishing meals, prepared every Sunday by the good ladies of the church. Bi-weekly housekeeping, provided by neighbors. Thanks to the mortgage insurance John purchased before his death, the house was paid off, and Leah had more than enough in the bank to keep food in the pantry and oil in the furnace tank for years to come.

Trouble was, Leah didn't have "years to come."

She had a plan, though, and after countless hours in deep and heartfelt prayer it became clear that God agreed with it, too.

There wasn't a moment to waste. So, after rewriting her Last Will and Testament, Leah began putting her plan into action.

In high school, they'd called Leah and Jade and Riley "The Three Musketeers." The caption beneath the yearbook photo of them, arm-in-arm outside the cafeteria, read "Friends for Life!"

For Jade Nelson, Student Council President and Riley Steele, the Eagles' star quarterback, the association went deeper than friendship.

But both had sworn Leah to secrecy and, being the type who believed in keeping confidences, she never let on that Jade loved Riley, or that he loved Jade. Ignoring her friendly advice to " 'fess up" and "tell it like it is," Riley went off to veterinary college in Virginia, and Jade followed her soon-to-be fiancé to California.

Their lives were busy and full, and both seemed happy—on the surface. But Leah knew better. They'd never stopped loving one another. She knew this because in every conversation with Jade, Riley's name came up—and vice versa. They were perfect for one another, and always had been.

Leah had faced the truth about her future, and it was time for Jade and Riley to do the same.

Because Fiona needed them as much as they needed each other.

Chapter 1

A ll during the long flight from California to Maryland, Jade alternated between feeling overwhelming grief—*How can I be losing Leah, my best friend for twenty years?* and rage—*Hasn't the poor woman suffered enough in her past?*

Jade had never been one to question life's dizzying twists and turns. Simple acceptance, she'd learned, steadied things. But Leah was dying. Did the Lord really expect her to accept that?

She daubed a tissue to red-rimmed eyes and took a deep breath. *Get a grip, girl; you have to be strong, for Leah.*

And for Fiona.

Fiona had been one of the main reasons she'd volunteered to move back to Baltimore. Why should Leah pay for full-time, live-in help while she was waiting for God to perform a miracle when her best friend had a nursing degree? Besides, things weren't working out as she'd planned in La-La Land, and it wasn't just because of Hank Berger, either.

Fiona.

She pulled out her wallet and looked at the photograph Leah sent with Jade's Christmas card. Chubby leotard-covered legs poked out from the ruffled hem of a red velvet dress that was mostly hidden by the huge stuffed bear Fiona had puckered up to kiss. She had her mother's honey-blond hair and her father's aquamarine blue eyes. "And a smile so sweet it could rot your teeth!" Leah was fond of saying.

Jade had been honored when Leah and John asked her to be Fiona's godmother, and took her duties seriously. No less than once a month, she sent books, toys, and cartoon video tapes by way of the Package Man. Every time she talked to Leah—and she could count on placing or receiving at least one long distance call a week—Jade insisted on talking to her godchild. It amazed her how quickly Fiona had grown, from a quietly cooing infant to a nonstop chatterbox.

Much as Jade loved the little tyke, she knew that no one on earth loved Fiona more than Leah. When she'd called to ask for Jade's help, the last thing Leah had said was, "I'm really gonna miss that little monkey!"

"Can I get you anything, miss?"

Jade looked into the sympathetic eyes of the flight attendant. "No, thanks," she said, smiling as she blotted her eyes. "I'm fine."

The pretty young woman put an extra bag of salted peanuts on Jade's food tray and gave Jade an understanding smile. "Death in the family?"

Leah wasn't blood kin, but she'd been family since that dreadful day—

It had been one of those freaky "in the wrong place at the wrong time" situations that had made Leah an orphan. She'd been in Jade's family room, teasing Riley for losing at Monopoly—again—as her parents and younger brother were buying soft ice cream to celebrate a Little League victory. The gunman barged into the store, panicking the clerk, and customers toppled like dominos as a result. And Leah had lived with Jade ever since.

The flight attendant took Jade's silence as a "yes." "Heading to or from the funeral?"

Funeral. Even the word sounded forlorn, final. That awful day could come in a month, six months, or a year. She had no choice but to hope and pray, right along with Leah, that a spiritual phenomenon would take place. "Excuse me," she muttered around a sob and hurried down the aisle.

"We'll be landing in just a few minutes," the attendant called after her.

In the safety and seclusion of the tiny rest room, Jade pressed her forehead to the cool metal wall. *You'll be landing soon*, she thought, *and Riley will be waiting at the gate.*

Riley. Big and burly, dark-haired and brown-eyed—

"He's been here every day since I got the news," Leah had told Jade on the phone, "running errands, cooking, cleaning, taking Fiona out so I can rest. . ."

That was Riley, all right. Though she'd been back in Baltimore dozens of times since moving to California, she hadn't seen him since Leah and John's wedding five years earlier. He was dating a cover girl at the time—no surprise to Jade, since every one of his dates had been tall and voluptuous and gorgeous—more evidence for her "I'm not beautiful enough for Riley Steele" argument. By then, she'd pretty much resigned herself to the fact they'd always be friends, and nothing more.

Although by then, calling him a "friend" was a bit of a stretch. Neither years nor miles had come between Jade and Leah, so why had time and distance separated Jade from Riley?

Had it separated them? Or had she only imagined the gap?

No. It was there, as broad and deep as the Grand Canyon. And Jade knew exactly when the crack began to widen into a chasm.

For years she'd managed to hide her emotions behind jokes and grins and playful shoves, but on graduation night, when excitement and pride and joy propelled her into Riley's arms, she had kissed him. It was supposed to say "congratulations!"—nothing more. But she'd felt so good in his arms, so complete. When the kiss ended, he'd gazed into her eyes, and in that unguarded tick in time, Riley must have recognized the look on her face for what it was: boundless love.

It must have terrified him, she thought, because he'd nearly took a pratfall backing away from her. Two days later, Leah told her he'd headed south to find a job and an apartment near the University of Virginia's School of Veterinary Medicine. Why hadn't he said good-bye? And why, whenever he visited his parents, had he made one excuse after another to avoid seeing Jade?

When Leah called last week to ask Jade to come help, she'd said, "Riley will be so glad to see you!"

"Yeah, right," had been her dry reply.

"No, really. He asks about you all the time."

"Uh-huh. Hoping I've finally married and settled down—outgrown that silly schoolgirl crush—"

"It wasn't a crush, and we both know it."

And there in the jetliner's minuscule bathroom, Jade admitted it was true. Always had been, and always would be.

A staticky baritone interrupted her thoughts. "Ladies and gentleman, this is Captain Tenet. We're making our approach at Baltimore-Washington International Airport, so if you'll all fasten your seat belts, we'll begin our descent. . ."

Heart beating double-time, Jade glanced at her watch. *Right on schedule, Captain,* she thought, swallowing the lump of fear that had formed in her throat.

Riley would be waiting at the gate, and she didn't for the life of her know what to say to him after all these years, after all this time.

❦

He'd been pacing back and forth in front of the window for nearly thirty minutes, hands pocketed and glancing at the monitor every minute or so. Flight 2254 from Chicago's O'Hare to BWI was right on time.

A quick check of his wristwatch told Riley he had ten or fifteen minutes before Jade deplaned. He'd called her from Leah's house—at Leah's insistence, now that he thought of it—to finalize the pickup arrangements. "I'm having most of my things shipped ahead," Jade had told him, "so we won't have to stand around waiting at baggage claim."

She'd sounded every bit as sweet as he remembered. And oh, he remembered!

His little black book was chock-full of names and phone numbers. He'd been engaged once and had come mighty close to it a second time. Some of the ladies had been beautiful. There had been smart girls, successful ones, some who liked to cook for him, others who seemed to take pleasure in tidying his house. But none had hair like spun gold or eyes the color of a summer sky. When they talked, he didn't think of cherubim and seraphim; when they smiled, he didn't see rainbows. In short, they weren't Jade.

Folks were beginning to gather near the wide picture window. "It's here!" a little boy squealed. "Grandpa's plane is here!"

Riley watched the little family huddle near the glass, pointing and chattering excitedly as the jumbo jet wheeled up to the terminal. Either their enthusiasm was contagious, or he was looking forward to seeing Jade even more than he'd allowed himself to admit.

Watch it, he warned himself, *or you could be in for one doozy of a roller coaster ride.*

He reminded himself how, just before they'd graduated from high school, Hank Berger proclaimed that he'd just been offered a job anchoring the news on a small TV station in southern California. "And Jade says she'll come with me!" big shot college man had announced. She'd dated Hank on and off over the years, but Riley hadn't paid the so-called relationship much mind. He saw Hank as a bigmouthed show-off—totally wrong for a girl like Jade. Riley had turned eighteen two days earlier, and couldn't remember anything hurting like that, not once in his life. Hank had gone on to explain how, since the best nursing school in the country was located near the studio, Jade's dad and his had put their heads—and their finances—together, and bought a duplex for their kids to share. "She'll live in the left-hand unit, and I'll live in the right," Mr. TV Personality had crowed; "brides stand on the left and grooms on the right on the altar, y'know. . ."

She'd always been a happy, energetic girl, but that night, Jade's blue eyes seemed to glow brighter, her smile wider. And then she threw her arms around him and kissed him.

Every time he kissed a date hello or good night—or good-bye—Riley had thought of that kiss. Her lips had been so soft, so warm and sweet and inviting, stirring something in him that he'd never experienced before. . .

. . .and hadn't felt since.

She'd gone off to California, just as Hank had said she would, returning for Thanksgivings and Christmases, and her parents' Silver Anniversary a few years back. She always made a point to call him when she was in town, and he made a point of avoiding her. *Couldn't let her see that she'd broken my heart!* he thought.

The little boy interrupted Riley's thoughts, jumping up and down and clapping his hands. "Grandpa!" he hollered. And turning to his parents, he pointed down the carpeted tube connecting the plane to the gate. "He's here! Grandpa's here!" The family surrounded the white-haired man and smothered him with hugs and kisses.

But Riley barely noticed. Leaning left and right, he searched for Jade.

And then he saw her.

She'd pulled her long, golden hair into a loose ponytail that swayed pendulum-like as she moved toward him on tiny, white-sandaled feet. She'd worn a formfitting jeans skirt, a short-sleeved white shirt, a wide bangle bracelet, and dangly earrings.

Of course, dangly earrings, he thought, smiling at the fond memory. Silver with turquoise, brass and coral, wolves and feathers and flowers had adorned her lobes for as long as he could remember.

He hadn't seen her since Leah and John's wedding five years ago. Hank was still in the picture then, and the big oaf hung on her like a permanent appendage. What she saw in him, Riley didn't know. But he knew what Hank saw in her.

She'd walked into the room in her pale pink maid of honor gown and turned every head, her long hair in—what had she called it?—a French braid, smiling a smile that brightened the room like the photographer's giant telescoping lamp. He thought she was even prettier now, if that was possible.

Riley stepped aside *The better to see you, my dear,* he mused, grinning.

She spotted him the moment he moved. He knew because her eyes and smile widened, and one tiny hand rose to send him a silent "hello."

The next moment reminded him of that old margarine commercial, where the guy and the girl ran toward one another in ultra-slow motion across a blossom-studded field, arms outstretched. Except Jade wasn't running, and her arms weren't outstretched. Well, he thought, grinning at the irony, at least there are flowers.

Life in California had changed her in small, subtle ways. Though time had been very gentle with her—she didn't look twenty-five, let alone thirty—a wounded, little-girl-lost expression had replaced her little-girl innocence.

"Hi," she said.

"Hi, yourself."

She thanked him when he took her suitcase, thanked him again when he handed her the flowers. "Riley, how sweet. You remembered."

"Remembered what?"

She fell into step beside him. "That daisies are my favorite flowers."

He remembered something else: At five-foot-two, she'd always had a hard time keeping up with his six-one stride. Riley slowed his pace. "They're really nothing but weeds, you know."

"I know. That's why I like them. They're pretty and delicate-looking, but tough and hardy, y'know?"

Yes. He knew. Because she was a lot like that.

"So how was your flight?"

"A little turbulence over Atlanta, but—"

"Atlanta?"

She gave a little shrug. "Don't ask me how the airlines figure their routes. All I know is we had a one-hour layover in Georgia."

"Buy any peaches?"

Jade rolled her eyes. "Same old Riley, I see."

He feigned hurt and shock. "Old? Who you callin' old? I'm what, six months older than you?"

Laughing, she shoved her face into the flowers. "Thanks, Riley," she said when she came up for air. "For these, and for picking me up, too."

"Hey. What are friends for?"

Lord, he thought, *why was that so hard to say?*

Because, came the answer, *you're crazy about her; always have been.* Riley exhaled. *If I have to settle for friendship—*

A blast of damp, hot air hit them the moment the sliding doors opened. "I'd almost forgotten how humid Baltimore can be in July," Jade said, wrinkling her nose. "In California—"

"I'm parked right on the other side of the road there," he interrupted. He didn't want to hear about California or anything that had to do with it. Hank Berger in particular. Although he had to admit, he did wonder why she'd never married the big blowhard. Leah had been tight-mouthed about the breakup, saying only "Things didn't work out, that's all."

Leah was like that. Telling her a secret was like dropping a penny down a well; chances for retrieval were slim to none. *I'm sure gonna miss her,* he thought.

"Speaking of Leah, do you suppose we could stop somewhere before we go to her house?"

Speaking of Leah? But they hadn't been speaking of Leah.

And then Riley recalled the way Jade used to be able to finish his sentences, and he hers. It was one of the things that sometimes got them laughing so hard it was all they could do to keep from drooling. Jade had explained it by saying their minds worked alike, and Riley had agreed. At least until Hank dropped his California bombshell. He didn't think he'd ever figure out why Jade had followed Mr. Stuck-on-himself to the west coast. "Sure we can stop. They've remodeled the Double-T—"

Jade groaned. "Don't tell me they upscaled it!"

"No. Just a face-lift. It still looks like a vintage fifties diner." He pointed. "That's my car over there."

"The convertible?" Jade wiggled her eyebrows. "Ooh-la-la," she cooed, grinning. "How many poodles did you clip to afford that?"

Chuckling, he unlocked the trunk. "Oh, couple hundred, I guess." He stuffed her suitcase into the small space.

"Are you going to put the top down?"

He stared at his own reflection in her mirrored sunglasses. He could only assume by the upturned corners of her mouth that Jade would enjoy feeling the wind in her hair. He could name only one other female who liked riding with the top down. . .

. . .Fiona, his godchild. Jade's, too, although some sort of Hank-emergency had kept Jade from being able to come home for the ceremony, and one of Leah's neighbors had filled in for her.

Thinking of the baby only made him think of Leah. There was plenty of time for that, later. Riley unlocked the passenger door. "Don't get in yet," he instructed, "till I get the AC fired up."

"Air-conditioner, fired up." Jade got into the car. "Real funny, Riley. Real funny."

"Hey. You know me," he said, sliding in behind the steering wheel, "I got a million of 'em. Ha-cha-cha-cha."

"You aren't old enough to remember Jimmy Durante."

"Then how'd I just do an imitation of him?" He paused. "A really good imitation of him?" he challenged.

Jade peered at him over the wire rims of her sunglasses. "Reruns?"

This small talk was beginning to wear thin. Sooner or later she was going to ask about Leah. Jade would be her round-the-clock caretaker, after all, starting tonight. And if he knew Jade, her head was swimming with questions. "Did they feed you on the plane?" he asked, hoping to put it off as long as possible.

Grinning, she nodded. "Yeah, but you know me. Those little trays just stimulate my taste buds, make me hungry for a real meal."

Yes. He knew her, all right. She'd cost him the lion's share of his allowance more times than he cared to remember. Riley gave her a quick once-over. She probably didn't weigh a hundred pounds soaking wet. *How does she do it?* he wondered, remembering how she could match a linebacker bite for bite.

They drove in companionable silence until the polished stainless steel exterior of the diner came into view. She made no comment about its newer, sleeker look, and did not remark about the big, blacktopped parking lot. "I wonder if they still serve breakfast all day long?"

"They do."

"Good, 'cause I'm in the mood for bacon and eggs. Hash browns. Rye toast. And tomato juice."

Riley held open the door, and as she walked inside, he said, "Mmmm-mmmm, 'Heart Attack on a Plate.' "

"No. That's fettuccini Alfredo."

Her soft, sweet voice had taken on a distinctive edge, and Riley had a feeling the small talk had just about ended. They followed the hostess to a booth in the back of the restaurant, ordered ice water and decaf coffee. The scent of the waitress's perfume was still in the air when Jade leaned forward on the tabletop. There were tears in her eyes when she folded her hands as if in prayer.

"All right," she said, "give it to me straight. How long do you think Leah has?"

He blew a stream of air through his lips and shrugged. "I haven't talked to her doctor lately."

One tawny brow lifted above her narrowed eyes. "So what does Leah say?"

He shrugged again. "You talked to her last night. What did she tell you?"

Jade rolled her eyes. "I've talked to her every night for a week, and I don't know a thing!" She began counting on her fingers: "She's holding her own. She's doing great—considering. She's lucky to have been given these last months to get everything in order." Running a hand through her bangs, she sighed. "I put a call in to her doctor, but we've been playing telephone tag all week."

"Leah thinks the world of him."

"Yeah, well, that remains to be seen."

It wasn't like her to be so cynical, and Riley said so.

"You'd be skeptical if you'd been doing what I've been doing for the past eight years."

He leaned on the table, too. "What have you been doing, Jade?"

"Watching people die, mostly."

She was angry, Riley noted, and didn't seem to be making any effort to hide it. Her eyes were flashing like blue diamonds, her full, pink lips thinned in exasperation.

"Most of the people I attend don't walk into the emergency room of their own accord—they're flown in by helicopter."

"You mean like on Shock Trauma?"

Jade nodded. "I've lost track of how many patients I've lost." Tears clung to her long dark lashes. Her gaze fused to Riley's as she laid her hands atop his. "I don't want to lose Leah," she whispered haltingly.

Bending forward as they were, mere inches separated Riley and Jade's faces. He wanted to wrap her in his arms, crush her to him and offer all the consolation she needed. He wanted to kiss away her tears and promise that one day, soon, everything would be the way it used to be between the three of them. But he couldn't, because Leah was dying; and because of that, nothing would ever be the same again.

Gently, he pressed a palm to each of her cheeks. "I don't want to lose her, either," he admitted, surprised at the sob-thickened huskiness of his own voice.

Jade closed her eyes, sending a silvery tear down one cheek. He caught it with the pad of his thumb and wiped it away. She nestled against his hand, then turned slightly and kissed his wrist.

Oh, how he'd missed her—missed everything about her—from the heart that was bigger than her pretty head to the inner strength that had her trying, even now, to tough this thing out. She'd always been a scrappy little thing, and it was apparent to Riley, Jade was still a fighter.

She hasn't changed all that much, he assured himself.

When Jade sat back to look for a tissue in her purse, he'd felt the chill as surely as he'd felt it when they'd walked from the muggy July air into the air-conditioned diner. He looked at his hands, empty now, save a glimmer of dampness, put there by her tears, and acknowledged silently that his heart had felt just as empty all these years without her.

Everything in him warned back off, before you get kicked in the heart—again.

"I'm sure gonna miss her," she said, sniffing and blotting her eyes with the tissue.

"Me, too."

She took a sip of her water. "How's Fiona doing? You think she knows?"

Riley shook his head. "Nah. She's too young to know more than her mommy rides around in a 'wee-cha,'" he said, mimicking the child's baby talk.

The parody put a slight smile on Jade's face. "'Wee-cha,'" she repeated, giggling softly. Jade, true to form, shook off the cloak of sadness. "She really is a cute li'l monkey, isn't she?"

"Couldn't love her more if she were my own."

If they noticed the curious stares of nearby diners, neither Jade nor Riley commented on it. This is our time, seemed to be the message for other Double-T patrons.

The waitress returned, and they ordered—Riley, a bowl of chili, Jade a full country breakfast.

"How does she look?" Jade asked when the waitress was out of earshot.

Grinning, he held his hand parallel to the floor. "About two feet tall. Big blue eyes. Rosy cheeks. And short, squatty legs that—"

"Not Fiona," she said, smiling, "Leah."

At the mention of their friend, their smiles evaporated and an awkward silence enveloped the table. He'd known exactly what Jade wanted him to say. But he hadn't been ready to talk death. Not when he felt fully alive for the first time in years.

You self-centered slob, he chided himself. *Leah is the only one who matters now. What she needs—that's the important—*

"I want you to promise me something, Riley."

How was it possible for her eyes to be bluer than he remembered? He waited for her to define the pledge.

"Promise you'll continue stopping by every day and calling when you get a chance—"

"Course I will." He tucked in one corner of his mouth, wondering why she'd even suggest such a thing.

"Not just for Leah," Jade said softly, "for me, too."

Now he was really confused.

"I've been right there, hundreds of times, when people died. Some wanted to be held—you know, like a baby—when the end was near; others just asked me to hold their hand. I've watched the life-light in their eyes fade away, heard them exhale their last breath."

Riley winced. "Gee. That's gotta be tough. You've gotta be tough, to do that."

"Not really. They need to be with someone at the end," Jade sandwiched his hand between her own. "But this is different, Riley."

"Different? How?"

"I've never lost anyone close to me before. I—" She bit her lower lip, looked across the room, toward the window wall. "I don't know if I'm strong enough to handle this alone." Jade met his eyes again, tightening her grip on his hand. "I'm going to need you at the end of the day." Shrugging, she sent him a feeble smile. "In the middle of the day, sometimes, I imagine—"

"Then I'll be there. I promise."

She tilted her head, gave his hand one last squeeze before letting go. "I'm gonna hold you to that."

He was about to say, "No need for that," when the waitress delivered their food. When she was gone, Jade leaned forward and whispered conspiratorially, "I was dying to ask you this at Leah and John's wedding—" She tugged gently at his beard. "What's that all about?"

"About an inch, I'd say, give or take a hair."

She laughed. Then, changing the words to the once-popular Top Forty song, Jade sang, "How long has this been growing on?"

"Eight, ten years. Why?"

She tilted her head again. "I was just wondering—"

"Wondering what?"

"What you're hiding from."

"Hiding!" Riley laughed. "Just 'cause a guy grows a beard doesn't mean he's hiding from something."

"Or someone." She winked. "Leah tells me there's someone special in your life these days."

"Yeah. Right."

"No one?"

Was that relief flashing in her eyes? he wondered. Well, a guy can hope. "No one." He grinned crookedly. "Unless you count. . ."

She stopped chewing, stopped dipping her toast into her egg, stopped breathing, it seemed. Riley's heart pounded at the possibility there was hope for them. ". . .unless you count Fiona," he finished.

His answer seemed to ease her concern, for she'd smiled around a mouthful of bacon. Only time will tell, he said to himself, so take it easy, real easy.

Chapter 2

Riley wheeled the convertible into Leah's driveway. "I have nothing but confidence in you, Jade." He stepped out of the car, walked around to her side, and opened the door.

"Thanks, Riley," she said, patting his hand. "I'm lucky to have such a loyal friend."

Something flickered in his dark eyes. *Was it relief that I've finally accepted our relationship as platonic, or something else?* she wondered.

"You'll be fine. And I'll help."

As the jumbo jet rocketed toward Maryland, Jade had prayed for a miracle for Leah, a flight without turbulence, that God would dim her feelings for Riley. It remained to be seen whether the doctors would find a cure for Leah, and the plane had flown through a series of rough air currents. And if her thudding heart was any indicator, the Lord had decided not to douse the flame flickering in her heart for Riley. At least, not yet.

He winked, gave her bicep an affectionate tap. "I promised, remember?"

"I'm counting on it."

She stood beside him, hands resting on the door, and gazed at the gathering thunderclouds overhead. "Looks like we're in for a doozy of a storm."

Riley got back into the car. "Go on in without me," he instructed. "You must be dying to see Leah."

Dying.

The word hung in the air like the rusting blade of an ancient guillotine. Their eyes met—hers misting, his glittering with self-reproach. Riley slapped the heel of his hand against his forehead. "Sorry," he groaned. "I've got to learn to be more careful about what comes out of my mouth."

She sent him a sad smile.

"I'll get your bag after I've put the top up."

Looking toward the front door, she hesitated, remembering what Riley had told her about Leah's appearance: Her once-beautiful blond hair was all but gone. Too weak to stand at the vanity, she wore glasses instead of contact lenses. Her movements had always been so graceful, so feminine—difficult to accomplish from a motorized wheelchair.

She closed her eyes and bowed her head. *Lord,* she prayed, *give me the strength to be whatever Leah needs. Make me an instrument of Your—*

"Jade?"

"Hmmm," came her distracted reply.

"You're gonna be fine."

Head down, she met his eyes. "So you said."

"Did you ever see that old Humphrey Bogart movie?"

"Which one?"

"I don't remember the title, but it's the one where Lauren Bacall tries to teach Bogie how to ask for help."

Her brows drew together in confusion.

" 'Just pucker up, and blow,' " he quoted Bacall.

Smiling, she closed the car door. "So you're saying—"

"If you need me, just whistle."

She grabbed her purse from the passenger seat, then headed up the walk. Finger poised to ring the bell, his voice floated to her on the sticky breeze. "I'm almost finished here." She turned in time to see him disappear beneath the convertible's canvas top.

Jade was still laughing under her breath when Leah opened the door. "What are you doing out there in this heat?" she scolded teasingly. "Get in here where it's cool and dry, and give me a hug!"

Bending at the waist, Jade wrapping her wheelchair-bound friend in a long and generous embrace. "Oh, Leah," she whispered, "it's so good to see you."

"All right, all right," she muttered into Jade's shoulder. "Turn me loose so I can have a look at you."

She stepped back, supposedly to allow Leah to inspect her. Instead, Jade trained her nurse's eye on Leah.

She'd lost weight, thirty pounds or more— a huge amount for a woman who'd never weighed more than a hundred twenty-five—and while Leah wasn't completely bald, shiny white scalp was visible through her thinning blond strands. Once, Leah's cheeks glowed with natural good health; now, Jade could see, the blush had been powdered on. But loving warmth still radiated from deep in Leah's soul, a fact that couldn't be hidden by the farsighted lenses of her tortoiseshell glasses or the lipstick that brightened her pale-lipped smile.

"Well," Leah said, grinning and spreading her arms wide, "what do you think? Should Miss Wheelchair America get ready to hand over her tiara, or what!"

"You're beautiful," Jade said truthfully, "and a sight for sore eyes, too."

"Why are your eyes sore? You've been lookin' at Riley for nearly four hours!"

"Four hours? It hasn't been—"

"It most certainly has. Your flight arrived right on time. Three o'clock sharp. I know," Leah said, wiggling her brows mischievously, "because I checked."

"You checked?" Jade pursed her lips. "Um, so where's Fiona?"

"Don't try to change the subject on me, young lady!" She crossed both arms

247

over her bony chest and, tapping her slippered toes on her wheelchair's footrest, added in her best housemother voice, "It's nearly eight thirty. That's half an hour past Fiona's bedtime. Now, then, where have—"

"Take it easy, Mom," Riley said, barging through the front door.

"Fiona's asleep. Don't sla—"

The slamming door punctuated Leah's abbreviated warning.

"Sorry," he whispered, chin tucked into his collar.

"Well?" Leah asked.

He looked at Jade, who shrugged and made a face that said, "I don't know, either."

Riley looked back at Leah. " 'Well' what?"

"Where have you two been all this time, that's what!"

"Oh." He chuckled. "Jade wanted breakfast, so—"

"So you took her to the Double-T." She sighed. "There are plenty of restaurants that aren't as far away, you know."

He nodded, looking every bit the tardy teenager. "But Leah, Double-T is my favorite—"

"Oh, this is going to be an interesting assignment," Jade interrupted, laughing. Propping a fist on her hip, she aimed a maternal digit of her own. "Well, let's get something straight right up front, girls and boys—"

Leah and Riley exchanged a puzzled glance, then focused their full attention on Jade.

"This may be your house, Leah Jordan, but starting right now, I'm in charge around here." She zeroed in on Riley next. "Got it?"

"Got it," they said in unison.

She softened her tone. "It's for your own good, you know."

Leah rolled her eyes. "Oh. I get it. This is one of those 'this hurts you more than it does me' scoldings, eh?"

Jade laughed. "Something like that." She clapped her hands once. "Now then, first order of business—Leah, when did you last have something to eat?"

She tapped a forefinger against her chin, squinted her eyes as she considered the question. Brightening, she held the finger in the air. "I had a chocolate bar at six."

"And. . . ?" Jade coaxed.

"And what?"

"And soup? A sandwich? Some salad?"

Leah lifted her shoulders and grinned. "I can't hold down rich food like that."

Jade shook her head and raised a skeptical brow. "Mmm-hmm. But have you had anything nourishing today?"

"Fiona hand-fed me a fish stick at lunchtime," she said in a small, defensive voice.

Sighing, Jade grabbed the wheelchair's handles and rolled Leah down the hall toward the kitchen. She parked her near the table, then began rummaging in the refrigerator, in the pantry, and in the cupboards. Ten minutes later, a steaming bowl of canned soup, a ham and cheese sandwich, oat bran pretzels, and a sliced apple sat between the spoon and paper napkin on Leah's place mat. "And you'll drink every drop of that milk, young lady," she said, putting a tumbler at two o'clock above the plate.

"But Jade," Leah whimpered, "I'm not hungry."

"Eat a few bites, at least; you'll sleep better with food in your stomach."

Pouting, she took a tiny bite of the sandwich, and popped an apple slice into her mouth. "Don't even like ham," she mumbled.

Jade gave her a sideways hug. "Then why did you buy it, sweetie?"

"Didn't," she muttered, grinning. "Church ladies brought it over."

"Which reminds me," Jade announced, "tomorrow, we're going shopping."

"For what?"

"Healthy, wholesome foods that aren't chocolate, for starters. And makeup, and a wig—"

"Makeup and a wig? It's nearly the Fourth of July, not Halloween."

Frowning, Jade shook a finger under her nose. "I know how important your appearance has always been, so we're going to make you feel as pretty as you are!"

Leah looked to Riley for support.

"Your bedside manner could use a little work, Jade," he said out of the corner of his mouth. And in response to her well-aimed stare, he held out hands in mock surrender. "Sorry, Leah, but Jade's in charge," he singsonged.

Bit by bit, the food on Leah's plate disappeared as the trio chatted. But despite the makeup on her cheeks and lips, her face paled. And despite the food she'd consumed, her shoulders slumped with weariness.

Jade faked an exaggerated yawn.

Leah patted her hand. "Aw, are we keeping you awake?"

"Must be jet lag," she said, stretching.

"California is three hours behind us, Jade." Then, grinning, she added, "You know, I'm a little bushed, myself. Think I'll go to my room and watch some TV," she said, winking at Riley, "so our sleepy pal, here, can get some much-needed shut-eye."

"Look at the pot calling the kettle black," he said.

Jade's brow furrowed with confusion.

"Your little patient, there, has been burning the midnight oil, night after night."

"Getting my affairs in order," Leah defended.

"Yeah, well, you haven't been getting much sleep these days."

Jade stood and started pushing the wheelchair toward Leah's bedroom. "Well, then. It's off to bed with you, Leah. But there's a catch."

"A catch?"

Don't go yet, Jade mouthed to Riley over Leah's head.

He nodded in agreement as Leah said, "A catch?"

"Riley is going to help me get you into bed, and then you're going straight to sleep. No TV for you tonight, young lady."

"Says who?"

"Says me." Jade leaned down to place a kiss on Leah's cheek. "That's who."

As if on cue, she yawned. "You gonna let her push me around this way, Riley?"

He grabbed the wheelchair's handles. "She's the boss," he repeated, rolling Leah down the hall.

"All right, but don't keep Jade up too late. She has jet lag, remember?"

Behind her, Jade's eyes widened and Riley's brows rose.

"I might be weak as a newborn kitten," Leah explained, "but I'm a mother-kitten," she aimed a warning finger over her shoulder, "who has eyes in the back of her head and sees everything."

Riley gently lifted her from the chair as Jade pulled back the covers on her bed. He fluffed pillows as Jade tucked the sheet under Leah's chin. Then, a palm resting on either side of her, Riley kissed the tip of her nose. "Yeah, well, it's time to go to get some rest, Mommy, so close all four of your eyes and go to sleep."

❧

Jade had ducked into the guest room to change into a T-shirt and sweat pants. "Think she's asleep yet?" she asked, padding into the kitchen on bare feet.

He nodded. "I think she was sawing logs even before we turned out the—" One look at Jade was enough to interrupt his sentence. "Why the long face, kiddo?"

Jade wrung her hands in front of her. "Oh, Riley, she looks so weak and pale. I hope I can do what she needs me to do right now."

"You're doing plenty, just by being here." He hesitated. "Leah told me you quit your job and sold your condo so you could be with her until—" Wincing, he gave a helpless shrug.

She sighed. "Don't feel bad. I can't say it, either." Then, almost as an afterthought, she added, "I'm not so noble as you think. Being here is sort of my grown-up way of running away from home."

"But Baltimore is your home."

Jade only nodded.

"I made us a pot of decaf," Riley said, changing the subject. "Everything we need is in the family room."

She hated seeing him like this, sad and powerless but trying his best to hide it. He stood a head taller than Jade, and likely outweighed her by seventy pounds, and yet something about his demeanor brought out the "mommy" in her. She wanted to comfort and reassure him, to make him smile again.

Humor had always worked when they were kids.

And so, crouching like a sprinter, she said, "I get dibs on the recliner!" and darted out of the kitchen.

The last time she'd visited Leah, the family room had been a warm, cozy place. The homey touches that were uniquely Leah—potted plants, a collection of wolves, dozens of old books—had been moved aside to make room for the huge hospital bed. Jade stood at the foot of it, arms limp at her sides, and took it all in—the I.V. pole, the oxygen tank, the adjustable rolling dinner tray, the green plastic cup and straw, the stainless steel bedpan. Shaking her head, she pressed both palms to her temples and closed her eyes tight.

Riley turned Jade to face him, pried her hands from her head, and wrapped her in his arms. "I know, I know," he offered, stroking her back, "it's awful, isn't it? Almost like a hospital."

"The only thing missing," she muttered into his chest, "is the antiseptic smell."

"And that annoying squeak the nurses' shoes make on the linoleum."

"Yeah," she giggled, "and that 'ding-ding' from the P.A. system."

"What about those nasal voices that follow the dings?" He pinched his nostrils shut. " 'Paging Doctor Kildare,' " he said in a mock falsetto, " 'Paging Doctor Kildare. . .' "

". . .those ugly stripes they paint on the floors."

He chuckled softly. "And a monster of a TV hanging from the ceiling."

A ragged sigh escaped her lungs. "First thing tomorrow, I'm going to make this look like a real family room again."

Smiling, he held her at arm's length. "I thought you were going grocery shopping first thing?"

She bobbed her head from side to side and rolled her eyes. "All right, second thing."

For a long moment, he simply stood there, hands clamped around her waist, gaze locked on her face.

"Why are you looking at me like that?"

Blinking innocently, Riley grinned. "Like what?"

"Like I have spinach on my teeth or something."

"Because you have—"

Jade gasped, covered her mouth with all eight fingertips. "I wonder where Leah keeps the toothpicks," she said, trying to dislodge herself from his embrace.

But Riley refused to let go. "There's no spinach on your teeth."

She rested both hands on his chest and frowned. "But you said—"

Laying a fingertip over her lips, he continued: "As I was about to say, you have the most beautiful blue eyes."

Involuntarily, her eyes widened.

And her heart hammered.

And her pulse pounded.

She'd had this dream dozens, hundreds-of times even: she, in the comforting circle of Riley's arms, he saying things like "you have the most beautiful blue eyes. . ." Was she dreaming now?

Or had the dream come true?

"I'm glad you're back, Jade."

"It's good to be back."

"I've missed you."

"I've missed you, too."

He looked genuinely surprised, and Jade wondered why. "Leah needs you," he said.

Her smile faded. *That's what I was afraid you'd say,* she thought. And then, *Jade! How can you be thinking romantic thoughts when Leah is in such terrible shape!* Jade heaved another sigh. "She needs us both."

Riley nodded. "Yeah, but you can do things for her that I can't."

"Well, that's no surprise. I'm a nurse, after all, so—"

"I don't mean those things. I mean friend things." Scrubbing a palm over his bearded chin, he shrugged one big shoulder. "I'm pathetic at 'girl talk,' for starters."

She brightened a bit. "What do you expect, with a voice like James Earl Jones?"

If he heard her compliment, Riley chose to ignore it.

"And I hate sitting through all those 'chick flicks' that Leah likes to watch," with one forefinger, he drew a circle in the air, "over and over and over."

Laughing softly, Jade reminded him that he was a master at Scrabble. "And I can't rack up a hundred points for the life of me!" she added, smiling.

"Yeah, well, you more than make up for it in Monopoly. Remember how you used to beat the stuffin's out of us?"

Jade nodded. "I still have the silly Tycoon Trophy you made me out of that old softball award of yours. I'm afraid I'd lose it if we played again, 'cause I haven't even seen a Monopoly board in years."

"But it was your favorite game."

All this talk of their warm past was taking its toll; she wanted—no, needed those feelings now. She looked at the stack of pillows at the head of the hospital bed, a stark white reminder that Leah was dying. *Your needs aren't important,* she scolded herself. *Only Leah matters now.* Lifting one shoulder, she said, "Hank thought it was a waste of time."

"What was a waste of time?"

"Playing games."

Riley blew a stream of air through his lips. "Well, remember how Leah used to beg you to sing?"

She shifted her weight from one foot to the other and said nothing.

His brows dipped low in the center of his forehead. "Don't tell me he thought that was a waste of time, too?"

"He—"

He held up a hand to silence her. "But you have the voice of an angel."

"Let's just say his taste in music and mine were—"

Riley gripped her shoulders, gave her a gentle shake. "What did you ever seen in that pencil-necked geek, anyway?" he demanded.

She recognized that tight-lipped, narrow-eyed stare; it told her he was angry. She hadn't seen the look since Leah's wedding. That day, Jade had blamed it on Riley's date—he'd never liked clingy girls, and that one seemed glued to him—but why was he angry now? He'd always seemed so disinterested in the boys she'd dated. And on graduation night, when she'd told him Hank asked her to come to California with him, Riley hadn't voiced a protest. In fact, he'd been in such an all-fired hurry to catch up with Suzie Anderson, Prom Queen, he hadn't said anything about the move at all!

"He isn't a pencil-necked geek," she said.

"I stand corrected." Riley's hard-eyed stare softened slightly as a silly smirk lifted one corner of his bearded mouth. "Actually, his neck is more like one of those big, fat crayons of Fiona's."

Jade tried unsuccessfully to bite back a giggle. "It isn't nice, you know, making fun of someone who isn't here to defend himself."

"And it isn't nice to ask the prettiest girl in school to follow you thousands of miles from home with a promise of marriage, and not deliver."

Shaking her head, Jade stared at the picture of Leah and John on the table beside the hospital bed, and remembered her last conversation with Hank. He'd developed a loyal following during his WIME-TV years, and they'd convinced him to run for state senate. "What will people say?" he'd demanded when he saw her suitcase near the door.

"Leah needs me."

"I need you!"

And it was true, after all. Hank did need her—to organize parties to impress the bigwigs, to applaud when he gave speeches, to help him entertain corporate officials and political dignitaries—

Riley's voice came to her as if from the end of a long, hollow tube, interrupting her reverie. "So why didn't that lout marry you?"

Jade hadn't given the matter much thought until then. Her work and volunteer activities and taking care of Hank's business interests left very little time for answering questions like that. But sometimes, in the quiet darkness before sleep overtook her, the truth seemed an easy thing to tell: "Because he didn't love me, and he never did."

It surprised her, saying it out loud for the first time. But it didn't hurt. Shouldn't it have hurt? she wondered, when she'd dedicated herself to Hank's happiness for nearly a decade?

"You left your family and your friends and started a whole new life for him. You don't seriously expect me to believe he never said—"

"Of course he said it." She met his eyes. "But people say things they don't mean all the time."

His intense scrutiny was unnerving, and Jade looked away. "I'm tired, Riley," she said quietly. "I think—"

"I think," he finished, "Hank Berger is a fool."

She took a deep breath and let it out slowly.

Riley gathered her close again, kissed the top of her head and said, "The biggest fool on two feet."

Being the firstborn, she didn't have an older brother, but Jade believed she knew how having one might feel, for Riley was behaving as any protective big brother would under the circumstances. *A friend loveth at all times*, she thought, reciting Proverbs.

Friend.

She had worried, during the flight home, that time and distance had damaged their friendship. But the moment she stepped off the plane, and saw his warm, welcoming smile, Jade had known the relationship had survived despite years of misunderstandings that had led to neglect. She sent a prayer of thanks heavenward, because in the months ahead, as they watched Leah slip farther and farther from them, they were going to need one another as never before.

"I'd better head out," he said. "I've got an early day tomorrow."

Jade walked him to the door. The clouds they'd seen earlier had finally begun to make good on their threat, and the refreshing scent of damp earth swished in on a summer breeze. "You be careful, now," she warned. "More accidents happen on newly-wet roads than on ice and snow, you know."

His smile warmed her all over.

"Something to do with oils on the blacktop, I think," she added.

"I'll be careful." His forefinger jabbed the air. "And you get some sleep. You have a pretty full day ahead of you tomorrow, too."

"Get a move on, Mr. Sandman."

He chuckled. "I'll call you around lunchtime to see if you need anything."

Another nod.

"I'll bring it by when I come over for supper."

He said it so matter-of-factly, as if he belonged here in this house, as if they were a family. The idea warmed her, and Jade smiled. "Okay."

He started for the car, stopping in the middle of the walk. It was raining harder now, the sound of it hissing and sputtering around them was like water on a hot griddle. "I'm really glad you're back, Jade," he said again.

Distant thunder rumbled overhead. "And I'm glad to be back. Now get going before you get soaked."

Riley snapped off a smart salute and half-ran toward his car. She watched as he slid in behind the wheel and fired up the engine, saw twin shafts of light perforate the darkness when he turned the headlights on. . .

. . .and continued staring after him until his taillights were nothing but tiny red dots in the darkness.

❧

She'd been on her hands and knees, pushing a hand-carved wooden train around on its oval track when the doorbell rang. "Now, who can that be?"

Fiona answered by giggling and beaning Riley with a stuffed bear.

And Riley rolled onto his back, taking her with him. "Hey, you know what happens when you mess up my hair." He quickly proceeded to blow air bubbles in the crook of her neck. The baby was giggling when the bell chimed again.

Jade stood on tiptoe and peered through the peephole. A tall, good-looking blond man stood on the porch, a well-worn black doctor's bag in one hand and a battered brown briefcase in the other. She opened the door as far as the chain would allow.

"Hi," he said, "I'm Dr. Peterson."

Jade swung the door open. "Of course. We've been expecting you. Won't you come in? Leah is napping, but," she said, glancing at her watch, "I don't expect her to sleep much longer."

He put his briefcase near the door and followed Jade into the family room as she said, "My name is—"

"Jade Nelson," he finished for her. "Leah told me all about you."

She cleared a spot for him on the love seat. "You'll have to forgive the mess; I'm trying to make the place a little more homey for Leah, since she'll be spending so much time here until—"

Peterson nodded as a look of silent understanding passed between them. "Never gets any easier."

"No. I'm afraid not."

Riley sat cross-legged on the floor and plopped Fiona into his lap. "So how's it goin', Doc?"

"Not bad. Yourself?"

"Can't complain."

Jade hid a frown. They were being civil with one another, but it was obvious by their cool, detached stares and stiff body postures that there was bad blood between them. "Can I interest anyone in a glass of iced tea? I made some fresh this morning."

"Tea?" Fiona repeated, toddling up to Jade. "Me, tea?"

Smiling, she scooped the child into her arms. "Sorry, sweet girl; the tea isn't decaffeinated. But I have something I think you'll like even better." She started for the kitchen, stopping in the doorway connecting the rooms. "I know how you like yours, Riley, easy on the sugar, easy on the ice." Focusing on Dr. Peterson,

Jade asked, "How do you like yours?"

He put his medical bag on the arm of the love seat, shrugged out of his suit coat. "Surprise me," he said, winking.

"I'll just give her a hand," she heard Riley tell Dr. Peterson. "Will you be okay in here alone for a minute?"

"Why wouldn't I be?"

In the kitchen, Jade gave Riley a stern look. "What's with you two? You're acting like old rivals."

"That's 'cause we are. Sort of."

She handed him Fiona and filled a toddler cup with fruit punch and snapped the cap on tight. "There y'go, sweet girl," she cooed, handing it to the baby. Then, as she dropped crescent-shaped ice cubes into three identical tumblers, she zeroed in on Riley. "How do you 'sort of' become rivals?"

Riley exhaled, and Fiona copied him. So he exhaled again, and the baby mimicked the sound.

"You two sound like a couple of broken-down accordions," Jade teased. "But you haven't answered my question."

Shrugging, he kissed Fiona's cheek. "I went out with his fiancée a couple of times."

Gasping, Jade's mouth opened in shock. "You did what?"

"Well," he said, wincing, "I didn't know she was his fiancée. She came into the clinic—her poodle had mange, see—and well, one thing led to another, and before I knew what was happening, I was accepting an invitation to have dinner at her apartment."

"She invited you to her place, and she was engaged to Dr. Peterson?"

Riley nodded. "It gets worse." Looking left and right, he added, "we were right in the middle of a very sweet good night kiss when the good doctor walked in."

Jade tamped down the jealousy that coursed through her. "Wait a minute—he had a key to her place, and yet she invited you to—"

"Um-hmm. Seems she'd been looking for a way to break it off with him for some time." He shrugged nonchalantly. "I was her ticket to freedom."

"How awful," Jade whispered, "for her to have used you like that." Then, in an even quieter voice, "How did he take it?"

"Let me put it this way: There's no love lost between Ron Peterson and me. Never was."

"You mean—? You knew him before the—"

"Yup. We were on the basketball team together at the University of Virginia." Riley wiggled his eyebrows, made a monster face, gave Fiona a noisy peck on the neck. He was grinning, and she was giggling when he added, "Old Ronnie boy wanted to be team captain."

Jade put their glasses, a plate of cookies, and some paper napkins on a tray. "But you got the job."

He held out one palm. "I was a better player, and—"

"And what?"

"Well," he said, shrugging, "well, the guys liked me more. What can I say?"

She tucked in one corner of her mouth as she lifted the tray. "You can say 'I'm the most humble man I know.' " Jade leaned close and whispered, "Course, it wouldn't be true.

"Here we go," she singsonged as they entered the family room. "Nothing like a nice tall glass of refreshing iced tea on a hot, humid July day, I always say."

"I never heard you say that," Riley said.

She saw the teasing glint in his eye and sent him a look that said "watch it!"

"Thanks," Dr. Peterson said when Jade handed him his drink. And after taking a sip, he added, "You weren't kidding when you said you brewed this yourself, were you?"

She wrinkled her nose. "Never cared much for that powdered stuff. Besides, it doesn't take much longer to make it from tea bags than to stir up the instant."

❧

"Now there's what I like," Leah said from the hallway, "a rip-roaring, intellectually stimulating conversation!" She rolled into the room smiling. "Hi, Doc," she said. "Good of you to come all the way over here this way."

"My pleasure," he said, holding up his glass. "Care for some iced tea? Or should we get right down to business?"

Leah rolled her eyes and gave a sigh of resignation. "I'd just as soon get it over with, if it's all the same to you."

Standing, he handed her his doctor's bag. "You hold onto that; I'll drive."

Peterson steered Leah to the end of the hall, then closed the door to her bedroom behind them. "What's this?" he asked, rattling the contents of a small brown bottle.

"You know very well what that is; it's the medicine you prescribed."

She watched as he popped the cap and emptied the pills into an upturned palm. "But Leah," he said, meeting her eyes, "you've only taken two."

"I'm saving them. For emergencies." And grinning mischievously, she added, "You don't want me to get addicted, now do you?"

He inclined his head. "Leah, don't be flip. This is serious busi—"

"They make me all groggy and dopey."

He dumped the pills back into the vial and gave it another shake. "They're not doing you any good in here."

"And I'm not doing Fiona any good half asleep from pain medication."

"But how do you stand it?"

She pointed to the corner of her room, where a small stereo sat on a wooden stand. " 'How Great Thou Art,' " she said.

Brow furrowed, he admitted, "I don't get it."

" 'The Old Rugged Cross,' 'In the Garden'— music," she explained, "soothes me. My favorite song is 'Amazing Grace.'"

Smiling, he perched on the corner of her bed and took her hand in his. "I remember thinking once that you have an amazing amount of grace and dignity."

"Oh, go on with you," she said, waving a hand. "I bet you say that to all your patients."

"Nope." He gave her hand a pat. "Only the brave ones." Peterson opened his bag and withdrew the stethoscope.

"So what do you think of Jade?"

He hung the instrument around his neck. "She's gorgeous." Then, as if the answer embarrassed him, he cleared his throat and quickly added, "She seems very efficient. I'm sure she's an excellent nurse. We're going to have a little talk, she and I, when you and I are through here."

"About what?"

"You."

"What's to talk about?" Leah asked flatly. "I'm dying—unless God comes through with a major miracle pretty soon."

Frowning, he listened to her heartbeat. "You sure don't believe in beating around the bush, do you?"

Leah shrugged. "Seems like an awful waste of time to me. Besides, it's unnecessarily hard on the shrubbery."

Peterson shook his head as his long, thick fingers palpated her neck. "So tell me, how long has Jade been a nurse?"

"Ten years, give or take."

He aimed the beam of his doctor's light into her right eye. "Does she have a boyfriend? Is she engaged?"

"What's with all these 'Jade' questions? You sweet on her?"

"Of course not!"

She watched his Adam's apple bob up and down as he swallowed.

"I'm only asking because I want to make sure she has the time to devote to you."

"I can assure you she's totally dedicated to me, Dr. Peterson."

"Ron," he said, looking into her left eye. "You agreed to call me—"

"Ron. I know. Sorry." She gave his stethoscope a light tap and set it to swinging like a pendulum. "Look, Ron, we both know all this examination stuff is a colossal waste of time, 'cause, hey, what are you lookin' for, anyway?"

"Irregular heartbeat, fluid in your lungs—"

"Ah," she said, nodding, "that dreaded pneumonia. I've read all about it. That's why I spend as much time as possible sitting up. Still," she said, riveting him with her eyes, "you don't need an excuse to come and see me." Wiggling what was left of her eyebrows, Leah smirked. "Go on. Admit it. It isn't Jade you're sweet on; you have a crush on skinny ole bald me."

Peterson chuckled. "I've said it before, I'll say it again: You're a piece of work, Leah Jordan."

"Yeah, yeah." Leah dismissed the compliment with a wave of her hand. "So what do you think? Do I have a couple of months left in me, or what?"

He straightened, busied himself by tucking his flashlight and stethoscope back into his bag. "I wish I knew. Could be six months, or two, or—"

She held up a hand to silence him. "I know. Or I could go in my sleep tonight." She sighed heavily. "It's just that it's tough, you know? Most people don't know when the end is going to come. Those of us who have a fairly good idea, well, we like to plan what's left of our future."

He knelt in front of her wheelchair and took her hands in his. "And what are you planning for your future, Leah?" he asked softly.

Leah glanced toward the closed bedroom door. "Not my future, Ron; Fiona's."

Chapter 3

"I love what you've done in here," Leah said, stretching. "Sometimes, when I look around, I almost forget that I'm—"

Jade looked up from the book in her lap. "I thought you were sleeping."

"I was."

She laid the book on the end table and quickly went to her friend's side. "What's wrong? Are you in pain? Is that what woke you?"

"No. I'm having a pretty good day, actually." Leah leaned forward as Jade plumped her pillows and smoothed the sheet over her knees. "Where's Fiona? Napping?"

"She's with Riley."

Leah nodded. "Oh, yeah. It's Saturday. How could I forget their summer Saturdays—a walk in Centennial Park, the swings at the tot lot, and an ice cream cone from Soft Stuff."

Jade returned to the chair. "He's really good with her, isn't he?"

"The best." She sighed dreamily. "It's a shame he never married. He'd be a great dad. He told me once he'd like to have about a dozen kids."

Laughing, Jade said, "Maybe that's why he never married."

"What do you mean?"

"Well, that's nine years of pregnancy. Maybe he couldn't find a woman willing to give him twelve kids!"

She paused, leaned forward a bit, and while they laughed at her little joke, added, "And while we're on the subject, why doesn't he have a wife? I mean, he's loving and thoughtful, handsome and successful, smart and—"

Leah pursed her lips. "Hmmm, if I didn't know better, I'd think you were applying for the job."

"Ha! As if the Perpetual Bachelor is even looking!"

"I happen to know that he is."

"He told you that? Riley actually said he's ready to settle down?"

"Actually, he said it years ago."

"Really." Jade did her best to appear only mildly interested and busied herself retidying the covers.

"Yup. Right after he enrolled in veterinary college."

"But that was," she began counting on her fingers, "but that was over eight years ago. What's he looking for—Mother Teresa, Ivana Trump, and Suzie

Homemaker all rolled into one?"

"Hmmm."

"Hmmm what?"

"Nothing."

Jade crossed her arms over her chest, lifting her chin in stubborn defiance. "I'm not interested in applying for the job, if that's what you're thinking."

"Of course not." But it was obvious by her smug expression and teasing tone of voice that Leah believed exactly the opposite.

"I'm serious!" Jade laughed, slapped her knees, and, with smile frozen in place, she added, "I mean, I want what's best for him, of course, because he's a friend, after all, but I'm certainly not interested in him—not in a romantic way." Nervous laughter punctuated her statement, because even as she told it, Jade asked God to forgive her lie.

"What was it Shakespeare said? 'Me think thou protest too much,' or something like that."

Jade opened her mouth to protest, but Leah held a finger in the air, commanding silence. "Shhh. You'll just prove my point."

Leah was right, and Jade knew it. She did as she was told.

"You and I have talked twice a week, minimum, since you moved to California, and every single time, Riley's name came up at least once." Leah raised what was left of her right eyebrow. "How is it you're only now asking about his love life?"

Love life? Her heart pounded at the mere thought of it. She didn't want to know anything about his love life. Because, in all honesty, Jade hoped he didn't have a love life—unless she was part of it.

"You're still crazy about him, aren't you?"

Again the nagging guilt that had attacked earlier when thoughts of a relationship with Riley came to mind. Much as she wanted it, it couldn't be. Maybe not ever, and certainly not now! *I'm not going to stand here and discuss such things*, Jade told Leah silently, *while you're lying there, helpless, and*—It was time to change the subject. Period. "How about a cup of tea? Or a nice glass of lemonade?"

Nodding, Leah smiled knowingly. "I was right. You are still in love with him!"

Jade hid behind one hand. "There's no talking sense to you today. Now what'll it be," she asked, "hot tea or lemonade?"

"How about the truth for a change?"

Gasping, Jade's mouth dropped open. "The truth—for a change? You've always said I'm one of the most honest people you know—that I use diplomacy and avoidance so I don't have to lie—even to spare people's feelings."

There was a moment of absolute silence before Leah asked, "What are you so afraid of, Jade?"

"Afraid? I don't know what you're talking about."

"Are you scared that if you tell him how you feel, he'll reject you?"

Yes, I've always been afraid of that, she thought, staring wide-eyed at her friend. "This is neither the time nor the place to be discussing such—"

"Did you ever consider that maybe he feels the same way?"

It was so preposterous, Jade could only laugh and roll her eyes. "Who? Riley? In love with me?" Another short burst of laughter, then, "I'd say you were high on pain killers—if you were taking pain killers—because that's just about the most ridiculous—"

"Look me in the eye and tell me you never gave it a thought."

Jade swallowed, hard. She'd managed to avoid the truth with others, but never with Leah, who could be a puppy to the root when on a quest for information. "As I said," Jade began, patting Leah's pillow, "this is neither the time nor—"

"It is precisely the time and place." Then, softening her tone a bit, Leah added, "Humor me, Jade; I've been a pretty good patient so far, haven't I?"

"You've been a very patient patient," she teased, smiling lovingly. And looking into Leah's nearly-lashless blue eyes, Jade shook her head. *You never could refuse her anything,* she told herself; *what makes you think you could refuse her now?*

She took a deep breath and plunged in. "You know very well that I used to think about Riley and me—not just as friends, but as. . .as. . .as a couple. I thought about it all the time."

"Seems to me I recall a couple of prayers, too."

She squared her shoulders. "True. But as you can see, they haven't been answered," she said without thinking. And upon hearing her blatant confession, Jade quickly added, "Besides, I was young and stupid then. Very young, and naive, too."

"Oh, and you're so much older and wiser now."

Jade tucked in one corner of her mouth and frowned. "You always did think you knew it all, didn't you?"

Shrugging, Leah said, "Hey, I believe in that old seventies cliché."

"Which is?"

" 'Tell it like it is.' "

Jade exhaled a sigh of frustration. "If I didn't know better, I'd say you were deliberately trying to make me mad." And grinning, she repeated, "And besides, it's 'as,' not 'like.' "

"Whatever," Leah laughed, waving the grammar lesson away. There wasn't so much as the trace of a smile on her pallid face when she said, "I'm not trying to make you mad, Jade; I'm just trying to make you see what's right under your nose."

"What I see," Jade said, standing straighter, "is that Riley likes sultry, mysterious women. You know the type—tall and voluptuous, with big brown eyes and long black hair." She spread her arms wide. "Look at me, Leah; I'm the complete opposite of that."

Leah regarded her with a careful eye, and nodding, said, "Can't see the forest for the trees, can you?"

Growling with frustration, Jade feigned a scowl and rolled her eyes, then laid a hand on Leah's forehead.

Leah giggled. "Stop that. What're you doing?"

"I thought maybe you'd spiked a fever; how else am I to explain that you're spouting clichés like some delirious—"

"You're the one who's crazy," Leah interrupted, grabbing Jade's wrist, "if you can't see how he feels about you." She paused, then continued: "I've seen the way he looks at you when he thinks no one is looking. He's feet over forehead in love with you, sweetie!"

She perched on the edge of the hospital bed, taking Leah's hand in hers. Heart pounding with joy at the mere possibility, Jade closed her eyes. *This is neither the time nor the place,* she reminded herself. What kind of person discusses issues of romance with a dying woman? She took another deep breath. A selfish, self-centered one.

"Leah, you know that Riley has always treated me as though I were his silly little sister. He's protective and sweet, but he thinks of me as a friend. Just a friend," she added, holding a warning finger in the air. "That's the way it's always been, and I see no reason to believe he feels differently now."

"Maybe you need to look harder."

"What?"

"Maybe you don't see a reason to believe he feels differently because you're not looking hard enough." She squeezed Jade's hand. " 'O fools and slow of heart to believe all the prophets have spoken.' "

Jade ruffled Leah's sparse hair and focused on the ceiling. *Lord,* she prayed, *help me put an end to this nonsense!* "Oh, and now she thinks she's a prophet, Lord," she said, shaking her head. Grinning, Jade returned her attention to Leah. "I think I'll just fix you that tea now. A nice big mug of chamomile. Maybe it'll put you to sleep so I won't have to listen to any more of this nonsense!"

Laughing, Leah shook her head. "You can run," she called to Jade's retreating back, "but you can't hide."

❧

"I can't hear you," came Jade's voice from the kitchen.

Tapping a finger on her chin, Leah gave a self-satisfied nod. "Well, Lord," she said to herself, "what do You think? Are things ticking along just fine, or what!"

Suddenly, she sucked a huge gulp of air between her teeth and grimaced. The pain always hit her this way, with no warning whatsoever. It was one of her only complaints, because if she had felt it coming, perhaps it could have been forestalled.

Trembling with rage and agony, Leah popped a tape into the recorder and hit the ON button. As the familiar notes of "Amazing Grace" floated around the room, she snuggled deeper into the pillows and focused on the words of the song, waiting for them to take effect.

Don't be angry, she told herself, *be loving, like Jesus was at the end.* And grinning slightly, she remembered Jade's English lesson. "As" Jesus was, she corrected.

"I once was lost," she sang along with the tape, "but now am found. . . ."

Think about the plan instead of the pain.

That the Lord had blessed her plan was so obvious! God had put the idea into her head; Leah had never been more sure of anything in her life.

Leah took a deep, cleansing breath. "Thank you, Lord Jesus, for giving me the idea that has given me such peace and contentment during this very trying time." And, grinning, she tacked on a silent, *Who says you can lead a horse to water but you can't make him, and her, drink?*

Jade had left a message for him at the clinic, and when Riley had returned her call at the start of his lunch break, the heaviness in her voice could have been weighed on a scale. "Just wanted to warn you," she'd said, "that Leah isn't doing very well today."

He'd made Jade promise to let him know whenever their buddy was having a bad day, so he could gird himself against letting Leah see shock or sadness at first sight of her.

"I almost talked her into taking some morphine today," she'd added, "but Fiona woke up from her nap, and the minute Leah heard her voice—"

Her own voice had waned away, and he could almost picture her, standing in that stiff-backed way of hers, shaking her head in frustration.

"What can I bring you?" he'd asked.

Her answer was still echoing softly in his ear. "Just you."

She'd cleared her throat, then asked, "What time can we expect you for supper?"

"Depends on what you're making."

"Spaghetti and meatballs, and a giant Caesar salad."

He'd known she was teasing because of the warm lightness in her tone. Besides, these days Leah couldn't hold down anything but bland foods—chicken, turkey, green beans—and Jade refused to cook anything spicy. "If Leah can't eat it," she said time and again, "we're not eating it. It just wouldn't be fair."

"Spaghetti and meatballs? That's right, torture me with talk of what I can't have," he'd said, laughing, "promising one of my favorite meals, and not delivering. I have a good mind to do something just as mean."

"Such as?"

"Such as, I'll have spaghetti and meatballs for lunch, and give you a big fat kiss when I get there so you can smell it on my breath."

She had giggled at that—a sound he'd come to treasure almost as much as the beautiful smile she always wore to greet him.

The rest of the day had slogged by, and Riley couldn't wait to see her again. He'd seen almost as much of her lately as he'd seen of her when they were kids, stopping by once, sometimes twice a day since Peterson had given Leah the final verdict.

The final verdict.

They'd gone round and round over that one—he and Peterson—Riley demanding to know if the so-called medical professionals had truly exhausted every possible avenue of treatment, the doc insisting they were doing all that could be done.

It wasn't that Riley didn't believe Peterson. He had a tendency to hold a grudge, but he'd earned his stellar reputation. Still, he couldn't help but question the doctor's confidence in his diagnosis. Cancer went into spontaneous remission all the time. Why wasn't Peterson looking into that, to determine if something had been overlooked? Leah had no one else to look after her interests; if his persistence made Peterson uncomfortable, so be it!

He'd made it his business to study the disease that was eating away at her, and stood beside her, every step of the way, which was exactly how he could be so certain that Peterson had done all that was humanly possible.

That, and he'd been praying about it every chance he got since Leah had given him the awful news. Mostly, Riley prayed for a miracle. If the eyes of the blind could be opened, and the ears of the deaf unstopped—if Christ could raise Lazarus from the dead and feed the multitudes from a few loaves and fishes, then there was hope for Leah.

Wasn't there?

Riley had long ago given up expecting an answer to why this had happened to his dear friend. "Hear, O LORD, when I cry with my voice," he'd read in Psalms, "have mercy on me and answer me." All his life, he'd been an obedient Follower and loved the Lord. Still, Riley thought he understood how Samuel felt when he said to Saul, "God is departed from me and answereth me no more."

He didn't know why cancer had invaded Leah's body.

And he didn't understand—or pretend to understand—why it couldn't be cured. But he knew only this: Leah was in God's hands now. " 'For thou art my hope, O LORD God; thou art my trust from my youth. . . .' " The verse from Psalms became part of his daily prayers.

And he would pray for Jade.

Because he still wanted her—more than ever—and believed it might well take a miracle to make that happen, too.

Riley winced inwardly as he parked the convertible in Leah's driveway. What kind of cold-hearted lout thinks about his potential love life when his best friend is dying?

He let himself into the house quietly, so as not to disturb Leah or Fiona, should they be napping. Jade was in the living room, lying on her stomach in front of the fireplace beside Fiona, a tattered copy of *Green Eggs and Ham* open on the floor between them. Neither had heard him open the door, or cross the foyer, or enter the living room.

Riley leaned a shoulder on the door frame, hands in his pockets, smiling and shaking his head, watching and listening.

" 'I do not like it, Sam I am; I do not like green eggs and ham,' " Jade read.

Her voice, as she recited the words, was every bit as animated as the rest of her. And he loved every minute part of her.

He'd never been the least bit envious of Fiona—till now: What he wouldn't give to have Jade snuggled up beside him, telling a story in that sweet, musical voice of hers!

Without looking at him, Jade said to Fiona, "Tell Uncle Riley that staring isn't polite."

The baby rolled over, and at the sight of him, scrambled to her feet and tottered to where he stood. Arms outstretched, she squealed with glee, "Wye-wee!"

He gathered her up and chuckled as she rubbed a chubby hand over each of his bearded cheeks. "Wye-wee fuzzy," she said, giggling. And turning to Jade, Fiona added, "Wye-wee fuzzy."

"Wye-wee hungwee," he said and blew air bubbles on her neck.

"You really shouldn't talk baby talk to her," Jade scolded gently. "It's hard enough for a child to learn English, let alone a language she can't speak once she's out of diapers."

He gave her a long, appraising stare. Nodding, a slow smile tugged at the corners of his mouth. "You're gonna be a terrific mommy some day." Riley watched her blush and fidget.

"Well, well, thank you. That's quite a compliment, coming from you."

"Coming from me?" he asked, taking Fiona's finger out of his ear. "What's that mean?"

Jade shrugged. "You're a confirmed bachelor, and it's been my experience they're the hardest men to please."

"I still don't get it," he mumbled past the eight tiny pink fingers wedged between his lips.

"You know what you want—and what you don't—and knowing makes you choosy."

Fiona pressed her lips to Riley's. "Wye-wee kiss," she babbled. "Wye-wee kiss."

He made a loud smacking sound against Fiona's chubby cheek. "How'd you know I was there? I didn't make a sound."

Inclining her head, Jade wiggled her eyebrows. "You shouldn't ask a girl to reveal her secrets."

"Secrets?"

"You know," she said matter-of-factly, " 'the wiles and ways of woman.' "

But he didn't know. In fact, Riley didn't have a clue.

It must have been written all over his face, because she smiled and said, "Oh, don't look so confused. From down there on the floor, I could see your reflection in that brass flowerpot on the hearth."

Chuckling, Riley shook his head. "You're a piece of work, Jade Nelson."

"Wok," Fiona repeated. "Wye-wee go wok?"

"No, sweetie," he said, grinning, "I'm off for the day. In fact," he added, digging in the outer pocket of his sports coat, "I'm not even available by beeper."

"Beep, beep, beep," Fiona said, reaching for the pager.

Quickly, he dropped the gadget back into his pocket and gave Fiona to Jade. "More story?" he said, pointing at the book.

Reminded of what they'd been doing when he came in, Fiona bounced up and down in Jade's arms. "Book," she said. "Book!"

"Why the sudden handoff?" she asked, putting Fiona on the floor.

"Wipe that smirk off your face," he kidded as the baby began flipping pages. "It's just that sometimes, like all females, she scares the daylights out of me."

"Scares you?" Jade laughed. "Dr. Dates-a-lot is afraid of women?"

"Not all women. Just pushy, aggressive ones who poke fun at their friends — and poke their fingers in my cars."

"I didn't mean to poke fun at you."

She might have convinced him she was sincere if she hadn't giggled and added, "But you're scared of Fiona?"

He gave a shy nod. "No. Well, she can be real bullheaded when she sets her mind on something. And I happen to know she likes my beeper." Riley shrugged. "I didn't know how else to distract her."

Jade glanced at Fiona, who was contentedly browsing the pages of the book. "Seems to me you know exactly how to distract her." Meeting his eyes, she smiled. "Leah's right. You would make a wonderful dad."

Riley felt the heat of a blush beneath his beard and scrubbed a hand over his face. There was nothing he'd like more than to be the father of four, six, a dozen kids like Fiona—provided Jade would be their mother.

"So when's supper?"

"The table is all set and everything is ready to go the minute Leah wakes up from her—"

"She's up," Leah interrupted, rolling into the living room.

Riley took one look at her and stood, feet shoulder width apart, crossed both arms over his chest. "Did you just lie there reading, or did you sleep?"

"I slept, 'Mr. Clean,' " Leah defended, "so wipe that scowl off your face and gimme a hug."

Immediately, his demeanor softened, and he leaned down, let her wrap him in a bony hug.

"What's for supper?" she asked Jade over his shoulder.

And when he straightened, Jade said, "Turkey, mashed potatoes and gravy, and—"

"I'm not very hungry. Would you mind very much if I watch the TV news while you guys eat?"

It was the very reason Leah had a hospital bed in the family room—so she could feel like a part of the household and rest properly. It hadn't seemed like such a bad idea to Riley, until he glanced at Jade.

Her stern expression and stiff posture made it patently clear: Leah had been skipping meals entirely too often to suit Jade. It could only mean one thing, and Riley didn't want to think about that.

"Oh, don't look so serious, you two," Leah scolded in her typically playful way. "I'm not dying. Yet."

Gasping, Jade ran to her side and wrapped her in her arms. "Don't say things like that. Not even in jest!"

"Sweetie, you're a nurse. You know the signs even better than I do. Isn't it time you faced the facts?"

"I may be a nurse," Jade insisted, hugging her tighter, "but I'm a Christian first and foremost." On her knees in front of Leah now, Jade grasped one of Leah's hands and reached out to Riley with the other. "We're praying for a miracle all along," she said emphatically. And looking to Riley for support, added in a lighter voice, "Aren't we, Riley?"

He knelt beside Jade and took Leah's free hand in his. "Jade's right," he agreed. "There's no reason to believe God won't come through for you."

There were tears in Jade's eyes when she said, "That's right! You can't give up, Leah. Fiona needs you, and. . .and so do I."

Leah sat back, giving Jade, a long, appraising stare. "I know what you're try-ing to do, Jade, but I'd like you to stop it."

"What am I trying to do?"

"You think you're helping give me hope. Well, I have plenty of that." She shook her head. "I ask you; what's wrong with this picture?"

Leah's speech had cut Jade to the quick. She'd been working night and day, getting very little rest in the process. Surely it was taking a toll on her. Riley wanted to wrap Jade in his arms, as he'd done the night she came home, because she looked every bit as frightened as a small child who'd gotten separated from her mother in the supermarket.

"I see I'm going to have to answer my own question," Leah said, wriggling her hands free of their grasp. "I used to be the weakling, the one who needed comfort and consolation."

"You were never a weakling," Jade insisted.

"You're sweet to say that," Leah said, "but we both know it isn't true. I moped around for months when I lost my family, and whined every time my heart got broken by whichever boy I had a crush on at the time. I was impossible to live with when my SAT scores kept me out of Stanford, and when John died—"

Leah looked at the ceiling, as if the description of that sad time in her life had been written up there in bold, black letters. "I don't know what I would have done without you two. Well, yes, I do," she added on a giggle, "I'd have fallen apart, that's what."

"Stop it, Leah," Jade scolded. "You're wearing yourself out with all this talk about—"

"I won't stop it. I have to make you accept this." She held out her hands, indicating first the wheelchair, then her puny body. "I've accepted it."

Jade bit her lower lip. "But you can't just accept it. You have to fight this thing!"

"I am fighting it, sweetie." Her voice, soft as a whisper, caught on a pent-up sob. "Don't you think I'm praying for a last minute reprieve from this death sentence? Don't you think I want to be here when Fiona loses her first tooth, and attends school for the first time, and goes to the prom?"

She was angry now and backed the wheelchair away from Riley and Jade. "I don't want to die, Jade. Surely you know that. But," she said, whirling the chair around to face them again, "if I have to—" She licked her lips. Swallowed. Bowed her head. And meeting their eyes again, added, "If I have to die, I want to do it with as much dignity as this detestable disease will allow."

Shaking her head, she covered her face with both hands. "I'm sorry for losing my temper," she said into her palms. "It isn't your fault this is happening to me." When she came out of hiding a moment later, Leah was fully composed again. "Well, Jade, you never answered my question."

Jade's voice trembled when she said, "What question?"

" 'What's wrong with this picture?' "

"Oh. That question." She blinked, sighed. "I don't know, Leah. What's wrong with it?"

It was the first time Riley had seen any evidence that the cancer—and the horrible effects it was having on Leah—was affecting Jade, too. She looked emotionally spent standing there, shoulders slumped, arms hanging limp at her sides as she tried her best to put on a happy face for her best friend. More than ever, Riley wanted to hold her, promise that everything would be all right.

But he couldn't, because if God didn't come through pretty soon with that miracle they'd all been praying for, Leah was going to die.

"Well," Leah said, grinning, "since you asked." She folded her hands. "Feels odd, me giving comfort to you guys for a change."

The grin never quite made it to her eyes. Still, Riley noticed, the effort was there.

"Weird, huh?"

He shook his head. "I've told you dozens of times over the years that you have a convenient memory."

When she aimed those lashless blue eyes of hers at him, Riley thought he might just cry, himself.

Leah propped her elbow on the arm of the wheelchair, rested her chin in her upturned palm. "What does my pitiful memory have to do with anything?"

"I can't speak for Jade, of course," he began, sliding an apologetic gaze in her direction, "but as for me—"

He'd never taken much credit for the fact that he could bench press double his weight; big muscles and strong bones were something he'd inherited from his father's side of the family. Since childhood, he'd hoped the solid, stable strength of his mother's people flowed in his veins. But he'd never really been tested—before now.

Lord God, he prayed, *show me what to do; tell me what to say to prove to Leah that I'm with her, all the way.*

It dawned upon him that what she needed most right now was to feel stronger despite the cancer—or maybe, because of it—than himself or Jade. So he put male pride aside and laid his head in her lap. And as she combed long, delicate fingers through his hair, Riley felt her relax, heard her take a deep, unwavering breath.

"I love you guys," she whispered.

"We love you, too," they said in unison.

Fiona toddled up and pushed Riley aside to climb onto Leah's lap. "Me wuv Mommy, too," she said, hugging her.

Connected by hearts and minds and clasped hands, the foursome formed a tight circle of love.

Chapter 4

S he let me give her something to help her sleep," Peterson said when he joined Jade and Riley in the family room.

Jade perched on one end of the sofa as the doctor sat on the other. "Well, that's welcome news. How did you talk her into taking it?"

He gave a halfhearted shrug and stuffed his stethoscope into the black bag on the cushion between them. "She told me Fiona is going to a birthday party tomorrow. Her first, as I understand it."

"That's right," Riley stated. "My brother's little boy is turning three. I'm picking her up at noon. We're going to spend the whole day together."

Peterson buckled the satchel, all but ignoring Riley's comment. "I convinced her that a good night's sleep might just give her enough energy to snap a few pictures before she leaves for the shindig."

Jade ran a hand through her hair. "Well, you deserve a medal. Riley and I can't even get her to take so much as an over-the-counter sleep aid. I honestly don't know how she's stood the pain all this time."

"A little stubbornness," Riley inserted, "and a whole lot of faith."

"Faith!" Peterson's bitter laugh cracked the quiet. "Faith in what?"

Riley leaned back in the easy chair, held up his hands in mock self-defense. "No need to bite my head off, Doc. Some of us got it, some of us ain't. Looks like you're standin' in the ain't line."

"And I'm standin' there willingly," he blurted, "because in my opinion, faith is for fools."

"I always say, people in the sciences are hardest to persuade of anything. You think because you can't measure it in a test tube or see it on an X-ray, faith doesn't exist?"

"My attitude toward faith has nothing to do with medicine," Peterson bit out. "The way I feel is the result of years of hearing people pray for divine intervention— to ease their pain, to cure their illness, whatever—with absolutely no results. Faith is for fools, especially blind faith, and your attitude proves my point."

"You honestly expect me to believe you've never witnessed a miracle? Never had a patient who, for no apparent reason, got better?"

"Sure I've had patients recuperate," he said. "But there are all kinds of rational explanations for it. And I resent that you're always questioning my professional opinion."

271

"I really don't give a hoot what you resent and what you don't. And in my opinion, your bedside manner could use a little work. Leah needs to know you believe she'll survive, and I resent that your so-called professional opinions are provin' just the opposite!"

"When I want your opinion, Steele, I'll ask for it. But don't hold your breath. As for my bedside manner, I reserve that for patients only. And while you're definitely trying mine, I—"

"Stop it!" Jade's hoarse whisper interrupted their argument. "Stop it, right now! What if Leah were to overhear the two of you, bickering like a couple of rowdy boys fighting over the only swing in the schoolyard? It's important for her to stay calm, and how's she supposed to do that if she hears you talking like this!"

Standing, she glared openly at each in turn. "I know there's bad blood between you, but for the love of angels, can't you act like adults for now and set it aside?"

Riley leaned forward, elbows balancing on knees, and hung his head. "Sorry," he said, clasping and unclasping his hands.

Peterson huffed out a deep sigh, moved his doctor's bag forward an inch, back again. "Yeah," he said nervously, "me, too."

Jade massaged her temples. "And I didn't mean to come off sounding like a grumpy old crone, either."

"You didn't," Peterson admitted. "We were behaving like a couple of spoiled, self-centered kids. We deserved a good scolding."

"Hey," Riley injected, grinning, "speak for yourself."

Jade watched as the men nodded courteously, thin-lipped smiles and smug stares declaring that, although it hadn't been announced formally, a temporary truce had been declared. She laughed softly, hiding her eyes behind one hand. "You two are priceless."

"Priceless?" Riley repeated.

Peterson stared at her, as confused as Riley.

"You looked like a couple of wolves just now, teeth bared, squaring off to determine who's leader of the pack." He watched her as she put his bag on the floor at his feet and slide onto the center cushion. "C'mere," she said to Riley, patting the one she'd just vacated.

When he was seated, she grabbed his right hand, then Peterson's. "Friends?" she asked, forcing them together.

"Friends," Riley said sullenly.

"Yeah," Peterson echoed, "friends."

And begrudgingly, they shook on it.

"There now," Jade said smiling, "that wasn't so hard, was it?"

❧

Too late, she discovered it was a question better left unasked, for the feral stares returned to their faces. Well, she told herself, Rome wasn't built in a day, and neither are friendships. For now, the focus should be on Leah.

"So tell me, Dr. Peterson—"

"Ron," he corrected.

"Ron." She smiled. "How's Leah today? I hate having to ask you the same thing every single time you come by, but if she doesn't want me in her room when you examine her, what am I to do?" She lifted her shoulders in a quick shrug. "I mean, I'm her friend, first and foremost, but I'm a nurse, too." She was rambling, and she knew it, but seemed powerless to stop the flow of words once they'd started. "I'm Leah's nurse, for goodness' sake! How can I take proper care of her unless I know what's—"

"No need to explain your concern to me," Peterson said, smiling gently. "I can see how much you care. As long as you don't ask me to violate doctor-patient confidentiality, I'll be happy to tell you anything you want to know."

"So cut to the chase, Doc," Riley butt in. "How's our girl doin'?"

Ron aimed a hard stare in Riley's direction, softening it a bit when he looked back at Jade. "Not well, I'm afraid."

Jade bit her lower lip. "It's close, then?"

"Pretty bad." A deep furrow formed on his brow. "Very close."

"How much time does she have?" Riley wanted to know.

The doctor shook his head. "A month. Maybe."

The three exhaled a collective sad sigh, ruminating over what seemed to be an irrevocable ruling, over what they had in common: Riley and Jade had their friendship with Leah; Jade and Peterson shared a medical concern for to her; Ron and Riley and Jade, utter sadness.

"Well," he said, shattering the moment of somber silence, "I'd best be on my way." He stood and gathered his things. "I'll stop by again tomorrow at about this time," he added, heading for the front door, "if that's okay."

"Of course it's okay," Jade said, grasping his hand. "And if you don't mind an ultra-bland diet—that's all Leah can eat these days—you're more than welcome to join us for supper."

His smile brightened at the invitation. "I might just do that." He gave her hand a little squeeze. "See you tomorrow, then."

She turned toward the family room and found Riley, hands in his pockets and one foot crossed over the other, one shoulder pressed against the door frame. She blamed his disapproving countenance on her supper invitation to Ron Peterson. He didn't want to share a meal with the man, and the proof was written on his face and in his stance.

But Ron had seemed so lonely and lost, despite all his tough talk. She'd worked with doctors for more than a decade now, and while some allowed themselves to care beyond the bounds of pills and treatments, most held to the theory that arm's length emotional involvement was the more professional behavior.

The sadness in Ron's eyes, and voice, told Jade that he considered Leah a friend. She believed he wanted to trust in faith, in the possibility of miracles. But he'd chosen oncology as his specialty, a discipline associated more often with death and dying than with life; faith in miracles could sometimes seem hopelessly impossible.

As a nurse, Jade understood it only too well. She was about to explain it to Riley when he lifted one well-arched brow and tucked in a corner of his mouth. "I'm gonna pour myself a glass of iced tea. Can I get you one?"

"Sure. Thanks."

As he rattled around in the kitchen, Jade checked on Leah, who was sleeping peacefully, a fact that brought her some much-needed relief. And after the bicker-fest between Dr. Peterson and Riley, she needed a moment of quiet and rest herself. She sat in Leah's recliner, leaned back, and closed her eyes. She'd given a good deal of thought to what Peterson's fiancée had done—using Riley to end the engagement. But something told Jade the ex-fiancée fiasco was only a very small part of the problem. *As long as their quarreling doesn't affect Leah, it doesn't matter how they feel about one another.*

If it had been that simple, why was she trying so hard to manufacture a friendship between the men?

Because, she admitted, helping build a relationship between them isn't sick and demented, like hoping that Riley will—

She forced the thought from her mind, focusing instead on the hard work it would be, bringing them together. *But even if they never become friends, at least in the meantime you'll have something to distract you from feeling the way you do about Riley.*

Her eyes snapped opened and she sat up straight.

How do you feel about him?

Fingertips drumming on the knees of her jeans, she counted his finer qualities. He's gentle and kind, and thoughtful, too. And terrific with kids. And except for that run-in with Dr. Peterson, he's always been easy to get along with.

Plus, Riley was completely devoted to his family, helping them any way he could, every chance he got. He'd always had a way with animals, so it came as no surprise to anyone when, in eighth grade, he announced that he wanted to be a veterinarian when he grew up.

Stubborn determination is what gave him the stick-to-it mind-set required to turn his dream into reality. And an old-fashioned attitude toward hard work and dedication had made his animal clinic one of Baltimore's most successful.

And then there was his "way" with women.

Leah often teasingly called Riley a "girl magnet" as much for his flirtatious charms as his dark good looks. And was it any wonder? It didn't matter one whit to Riley whether a female was five or ninety-five, overweight or not. He made every woman feel beautiful, intelligent—like the center of the universe.

She sighed dreamily. *He makes you feel like that,* Jade admitted. *Maybe you're just another one of his many admirers, basking in the warmth of his handsome gaze.*

There was no denying his physical attributes. Why, Jade had never been overly fond of facial hair, but Riley looked so good in his neatly-trimmed dark beard that she completely forgot her preference for clean-shaven men!

And he was a terrific kisser, too. There had only been two kisses between them, the one after graduation, and the one he'd given her the night she came home. But Jade knew she needn't kiss a hundred men to know that this was the man she wanted to be with, morning and night, for the rest of her life.

The rest of my life.

Would she have had such a thought if she didn't love him?

The answer, quite simply, was "no."

All right, so I admit it; I love Riley Steele! But she couldn't admit it aloud, ever, especially not to Riley.

The creepy-crawly sensation shrouded Jade again. It happened every time she had romantic thoughts about him. *You're a hideous, despicable human to be contemplating a future with Riley at a time like this!*

Prayer was the solution. The only solution. She would cleanse her mind and heart of Riley, by praying him away.

The idea made her grin a little, and a line from an old tune jangled in her head: *Gonna pray that man right outta my hair,* she sang silently.

"Care to share the joke?" Riley asked, handing her an icy glass.

The smile and the mood that had caused it disappeared. "Thanks for the tea," she said. And to herself, Jade added, *You're going to have to be more careful—a lot more careful—because he's always been able to read you like a—*

"I peeked in at Leah."

"Is she asleep?"

Riley nodded. "Yeah. I guess whatever Doc gave her finally kicked in."

"Good. She needs her rest."

"What she needs is a miracle."

The only sound in the room was the tinkling of ice in their glasses. Riley broke the silence. "Will you pray with me, Jade?"

Her heart fluttered in response to the intimacy of his invitation. "Of course."

They bowed their heads—she in the recliner, he in the easy chair—and folded their hands. And eyes closed, Riley began: "Lord Jesus, we thank You for our blessings: good friends, satisfying careers, all our material needs met. But we have a need that has not been satisfied.

"You said that with faith the size of a mustard seed, we could move mountains. You can read our hearts, so You know the size of our belief. And You know how much we need Leah in our lives!

"We believe You have the power to heal her, if it's Your will. We ask it now in Your most holy name. Amen."

"Amen," Jade echoed.

She'd never realized before that he became a different person when he prayed. He did not attempt to impress or educate, as when speaking before colleagues;

wasn't trying to comfort or console, as he must when talking to pet owners in his clinic; seemed to have no desire to dazzle and fascinate, as when wooing the ladies. In prayer, he looked more appealing than ever—because he was one hundred percent the man God had intended him to be.

Jade picked up her glass, clinked it against his. "To miracles," she said softly.

He nodded gravely. "To miracles."

※

She had heard the door open, and from the corner of her eye, saw Riley peek into her room. Leah hadn't dared stir, for fear he'd take one look at her eyes and know about the tormenting pain that was wracking her body.

He'd tiptoed up to the bed, and she sensed him hovering over her. "Ah, Leah," she'd heard him sigh, "why?"

It had taken every ounce of self-control to remain silent and still, to keep up the pretense of sleep, because she'd wanted to grab him by the scruff of the neck and shout, "If only I knew!" or to hold him close and comfort him, saying, "Don't be sad, Riley."

The sound of his running shoes scuffing across the thickly-napped carpet was the only indicator that he'd left. Leah might not have opened her eyes at all, if she hadn't needed to find a tissue to blot the tears.

She didn't want to die. At least, not at thirty. *How ironic,* she grinned, *that the flower generation said you couldn't trust anyone over thirty; and here I am, just reaching the age where I can't be trusted, and I'm dying!*

But in all seriousness, Leah knew that she would die—soon, if she was reading the signs correctly—despite the thousands of prayers she'd sent heavenward pleading for a cure.

Leah would hold fast to the possibility she would recover, right to the end. But having never been one to leave things to chance, she believed in being prepared. It was what prompted her to carry a purse the size of a carryon suitcase filled with bandages and antibiotic ointment, baby aspirin, and wet towelettes just in case Fiona needed something when they were away from home. The same attitude drove her to keep the pantry well-stocked, the laundry washed and folded, the house tidy at all times.

And that mind-set was also responsible for her plan.

If she wanted things to turn out well for Fiona, for Jade and Riley, Leah knew she must act now.

And so she eased herself into her wheelchair and rolled quietly toward the sound of voices in the family room. Riley's prayer stopped her, though, a prayer that was both poignant and powerful as he asked God to perform a miracle.

She'd come out here, fighting the effects of the medication Peterson had given her, to lay it all on the line, to ask Jade and Riley to help her put the finishing touches on that plan. But hearing his heartfelt appeal only served to underscore her own worries. Yes, she would continue hoping to win her battle against cancer, but the likelihood of victory was slim, at best.

Cancer was a woeful, wretched disease. "The Great Pretender" Leah had called it, because, while it simulated the camaraderie of friends and neighbors who gathered round to comfort and console, it left its victims to suffer in silent solitude the fears and doubts of a precarious, unpredictable future.

Leah could not face them this way—afraid, uncertain—vacillating between the strength of her convictions and the weakness of her human spirit. In order for the plan to work, it must be presented as the only viable alternative left to them; it must be presented in a clear, convincing voice that established the very rightness of it.

She maneuvered the chair backwards down the hall, rolled up to the bed, and climbed under the covers. *Help me hold on, Lord, until I've seen to Fiona's future.* When she could see for herself that things were firmly in place, Leah told herself, she could exchange alarm for assurance; cowardice with courage. Then she could face Jade and Riley, and present her case.

With trembling hand, Leah lifted the telephone from the nightstand, put it in her lap, and dialed the number she'd memorized that day, more than a year ago, when Dr. Peterson told her she could die.

"Jules?" she said when a man answered.

"The one and only."

He was a kind man, an honest man, and when he'd promised to help her in any way he could, Leah had taken him at his word. "It's Leah Jordan. I'm sorry to call so late, but—"

"It's only eight thirty," he said, chuckling. "What can I do for you?"

"I—I need to talk with you. As soon as possible."

She read the lengthy pause to mean he was likely considering possible reasons for the urgency in her voice. But only one reason mattered.

"How about if I stop by at lunchtime tomorrow with the paperwork? All we need is your signature on a couple of documents, and everything's ready."

"Everything?"

"Well, there's one that isn't quite complete, but you can't sign that one."

"And I'm working on that."

"Any luck?"

Laughing softly, she whispered, "Well, there are a few signs and symptoms that it'll be a success. Now, if I can just keep it together a few more weeks—"

She heard a woman's quiet voice in the background. "Who is it, Jules?"

The lawyer must have put his hand over the mouthpiece, because his reply was muffled: "Leah Jordan," was his whispered reply.

"Oh, that poor young woman!" said his wife. "Tell her she's in our prayers."

"Melissa sends her love and prayers," Jules told Leah.

"Thank her for me, won't you? I can use all the help I can get."

Death is a funny thing, Leah thought during the uncomfortable pause. *We all know we can't escape it, and yet it terrifies us, even when it's not our own death we're facing.* "Hang in there, Leah, we'll get you through this. I promise."

"See you tomorrow, then," she said around the lump in her throat.

She put the phone back on the nightstand and collapsed onto her pillows. Never before had Leah felt she could relate on a personal level with Christ's life. Even when He walked the earth as a man, He'd been so pure, so perfect.

But one incident stood out in Leah's mind, when He'd behaved more like a human than at any other. . .

. . .at Gethsemane.

Afraid, sorrowful, anguished by the knowledge that He would be betrayed, Jesus left His disciples so that He could pray. And falling on His face, He called to the heavens: "O my Father," He'd said, "if it be possible, let this cup pass from me: nevertheless not as I will, but as thou wilt." He'd said it three times that night, alone in the garden. And yet, though His plea was hopeful and heartfelt, He was not spared.

He could not be spared, for He was the Savior! His blood, shed at Calvary, had been a requirement, to cleanse the sins of all men, for all time. It had been the supreme sacrifice, the most glorious of loves—dying, so that others might live. Humbled by such devotion, Leah gave thanks, as she did every morning and every night.

But she was no one special. Her only accomplishment in life had been Fiona. *What possible good can come of my death?* she'd demanded time and again.

The thought had forced her to seek the Father's forgiveness, time and again, too, for even asking the question. It wasn't for her to second-guess God's plan, after all. Though for the life of her, Leah didn't know how her death was part of His plan.

She'd asked all the typical things: *Why me? Why now?* She didn't know why cancer had invaded her body, eating away at her like a ravenous beast. And it wasn't likely she'd ever know any of those things. At least, not while she walked the earth.

But Leah knew this: the Lord loved her, and if He chose to take her home now, she would not fight it.

Oh, she'd continue asking the questions and crying for answers, to be sure! And she'd keep right on praying for a miracle. Mostly, though, she'd stick to the appeal that brought her the most peace:

"Father in Heaven, give me the strength to endure, uncomplainingly, whatever awaits me."

She turned out the light and rolled onto her side. The pillowcase was damp with her tears. But Leah didn't mind. She looked at it as proof she was still alive enough to shed them.

"I'm not afraid to die, Lord," she whispered, "but I am afraid to leave Fiona without loving parents." She paused, chewing her knuckle until the pain lessened enough to allow her to continue. "Thank You, Jesus, for helping me devise a way to protect her."

She closed her eyes and held her breath to forestall another wave of pain. "I'm tired, Lord. So tired of fighting, of pretending it isn't so bad. Bless me with strength and energy, at least until—"

The room was dark and, except for the sound of her own ragged breathing, quiet. And yet, from deep in her memory, she heard the lovely notes of the old hymn. Leah sang the first line softly, reciting the second in her mind.

She was asleep before she could intone her favorite part, but its echo carried her toward peaceful slumber, nonetheless: "I will cling to the old rugged cross, and exchange it someday for a crown. . . ."

❧

"Riley will be a little late," Jade told the doctor as he stepped into the foyer. "He had an emergency at the clinic."

"Emergency?" He put his medical bag near the door. "What kind of emergency?"

Jade ignored his scoffing, sarcastic tone. "Riley was getting ready to leave when he saw a little boy crossing the parking lot. He was carrying a small dog wrapped in a blanket. Seems the pup had been run over by a car. There isn't much hope, Riley says, but he had to try, for the boy's sake."

Peterson tucked in one corner of his mouth. "Okay, so he has a heart, after all."

"You'd be surprised just how big it is," Jade said, leading him into the kitchen. She poured him a glass of iced tea.

He thanked her and sat at the table. "So tell me, Jade, what are your plans for the Fourth of July?"

"I'm making turkey burgers and chicken hot dogs, served with boiled potatoes. I figure if I decorate with red, white, and blue, no one will notice there's no cole slaw or baked beans."

"Planning to see the fireworks?"

She sat across from him, a glass of tea in her hands. "Yes," she nodded excitedly, "the neighbors say you can see them from the backyard. I'm going to pad Leah's patio chaise lounge with blankets, and Riley's going to carry her to—"

"Riley," Peterson interrupted, "our hero."

Jade raised one eyebrow. "Can I ask you a personal question?"

He shrugged and wrapped both big hands around his tumbler. "I guess."

"Why don't you like him?"

Peterson told her the story of how he'd walked in on his ex-fiancée, lip-to-lip with Riley.

Jade waved it away. "That isn't why you dislike him."

It was Peterson's turn to raise a brow. "Oh, really."

"You know as well as I do that Riley didn't know she was your fiancée." She hesitated, then added, "Don't you?"

"Yeah. I guess I do," was his response.

"Then what's the real reason you look as though you'd just sniffed a rotten egg when he walks into a room?"

Chuckling, Peterson shook his head. He stared into his glass, poked an ice cube with a beefy fingertip. "Sometimes things don't have easy answers, Jade." Only then did he meet her eyes.

"Easy answers? Are you talking about us, Ron?"

"Maybe."

"Sometimes the problems of two people don't amount to a hill of beans in this crazy world."

"Huh?"

"Casablanca?" She paused. "The point is, there are bigger problems than your hurt feelings."

He nodded.

Jade rested her chin on a fist. "They say curiosity killed the cat."

"And they say cats and women have a lot in common," he countered, smiling.

"Far as I know," she said, folding both hands on the table, "I've only taken one chance in my whole life. Way I see it, I have eight lives left."

Laughing softly, Peterson wrapped both big hands around her slender wrists. "You're a piece of work, Jade Nelson."

"Hmmm," she said, smiling, "something tells me I'm not going to risk a life today."

He made a "you got it" face and took a sip of his tea.

"So what are your plans for the Fourth, Doc?"

"I haven't any to speak of. I have an open invitation to several friends' cookouts."

"Well, good for you! But don't you have any family in town?"

"No family period."

"My folks used to live in here in Ellicott City," Jade said, "but they moved to Colorado when my dad retired."

"Not Florida?"

"Nope. They went out west for their anniversary several years ago and fell in love with the place."

"So being different runs in the family, eh?"

Jade's brows drew together in confusion. "Different?"

"You're hardly what I'd call typical. Not in any way, shape, or form."

"Is that so?"

"I'll say. Your approach to nursing would drive most docs nuts. You've questioned everything I've done—and some things I haven't," he said, counting on his fingers. "You refuse to accept the inevitability of Leah's future, and—"

"I don't refuse to accept it, Ron. But more than anything, Leah needs hope.

And I can't give her that unless I have it myself."

"You mean, a miracle?"

"Sure. Why not?"

"Because there's no such thing, that's why not."

Jade shook her head. "If you really believe that, then I feel sorry for you."

"Sorry? For me?" He met her eyes. "You're not the one who's dying."

"We're all dying, Ron. If we're lucky, we'll be old and gray and go in our sleep. But some of us get cancer, some of us have heart attacks." She paused, then gave the tabletop one soft slap. "And some of us die long before our souls leave our bodies, of fear, and lack of faith."

"I have faith," the doc said. "Plenty of it."

"In science. So you said."

"What's wrong with that? It's trustworthy. It's predictable. It's—"

"It's safe," she finished for him, "and doesn't require belief in the impossible."

He looked into her eyes for a long time before saying, "Maybe you've got a point."

She grinned. "Maybe?"

And so did he. "My grandfather on my mother's side was a born and bred Texas cowboy; he had a saying for folks like you."

"Folks like me?"

"People who dig at a thing till they unearth the answers they're looking for."

"Bullheaded?" she guessed.

Peterson chuckled. "He would have said you're like a puppy to the root."

"Hmmm," she said again. "It's sure a lot nicer than being called stubborn."

He took another swallow of tea.

"Why don't you join us tomorrow?"

"For turkey burgers and chicken dogs?"

"And vanilla pudding pie and fireworks."

"Fireworks, eh?" He chuckled. "Maybe sparks will fly."

She raised one brow. "Don't get your hopes up."

"Touché," he said, grinning.

"Now then, why don't you tell me what you don't like about Riley?"

"I declare."

"Puppy to the root?"

"Exactly."

"Want a refill on that tea?" she asked, standing.

He shoved the glass nearer. "Sure."

"There's what I like," Jade said, winking, "a man of few words."

"Well, I'm not going to tell you what I like," Peterson countered.

She dropped three fresh ice cubes into his glass. "Why not?"

"Wouldn't be professional. At least, not right now."

Chapter 5

I tell you, Leah, he's in love with Jade!"

"Don't be silly, Riley. Ron is completely—"

"Professional? I hope that isn't what you were going to say, 'cause doctors have been falling for nurses—and the other way around—for centuries. I don't know what it is. Maybe all those starched white uniforms are a turn-on."

Leah smiled weakly. "Well, even if you're right, and Ron does feel something for Jade, there's no reason to believe she feels the same way."

"You didn't see what I saw," he ground out. His voice deepened and so did his sarcasm. "They were sitting in the kitchen, holding hands and making goo-goo eyes at each other." He shook his head and threw both hands into the air. "She invited him to our July Fourth celebration, for goodness' sake!"

"Maybe Jade knows something we don't know."

"Like what?"

"That Ron is lonesome?"

"Don't make me laugh."

Leah smiled. "I don't think David Letterman could make you laugh right now!" She sighed. "You're jealous."

"Jealous?" He scowled. "Now who's being silly?"

"Go ahead, admit it. You're in love with Jade, and the very idea of another man being interested in her is making you crazy."

In love with Jade.

He'd never put it quite that way before. And yet—

For as long as he could remember, Leah had been reciting clichés. The more commonplace they were, the better she liked them. In love with Jade, eh? One of her favorite clichés fit this situation perfectly: *You've hit the old nail on the head this time, Leah.*

But admitting that he loved her only served to remind him that any thoughts of romance now were out of the question. "I just don't want him taking advantage of her. She's vulnerable right now, what with Hank breaking off the engagement and—"

"Whoa, there big fella," Leah interrupted. "Where'd you get a nutty idea like that?"

"What? About the breakup, you mean?"

She nodded.

His brows drew together in a puzzled frown. "From Jade. Where else? She seems so sad and disappointed when she talks about leaving California. I just naturally figured it was because he'd ended the relationship."

"Hank would have been more than happy to keep Jade on a string forever. In my opinion, Hank wanted a mother more than he wanted a wife. If she told me once, she told me a hundred times how she saw to it he ate smart and exercised, got plenty of sleep, and rested up after a long, hard day."

Riley swallowed. "I didn't know they were, um, living together."

"They weren't." She leaned forward in her wheelchair. "Oh, my goodness, you thought they were, didn't you?" Clucking her tongue, Leah said, "Riley, I'm surprised at you. She was born and bred a good Christian girl. She would never—"

"I thought I knew her, but she was living in an L.A. suburb, don't forget. And besides, we haven't exactly been close all these years. People change."

She gave an exasperated sigh. "Don't I know it!" Frowning, she shook her head. "Wait. I retract that. Granted, you two haven't been in much contact, but you have so been close." Leah pressed a palm to her chest. "You've kept her right here, and that's where she kept you, too. People can't get much closer than that."

"You look tired, Leah. I'm so sorry."

"For what, sweetie?"

"For bothering you with my pathetic concerns." He stood, started picking her up from the chair, intent upon putting her back to bed. "Now, let's get you—"

"Stop it, Riley."

Her angry tone surprised him. "Stop what? You don't want to go to bed?"

"As a matter of fact, I do. But that isn't what I'm talking about."

Gently, he positioned her in the center of the mattress, then pulled the covers up over her knees. "You'll have to forgive me, Leah, but I'm just a thickheaded man, and I don't have a clue what you're talking about."

"Riley, drop the 'thickheaded' routine. What I'm talking about—" She inhaled sharply, closed her eyes, clamped her lips together.

Riley wrapped her in his arms. "What? Is the pain worse? Can I get you something? What can I do?"

"Ooo ammm ett eem oh, orr arrtrrs," she mumbled into his shoulder.

He loosened his hold. "What's that?"

"You can let me go, for starters," she translated. Grinning mischievously, she added, "Wouldn't it be ironic if you smothered me before the cancer could kill me!"

Riley winced. "Leah, that's not funny."

"It left me breathless," she said, still grinning. "I'm fine," she assured, patting his hand. "Really. But this is what I'm talking about, actually. I know it's getting harder and harder to act as if I weren't sick, but you have to try. Pampering and protecting me won't help a bit. In fact, it'll hurt more than it'll help, because I need to feel like I'm still a whole human being, who can conduct normal conversations with my friends, who's able to give advice, and—"

"And take it?"

She gazed deep into his eyes, so deep that Riley was tempted to squint, for it felt as though she were reading his soul.

"And take it," she conceded.

"All right then," he said, dropping a kiss onto her forehead, "here's some friendly advice: Get some sleep so you'll have enough energy to sit at the table with us for a change. Jade will have supper on in an hour or so."

She grinned crookedly. "Keep that up and I'm going to get the idea you guys miss me."

"We do." *We will*, he added silently.

✣

She waited for him to close the door before sliding the big envelope from her nightstand drawer. Earlier, she'd barely finished signing on the dotted lines when they heard footsteps coming down the hall this afternoon. "Put it in there," she'd whispered, pointing at the narrow drawer. "I don't want them to see this yet."

When Jade returned from her quick trip to the grocery store, she seemed surprised that Leah had a male visitor. "I don't believe we've been introduced," she'd said, extending her hand.

"Just call me Jules," he'd said. "I'm a friend of Leah's."

"How did you get in?"

"Leah told me the back door would be unlatched."

"But I'm sure I locked it when I left."

"And I unlocked it," Leah had said. If her cross tone had hurt Jade's feelings, she would have felt bad about that, but what else could she have done? Jade and Riley had to be kept in the dark until everything was set to go, or nothing would turn out as she wanted it to.

With any luck, Leah would have a few minutes of undisturbed privacy now to go over the paperwork.

Rifling through the envelope, she scanned the deed to her house. Correction. The deed to Jade and Riley's house, she thought, grinning. The title to her car now bore their names, as did her savings and checking accounts. When her husband John died, Leah had invested the insurance money, and her stock portfolio was now registered to Riley and Jade. The Certificate of Adoption, in her opinion, was the most important piece of paper in the file, for it would guarantee her innocent little girl had a chance at a stable, loving family, with parents who shared the same last name.

Of course none of it would be possible unless Jade and Riley signed the paper she held now.

Footsteps alerted her that Jade was on her way into the bedroom. Leah would recognize the sound of that surefooted, energetic walk anywhere.

Hurriedly, she stuffed the documents back into the file and slid the file back into the envelope. There wasn't time to put the folder back into the drawer so she tucked it under the covers instead.

First, there came the familiar soft knock, followed by Jade's pretty face peeking between the door and its frame. "Why do you look like the cat who swallowed the canary?" Jade wanted to know.

"Because I just woke up from the nicest dream," she admitted. "I made a wish some time ago, and it's about to come true, you see."

"A wish?" Jade plumped the pillows, then sat in the chair beside the bed. "What kind of wish?"

"A wedding wish."

Giggling, Jade rolled her eyes. "A wedding wish! Who's the lucky couple? Anyone I know?"

"My stomach has been growling for half an hour," she said, hoping to change the subject. "When's supper?"

Jade eyed her suspiciously. "Right now, if you think you're up to it."

"You know how I have good days and bad days?"

Jade nodded.

"Well, this is a pretty good day, all things considered."

"I'm glad." She gave Leah a sideways hug. "Want me to get Riley? Have him help you to the kitchen?"

"That'd be nice."

The minute Jade was out of sight, Leah buried the file under the stack of magazines and the Jordan family Bible. She'd barely gotten the drawer shut when Riley strode into the room.

"Ready to eat?" he asked, rubbing his hands together.

"Ready."

He slid one arm under her knees, wrapped the other around her waist, and lifted her gently from the mattress. "You'll let me know if I hurt you."

Leah nodded. But since everything hurt these days, she saw no point in singling out any particular activity. Especially one that involved joining the family again.

The pain was almost constant now, and to hide it from Jade and Riley, and especially Fiona, Leah had been spending more and more time in her room. Jade seemed to recognize the signs, but Leah had continued to deny her discomfort. Only Ron knew the truth for sure, and he'd promised not to tell. She had to find a way to conceal it in the coming weeks, because the sands were quickly sifting to the bottom of her hourglass. As her grandma used to say, "You've gotta make hay while the sun shines."

She would tell them everything tomorrow, right after the fireworks.

Because something told her the sun wasn't going to be shining on her much longer.

Jade was proud of them, and as they stacked paper plates and cups to carry them inside, she told them so.

"Aw, shucks, Ms. Nelson," Peterson said, "you're gonna make me blush."

The comment prompted a laugh from Riley, and unless he'd been taking acting lessons lately, it seemed genuine.

"I hope she's strong enough to stay out there till dark," Jade said. "It seems she gets more pale by the minute."

Riley spun the trash bag he'd filled, secured it with a twist of the tie. "Which is exactly why we have to let her stay out there. What do you say, Doc?"

"Much as I hate to agree with anything that came out of your mouth," Peterson said, forcing a grin, "I think you're right."

"Fiona is awfully cranky today; do you think she knows?"

"Jade, honey," Riley said, kissing her cheek, "everybody is cranky in this humidity. I've done a lot of reading on the subject, and from everything I've seen, Fiona's too young to understand what's going on."

"Riley's right," Peterson said. "I've seen this dozens of times. Kids under the age of three have no preconceived notions of life and death, so they accept things at face value."

"Well, mama pin a rose on the experts." Jade put the last of the silverware and glasses into the dishwasher and turned it on. "I'll leave you two to read up on what she's feeling; I think I'll ask her myself." She paused, then added, "She knows that she loves her mother."

"What's goin' on in there?" came a quiet voice from the other side of the screen door.

Despite the hum of the refrigerator and the churn of the dishwasher, the room seemed cloaked in deafening silence.

"Where's Fiona?" Jade asked to change the subject.

"On the swing set with Riley's sister-in-law."

Peterson pocketed both hands. "She's something with the little guys, isn't she? I told her she ought to have a whole passel of young'uns."

"The weatherman says we're in for a humdinger of a storm tonight." Riley ran both hands through his hair. "I hope it holds off till after the fireworks."

"For goodness' sake, I wish the three of you would stop looking so guilty." Leah aimed a maternal digit at Riley. "Remember what I told you."

He nodded. "Yeah."

"What did she tell you?" Jade asked.

"That we have to treat her as if she's healthy as a horse. No pampering, no trying to protect her from the truth."

"That's right. Now either get back out here," Leah instructed, "or let me in. I miss you!"

It seemed to take an eternity for Riley and Jade to tuck Fiona in. Leah impatiently drummed her fingers on the mattress, stopping only to rearrange the file folder on her lap. They'd always paid her a brief visit after putting her little girl to bed, but Leah had never specifically invited it before. If she didn't know better, she'd say they knew, somehow, what she was plotting, and were deliberately stalling.

You should have rehearsed it, she thought. *At the very least, you should have written down what you want to say.*

She took a deep breath and let it out slowly. The matter was entirely in God's hands, and the success or failure of her plan depended upon the words He called her to speak.

Jade's familiar soft knock sounded on the door, startling Leah from her reverie. Suddenly, she found herself wishing they had been stalling—and that they'd done a better job of it.

Be with me, Jesus, she prayed.

"So what's up?" Riley asked, pulling a chair near the bed.

"The ceiling? The sky? The price of gasoline?" Leah joked.

"Very funny," Jade said, sitting cross-legged at the end of the bed. "You've been acting funny all day. What's up?"

"Yeah. Hilarious," Riley agreed, stifling a yawn. "Now quit stonewalling. It's late, and you need your sleep."

Leah took another deep breath, then slid the folder from its envelope. "I have a few things here that I'd like you to look over."

"Legal documents?" Riley asked, nodding toward the stack.

"Legal documents." Leah cleared her throat. "I've given the matter a lot of thought and prayer, and I've come to the conclusion that this will be best for all four of us."

"All four of us?"

"You, Riley, Fiona, and me." She handed Riley the deed and handed Jade the Certificate of Adoption. "But for any of this to work, I need both your signatures, on everything."

"Our signatures? On everything?"

Leah stuck a finger in her ear and wiggled it. "Is there an echo in the room, or have I lost my mind?"

"I'm sorry," Jade said. "It's just—"

"Surely you didn't expect me to let Fiona end up in foster care. You had to know one of you would get custody."

Jade and Riley continued to fidget with the papers she'd handed them.

"Really, now. Who did you think I'd leave her with? You two are my only family."

Riley flipped the first page of the deed. "Leah—"

"Yes, sweetie?"

"It says here you're leaving your house to us."

"That's right." She grinned. "I don't want my little girl living with homeless people."

"But," Riley put in, "I already have a house."

Leah lifted her chin and assumed a smug demeanor. "You can never be too thin or too rich," she said, quoting the women's magazines, "and," she added, her grin growing, "you can never have too many houses."

She took one look at their shocked expressions and said, "Don't look so shell-shocked. What I'm suggesting isn't so strange. There was a time when arranged marriages were as common as dirt. Back then, only the fella got a dowry; in this case, you're both getting one! You can invest the money for your children's education."

Jade gasped involuntarily. "Our. . .our children?"

Riley showed her the first page of the deed. "She's serious," he said, pointing.

" 'Mr. and Mrs. Riley Steele,' " Jade read aloud. Eyes wide and mouth agape, she stared at Leah.

"No, it isn't a mistake. You read correctly." Leah gave an affirmative nod of her head. "I may be near the end of my life, but I want to be part of giving you two a new beginning. You'll get the house and everything in it—once you're man and wife."

Jade wanted to look at Riley, to see if he was having as much trouble with this as she was. But she couldn't seem to tear her eyes away from the title line.

"There's an organization," Leah said, commanding their attention. "I don't remember the name of it, but I know it exists expressly to grant dying children one last wish."

Jade covered her eyes with one hand. "Dear, God. . ." she prayed.

Riley merely shook his head.

"Oh, stop feeling sorry for yourselves," Leah scolded. "I know this makes you uncomfortable, but it had to be done. We all know that." She smoothed the top sheet and lifted her chin. "Now, listen to me, kids, I'm no child, but I have a last wish."

Riley put the deed back on the bed, sandwiched her hands between his own. "But I thought you said the organization was for—"

"They're not going to grant my last wish, you are."

"We are?" Jade echoed.

"How?" Riley asked.

She stared him straight in the eye, then zeroed in on Jade. "I want to schedule a wedding."

Jade swallowed. "For. . .for Riley and me, you mean?"

"Exactly." The corners of her mouth turned up in a trembly little smile. "I just so happen to have a calendar here."

She slid a pocket-sized date book from the folder, then Jade and Riley met one another's eyes. "But Leah," Jade said, "we're not—"

"Yes, you are," she said emphatically.

"You don't even know what I was going to say."

"Whatever it was," Leah said with a wave of her hand, "I can explain it away."

She signaled them closer, then held tight to each of their hands. "Look, you guys are all I've got. More importantly, you're all Fiona has." Blinking away tears that had pooled in her lashless eyes, she summoned a halfhearted grin. "Tell you what, don't give me an answer right now. Go out there and talk it over some. Pray about it." She winked. "And see if you don't come to the same conclusions I did."

Leah gathered up her legal documentation and shooed them away. "Now scram. It's been a long day, and I need a nap."

They got up and moved woodenly toward the door.

"Go on. And don't come back till you can tell me you're getting married." She turned off the light and put her back to them. "And close the door behind you, please?"

Riley and Jade sat across from one another at the kitchen table, silent and frowning, shaking their heads.

"I kind of expected her to ask one of us to adopt Fiona," Jade said at last, "but I never dreamed she'd do anything like this."

"Me, either." He got up and filled the teapot with water. "I don't know why, but I'm in the mood for something hot." ·

Jade nodded. "Warm things are comforting at a time like this."

"I guess."

"She's sure stirred up a tempest this time, hasn't she?"

He turned on the flame under the kettle. "You can say that again."

But aside from that, they didn't seem to know what more to say about Leah's shocking proposal.

"Here's a question for you." Riley looked left and right, lowered his voice and scooted his chair nearer the table. "Just between you and me, if she hadn't been cooking up this scheme all these weeks, which one of us do you suppose she'd have wanted to adopt Fiona?"

Jade sighed. "It was a toss-up, really. Sometimes I was positive she'd choose you, because you're so playful, and Fiona simply adores you. And sometimes I believed it'd be me, since I'm a nurse, and a woman, and—" She matched his grin, dimple for dimple. "Okay, out with it. Who did you think she'd pick?"

He feigned a look of arrogant certainty. "Me, of course."

They shared a brief round of hearty laughter, which came to an abrupt end when the teapot whistled.

Jade dropped tea bags and sugar cubes into two oversized mugs. "Hmmm," she said, pouring water into each.

" 'Hmmm' what?"

"Never thought about it before, but we have a lot in common with these herbs."

Chuckling humorlessly, Riley nodded. "What? We suit each other to a tea?"

"I was thinking more along the lines that we're in hot water right about now." Grinning, she put the mugs on the table. "What are we going to do, Riley?" she asked, grabbing his hands.

He brought hers to his lips, kissing the knuckles. "I don't see how we can refuse her, kiddo."

Heart hammering, Jade's eyes widened. She'd dreamed of becoming his wife so many times, she'd lost count. But not this way. A dying woman's wish was compelling, but hardly romantic!

Riley turned her loose and wrapped his hands around his mug. "Well, we have a couple of things going for us, right from the start."

"Like what?"

"Well, we're best buddies. We already know each others' quirks and faults, so—"

"What quirks?" she asked, grinning. "Everyone knows I have no faults."

"Everyone but me."

His hands, still warm from the hot mug, covered hers like a comforting blanket.

"I know that you're scared of thunderstorms," he began, "and that you're terrified of anything that stings. You hate lima beans, and after you sweep the floor, you always leave a pile of crumbs in the corner behind the broom."

She hid a blush behind one hand. "Only until I get around to finding the dustpan."

"No need to defend yourself to me, Jade." He tightened his hold on her hand. "I'm not complaining. I love everything about you." He winked. "Even the way you insist that the toilet paper absolutely must roll over the top."

"That's the right way to do it!" she teased.

"Unless you prefer it the other way."

"Well," she countered, "what about the way you make a huge mess of the Sunday paper, and flip through the channels at breakneck speed? And the way you never push in a chair when you leave the table?"

"You've got me dead to rights, there," he admitted, "and you've just proven my point."

Jade wrinkled her nose. "Ah, I'm afraid I've forgotten the point."

"We won't annoy one another while we get used to all that stuff."

She rolled her eyes. "What an annoying thing to say!"

Again, they shared a moment of quiet laughter.

"Riley?"

"Hmmm."

"Let's pray on it."

"Good idea." He took her hands as they bowed their heads and squinted. Two, perhaps three seconds passed before he said, "Amen."

"Amen! You mean that's it? Riley, you barely spent a—"

"We were talking to The Almighty. How much time do you think He needs?"

After taking one look at her serious expression, he said, "All right. Let's try this again. Lord," he began, "give us a sign, if this isn't Your will."

Jade waited a moment, then opened one eye. "That's it?"

He shrugged one shoulder. "What more is there to say?"

Smiling, she shrugged, too. "You make a good point."

"I'd say God just answered our prayer."

"He did?"

Riley nodded. "I asked for a sign, didn't I?"

"Yeah, so?"

"So when I told you why I didn't say a long, drawn-out prayer, you agreed with my reason."

"Okay."

"We're gonna get along great, Jade," he said, grinning, "as long as you continue being so agreeable."

Jade rolled her eyes. Outwardly, she went along with his little joke. But inside, where her heartbeat had doubled and her pulse was pounding, Jade acknowledged the comfortable compatibility that had always been part and parcel of their relationship.

"Seriously," Riley said, interrupting her thoughts, "it's sure gonna be nice, knowing you'll be with Fiona while I'm at the clinic."

"And that you'll be with her when I'm at the hospital."

He raised both eyebrows. "You're going to continue working after—?"

"After we're married?" she finished.

Riley nodded. "Yeah. After that."

"Would you mind?"

"No. Not if it's what you want to do. I'd never stand in the way of your happiness."

"Actually, if it's all the same to you, I'd rather stay home. For awhile, at least. I think it'll take us all time to adjust. Fiona, especially. It's important to build a firm foundation for her, a stable routine." She shrugged. "Maybe in a year or so, I'll go back, but for now—"

Smiling and nodding, he gave her hand an affectionate squeeze. "I was hoping you'd say that."

"Really? Why?"

"Like I said. It's gonna be nice, knowing you'll be here, waiting for me."

Waiting for him?

Jade read the warm light emanating from his dark eyes, the soft smile that turned up the corners of his mouth. If she didn't know better, she might have said they were signs that he loved her. But Riley hadn't said it. Hadn't so much as hinted at it. He was doing this for Leah and Fiona. Because he had always loved them both so deeply.

He was right, after all; they had half the battle licked even before they exchanged I do's. They'd gotten along well as kids, had been getting along well since her homecoming. That should be enough.

So why wasn't it?

Aw, who knows? Jade wondered. *Maybe we'll be like one of those mail order marriages that started out as a matter of convenience, and blossomed over the years into a full-blown love affair!* She sighed wistfully. *A girl can dream*, she added.

"When do you think we should do it?"

"Yesterday, if Leah has her way," Jade kidded.

"She's probably got a preacher and a church all lined up."

She bobbed her head back and forth, emulating an empty-headed California surfer girl. "Do you suppose she sees me in a long, flowing gown? Or a simple two-piece suit?"

He looked completely serious when he said, "Oh, a gown, by all means." His expression turned sour when he added, "I wouldn't be the least bit surprised if she's already rented me a monkey suit, too." He groaned. "But I draw the line at a top hat and tails. There's only so much a guy will do for a pal, y'know."

"Well, if you can put your foot down, so can I: I will not drag a fussy old train behind me down the aisle."

A small grin slanted his mustache. "This is weird."

"What is? All this wedding talk?"

"Yeah." He nodded. "Weird," he said again. "But you know something? I feel good about this, like it's the right thing to do. And I really think we can make a go of it."

Jade's heart did a little flip. He looked genuinely happy, saying that. So happy that she couldn't help but wonder yet again if maybe he could fall in love with her—in time.

She'd be a good wife to him, as good a wife as she knew how to be. Which wouldn't be hard, because Riley had always been easy to please. "Three squares and clean sheets," he used to tease, "that's all I want outta life." Well, she'd give him that, and so much more. She'd see to it his lab coats were always bright white. He hated floral-scented soaps—she wouldn't buy them, ever—and chairs with ruffles, so they'd have none in their home.

Their home.

The picture made her breathe a soft, wistful sigh.

Though male pride forbade him from admitting it, Jade had always known that he enjoyed flowers. "Stinky posies," he'd called them to hide his appreciation.

But she remembered the way he'd always lingered in her mother's rose garden, and the way he drove a little more slowly up the streets in springtime, when the cherry blossoms were in bloom. Jade intended to plant petunias and marigolds and zinnias—so many he'd go color-blind looking at the blooms!

His favorite meal was lasagna with garlic bread and Caesar salad; she'd fix it every year on his birthday, along with his favorite dessert, fudge-frosted brownies. She'd be sure to keep plenty of milk on hand, because he drank a gallon a day, it seemed, and a steady supply of peanut butter, because—

"So what do you say?" he asked, standing. And holding out his hand, Riley added, "Should we see if Leah is still awake?"

Nodding, she put her hand into his and hoped he wouldn't feel it trembling. "If this news doesn't give her a peaceful night's sleep, nothing will."

Chapter 6

Just as they'd expected, Leah had indeed lined up a preacher. But, much to their amazement, she'd arranged to hold the ceremony in the backyard rather than a church.

"Look at you," Leah remarked when she rolled into Jade's room, "you're gorgeous!"

Jade stood in front of the mirror, hands clasped under her chin. "You think so?" she asked, adjusting the mesh veil that covered her face.

"Yup. I think so." She gave an approving nod. "Something told me you'd prefer a simple suit to a frilly dress. I can see I was right."

Tugging at the hem of the fitted white jacket, Jade grinned at her reflection. "It's beautiful. I don't know how to thank you, Leah."

"Thank me!" Laughing, she shook her head. "I should be thanking you, and Riley, too, of course, for going through with this. You don't know how happy you've made me."

Down on one knee, she wrapped her arms around Leah's shoulders. "Hush. You'll wear yourself out, and we have quite a day ahead of us, thanks to you."

"Boy. Don't I know it."

Standing, Jade smoothed the slim skirt. "What I want to know is, where did you find time to arrange all this?" She pointed toward the backyard, where giant, white paper bells and huge white satin bows decorated the fence posts, the gazebo, and deck rails. She'd had the grape arbor painted white, accenting the red mini rose vine that clung to its slats. Three dozen white folding chairs stood in straight rows alongside the wide, white cloth path that split the yard in two, and white pillars flanked the arbor, the bright green fronds of a potted fern dangling down from each.

"It was all taken care of, even before you came home."

"But how did you know we'd agree to this?"

"Because I had God's assurance." Leah snickered behind a white-gloved hand.

"God's assurance?"

"You don't think I'd do all this on a whim, do you?"

Jade took another look at the beautiful yard. "No, I suppose that would have been taking an awful chance."

"Riley's gonna flip when he sees you."

"I doubt that."

"And wait till you see him. I tell you what—not every man looks good in a tux, but that one—" Leah shook her head. "Mmm-mmm-mmm."

She'd seen him in a suit before and had thought he was quite striking; Jade could only imagine how much more handsome he'd be in a tuxedo.

"Stop worrying, sweetie."

She thought she'd been doing a good job of hiding her anxiety. "You know me too well," Jade said, smiling fondly.

"Which is precisely why I know you'll be fine."

"I'll take good care of her, Leah. I promise."

"Fiona? Course you will! I'm talking about Riley. Things are going to be swell. You'll see."

Jade only sighed.

"He loves you, you know."

An nervous giggle popped from her lips.

" 'He who laughs last,' " Leah quoted, shaking a finger of warning in the air. "Mark my words, before you know it, you're going to have to admit that I'm right!"

Another sigh.

"The flowers ought to be here by now. You want me to roll on into the kitchen and check on' em?"

"No, there's plenty of time for that. Just sit here and talk with me for a minute." Jade sighed. "Next time we have a chat, I'll be a married woman!"

" 'The more things change,' " Leah said, " 'the more they stay the same.' "

"Have I told you how pretty you look today?"

"You think?" Leah struck a model's pose in the chair, tilting her head to emphasize the pink silk scarf she'd tied around what used to be her hair. False eyelashes and drawn on brows gave her back a semblance, at least, of her former natural beauty. "I'm going for the gaunt look."

Jade winced.

"Aw, sweetie, I'm sorry. My sense of humor can be maudlin at times; I didn't mean to spoil your day."

Squaring her shoulders, Jade forced a grin. "That's a very pretty dress."

"Oh, this old rag," she said, smoothing the flowing skirt. "I've had it for ages." Giggling, Leah added, "I'm surprised it fit." She patted her flat tummy. "Middle-aged spread, y'know?"

The doorbell rang for the twentieth time, announcing the arrival of yet another guest. There would be fifty in attendance, counting Jade's family, and Riley's, and Leah's friends from church.

"I saw Pastor Jones out back," Jade said, glancing at the clock. "I guess it's time we went outside."

❧

The moment Jade took her place on the lawn, Riley's palms began to perspire.

His best man gave him a playful elbow jab to the ribs. "Keep that ticker of yours quiet, will ya," Pete teased, "before somebody dials nine-one-one."

Grinning, Riley rolled his eyes. "Put a lid on it." Of course his brother couldn't really hear his heart beating—could he?

Riley took a deep, calming breath, just in case.

Even from the distance between the deck, where she stood, and the makeshift altar, and despite the gauzy veil that covered her face, he could see that she'd fixed her blue-eyed gaze on him.

He'd heard women described as dazzling. Pretty. Handsome, even. The only word Riley could come up with to describe Jade had been one worn thin by overuse. Still, it was the only word that would do: Beautiful.

Riley had never been a vain man, so the thought that ran through is mind made him frown. "Do you think I look okay?" he asked his brother through clenched teeth.

"What do you mean?" Pete whispered back.

Annoyed, he snorted, "I mean, do you think she thinks I look all right?"

Shrugging, Pete said, "Sure."

"Sure what?"

Pete leaned back, and grinning, said, "Sure, you look okay."

Riley expelled a grateful sigh. "Thanks."

"Thanks for what?"

Rolling his eyes, Riley said, "Never mind."

And chuckling, Pete elbowed him again. "You're welcome, little brother."

Riley tugged at the sleeves of his tux as the music started—Leah had even seen to that—and he thought his heart might leap out of his chest.

Leah rolled down the aisle, grinning like the Cheshire cat as she scattered rose petals left and right. She parked the wheelchair and turned to watch Jade, who floated toward him like an angel riding a soft white cloud. The satiny sheen of the fabric of her knee length suit reflected sunlight. He blinked. Rubbed his eyes, hoping she was real and not another of the many dreams he'd had over the years.

She was real, all right. More real than any woman he'd known to date. The way she'd described the suit Leah had ordered from a catalog had made it sound attractive enough. But seeing it now, wrapped around. Even Robert Frost couldn't have done the description justice.

The wedding procession ended, and Mr. Nelson left Jade there, alone beside Riley under the arbor. The pastor read from the Good Book and led the guests in heartfelt prayer, then said a blessing on the couple who stood trembling before God. He felt a little sorry for Jade; his fear wasn't visible, but Jade's was apparent by the constant quaking of the roses in her bouquet. As though she could read his thoughts, Jade turned and handed the flowers to Leah.

The pastor's droning voice penetrated his frightened fog. Squaring his shoulders, he blinked. "Riley Steele, do you take this woman, Jade Nelson, to be your lawfully wedded wife?"

He turned to face her. Took her hands in his. "I do," he said softly, staring deep into teary blue eyes that shimmered like a spring-fed lake. Tears? he wondered, frowning slightly. Is the prospect of a lifetime with me that unbearable?

Riley's heart ached. Or is she wishing it was Hank Berger standing here, instead of me? He'd thought about little else last night as he tossed and turned the hours away, because while she'd said on the night she'd arrived that Hank never loved her, never had, Jade never said how she felt about Hank.

But she had come home to stay.

So the tears in her eyes now, they could be tears of joy—couldn't they?

"And do you, Jade Nelson, take this man, Riley Steele, to be your lawfully wedded husband?"

Even through the veil, he saw the long, lush lashes flutter, sending a tear down her cheek. She sank her teeth into her lower lip, then whispered, "I do."

She had hesitated for at most a fraction of a second, but the infinitesimal tick in time was enough to cut him to the quick, for Riley had hoped that secretly, Jade had wanted this marriage every bit as much as he did.

"I now pronounce you man and wife." The pastor turned to Riley and smiled. "You may kiss the bride."

He lifted the filmy fabric that veiled her face and lay it gently atop her hat. She seemed so small, so vulnerable, standing there blinking up at him. Setting aside his own dashed hopes, male instinct made him want to wrap her in a protective embrace and shield her from all harm, from all pain, for a lifetime. He'd tried for years to convince himself he didn't love her—wouldn't love her.

But he did.

Gently, Riley pressed his palms to her cheeks and let his thumbs tilt her face up to receive his kiss. He'd intended it as a light brush of lips, nothing more. But the moment his mouth met hers, Riley's spirit soared, and the gloom that had enveloped him since learning of Leah's illness lifted, as if carried away by angels. "Once I was lost, but now I'm found" had been Leah's favorite line from the song "Amazing Grace." *Ironic*, Riley thought.

A man's voice shouted "Atta boy, Riley!" Another whistled. Everyone else applauded. And the noise shattered the moment. Riley ended the kiss and stood back, his palms still cupping her lovely face. Slowly, her eyes fluttered open and met his. For a moment, he thought he saw love sparkling there amid the green and gray flecks that deepened the blue of her eyes, and his heart pounded harder still.

There was a chance that she loved him already. But even if he'd been mistaken—and what he'd seen in her eyes had been relief that this arranged wedding was over at last—he would do everything in his power to take good care of her.

For the rest of his life.

In the receiving line, Riley's sister-in-law told Jade she had it on good authority that the groom hadn't eaten a proper meal in days. "Is that right?" Jade had asked, one brow high on her forehead.

Later, at the reception, Jade insisted on performing her first official wifely duty, and forced Riley to sit at the picnic table. "Now, you wait right there," she instructed, laughing. "Don't move. I mean it!"

She filled a plate with food prepared by the Ladies Auxiliary, put a polished knife and fork beside it and tucked a napkin into his collar. "If you don't eat every bite," she said, winking, "I'll just have to force-feed you!"

He folded his arms across his chest. "Is that so?"

She inclined her head and grinned. "You think I won't do it?"

Riley glanced around at friends and relatives who'd gathered to wish them well. Meeting her eyes again, he shook his head. "Not a chance."

Jade looked around, too. She'd known most of these people her whole life. There was no reason for the flutter in her stomach, and so she sat down beside him. Never taking her eyes from his, she slowly and deliberately removed her gloves, one lace-covered finger at a time.

Ignoring the lazy heat smoldering in his dark eyes, she lay the gloves carefully on the tabletop, patting them flat and smooth before lifting the fork she'd placed beside his plate. Spearing a slice of ham, she leaned in close and whispered, "Open wide, Riley, and let the yummy food inside."

As though controlled by some benign force, his lips parted. It amazed him that he'd so quickly done as he was told. But he saw the warmth glowing in her blue eyes as she slipped the chunk of meat past his teeth. The glow intensified as he closed his lips around the tines and clamped down, allowing her to withdraw the empty utensil. She pierced a potato next, and this time, her own lips parted as she aimed the food at his open, waiting mouth.

Bite by bite, Jade fed Riley every scrap of food on the plate, stopping occasionally to hold a glass of sparkling water to his lips. She hadn't said a word through the entire meal, and neither had he.

But oh, they'd communicated in those moments.

Unable to stand another minute of it, Riley wrapped his fingers around her delicate wrist, forced her to take the fork from his mouth. He chewed and swallowed, watching as the tip of her pink tongue slid over her lips, mimicking his movements. They were nose to nose when he said through clenched teeth, "For two cents, I'd kiss the livin' daylights out of you, right now."

Emboldened by the intimacy of the meal, she looked away only long enough to open her tiny, white satin purse. Withdrawing two coins, Jade slapped them on the table and, meeting his eyes, said in a mere whisper, "A wedding gift from me to you, Mr. Steele; now why don't you put your money where my mouth is?"

Everything in him warned Riley to stand up. To walk away from the table and pretend to visit with the wedding guests. But she looked so lovely sitting there, curvy torso leaning close as her full, slightly-parted lips beckoned him. What choice did he have but to lean forward himself and press his mouth to hers?

He hadn't expected the silken sigh that escaped her lungs, nor the soft purr that rumbled deep in her chest. Hadn't expected her hands to comb through his hair, then come to rest on his shoulders. Nor was he prepared for the sight of her thick-lashed closed eyes, right there near his, or the way she'd tilted her head back, inviting him to have another taste.

Riley was aware, suddenly, that the atmosphere around them had changed. Grinning, he placed both hands on her shoulders and gently pushed her away. "You don't know how it pains me to do that," he admitted, gazing longingly into her eyes, "but it seems we've got ourselves an audience."

Jade's eyes fluttered open. The gleam of passion quickly became a teasing glimmer as she looked around and took note of the curious onlookers all around them. She stood, gathered her purse and gloves, and bent at the waist, putting them eye-to-eye.

He nodded toward the dessert table. "I sure could go for a big fat slice of cake."

She raised a brow and left him sitting there alone, wide-eyed and gap-jawed.

❧

A smattering of laughter floated around them as the guests who'd gathered disbanded. Jade pretended not to hear it, pretended the flush in her cheeks had been put there by the hot July day, rather than the tantalizing kiss she and Riley had just shared.

She'd never behaved with such wild abandon!

But then, she'd never been Mrs. Riley Steele before.

They'll be calling you the Shameful Mrs. Steele, she told herself, *and you'll deserve it, after that brazen behavior!*

Halfway to the dessert table, she turned and looked over her shoulder, mildly stunned to find Riley still staring after her. Jade didn't know what possessed her to do it, but she held up her hand and sent him a flirty little wave, then added a merry wink and a saucy smile for good measure.

Put that in your pipe and smoke it, she told him as she plopped a thickly-iced slice of wedding cake onto her plate.

❧

When the guests were gone and Fiona and Leah were tucked into bed, Jade and Riley sat on the back deck, staring up at the stars. Still wearing their wedding clothes, both had kicked off their shoes.

"About that little scene at the table," she began, breaking the silence, "I don't know what came over me."

Chuckling under his breath, he said, "Darlin', I enjoyed every lip-smackin' minute of it. Believe me!"

Jade shook her head. "But what must people be thinking? What are they saying about the way I behaved?"

"How did you behave?"

"Like a wanton hussy, right there in front of the preacher and all our friends! We'll be the talk of—"

"I was the envy of every man in the yard," he said, "and I was proud as a peacock to have you paying so much attention to me."

"Really?"

"You betcha. But I have to warn you."

"Of what?"

"Well, if I wasn't sure before, I'm sure now!"

"Sure? Sure of what?"

He clasped both hands behind his head and stared at the star-studded sky. "Nothing. Forget I mentioned it."

Jade sat up, planted both stockinged feet on the deck. "I didn't mean to put you on the spot that way, Riley. I mean—" She stared at the boards beneath her feet. "I mean, the deal was to get married. We never talked about what we'd do about the. . .about—" She took a deep breath. "I'm sorry."

"Jade, there's absolutely nothing to apologize for." He turned slightly to face her. "Honest."

She was crying quietly, and he didn't for the life of him know why. But it wasn't like her to give in to tears without a good reason. Riley remembered that moment of hesitation during the ceremony. Were the tears connected somehow?

He hoped not. Because he wanted to believe that she'd so quickly consented to marry him, not only for Leah and Fiona, but because she loved him. Or, at the very least, that she believed she might love him someday.

Riley wanted to comfort her, to promise her that nothing in life would ever make her cry again. But that was impractical at best.

It had been a long time since a woman had stirred anything in him—since his high school graduation, to be exact—when Jade had given him that delicious kiss of congratulations. Her sassy behavior at the reception had reminded him of that night. Would she have been worried that her actions had embarrassed him if she didn't care, if she didn't love him, or at least, believe she could?

Riley sat beside her on the patio chaise and wrapped her in his arms. She melted against him like butter on a hot biscuit, and it felt right, felt good, having her nestled in the crook of his neck.

It had all happened so fast that neither of them had had a chance to sort it out, to make sense of it. But there was time for that later.

"That was some day, wasn't it?"

Nodding, Jade said, "Mmmm-hmmm."

"Good thing we only have to do something like that once; I don't think I'd survive another wedding."

She laughed softly. "Oh, it wasn't all bad. I got a couple of neat pot holders out of the deal."

Riley harumphed. "No fair. All I got was a chef's hat that's two sizes too big for my head."

Sighing again, she sat up. "I'd better check on Leah."

"I'll come with you. We're in this together from here on out, remember?"

The moon had slipped behind a cloud, leaving just enough light to illuminate her sweet, grateful smile. Oh, how he loved her, and one day soon, he'd have the freedom to admit it.

Somehow, he'd convince her that he'd loved her for years. He didn't know how, but Riley wasn't worried; he had the rest of his life to find a way.

Didn't he?

"Sit with me a minute longer," he suggested.

She snuggled close as a clap of thunder sounded in the distance. "Looks like we're finally gonna get that storm the weatherman promised on the Fourth."

"Think it'll be an all-nighter?"

"I hope so. I love the sound of rain on the roof."

He hugged her closer. "That breeze feels good."

She tilted her face heavenward. "Smells good, too."

Gently, he kissed her. And chuckling, Riley said, "Aren't you supposed to close your eyes when you kiss?"

"Hmmm?"

"Isn't that what you gals say? That it's more romantic that way?"

Jade closed her eyes and puckered up. And stayed that way until he gave her another kiss. Her fingers combed through his hair, and he wondered how in the world he was going to keep his distance until they'd discussed the incidentals of their marriage.

She wrapped her arms around him, pressed her lips to his bearded cheek. Riley's blood ran hot and fast, his pulse pounded. "I've never been kissed that way before," she whispered.

Her admission kindled something in him, fanning the flames already burning in his heart. "Neither have I."

When his lips found hers again, her mouth softened beautifully for him. He felt her desire, like the taut and trembling strings of a violin. And she'd make music with him now, if he asked it of her. *Nothing wrong with that,* Riley thought. *We're married, legally and in the eyes of God.*

But he owed her more than that. Owed her the time and patience to believe in their love. And before that could happen, he had to earn it.

Lightning sliced the sky, brightening her features. If she didn't love him, Jade was certainly a talented actress, Riley thought. He'd never felt so loved.

Surrounded and overwhelmed by the plainness of it, he buried his face in her hair. His eyes were moist with emotion when he said, a soft smile playing at the corners of his mouth, "Oh, Jade."

Her next kiss came at the exact moment as a violent clap of thunder, and Riley couldn't be sure which had caused the furious beating of his heart, nature in the sky, or nature in his arms.

"We'd better get inside," she said, "before we're electrocuted."

Chuckling, he held her at arm's length. "Too late for that," he said under his breath. "I can already feel the electricity."

"What?"

He sighed. "Nothing. I'm a lucky guy, is all."

"Lucky?" she repeated, standing.

"How many men are so blessed?"

"Blessed?"

"Polly want a cracker?" he teased.

Jade held out her hand. "It's starting to rain. Let's go in, now."

"What's the matter, sugar?" he asked, closing the door behind them. "Afraid you'll melt?"

"No," Jade said, smiling. "I'm not that sweet."

They stepped into the hall. "That's a matter of opinion."

"Shhh, Riley; you'll wake them."

"Sorry," he whispered. "I don't mean to behave like a hyperactive brat, but I can't help myself." He did a little jig outside Leah's door. "I'm happy, Jade. Really happy."

She took his hand. "Me, too, Riley. Me, too."

Then, pushing the door open, Jade held a finger over her lips, signaling silence.

"No need to tiptoe," Leah said. "I'm awake."

"How ya doin', kid?" Riley asked first thing.

Leah patted the mattress. "Sit down here, both of you."

Jade perched on the edge of the bed while Riley leaned both palms on the footboard.

"Did you have a good time at the wedding?" Riley wanted to know.

"I. . .I had a. . .terrific time."

"Leah," Jade said, taking her hand, "what's wrong? Are you having trouble breathing?"

"Yes. Yes, I am."

Immediately, Jade reached for the oxygen tank, fastening the breathing tubes to Leah's nose. "There you go. Nice deep breaths, now. Slow and easy, that's it."

"Thanks, sweetie."

Leah closed her eyes, and for a moment, Riley and Jade thought maybe she'd fallen asleep, or was unconscious.

Jade smoothed the hair from her forehead as Riley tucked the covers up under her chin. Then, exchanging melancholy smiles, they headed for the door.

"Where. . .where do you. . .think you're going?"

"Get some sleep, Leah," Jade instructed.

"I will," she promised, "soon as I say this."

They moved closer, and waited.

"H. . .help me sit. . .up."

Riley got behind her and propped her upright. "There y'go, doll-face. Go ahead, spill the beans."

"I just. . .wan. . .ted to thank you." She managed a weary smile. "Y. . .you're swell."

"We know," Riley said, trying to sound lighthearted. "And we think you're swell, too."

"You're gonna be. . .gonna be great for. . .for Fiona. She's lucky, so lucky to have—"

"Leah," she interrupted, joining the hug, "Leah, please be quiet. Just rest. Please?"

"Okay. I'll rest. But first. . ." She grabbed Riley's hand, put it into Jade's. "First I have to know—"

"Know what, Leah?" Jade asked around a sob.

"That you'll try. Just say. . .just say you'll try."

Their eyes met, locked, and overflowed with tears. Try? Try what? was the question that passed between their gazes.

"Oh, Jade," Leah whispered. "Don't be sad. Please don't cry for me."

"All right, Leah. I won't. Not if you'll promise to go to sleep."

She gave a feeble nod and closed her eyes. "Okay. Okay, I'll sleep."

Gently, Riley laid her down. She was asleep even before they walked out the door.

In the kitchen, they stood in the halo of the overhead lamp. "Oh, Riley," Jade said, falling into his arms. "She's so weak and pale. It's as though she was holding on all this time, just to bring us together."

"Yeah," he choked out. "And now that we're married—"

Jade lay her fingertips over his lips. "Shhh. Don't say it. Please don't say it."

He held her tighter. "Think we oughta call Peterson?"

She nodded against his chest. "Maybe. I don't know what he can do, but—"

"To make her more comfortable, you mean?"

Another nod. "Every breath is a struggle for her now. Why didn't I see it before, Riley? Was I so wrapped up in my own—"

"Stop it, Jade." He held her at arm's length, one hand gripping her shoulders, and gave her a gentle shake. "We didn't see it, because she didn't want us to."

She stepped out of his embrace and dialed the doctor's number and quickly rattled off the pertinent information about Leah's condition.

"What!" she nearly shouted into the receiver. "But you're the specialist."

Riley watched her lovely face crinkle with anger. "Tell me something, anything that'll help, till you get here!"

A moment later, after she'd hung up, Jade said, "He's on his way."

Tenderly, he cupped her face in his hands. "What did he say to get you so riled up, kiddo?"

"He said there's nothing we can do but pray."

Riley slid his arms around her, but this time, the hug was more for his benefit than Jade's. "Dear God," he said, "let her last till morning; she'll want—"

A sob strangled the words from his throat.

"She'll want to see Fiona," Jade completed for him, "so she can say. . ."

". . .good-bye," they said together.

Chapter 7

O n the Fourth, Peterson had worn shorts and a T-shirt. When he stopped by on Saturdays and Sundays, he was usually in blue jeans and collarless shirts. Once, as an afterthought, he'd dropped in on his way to the track, outfitted like an Olympic runner. Without exception, the doctor had always looked as though he'd stepped straight from the pages of a catalog.

Not so tonight.

His maroon and gold football jersey didn't match the pale blue sweat pants; one white sock bore a popular tennis shoe logo, the other was blue. His shoelaces were untied, he hadn't shaved, his eyes sleep-puffy. "I got here soon as I could," he said when Jade opened the door.

"I brewed a pot of coffee," she said, stepping aside to let him in. "Care for a cup?"

The doctor nodded. "Double-double," he told her.

And Jade smiled sadly. "Except for adding the coffee, your mug is all ready for you—two sugars, two creams, just the way you like it."

"She's a born caretaker, isn't she, Doc?"

It was the first time since his arrival that Peterson acknowledged Riley's presence. Like Jade, he'd changed out of his wedding garb. "Yeah," he said, stuffing his hands into the pockets of his sweat pants, "a natural."

"It's no wonder she went into nursing."

"Doesn't mean a thing," Peterson said, running a hand through his hair. "Some of the worst housekeepers I've ever known have been nurses. Couple of my buddies married nurses, and about all the 'care' they get from their wives happens on payday." His gaze seemed to take in everything—her white socked feet, capri-length stretch pants, baggy T-shirt, and the loose braid that held her blond tresses back from her face. "Either you're a nurturer," he said, smiling, "or you aren't." Resting a hand on her shoulder, he added, "Jade would have been this way no matter what line of work she chose."

Jade frowned. "The coffee," she reminded the men, "is in the kitchen."

They followed her down the hall and quickly seated themselves at the table. Jade placed napkins and spoons beside their mugs, slid a slice of cherry pie near each.

"We're sorry you couldn't make it to the wedding," Jade said, sitting beside Riley. "How's your sister?"

His cheeks turned nearly as red as the fruit when he said, "She's fine, just fine."

Riley looked from Jade to Peterson. "Your sister? What happened to your sister?"

Peterson's blush deepened. "She, ah, her, um, her dog ran off. She's really attached to the mutt now that the kids are all off on their own."

Frowning slightly, Riley said, "Ah-ha. So did you find him?"

" 'She.' And yes, we found her."

"Well, good. I'm glad she's safe and sound." Harumphing, he added, "That's more than we can say for Leah."

He tucked in one corner of his mouth and met Jade's steady gaze. "You said her breathing has been labored?"

Jade nodded. "She was fine all afternoon. Fine this evening, too. And then—" Her voice faltered, then faded.

"She's sleeping now, I presume?"

"If you want to call it that."

He took a sip of coffee. "It's perfect," Peterson said. "Like you."

She cut a glance toward Riley in time to see that he'd clenched his jaw and raised a brow. *Boy, you really don't like this guy, do you?* she silently asked him.

Peterson scooted his chair back and stood. "I'll just go and have a look at her." And when Jade started to join him, he held a hand level with the table top. "No," he said, "you've had a—" He looked away, cleared his throat. "You've had quite a day. Take it easy while you can." And then he was gone.

"Well, well, well," Riley said, staring after him.

" 'Well, well' what?"

"Looks to me like the good doctor has a crush on you," he began, focusing on Jade, "Mrs. Steele."

She frowned. "He's here for Leah. Period."

"Mmm-hmm. And that's why he turned beet red when you asked him why he missed the wedding."

She was about to ask him if he realized how ridiculous he sounded when Peterson leaned into the kitchen. "I think you guys better get in here. Now."

Riley leaped up so fast, his chair toppled over. The feet of Jade's chair screeched across the tiles like fingernails on a chalkboard. "What?" she asked breathily, joining Peterson in the hall. "Is she—?"

"She's still with us," he said gravely, "barely."

Leah looked so tiny and fragile in the middle of her queen-size bed, it was difficult to determine where she began and the starched white linens ended. Lifting her hand, she grasped Riley's. "You have a birthday coming up. I haven't missed one of your birthdays since we were little kids."

He feigned a smile. "I'm too old to celebrate birthdays."

"Thirty-one isn't old."

"I suppose not," he shrugged. "I guess I've lived alone so long, I feel ancient sometimes."

"Well, Fiona will be good for you, then. By the way, is she asleep?"

"For an hour already," Jade answered.

An almost indiscernible sigh escaped Leah's lungs. "Amazing, isn't it?"

"What's amazing?" Jade wanted to know.

She took Jade's hand, too. "The way God brings people together exactly when and where they need each other most." Her blue gaze bored hotly into Jade's, into Riley's. "You'll be good for each other, too."

Deliberately, they avoided looking at one another.

"I'm so happy Fiona will be growing up in a house with a mommy and a daddy who love each other."

Jade looked toward the door as Leah added, "It gives me such peace, knowing that."

Taking Leah's brush from the nightstand drawer, Jade perched on the edge of the bed and began gently running it through thin blond strands. "Feels nice," Leah sighed, closing her eyes. "Reminds me of how my mother used to do it." And within seconds, it seemed, she was asleep.

The only sound in the room was the hushed hiss of oxygen.

The doctor had been standing quietly, unobtrusively at the foot of the bed. "She seems to be resting peacefully," Jade said to him. "She must have let you give her something for the pain."

He shook his head. "She said there were things she had to say, and morphine would cloud her judgment."

Suddenly, Leah opened her eyes. "That's right," she said. And then, "It's time."

"Time? Time for what?" Jade ventured. But it was obvious from her solemn expression that she already knew the answer. Jade bit her lip, and Riley clamped his teeth together as Peterson's fingers tightened around the bedpost.

"I have something. . ." She winced with pain. ". . .something to tell the two of you."

When Leah motioned them nearer, they got onto their knees and leaned in close.

"Don't feel guilty any more, okay?"

"Guilty?" Riley repeated, gently tucking a lock of hair behind her ear. "What do we have to feel guilty about?"

"I've been watching. . ." Another grimace. "I've been. . .watching the both of you; you're so oppressed by guilt, it's a wonder you can stand up straight." She raised one hairless brow, lifted a frail hand and pointed, first at Riley, then at Jade. "You have nothing to feel guilty about. The love you feel for each other? I've been praying for it. Get this through your hard heads: It's God's will!"

Jade stood and straightened her shoulders, as if trying to summon the self-control required to hold back her tears. "Leah, rest, why don't you, so that—"

"Sweetie," she interrupted, "you know that I love you, but"—she gave Jade's hand an affectionate squeeze. "All too soon, I'll be resting for eternity." Another squeeze and a smile and then, "So shut up, will you please, and let me have my say?"

Nodding, Jade smoothed back Leah's sparse bangs.

"There's a good gir—" Leah took a quavering breath and winced, squeezed her eyes shut and bit her lower lip.

"Let Jade give you something for the pain, kiddo."

A frail smile curved her pale lips. "No, Riley; Ron already told you why."

When she coughed, Jade helped her sit up a bit and held the plastic straw from the drinking glass between her parched lips. One tiny sip, then two, and Leah lay back. "Now then, what was I saying?"

A millisecond passed, perhaps two, before she focused on Riley. "Would you wake Fiona, please? Bring her in here, so I can—"

One hand on either side of her head, he leaned down and kissed her cheek. "Lie still now. I'll be right back." He pressed a second kiss to her forehead, then started for the door. When he hesitated in the doorway, Leah said, "Don't worry, I'll hang on till you get back."

Though she was smiling bravely, Jade knew that Peterson had been right; the end was near. Very near. And the proof was Leah's joyless monotone. It broke her heart to see such sadness in her friend's eyes. Jade wanted to fling herself across the bed and sob about the unfairness of it all.

But Leah deserved to be surrounded now by the same kind of strength she had displayed throughout this ordeal. "Did you hear Fiona tonight?" she asked, tidying Leah's covers. "Every time I read the word 'beauty,' she pointed at Belle." Plumping the pillows, she continued in a bright, cheery voice: "She's so smart, it's a little scary. I mean. . ."

She repositioned the water glass, the alarm clock, and the telephone on the nightstand. ". . .if she's recognizing words already, and she's only two, well"—she forced a laugh—"I'd hate to be her kindergarten teacher!"

Riley entered the room, carrying the tousled little blond. One chubby cheek, still slumber pink, boasted brighter pink sheet wrinkles; the other rested against his shoulder. He tenderly eased her under the covers to nestle beside her mother. "Mama," Fiona whimpered, snuggling close and rubbing fat fists into her eyes, "Fee seepy."

Leah drew her little girl close. "I know you're sleepy, sweet girl," she whispered, kissing her temple, "and you can go back to bed in a minute. Mama just wanted to hug you, that's all."

Jade had no idea how much time had passed as they cuddled quietly, Leah humming a sweet lullaby as she wound strands of flaxen baby hair around a forefinger, Fiona contentedly sucking her thumb. She wanted to memorize this moment, wanted to fuse it to her memory for all time.

Grinning slightly, Fiona began to sing the words to her mother's tune: "Rocky bay-bee inna twee top."

It must have been too much, too sweet for Leah, because she bit her lips and closed her eyes, ending the song. "Aw, sweetie," she sighed, hugging Fiona tighter still. "My sweet girl."

"Everything is going to be all right," she whispered into her daughter's ear, "I promise. Mama asked Jesus to take care of you, and He did. He made sure you'd have a mommy and a daddy to love you and watch over you after—when I'm—"

Tears filled her eyes as she kissed Fiona's forehead. "Oh, how I love you, my sweet Fee. Mama's going to miss you, going to miss you, so much!"

Suddenly Leah cleared her throat. "Put her back to bed," she instructed Riley in a voice that belied her condition. "It's bad enough she's had to see me fall apart like an old toy; I don't want her to see what's about to happen."

He made a move to scoop the baby into his arms, but Peterson stepped forward, laid a hand on Riley's forearm. Nodding understandingly, he said in a soft, cracking voice, "I'll take her. You stay here, with Leah."

A brusque, yet sincere, "Thanks, Doc," scraped from Riley's throat as he handed Fiona over.

The minute Peterson and the baby were out of the room, Riley cupped Leah's face in his hands. His voice trembled when he spoke: "You know what you remind me of?"

She gave a fragile laugh. "A dish rag? A wet noodle? A—"

He lay a finger over her lips. "Shhh. I'll tell you what you remind me of. Remember my mother's Christmas angel?"

Nodding weakly, Leah smiled. "The one she topped the tree with every year?"

"That's the one."

"I always thought she was so beautiful."

"And she was," he agreed. "She was really nothing more than a china doll, with a halo and wings and a white dress. And her smile—sometimes I'd stare at her so long, I imagined her lips were moving. Even now, I can't help but—"

"Careful," Leah teased, "or your 'tough guy' routine will be exposed for the sham it is."

Her words, caught on the ragged edge of pain, stuck in her throat. "Oh, Lord," she prayed aloud. "It hurts, guys. Hurts bad."

"I'll get Ron," Jade said, "see if maybe he brought something to ease the—"

"No!" she rasped. "I want to be aware, right to the end."

Riley straightened, turned his back to the bed. Jade watched as he ran both hands through his hair, then stood there, fingers clasped at the base of his skull. She wanted to go to him, throw her arms around him, and console him as he'd consoled her so many times. But there would be time for that later. Right now,

Leah needed her comfort more.

Climbing onto the bed, Jade stretched out beside Leah and held her in her arms. "We're here," she said, hugging her tight, "right here with you, all the way."

One corner of Leah's mouth turned up in a weak smile. "Did you have onions for supper?"

Despite the moment, Jade grinned. "Leave it to you to make light of a heavy situation."

"Well, the joke's on you," Leah teased, " 'cause I'm not goin' anywhere just yet. Not till you promise."

"Promise what?"

"I know you'll take good care of Fiona, but I want you to promise you'll take care of each other, too."

"Done," Riley said without hesitation.

"Whatever you say," Jade agreed.

"Promise?"

"We promise," they said in unison.

Leah exhaled a long, relieved sigh. The furrows that had wrinkled her brow smoothed, as if her pain had been overpowered by their simple, heartfelt pledge.

"Thanks, guys," she sighed, patting their hands.

It was happening right before their eyes, and they were helpless to prevent it. "Oh, Leah," Jade cried, gathering her closer. "I love you."

Eyelids fluttering, she met Jade's eyes. ". . .love you, too, sweetie." And turning to Riley, Leah added, ". . .you, too."

"Yeah, yeah," he said, trying unsuccessfully to smile past his own tears.

"It's been quite a life, hasn't it?" Leah husked.

"That it has, kiddo."

She looked at each of them long and hard, then smiled serenely.

" 'And lo, I will tell you a mystery,' " Riley recited in a broken voice.

" '. . .in the twinkling of an eye,' " Jade continued, " 'the trumpet will sound. . . .' "

" '. . .and the dead will be raised imperishable,' " they prayed together, " 'and we will be changed.' "

Tears trickled from the corners of Leah's eyes. "Don't let Fee forget me."

"We won't," they assured.

They clung together for those last moments, forming a three-way hug as they'd done so often in the past.

"It's. . .it's been. . .a pleasure," Leah said.

When she went limp, they knew her spirit had left her.

Jade and Riley continued to hold her for a long, silent moment, their tears dampening the soft cotton flannel of her blue-flowered nightgown.

"The pleasure was ours," Riley said, gently settling her back onto the pillows. "All ours."

If Leah had said it once, she'd said it a hundred times: "Wakes are a barbaric, paganistic ritual. I don't want people gawking at what used to be me when I'm gone. And I don't want 'em sending flowers that I won't be able to enjoy!"

So it was no surprise that she'd arranged a private memorial service, to take place immediately before the burial. Her favorite hymn, "Amazing Grace" played in the background as the preacher's booming voice recited her favorite Bible verse: " 'There hath no temptation taken you but such as is common to man,' " he read from 1 Corinthians 10:13, " 'but God is faithful, who will not suffer you to be tempted above that ye are able; but will with the temptation also make a way to escape, that ye may be able to bear it.' " She'd lived by that verse and, as it turned out, died by it, too.

She'd thought of everything, right down to her black and white photo, which appeared beside her obituary in the Saturday edition of The Baltimore Sun. The plain gray casket, picked out and paid for long before she left them, was slowly lowered into the deep, dark rectangle carved into the earth beside John's grave. And the headstone she'd commissioned read simply, "Leah Marie Jordan, 1968–1998, beloved wife, mother, friend."

"It's supposed to be raining," Jade said glumly as they stood, stock-still and stiff, watching the groundsmen prepare to fill the gaping hole. "It's supposed to be bleak and cold, ugly as death itself."

Riley scanned the lush green cemetery lawn. Ancient, stately oaks shaded cherubs and archangels, carved from white marble, that guarded the tombs. And in the branches of birch and willow trees, birds tried to out-sing one another. Flowers of every color and variety bloomed along neatly-trimmed hedgerows that were home to chorusing crickets.

A sweet summer breeze riffled Jade's blond hair, lifting it like a butter-yellow cape that fluttered behind her. And the sunshine shimmered down, its golden fronds stroking them like the warm, reassuring fingers of a loving parent.

It was anything but a dreary day. "Leah planned everything else," he said, smiling "If she could have ordered the weather, it would have been a day just like this."

She heaved a deep sigh. "I suppose you're right. It's just that I'm so tired of being stoic, of pretending everything's all right, of behaving like I'm willing to go along with—" She pointed at Leah's grave. "With that."

He slipped an arm around her waist. "Come on. Let's go and pick up Fiona."

Jade let him walk her to the car. "She's a smart little thing; she's sure to know."

Nodding, he said, "For a while. But she's awfully young."

She stepped back as he opened the passenger door. "Well, we'll make sure she never forgets. We'll show her pictures and tell her stories and—"

He wrapped her in his arms and held her tight, his tears dampening her hair, her tears soaking into his shirt. " 'Course we will," he sobbed. " 'Course we will."

A man in a dark suit stepped up beside them, removed his aviator-style sunglasses. "Sorry to intrude," he said, pocketing the shades. He extended his right hand. "I'm Jules Harris, Leah's attorney." He shook Riley's hand, then Jade's, and held out the manila envelope he'd been holding in his other hand. "She asked me to wait till after the funeral to give you this."

For a moment, Jade merely stared at it, as if she expected it might explode. When she finally accepted it from Jules Harris's outstretched hand, she frowned slightly. "Feels like a videotape."

"That's exactly what it is," Harris said, running a hand through his dark hair. "Don't ask me what's on it, because I haven't looked." He glanced toward the navy sedan parked across the way, gave a little wave to the redheaded woman in the passenger seat. "Well," he said, putting the sunglasses back on, "I'd better go." He smiled. "My wife's eight months pregnant, and if I know her, she's desperate to find a ladies' room."

He wasn't smiling when he added, "Leah was some terrific lady. Wish I'd known her better, and under better circumstances."

Riley nodded.

Jade smiled sadly.

He started to leave, then stopped and faced them again. "She thought the world of you two. But I guess you already knew that."

Another nod from Riley.

A second sad smile from Jade.

Without another word, the lawyer turned and walked away.

Jade slumped onto the passenger seat, and Riley closed the door. They drove back to Leah's house—the house she'd signed over to them—in total silence. . .

. . .the videotape lying on the seat between them.

He'd moved a few of his things into the main bathroom, hung a few shirts and several pairs of trousers in the hall closet, stuffed jeans and rag-knit socks and colorful T-shirts into the antique bureau in the family room.

He slept on the couch in the family room, which was too short and too narrow to provide a decent night's rest. But he couldn't bring himself to sleep in the master bedroom, in the brass bed that had been Leah's. He'd given a thought or two to bringing his own bed from home, but it would still be Leah's room.

The big ugly hospital bed was gone now, and when the medical supply company picked it up, the attendants had also taken away the tanks and clear plastic tubing that had carried oxygen to Leah's exhausted lungs.

Memory of her was everywhere.

She smiled at him from the family portrait taken of her and John and brand-new Fiona. Her favorite books filled the shelves in the bookcases that flanked the flagstone fireplace, her lush green plants stood in every corner and on the hearth. The pink-and-cream afghan she'd knitted in her high school home economics class was draped over the arm of the love seat. Her collection of ceramic wolves perched on end tables, the mantle, and window ledges, and the well-worn family Bible she'd always kept within easy reach lay on the coffee table.

And there was the videotape, delivered by her lawyer at the graveyard, sitting on the VCR, still wrapped in its gold envelope.

They'd been too tired that first night to watch it. And in the two days that had passed since, one thing or another—Fiona's out-of-character fussiness, friends who stopped by to pay their last respects—kept them from seeing the last-minute message Leah had recorded for them.

How she'd recorded it in her condition, without anyone knowing, was anybody's guess.

But Leah had thought of everything else. Riley suspected that, when the finally got around to watching the tape, that question, too, would be answered.

Any minute now, Jade would finish up in the kitchen. Fiona was sound asleep, and had been for nearly an hour now. There would be no more excuses, no more procrastinating. Difficult as it would be, they would watch the tape.

Riley shook the tape from its envelope, fully intent upon setting up the TV and VCR. But a note fluttered to the floor, capturing his attention as it landed face-up on the carpeting. Immediately, he recognized Leah's oversized, childlike script. The date above the salutation read January 5.

It's August tenth, he thought. Had she made the tape on the day she'd written the note? Riley's head ached as he considered the probability that Leah had been prepared for her death, a full seven months in advance. He could only hope Jade and he had made her stoic acceptance easier to bear.

Squatting, Riley gently grasped the single sheet of pale pink stationery. His gaze fell upon Leah's fanciful calligraphy initials top and center. "Dear Jade," the first line said.

Riley read no further.

Standing, he slid the tape and accompanying note back into the envelope. He was about to put it back on top of the TV when Jade entered the room. She took one look at the package and said, "I guess we've put it off long enough."

"That's what I was thinking when I opened the envelope." He handed it to her. "It's addressed to you."

She turned it over, over again. "But there's no writing on it. How do you—"

"There's a note inside. I read 'Dear Jade' and put it right back." Fighting tears, he scrubbed a hand over his beard. *What is wrong with you?* he demanded. *It isn't as though you've never dealt with death before.* He'd lost a beloved grandparent and an elderly aunt. When he was ten, his favorite cousin died in a car accident, and a little more than a year ago, his college roommate passed on after a monthlong bout with pneumonia.

Disgusted with his weakness, Riley shook his head. "I'll be in the kitchen. If you need anything, just—"

"Please don't leave," she whispered, extending her hand. Grinning slightly, Jade added, "We've always shared everything. I see no reason to start keeping secrets, just 'cause we're married now."

Returning her smile, he gave her hand a little squeeze and sat beside her on the sofa.

Jade dumped the contents of the envelope into her lap. "I'm glad Fiona was sound asleep when I checked on her just now." She rolled her eyes. "If I thought she might see my reaction."

Placing the tape on the coffee table, she held the letter in trembling hands. " 'Dear Jade,' " she read aloud. " 'I got some bad news this morning, and if my suspicions are correct, it's going to affect Fiona and Riley and you, too.' "

Jade hid behind one hand. "I can't believe what a weakling I've been through this whole thing." She held out the note. "Would you mind?"

"What makes you think I'll do any better?" he asked, one side of his mouth lifting in a sad grin. But he took the note from her, smoothed it flat, and picked up where she left off:

" 'You know how terrible I've always been at things like this. That's why I've made a videotape for you to watch. And if you're reading this, it means I was right and the worst has already happened. (Well, not the worst; the worst would be if something happened to my sweet little Fee.)' "

A ragged sigh escaped his lungs as he Riley pinched the bridge of his nose between thumb and forefinger. " 'Anyway,' " he continued, " 'watch the tape. And please don't be sad, because I'll be watching you. . .' "

He stopped, a pent-up sob preventing him from reading the last words aloud.

" '. . .from heaven,' " Jade finished.

" 'Love you always,

" 'Leah.' "

She held the note to her chest and bit her lower lip. "I'm almost afraid to look at the tape," Jade said, folding it neatly. She took a deep breath. "But knowing Leah, there's a list of instructions five feet long on it." Sighing again, she stood resolutely and turned on the TV and VCR. And holding the tape in one hand, she said, "We may as well get it over with, right?"

Riley nodded. He scooted to the edge of the sofa cushion, prepared to stand. "You want me to fix you a cup of tea or something first?"

She smiled understandingly, lovingly. "No, but we'll probably need something soothing when it's over, though."

Chapter 8

The bright blue TV screen flickered, then gave way to a hodgepodge of black and white haze before the fuzzy image of Leah's family room came into view.

She'd aimed the camera at the couch, where Jade and Riley were sitting now. "Bear with me," came her bubbly voice from behind the tripod. The picture clouded further, then came into sharp focus. "There. I think that's got it."

A moment later, she hop-skipped in front of the lens and flopped onto the center sofa cushion, blond waves spilled over her shoulders, catching the sunlight that filtered in through the windows. She'd worn her customary violet eye shadow and black mascara to highlight her beautiful blue eyes, and a coat of coral lipstick to emphasize her perky smile. A sheen of powder did nothing to hide the freckles that had always dotted the bridge of her nose, and when she smiled, a dimple dented her right cheek.

"She looks beautiful," Riley said, smiling wistfully.

"So healthy and—"

Leah spread her arms wide and wiggled her well-arched brows. "Well, sweetie, feast your eyes. I don't imagine you've seen me looking like this in a long, long time!"

Criss-crossing her legs, Leah leaned her elbows on her knees and took a deep breath. "Well, now. Where to begin?" Squinting, she tapped a forefinger against her chin, then rolled her eyes. "At the beginning, right?" She giggled. "Okay, here goes.

"I saw the doctor today." Tapping both sneakered feet flat on the floor, Leah's fists lightly pummeled her jeans-clad thighs.

"She never could sit still when she was nervous," Jade observed, smiling sadly. "Just look at her, fidgeting."

"Anyway," Leah continued, "he seems to think there's no hope for me." She held both arms akimbo again. "As you can see, I've already lost about twenty pounds. Under other circumstances, I'd be giddy with glee to be stuffing my carcass into size six jeans, but—"

Riley bowed his head. "God bless her 'take it on the chin' attitude, huh?"

Jade nodded her silent agreement.

"From the moment I learned about the, ah, the cancer," she said, looking away from the camera's lens, "I've been giving a lot of serious thought to Fiona's future."

She wasn't smiling when she added, "I came up with this idea, see, and I've been praying and praying about it, and I believe my plan has God's blessing."

Fiona's voice, coming from her room down the hall, interrupted them. "I'll get her," Riley offered. "You go ahead and watch the rest. I'll catch the end later."

Ordinarily, she'd have stopped him and would have gone to Fiona, herself. But something about Leah's word choices made Jade believe this film had been intended for her eyes only.

The temporary distraction caused her to miss the part where Leah heaved a deep sigh and folded both hands in her lap. But by the time Riley had gone down the hall and into Fiona's room, Leah was looking straight into the lens again. "I won't pussyfoot around, Jade," she said in that no-nonsense way of hers. "We both know how you feel about Riley—"

You were right; the note was addressed to you, because the tape wasn't intended for Riley's eyes, or ears. Heart hammering, she grabbed the remote and quickly turned down the sound.

"—how you've always felt about Riley. If you weren't so proud and stubborn, he'd know it, too, because you would have told him by now. And more than likely," she said, wagging a finger in the air, "you'd be married and have a couple of kids already!"

Children? Hers and Riley's? The image of it, sweet and warm, flashed in her mind's eye, making her heart beat double-time.

Leah's voice called her attention back to the TV screen. "You're a sweetie," she was saying, rolling her eyes, "but you sure can be frustratingly bullheaded sometimes!"

"Puppy to the root," the doctor had said.

Jade smiled as Leah gave a little laugh. "Like I said, I have this plan, see, one I'm certain will be best for everybody." She tilted her head slightly, tucked in one corner of her mouth. "Knowing you and Riley, it's gonna take a while before either of you admit it, but trust me, you'll thank me in the end."

I hope you're resting easy, Leah, because everything went exactly according to your plan, Jade admitted. *Riley and I are married, your house is legally ours—*

Leah propped the soles of her shoes on the edge of the sofa cushion and, hugging her legs, smiled. "So you're married! Isn't it just the most wonderful thing!" She bobbed her head from side to side, grinning like a schoolgirl as she sing-songed, "There you are, in your own little house, with the baby sleeping down the hall, waiting for your good-lookin' husband to come home from work.

"And he's across town, watching the clock and counting the minutes till he can go home to his little family." She heaved a wistful sigh. "It's so-o-o ro-man-tic."

Leah retied one sneaker, patted the neat bow. "Can you hear that?" she asked, looking toward the bedrooms down the hall. "No, I don't suppose you can. Well," she whispered, gaze on the camera again, "Fiona is waking up from her nap, so I'm going to have to make this short and snappy."

"I hope I had the presence of mind to tell you in the, ah, at the end, that you shouldn't feel guilty for loving Riley. And he shouldn't feel guilty about loving you, either."

She'd pretty much said the same thing on her death bed. But how had Leah known they'd feel this way?

"I've known the pair of you a lifetime," she said, as if cued by Jade's thoughts, "and I'd be surprised if you're not feeling guilty, well, suffice it to say I'm pretty sure you are.

"So stop it. Stop it right now! It's okay to need one another. In fact, it's better than okay. It's good. Really, it is!"

Leah went into singsong mode again. "You're probably thinking there's something bad about wanting a happy future with Riley, because you think it's somehow disloyal to me."

Jade had heard it said that true friends can read one another's hearts. She'd pooh-poohed the idea—until this moment.

"That's nonsense, Jade, just plain nonsense. The love you feel for Riley is proof of your loyalty to me. I mean, you went through with the wedding, without knowing for sure if he loves you, if he'll ever love you, to fulfill my last wish." She held her forefingers aloft and drew parentheses in the air. "You wouldn't be looking at this movie if you hadn't, 'cause I instructed Jules to give you the tape only if you and Riley got married before I—" She took a breath. "Before I died.

"There. I said it." A little giggle popped from her mouth, though Jade noted that the smile didn't quite make it to her eyes. "That wasn't as tough as I thought it would be."

And completely straight-faced, she gazed into the camera lens. "Things won't be as tough as you think they'll be, either. You have my word on it. Because whether you know it yet or not, Riley loves you. Always has. Always will."

Jade rolled her eyes. *Yeah, right.*

"Don't roll your eyes, missy. You'll see. I'm right!"

Jade could only shake her head in awe as Leah stood suddenly, crossed the room and disappeared behind the camera. She leaned in front of it for a moment, her lovely, loving face filling nearly the entire TV screen. "Better than that, you have God's Word on it!"

The grainy snow that had preceded the recording returned, followed by an annoying hiss and crackle. Jade hit the remote's STOP button, then rewound the tape. She turned off the TV and VCR, put the tape back into its protective sleeve, and stuck the note and the envelope in the cabinet beside the fireplace. Later, when Riley and Fiona were asleep, she'd sneak the package into Leah's room and watch it again.

"Our girl completely unmade her crib," Riley announced, marching into the room with Fiona on his shoulders. "But not to worry," he said, wincing as she filled her hands with his hair, "we put it back together, didn't we, Fee?"

At Leah's suggestion, they'd both been calling her Fee, practically since the day Jade came back from California. She'd never actually heard Leah telling Fiona to call them Daddy and Mama, but how else was she to explain that the baby referred to them in exactly that way?

As for herself—despite how sweet it felt to have the title Mother associated with her name—Jade had always corrected the toddler. "Jade," she'd say sweetly, one hand pressed to her chest. And pointing at Leah, she'd add, "There's Mama." Until now, she'd attributed the annoyance on Leah's face as proof she was having difficulty listening to another woman scold her child, even in the gentlest voice.

Riley, on the other hand, appeared completely comfortable with his role as surrogate father, so natural and confident that it seemed he thrived on the label and the duties that went hand and hand with it. Like a boy shoving to be first in line at the movie counter, he volunteered to feed Fiona. Every day, as Jade bathed Leah, or massaged lotion into her skin to prevent bed sores, or changed the linens, she could count on Riley to be there, entertaining Fiona. He didn't even mind changing dirty diapers! When Fee called him "Dah-dee" in her exuberant, loving way, he positively glowed. And Jade had to admit, the title fit.

As she watched him now, blowing air bubbles on Fiona's chubby cheek that inspired gales of baby giggles, she loved him more than ever.

And she'd loved him wholeheartedly before.

Could Leah have been right about Riley loving her, too? Or had he agreed to go through with the wedding because he couldn't say no to anything Leah asked of him, especially not at a time like that.

Leah had assured Jade that even the idea of bringing Jade and Riley together had been put into a lowly human mind by the Creator. The marriage itself, she'd insisted, had been designed and blessed by God Himself.

Perhaps romantic love would one day be a part of that marriage. But even if it didn't—and they continued to devote life as they'd been living, devoting themselves to Fiona—it would be a deep and abiding relationship. There were no doubt thousands of couples who'd gladly settled for that. How could it be otherwise, when it had been built on a Godly foundation!

But what was it that William Wilde Curringer said? Something like, "The thing that really separates human beings is the gap between what each of them wants. . .and what each is willing to settle for."

She'd been saying this an awful lot lately: That should be enough. Why isn't it enough?

※

It had been a week since Jade viewed that videotape, and she hadn't been herself since. Riley couldn't help but wonder what message Leah might have taped that would have such a strangely sobering effect on Jade's normally upbeat and energetic personality. One thing was certain: Leah had intended it for Jade, and Jade seemed resolved to honor that intention.

It was more proof, as he saw it, that "Riley's girls" (as they'd often affectionately referred to themselves), sometimes shared things that didn't include him. Because even if they had tried to explain why some things got them giggling, and other things started their eyes to leaking, he had a feeling he wasn't supposed to understand.

He'd decided early on that every red-blooded male had better learn one lesson by the time he's six: Guys and girls are different, period.

Their secrets, which he had always strongly suspected involved things that were of no interest to him, anyway, as part of that difference. Besides, who had they turned to for answers to their "really important" questions, such as whether or not boys really liked girls to wear makeup and fingernail polish, as the teen magazines claimed? And when their feelings were hurt or they were scared, who had they gone to for comfort and protection?

As they grew up, the things Jade and Leah had considered "important" matured as well. He found himself included in far more of their "girl talk," and realized he understood far more about them than he had when they were little kids. The only explanation he could come with was that, in matters of the heart, grown-up guys and girls weren't as different as he'd once believed.

That Leah would make a movie just for Jade hurt, and admitting it hurt worse because the confession made him feel small and shallow and, worst of all, like a milksop.

Riley had prayed on it, long and hard, had come to the conclusion that the best way to deal with his feelings was not to deal with his feelings. He would concentrate on Fiona. And on Jade. Which, he guessed, wouldn't be a difficult task, she'd more or less been the center of his life since that night he'd picked her up at the airport, anyway.

Leah had been the one whose illness required round-the-clock care, and that sort of put her "front and center" whether she liked it or not. But Jade had been the one to give that care, whenever, wherever it was needed. And she'd given it joyfully, generously, and without a word of complaint. He'd watched her smile as she hand-fed Leah when their friend was too weak to feed herself and heard her laughing and making jokes, as if watching a loved one die was no hardship at all.

It had been a hardship, of course. Not just the backbreaking day-to-day work that went hand in hand with nursing a terminally ill patient. This terminally ill patient had been Jade's lifelong friend, more beloved than her flesh and blood sister.

She saved her tears for moments that Leah couldn't see, and Riley greatly admired her for that. Sometimes, once she'd seen to Leah's immediate needs, she'd go into her room and close the door, and he'd hear her soft sobs though he could tell she'd tried to muffle them in a pillow. It had taken all the strength he could muster to keep from barging in there and holding her close!

He'd caught her once, moments afterward when she'd been red-eyed and sniffing. "I heard you in there," he'd said, "you don't have to go through that alone, you know."

She'd straightened her back and said, "Yes, I do." She'd immediately followed it up with a bright smile and a tiny laugh. "You trying to deprive me of my Personal Pity Parties?"

He'd never mentioned it again.

But he didn't deserve any credit for that, because Jade had never let him catch her crying again.

She stood no more than five-foot-two, barely weighed in at a hundred fifteen. And yet, she had more strength of character than any man he could name—than any ten men he could name—and sometimes, that included him.

So he'd known well in advance that his decision to put Jade at the center of his focus wouldn't be hard. Especially these days, when the only time she seemed her old self was when she spent time with Fiona—particularly if she thought the two of them were alone. Her laughter, her smiles, her enthusiasm—everything was at full tilt during those moments of private, pleasant play.

He'd taken a course while in veterinary school, "Dealing with Grief," or something along those lines. Their purpose was to help people cope with the loss of a beloved pet. "Some folks get more attached to their animals than others get to the people in their lives," the professor had said. "The best medicine," he'd insisted, "is communication. Only when people must admit how they feel about the death—only then can the healing begin."

The lesson had been intended for pet owners, but Riley had always been a staunch believer that good advice was good advice, no matter who gave it, or to whom, or why. Seemed to him that advice might just do Jade some good right about now. And it didn't hurt that he agreed, wholeheartedly, with the message!

Being part Irish, Riley understood something about that. His first real loss had been at the age of ten, when his grandfather died. Family and close friends had gathered after the funeral at the old man's house. He'd been stunned, days later, when Irish neighbors three doors down told his grandmother that long after they'd left the house that night, they'd heard the talking and the laughing, all the way upstairs in their bedroom!

What was all the good cheer about? he'd wondered then. Shouldn't they have been crying and shaking their fists at the heavens, demanding to know why Grandpa had been taken from them? If they'd loved him at all, wouldn't it show by the depth of their mourning!

Nearly a week had passed when the angry and confused boy put those very questions to his grandmother. There had been tears in her eyes and a loving smile on her face when she said, "Ah, but there's good reason for the joy y'saw, Riley, m'boy. Yer grandda has gone on to a better world, where he can sing with the angels an' talk with Jesus, face-to-face."

His grandfather loved to sing. And the life of Jesus had always been one of his favorite topics.

As she spoke, he saw the love she'd felt for her husband on her face, and heard it in her voice: "There's no more pain in his bones, and he can see again, 'cause in Paradise, y'see, there ain't no sufferin'. . .and man is perfect for the first time in his life."

Gran had been fifty-one when the title 'widow' had been forced upon her, and though Riley knew for a fact that she'd been asked his Gran never remarried. Many years after his grandfather's death, her inquisitive grandson asked why. "Oh, but 'twouldn't be fair, 'cause I'd always be comparin' the poor bloke to yer grandda. And since there's no way he could measure up, he'd be miserable!

"Besides, I've got yer folks; I've got you and yer brother." Smiling wistfully, she'd added, "And I've got me lovely mem'ries; what more do I need?"

She missed her man. The proof was in her eyes, in her voice, in the spell-binding stories she'd tell when a chip in a tabletop or a tree in the yard or a song on the radio reminded her of a moment in the life they'd shared. She seemed content to focus on the wonderful life they'd shared, rather than the moment of his death.

Maybe all Jade needed was an opportunity to talk about Leah, about the good times the three of them had shared, and about the sorrow he and Jade felt now at having lost her.

He'd start out by reminding Jade of the time when, at eight years of age, the threesome packed lunches and walked miles to the Patapsco River railroad trestle, determined to disprove Billy Jacobs' story. Fact was, they hoped Billy had been right when he said if they were quiet enough and patient enough, a fawn might nibble sunflower seeds from their hands, too. Well, they hadn't seen anything move that day—except for that runaway caboose. The railroad car wouldn't have hit them, even if they'd been frozen to the spot. Still, it was a story that got them rolling in the aisles every time they talked about the way Leah lost her retainer, Jade swallowed her gum, and Riley tore his brand new jeans as they scrambled up the steep embankment to escape "certain doom."

Grinning at the memory, he barged into the kitchen, and found Jade at the sink, holding her face in her hands. His smile faded. "What's wrong, kiddo?"

She nodded at the table, where three place mats, three napkins, and three sets of silverware awaited the meal she'd prepared for supper; Fiona's baby cup and matching plate and tiny spoon lay on the tray of her high chair. "I set a place for Leah," she said, voice cracking. "I must be losing my mind. It's the second time I've done that since—"

Hugging her from behind, he rested his chin on her shoulder. "Don't worry, kiddo; if you're goin' nuts, you'll have company. No more than an hour ago, I walked into her room to see if she was hungry."

She turned her tear-streaked face to him.

"And a few days ago," he said, focusing on Leah's place setting, "I could have sworn I heard her calling my name."

She flopped onto a kitchen chair. "I know the mind can play tricks at a time like this. I took a course in grief management, and—"

"Grief management," he repeated dully.

She sighed. "I know the stages." She rattled off the list, counting on her fingers: "Anger, sadness, depression, hopelessness, guilt, loneliness, helplessness, frustration. I know not everyone goes through every stage; I know we don't necessarily go through them in order; but at some point, you have to get to acceptance."

Jade propped both elbows on the table as Riley sat across from her. Resting her chin on upturned palms, she said, "Good thing I'm not being graded; I'm not doing this very well, am I?"

He tucked a strand of hair behind her ear. "You're doing fine. We're doin' fine. It's only been a couple of weeks. And we're living in her house, surrounded by her things. Give yourself a little credit where credit is due. You see her everywhere, all day long." Riley paused, then said pointedly, "Do you realize this is the first time we've actually talked about her?"

She met his eyes. "I suppose you're right."

He raised both brows. "You suppose? Course I'm right." Tenderly, he touched her cheek. "Remember what I told you the night you agreed to marry me?"

A half-grin brightened her face, telling him she knew exactly what line of their dialog he was referring to. But, "Hmmm, I'm not exactly sure," is what she said.

Riley chuckled. "Well, then, let me refresh your memory. I said we'd get along fine, as long as you—"

"Continued being so agreeable."

"Exactly."

"Then I have a piece of advice for you, Mr. Steele."

He read the teasing glint in her eyes and matched it with one of his own. "I'll be agreeable, when you're right."

"Seems to me the true test of a wife's devotion is to be agreeable, when her husband is wrong."

Standing, Jade tucked in one corner of her mouth. "I never did like tests," she said humorlessly, picking up Leah's dinnerware.

He stood beside her. "Look, Jade, I know it hurts, but—"

She focused on the long thick fingers, wrapped around her wrist, that stopped her from putting Leah's dishes away. "Nah," she said, forcing a smile, "you're not nearly as rough and tough as you think you are."

"Not this," he said, giving her wrist a gentle shake. "Of course it doesn't hurt; I'd never hurt you, not for anything in the worl—"

She put the dishes down and wrapped her arms around his waist, rested her cheek against his chest. "You're right. It hurts," she husked out. "I knew I'd miss her, Riley, but I never imagined it would be like this."

"I know, kiddo. I miss her, too." Combing his fingers through her silken locks, he kissed the top of her head.

"It's going to take a long time, I think."

"What is?"

"Getting used to life without her." She stepped away from him, wiped her eyes on a paper napkin and tucking it into her jeans pocket. "I feel like such a monster," she said, slamming door and drawers as she put Leah's plate and silverware away. "Why didn't I call her more often? Why didn't I hop on a plane and—"

"If you're gonna beat yourself up, you have to throw a punch or two my way," he interrupted. "I was right here in town," he said, pocketing his hands, "and I only saw her a couple times a year."

"At least you called every week," she insisted, facing him head-on.

"How do you know?"

"Because," she blurted, "she told me so."

"When?" he challenged.

"When I—" Biting her lower lip, Jade looked away.

"When you called her every single week."

"It wasn't enough." She huffed and shook her head. "I could have come to see her more often. I didn't have her responsibilities—home, husband, kid."

"Leah was happy, Jade. She didn't need us in the same way after she married John."

"That's exactly what I'm talking about. Why didn't I visit more after John's accident! I—"

"You stayed with her for more than a month, as I recall, after his funeral."

She shrugged. "What's your point?"

Three, perhaps four feet of space separated them, so why did she seem miles away? "Look at me, Jade," he said softly.

A second passed, then two, before she did as he asked.

He held out his arms, fully expecting her to take those three or four steps, and press up against him, as she'd done earlier.

Instead, she walked to the stove, began lifting lids, stirring the contents of each pot and pan. "Well," she said in a fake cheery voice, "supper is ready. Would you mind getting Fee for me?"

Pocketing one hand, he pinched the bridge of his nose between thumb and forefinger. The space between them had grown just then, and though he couldn't say how or why, Riley knew this: It hurt as much as losing Leah. "Jade, don't—"

"She shouldn't need a diaper change. I checked her before I put her into the playpen a few minutes ago."

"I was about to ask you not to shut me out, but that's exactly what you seem determined to do." He let a silent moment pass, hoping she'd fill it with a denial.

When she didn't, he pressed further. "Why, Jade? Why are you so determined to keep me at arm's length?"

Her eyes widened at the angry harshness of his tone. "I. . .I'm not. It's just—I can't talk about it right now, okay?"

"Can't? Or won't?"

She put her back to him and began filling serving bowls. "Fee had a doozy of a nap this afternoon; she'll probably eat like a horse!"

"Yippee," he ground out, then plodded from the room.

❧

"So how's married life?" Amber wanted to know.

Jade recalled their near-silent dinner last night.

Amber handed her little boy another cookie. "I always knew the two of you would get together eventually."

Gently, Jade wiped a blob of jelly from the corner of Fiona's mouth and raised an inquisitive brow. "You did?"

"Didn't everybody?"

"Really. Everybody?"

Laughing, Amber rolled her blue eyes. "Well, it was never a big secret, was it, that you and Riley were crazy about each other? I mean, we used to make guesses about when he'd pop the question."

She tucked in one corner of her mouth. "Who 'we'?"

Grinning mischievously, Amber shrugged. "Mom, Dad, me," she counted on her fingers, "Riley's folks, and his brother Pete." She leaned forward and giggled. "I love 'how we met' stories. But since you guys have known one another since the cradle, practically, I guess I'll have to settle for a 'when I knew I loved him' story. Come on, you can tell me; when did you know Riley was 'Mr. Right'?"

Jade met Amber's steady gaze and smiled. "I think I always knew."

Her sister's hand shot into the air, two fingers forming the victory sign. "Ha! I was right!"

She sobered suddenly, lay a hand atop Jade's. "Listen, I know you miss Leah. She was a great lady." She patted the hand. "But so are you. You helped make her last days as happy and comfortable as possible." She held a finger aloft to add, "And let's not forget that you've changed your whole life to grant her last wish!"

"But how—? You—? What makes you think—"

"I don't think," she said, giggling, "just ask Neil; he says I'm the only woman in America who gladly handed over thinking privileges to her husband!" Another laugh, then, "But seriously, Leah swore me to secrecy. Remember that time I came to visit her, and she—"

"And she sent me into the kitchen to fix her a sandwich." Jade shook her head, smiling at the memory. "She never did eat it, as I recall."

"I've always looked up to you and admired you, but Jade, never more than now. What you did for Leah, well, you're a hero in the truest sense of the word, that's what. I've never known anyone with a heart like yours."

Blushing, Jade gave Amber's hand a gentle squeeze. "You ought to concentrate a little less on me and a little more on your hostess duties," she teased, pointing at her empty mug. "I've been out of coffee for nearly two whole minutes, now."

Laughing, her sister rose to refill the cup. And while she was away from the table, Jade admitted that she'd arranged these mid-week breakfasts with her younger sister in the hopes of turning her into a surrogate best friend. Unfortunately, the get-togethers only served to accent the fact that no one, not even dear sweet Amber, could replace Leah.

Oh, she'd loved her little sister, there was no denying that! But they'd never had much in common, growing up. Jade liked playing dress up, Amber preferred climbing trees; Jade enjoyed cooking, while Amber's main interest in the kitchen were the meals created there; Jade liked to keep her room tidy and clean, whereas a person could sprain an ankle walking through the debris on Amber's bedroom floor. Jade had so much more in common with best friend, and what she missed most was Leah's fun-loving, exuberant involvement in every aspect of life, no matter how mundane.

It was as she watched Amber's bright eyes just now that Jade realized how many of Leah's admirable traits—like intelligence and wit and generosity of spirit—were part of Amber, too. She kept a spotlessly clean house now that she was a wife and mother, and the little girl who loved shoving dump trucks through the mud had grown into quite a talented interior decorator. Jade would have had a friend in Amber all along—if only she'd taken the time to look.

A person doesn't have to be a gun-toting criminal to have some nasty character traits, she admitted. Her father had likened children to diamonds in the rough; if he said it once, he said it a hundred times: "Life wears off the hard, sharp edges. . . ." *You have a whole lot of living to do,* she told herself, *before you "shine" to your full potential—and something tells me God has had His polishing cloth out for quite some time now.*

"Thanks," she said when Amber put a newly-filled mug in front of her.

"You're welcome."

Damp eyes and trembly smiles and tightly clasped hands made it clear that, pleasant though it was, hot fresh coffee was not what the sisters were most grateful for.

Chapter 9

Jade decided after leaving Amber's yesterday morning that she would pull herself together. It hadn't been a hard decision to make, really, once she got onto her knees and asked for God's help. She hadn't been in prayer a full minute when the question flitted through head: What would Leah do under similar circumstances?

She'd throw back her shoulders and square her chin, that's what, and keep on keeping on, just as she had when her family was taken from her, when John died, when she learned her own death was certain. She'd endured so many losses in her short life, and she'd done it matter-of-factly, with courage and fortitude like none Jade had seen to date.

Jade, on the other hand, had lived an easy, pampered life, surrounded by loving family and caring friends. So why was she slogging through life these days like a woman with the weight of the world on her shoulders? *How dare you behave like a spoiled little brat!* she scolded. *Riley and Fiona deserve better than what you've been giving them. And starting right now, they're going to get it!*

Ashamed of her childish, self-centered behavior of late, Jade fell to her knees in the middle of the kitchen floor, hands clasped beneath her chin and eyes tightly closed. "Forgive me, Father," she prayed, "for forgetting what You instructed through Paul in Philippians: 'Do all things without murmurings and disputings. . . .'" She quoted Psalms, then: "'. . .for with the Lord there is mercy, and with Him is plenteous redemption. . . .'"

Secure in the knowledge that He would help her atone for her sin of self-centeredness, Jade got to her feet as the back doorbell chimed.

"Ron," she said, smiling as he stepped into the kitchen, "what a nice surprise. What brings you by?"

"I was just in the neighborhood, thought I'd say hi." He hesitated, as if he didn't know what he'd like to say next. "It's good to see you, too, Jade. How've you been?"

"Fine." And for the first time since Leah's burial, she meant it.

"You look a little pale, if you don't mind my saying so."

She waved his concern away. "I'm okay. Honest." She headed for the fridge, and said over her shoulder, "Fiona's taking a longer-than-average nap this morning; I didn't expect to get nearly so much accomplished. I was about to pour myself a glass of lemonade to celebrate. Can I fix you a glass?"

"That'd be nice." He settled himself at the table. "Where's Riley?"

"At the clinic." She sent him a wry grin. "Life must go on, or so the sages say." Ron nodded.

"And how's Fiona?"

She put napkins and glasses of fresh-squeezed lemonade on the table, then sat across from him. "It's amazing, really, how resilient children are. I mean, it's obvious she realizes something is drastically different, because she asks for Leah all the time, but she doesn't seem the least bit sad. I like to think it's because she knows her mommy has gone to a better place, free of pain, and—"

The look on his face stopped her. Jade didn't know him well enough to determine if it was outright anger or utter sadness that furrowed his brow. "So tell me," she said, changing the subject, "do you agree with the weather bureau?"

He tucked in his chin. "What?" he asked, grinning.

"They say we could get four feet of snow."

Chuckling, he shook his head. "That's what they said last year, remember? But thanks to El Niño, we had one of the shortest, mildest winters on record."

"I must say, you're awfully cynical, for a man of science."

He snorted. "Maybe it's because I'm a man of science that I'm a pessimist." He shook his head. "Sorry. Maybe this was a mistake, coming over here. It's just that—"

Jade leaned an elbow on the table, resting her chin on a fist. "We haven't known one another long, Ron, but what we went through together because of Leah—" she smiled slightly. "I like to think the one positive thing to come of it was that you and I became friends."

He met her gaze, tucked in a corner of his mouth. "That's good to hear. Especially now."

"Why especially now?"

"Because since Leah died, I keep asking myself what I could have done differently—if I overlooked something—whether I accepted the claims of 'science' too soon."

"I saw her chart; all the tests said the same thing: There was nothing more on earth you could have done for her."

"Nothing on earth," he repeated dully.

"She was in God's hands."

"Which raises a very important question."

"Which is?"

"You were praying, Riley was praying, both of your families and Leah's fellow parishioners were praying. If He's up there, all-merciful like He wants us to believe," Ron said, eyes narrowed and lips thinned in outrage, "why didn't He save her?"

" 'Who can know the mind of God?' "

"Don't add insult to injury by spouting biblical principles. They're about as useful as lips on a chicken, if you ask me."

"I didn't ask you; you asked me, remember?"

He only continued to glower.

"Whew," she said, fanning her face, "and I thought I was angry."

He frowned. "Angry. You? You're one of the most even-tempered people I've ever met."

She quirked a brow. "You think you're the only one who questions God?"

"So what keeps you believing, then—since you admit you can't get satisfying answers from Him?"

"I never said He didn't provide satisfying answers."

"He didn't save Leah."

"No," she said softly, "He didn't, did He?"

"And you accept that?"

"Yes."

"Why?"

"All He asks of us is that we have faith."

"Ah, yes," he said, imitating W.C. Fields, "the ever-present, super-popular, all-powerful Faith."

Brow furrowed, Jade said, "Why did you come here? To make fun of me because despite the fact that I'm a nurse, I've chosen to put my faith in a Being more powerful than your precious science?"

"No," he whispered, leaning forward. "I came to see how I could share in it. I want to believe, Jade; I want to have faith, but—"

"But you've seen where it gets people."

"Right. They put all their hopes and dreams in God, and where does it get them?"

"It gets them faith, don't you see? Faith isn't something you order from a catalog. It's a gift, and it's yours merely by asking for it."

"That isn't true, and you know it. The minute you ask for faith, something ugly happens to test it. Frankly, I don't get it. How can people keep looking to heaven like wide-eyed trusting children, expecting miracles, knowing they'll be tested?"

"Because sometimes they get miracles."

"Yeah," he countered, "but mostly they just get kicked in the head."

"They don't see it that way. Of course there will be hurts and disappointments in life, but if you choose to believe, if you choose faith, your pain is short-lived." And she ought to know, because she'd so recently learned the lesson herself!

"How long did you know Leah, Ron?"

He shook his head. "Long enough to wish I could have saved her," he snapped. "What does that have to do with anything?"

"How long?" she persisted.

"Puppy to the root," he reminded her, running a hand through his hair. "I dunno. Goin' on two years, I guess. Why?"

"Long enough to have learned about her love of clichés."

He frowned. "What?"

"She collected them like kids collect sea shells! 'It's always darkest before the dawn.' 'Don't put your eggs all in one basket.' 'You can't see the forest for the trees' was one of her favorites. And that, Dr. Peterson," Jade said, narrowing one eye at him, "is your main problem."

"Those are proverbs, not clichés."

"Maybe," she snapped, "if you'd listen once in a while, instead of behaving so above it all, God could reach you!"

Ignoring the wince her angry words had put on his face, Jade continued. "And maybe those 'sayings' Leah liked to quote started out as proverbs, but they got repeated so often they became clichés!"

He nodded.

"You want signs and symbols to explain why people believe."

His brow crinkled with confusion.

"Miracles, Ron! We all want to believe in them, hope and pray for them when times are tough, but that isn't why we have faith. You said it yourself a moment ago; we look to the heavens, like wide-eyed trusting children. That's where we get our faith, from our childlike belief that God is our Father, that He'll watch over us, do what's best for us, even though we might not see eye-to-eye with Him when He does." She paused. "I don't know why Leah got cancer, why she suffered, why she died, but God knows. And I have faith there's a good reason. A very good reason for it."

She took a deep breath. "Like it or not, you're a child of God, too, you know."

He looked genuinely surprised. "Who, me? No way."

She grabbed his hand, gave it a squeeze. "Yes, you. . .with a head full of scientific facts and a heart hardened by the suffering and death you've seen. Especially you. Why not you?"

"Because. I'm a self-centered know-it-all."

Jade laughed softly. "Oh, Ron, don't you see? God has a special place in His heart for arrogant, hardheaded know-it-alls like you."

"Hardheaded!" he repeated. And grinning a bit, he added, "Arrogant?"

"Well, you have to admit, you don't exactly take to new ideas easily, especially if they can't be worked out on a calculator or measured in a lab experiment."

He glanced at her hand, resting atop his. "I declare, Jade, if you weren't Riley's wife."

She read the gleam emanating from his eyes and realized for the first time that what he felt for her had very little, if anything, to do with friendship. And it certainly had nothing to do with religion! She pulled her hand from beneath his. "Drink your lemonade, Ron, " she instructed lightly, "the ice is melting and it's getting all watery."

"Then again," he continued as if she hadn't spoken, "it's not like you guys are really married; you only went through with that sham of a wedding to make Leah happy in the end. I mean, it's not like you're in love with the guy or anything, right?"

Jade stood so fast that her chair teetered and tottered before coming to rest on all four feet again. She hadn't been eating properly, hadn't been sleeping well, either, and standing so quickly sent a rush of dizziness coursing through her that made her stagger and stumble.

Peterson was on his feet in a whipstitch, arms outstretched to save her from the hard fall. Gathering her near, he held her for a long, silent moment. She was a nurse, he a doctor; both knew how to treat a fainting spell—lay the patient down, get the feet higher than the head—but neither seemed able to make the necessary move. Jade concentrated on taking deep, cleansing breaths—in through her nose, out through her mouth—as he gently stroked her shoulders.

Once her tremors calmed, he lifted her face on a bent forefinger, and she felt, rather than saw, the intensity of his gaze. When he pulled her nearer, she locked her elbows and pressed both palms against his chest to ensure the distance, and felt his hard-pounding heart beneath her hands.

She sensed that he wanted to kiss her. Sensed, too, that he wouldn't—not if she didn't want him to. And Jade most definitely did not want him to!

She didn't speak. Didn't dare, for the words churning in her head would likely have singed his ears. *How dare you so much as suggest that I don't love Riley,* she told him with her hot gaze, *when he's the single most important human being in my entire life!*

Taking a deep breath, she prayed for the strength to stay on her feet, prayed that her head would clear. Almost immediately, the waves of nausea and lightheadedness disappeared. "Ron," she managed to croak out, "I—"

"I know," he said, looking away. "I know." After a long, silent moment, Peterson stepped back, still unable to meet her eyes. "Maybe later?"

"No," she said in as gentle a voice as she could muster under the circumstances.

As it turned out, it wasn't a very gentle voice at all, and the proof could be seen in the doctor's wide, surprised eyes.

"Not now, not later, Ron. I'm Riley's wife, in the eyes of God and the State of Maryland, and most important of all, in my heart. And that isn't going to change. Ever."

His brows drew together in the center of his forehead. "So you really love him, then?"

"Yes," she whispered, smiling as she admitted, "I do."

He shrugged one shoulder and held out his hands, palms up. "Well," he said, grinning, "you don't hate me for trying, do you?"

She returned his smile. "How could I ever hate the man who tried so hard to save Leah?"

As he quietly let himself out the back door, Jade dropped onto the seat of the nearest chair, sent yet another prayer heavenward: *Lord, give me the wisdom to know when I should tell Riley what I just told Dr. Peterson!*

※

He thought it might be fun to stop off at the local burger joint on the way home and buy a couple bags of those French fries Fiona seemed to love so much. He'd been grinning like a fool at the picture of Fee's little face when he handed them to her. . .

. . .and then he saw Peterson's car in the driveway.

Glowering, Riley's heart began beating like a parade drum. *What's he doing here?* he demanded, slamming the car door.

Leah's house—correction, his and Jade's house, now that he had his place on the market—was a tri-level affair with a layout that pretty much guaranteed that if Jade was in the kitchen and he came in through the laundry room, he could tap-dance on the washing machine and she wouldn't hear it. He'd taken to whistling softly, so as not to startle her.

Riley didn't even bother to pucker up today.

He had every intention of barging into the kitchen and making it clear to Peterson that this was his house; that Jade was his wife.

But her soft, sweet voice stopped him cold:

"I like to think the one positive thing to come of Leah's death was that you and I became friends."

The one positive thing? Not Fiona, or their marriage, but a relationship with Ron Peterson! Holding his breath, he ground his molars together. *I oughta march in there and deck that fat-headed cretin. I oughta—*

Their conversation turned suddenly to God, of all things, and he listened, grinning with pride as Jade appeared to be putting the pompous Doctor Know-it-all in his place. Her soft laughter, like a magnet, pulled Riley forward a step or two, and he almost allowed himself to be drawn into the kitchen by the warm inviting sound of it.

"I declare, Jade," he heard Peterson say, "if you weren't Riley's wife. . ."

If she weren't my wife, what? Riley demanded, fists clenched at his sides.

She said something about waterlogged lemonade, to which the doctor responded, "It's not like you're really married; you only went through with that sham of a wedding to make Leah happy. . ."

Pulse pounding in his ears, it was all Riley could do to contain himself. But he had to keep a lid on his emotions. It would be easy to stomp in there and enforce his husbandly rights, like some uncivilized cave man; far better to bide his time—see how Jade would handle the situation.

He said a quiet prayer under his breath: "Let her tell the big blowhard to get lost," he whispered, seething.

"I mean, it's not like you're in love with the guy or anything, right?" Peterson asked.

There was a long, deafening pause that tugged at him even harder than her laughter had seconds ago. Riley took a chance and peeked through the fronds of the Boston fern at the bottom of the stairs just in time to see Jade leap up from her chair. It seemed she was about to fall over in a dead faint when Peterson reached out and steadied her.

Why, the no-good, lousy dog is going to kiss her! He shook his head. *You're a vet; to call him a dog is an insult to all canines; he's a snake in wolf's clothing, that's what, and—*

He watched through narrowed eyes as Jade pushed Peterson away. "Ron, I—"

"I know," the doctor interrupted. "Maybe later?"

Riley couldn't see Jade's face, but he could see Peterson's. The hangdog expression told him the doc was hoping that Jade would give him the go-ahead to try again later.

"No," she said emphatically. "Not now, not later. I'm Riley's wife, in the eyes of God and the State of Maryland, and most important of all, in my heart."

His heart swelled with relief and pride and love, and he wanted to wrap her in his arms and press a grateful kiss to her lips.

"So," Peterson said, "you really love him then?"

"Yes," she whispered, "I do."

The doctor shrugged. "Well, you don't hate me for trying. . . ?"

Her back was still to him, but Riley knew from her tone of voice that Jade was smiling when she said, "How could I ever hate the man who tried so hard to save Leah?"

And she was right, Riley admitted. There was that reason, at least, to keep from hating Ron Peterson. And grinning, he told himself if the doc hadn't already let himself out through the kitchen door, he might just give him a great big hug, himself.

The man wants something he can never have because Jade has chosen to give her heart to you instead. Not now, not ever, she'd told the doctor. Jade was his, as the wedding vows said, until death them do part, and Riley intended to thank God for that, every last one of those days.

He'd see her through these trying times as they adjusted to life together, to parenthood, and a future without Leah. If she held him at arm's length for a while longer, well, it would hurt, but he'd focus on the days ahead, when she'd drop her defenses, put the loss in perspective, and move forward. She'd always been spunky and plucky; he had good reason to believe she would.

Riley headed back through the house, intending to go out the way he'd come in, make a second entrance, this time the way Peterson had done it. He'd take her in his arms and confess it all—that he'd fallen feet over forehead for her the first time he saw her, and that every day that had passed since, he'd only loved her more. And if God saw fit to answer his most current prayer, Riley would make her his wife in every sense of the word.

The burgers and fries would no doubt be colder after they exchanged their latest vows, but hey, he said to himself, grinning, isn't that why the microwave oven was invented?

❧

She was wide-eyed and frantic when he walked into Fiona's room, beaming as he held out the white paper bag filled with burgers and fries. "Oh, Riley, thank God you're home early. I was just about to call her pediatrician!"

He dropped the sack on the changing table and took the baby from her. "She's burning up!" he said, one big hand covering Fiona's forehead.

"I read in the morning paper that a little boy died of meningitis just last week," she said, half-running into the kitchen. "It really isn't the season for it, but," she shook her head, "the virus that causes it can be terribly contagious; just yesterday, Fee and I went to the grocery store right up the street where he lived." Jade grabbed Leah's personal phone directory, looked up Fiona's doctor's name.

If she'd been in the same neighborhood as the boy who'd died, it was entirely possible Jade and Fiona had come into contact with the airborne germs that caused the potentially deadly disease. "What's the incubation period?" he asked.

She finished dialing the phone. "Could be hours, could be days; depends on how healthy you are when you're exposed."

Fiona continued to snooze against his shoulder. "But she hasn't been sick."

"Hasn't been her usual self, either. Remember how she's been pushing her food away the last few days?"

It was true. Ordinarily, Fiona had a voracious appetite, but lately, she'd barely touched a bite. She'd been sleeping in fits and starts, too. They'd sloughed it off as the result of the drop-in guests, the interrupted naps, missing Leah. "Couldn't she be teething, like we figured?"

"Sure, but we can't take the chance. Not with something like that going arou—

"Yes," Jade said into the phone. "I'm," She hesitated, but only for a moment. Leah had seen to it that all of Fiona's records had been changed, including those on file at the pediatrician's office. "I'm Fiona Steele's mother. She's burning up with fever, and I'm leaving for the emergency room as soon as we hang up. I want you to get a message to Doctor O'Dell, have him to meet her father and me at the hospital as soon as possible."

She listened for a moment, then snarled, "I don't care if he's about to shoot a birdie; get him off the golf course and over to the hospital, stat!"

Riley had never seen her this way before. Normally, she was cool under pressure and gentle as a deer. Throughout Leah's illness, and even as she lay dying in their arms, Jade had held her emotions in check. She gave into tears—who wouldn't have under those circumstances?—but never to the point that the job didn't get done, and never in front of Leah. There must be something to this maternal stuff, he thought, because she'd turned into a fire-breathing dragon right before his very eyes at the mere possibility that her child might be in danger.

Under different circumstances, he'd have offered a victorious high-five hand-clap to prove just how proud he was of her grit and determination. Right now, he'd have to settle for a supportive smile and a loving glance.

"I'll rev up the car," he said, heading for the garage.

She hung up the phone. "I'll be right out; I just want to grab a few diapers, her Teddy and favorite blanket."

The baby hadn't said a word since he took her in his arms, and that wasn't like her. What worried Riley most wasn't the high temperature itself—he'd seen her spike a fever before—but nothing, not even that bout with the croup had managed to keep her from chattering like a chipmunk. *Lord Jesus,* he prayed, *lay Your healing hands on our girl.*

They drove to the hospital with the emergency flashers going and the head-lights turned on bright, Riley honking as he zoomed around other drivers who were obeying the posted speed limit. "Where's a cop when you need one?" he wondered aloud. "If we got stopped for speeding, we could get a police escort."

"We're nearly there," she assured, patting the hand that white-knuckled the gear shift knob, "and you're doin' swell."

"You sounded like Leah when you said that."

She nodded. "I thought the same thing the minute the words came out of my mouth. I'm going to take that as a good sign."

Fiona snuggled a little closer and held Jade a little tighter. "You'll be fine, sweet girl," she cooed, kissing the child's temple, "just fine. Mommy and Daddy are going to take you to the doctor so they can fix your boo-boo," she added, smoothing soft, silken locks from her fevered forehead.

Mommy and Daddy.

Suddenly, it didn't sound at all foreign. Instead, it sounded normal and natural and strangely comforting under the circumstances.

"And before you know it," Jade was saying, "you'll be all better again, and Daddy and Mommy will take you home, and we'll eat cookies!"

"Cookie?" Fiona whimpered.

It was the first word Riley had heard her speak since he'd arrived home. He took it as a signal, a sign from God that all would be well, just as Jade had promised Fiona.

Riley steered the car under the protective overhang at the emergency room entrance. "You go on in," he instructed with an encouraging wink, "while I find a parking space."

She quickly gathered the baby and her things and stepped onto the concrete ramp that led to help, and hopefully, to healing. "Don't be long," she said meaningfully; "we need you."

He nodded and drove off, nerves jangling and muscles tight as a tambourine. Something told him he wouldn't feel calm, or complete, not until he was with them again.

⁓

It seemed to take hours instead of moments for Riley to park the car, which struck Jade as odd in more ways than one.

For one thing, she'd always prided herself on being independent, self-sufficient, and reliable. Plus, she had extensive training as an emergency room nurse. This was very familiar territory—from the ebb of calm moments to the tide of critical ones—and she should feel comfortable, surrounded by the lifesaving staff and equipment.

But today, Jade was just another frightened mother hoping that these people and their machines could save her child.

Riley's presence had a calming, soothing affect on her, especially lately, and she didn't quite know how to feel about that. Because on the one hand, her training should have provided her with the strength to do what had to be done on the night that Leah died; by all rights, she should have been the steadfast one, the one doling out assurances that night, because Jade had been the one who'd been there at the end for hundreds of strangers.

On the other hand, it was pompous and arrogant to presume that, just because the suffering Riley saw every day in his practice was of the animal rather than the human variety, he didn't understand the full ramifications of a life lost.

There was another, very real element to consider: His nearness seemed all she'd needed to keep her emotions in check that harrowing, horrible night when Leah left them; one look at his intense self-control was enough to gird her own fortitude, an unfair position to put—and keep—him in, especially considering that he had loved Leah every bit as much as she had.

She would not put him through such an ordeal, not this time. He adored Fiona, and she'd seen the fear in his dark eyes the moment he realized how serious her condition might be. He'd certainly earned the right to let down his guard, to accept rather than constantly give comfort, and while it terrified Jade more than she cared to admit to see Fiona in this state—frail, fevered, afraid—she would hide her worries, for Riley's sake.

Jade recalled the verse from Isaiah she'd memorized as a child as a Sunday school assignment. "He giveth power to the faint; and to them that have no might he increaseth strength. . ." she recited mentally, tightening her hold on Fiona as they awaited a doctor's attention, ". . .they that wait upon the Lord shall renew their strength; they shall mount up with wings as eagles; they shall run, and not be weary; and they shall walk, and not faint."

She had God's assurance, then, that the strength required of her would be available when she needed it.

Riley shoved through the doors just then and walked toward her in that sure, solid way that was uniquely his. His gaze fused to hers and warmed her, despite the over–air-conditioned temperature of the waiting room. Connected as they were by threads of honor and respect, he managed a shaky smile, which she returned with a hopeful, confident look.

"How's our girl doing?" he asked, sitting beside her.

"No better, but no worse, either," she answered as he slid his arm across her shoulders.

He nodded toward the double doors that barred entrance to the emergency room itself. "How much longer?"

"Five, maybe ten more minutes, according to that nurse over there."

He followed her gaze, then looked into her eyes and raised both dark brows. "Ten whole minutes? And she's still walkin' around with a head on her shoulders?" Giving Jade a sideways hug, he grinned slightly. "I'm surprised you didn't bite it off and threaten to stuff it into her pocket for making Fee wait ten seconds."

Jade recalled the brief set-to she and the admitting nurse had when she'd walked up to the counter. She'd explained in no uncertain terms that, as one who had walked emergency room halls herself, she knew procedure and would not be kept waiting unnecessarily long. "Oh, trust me," she said, "she understands the seriousness of the situation."

Riley pressed a kiss to her cheek, then laid a hand on Fiona's forehead. "I sure do wish they'd hurry up back there; Fee's not getting any better sitting out here in this drafty waiting room."

This was the way God had intended marriage to be, Jade believed. Each partner intent upon working at full throttle so that when one half of the team wasn't up to it, the other could pull the load, temporarily. That's what the Lord meant when He described equality in a love-filled marriage through the Apostle Paul in Colossians.

"My little children," John had written, "let us not love in word, neither in tongue; but in deed and in truth."

One of Jade's favorite Bible passages had always been I Corinthians 13:7–13, and she whispered it aloud:

" 'Love bears all things, believes all things, hopes all things, endures all things. Love never ends.' "

Riley pressed a gentle kiss to her temple, then whispered into her ear: " '. . .if I have not love, I have nothing. . . .' "

She leaned her head on his shoulder and together, they hugged Fiona's feverish, shivering body. Despite the fear—or perhaps because of it—they shared a curious calm, as though God Himself had blessed the moment.

"Mr. and Mrs. Steele," the nurse called, "will you come with me, please?"

Relieving Jade of Fiona's limp weight, he guided her toward the entrance with his free hand. " '. . .so faith, hope, love abide, these three,' " he whispered as they walked, " 'but the greatest of these is love.' "

It would, perhaps, be a long and harrowing night. But Jade was filled with a peace and contentment like none she'd known before, for God was with them, right here in the emergency room.

And, she knew, He would be with them, no matter what, for the rest of their days.

Chapter 10

"C erebrospinal meningitis," the neurologist on duty explained, "is an acute inflammation of the membranes of the brain or spinal cord or both." He held the X-rays in front of the window and used the tip of his silver ball point pen as a pointer. "We'll know once we see results of the blood work if its cause is by bacteria, viruses, protozoa, yeasts, or fungi."

"Cut to the chase, Doc," Riley interrupted. "How bad is it?"

The white-haired gent peered over the rims of his half-glasses to study Riley's face. "Sorry," he said. "Didn't mean to pontificate." He smiled apologetically. "I've become a spoiled old man, I'm afraid, whose work these days consists of mostly of teaching at the University of Maryland. When I volunteer for E.R. duty, I don't get the sleep I'm accustomed to and sometimes, frankly, I forget where I am."

He cleared his throat and turned to Jade. "Now then, young lady, when did you first notice symptoms?"

"Ordinarily, Fiona has a very pleasant disposition. It isn't like her to be so fussy, but then, these are not ordinary circumstances."

Frowning, he tilted his head. "Circumstances?"

Jade explained how she and Riley became Fiona's parents, and how they attributed the child's recent behavior on changes in the household.

Nodding, the doctor said, "Easy to see why you'd think it was emotional, rather than physical."

Riley took Jade's hand, gave it a supportive squeeze as she continued. "But then I noticed she was putting her hands to her head, moving as though she might have a stiff neck. Her temperature only registered a hundred and two—which I know isn't as dangerous for a child of two as it might be for an adult—but because of the story in the papers, I decided there were enough warning signs to warrant a trip to the hospital."

She glanced at Fiona, who'd been sleeping quietly on a high, narrow cot in the E.R. cubicle for the past few minutes. "I'd rather be labeled a fussbudget by the hospital staff than risk her taking a turn for the worse. I'm well aware that meningitis has a tendency to worsen quickly—climbing temperature, projectile vomiting, convulsions, coma—"

"It's not every fussbudget who knows so much about meningitis," he said, smiling gently. "Don't tell me you teach at Maryland, as well?"

Flushing slightly, Jade explained her lecture. "Until very recently, I worked at L.A. General; we handled a meningitis epidemic some years back. For the patients who got to us in time, we managed to control it with sulfa and antibiotics, but not everyone was so lucky." Shaking her head, she proceeded. "Some patients lost their hearing or went blind because of infections of the iris, a few developed arthritis, others—the ones with extensive spotting of the skin—became delirious and went into comas."

"How many did you lose?"

"Half a dozen or so, total; two, on my shift." Another sigh. "Give me boring lectures in the gallery, complete with gory slide presentations any day over actual human suffering any day. That was quite an education."

"I imagine it was." Like a protective grandfather, he patted her shoulder. "Well, you did a fine job, diagnosing your daughter, a splendid job. And as soon we can have a look at the lab work, we'll know how to proceed. Meanwhile," he said, looking over at Fiona, "it's a good sign that she's resting."

"How soon will you know something?" Riley wanted to know.

The older man slid a gold pocket watch from his vest, popped open the lid. "It shouldn't be long now." Winking, he snapped it shut again. "But just to be sure," he said, putting the timepiece away, "why don't I just call down there and see if I can't hurry things along." He gave Jade's shoulder another paternal squeeze. "Would that help you rest easier?"

Nodding, she smiled. "Yes, it most certainly would. Thank you so much, Doctor—"

"Stewart."

"Not Anthony Stewart—who separated the conjoined twins connected at the skull back in the sixties?" Riley asked.

The physician removed his half-glasses and nonchalantly shrugged one shoulder.

"You invented the process that doctors today are—"

Chuckling good-naturedly, the doctor held up a hand to silence Riley's praises. "I don't know as I'd go so far as to say I 'invented' anything," he said, chuckling. He dropped the glasses into his lab coat pocket, and glancing at Fiona's chart, said to Jade, "If you ever decide to come to work at Howard General, Nurse Steele, I'd very much appreciate it if you'd arrange to work on my shift."

She smiled appreciatively. "That's quite a compliment, coming from you." She glanced at Riley before focusing on the doctor again. "When my husband and I decide it's time for me to go back to nursing, you'll be the first to know."

❧

" 'The prayer of faith shall save the sick, and the Lord shall raise them up,' " Riley prayed. While Jade rocked Fiona to sleep, he'd gone to the hospital chapel. On his knees at the simple little altar, he recited every verse he'd every memorized

339

that dealt with healing and medicine:

" 'He gave them power against unclean spirits, to cast them out, and to heal all manner of sickness and all manner of disease. . . .' 'The Lord will strengthen him upon the bed of languishing. . . .' '. . .who forgiveth all iniquities; who healeth all thy diseases. . . .' '. . .sickness not unto death, but for the glory of God. . . .' "

At the end of it all, weary yet strangely energized, Riley stood and faced the Cross. Leah's death had taught him many things, among them that life was fleeting, at best. He had no idea why Leah had been taken, but he knew this: Fiona would not join her. Not for a very long time. Riley believed that as strongly as he believed Leah had been right when she'd said his marriage to Jade had been the Creator's handiwork, and Riley would not waste one more precious moment waiting for—

What had he been waiting for? A voice from on high, thundering permission for them to live as man and wife? A message written in the clouds, granting authorization to become one?

He loved Jade with all his heart. If she didn't know that already, well, he had the rest of his life to demonstrate it, didn't he?

Riley remembered the day they were married, when he'd wondered if her tears were the outward symbol of her aversion to the marriage. He couldn't have been more wrong! The signs of her love for him were everywhere—in the special and loving things she did for him, every day of his life, in the warm, affectionate light that glowed in her eyes only when she looked at him, in the sweet lilt that brightened her voice when she talked to him. Jade was devoted to Fiona, but not even her deep affection for the child could stir the one-of-a-kind expressions reserved only for him. Besides, he had a feeling the loving looks and warm words and gentle gestures she'd been showering on him were but a fraction of what Jade had to give her friend and life-mate and lover.

The Lord had not brought them together to share a home and years and life as mere pals; friendship was all well and good, a necessary part of marriage, but it was only one thread in the colorful fabric God had woven for husbands and wives.

And as soon as Fiona recuperated, Riley aimed to see that they started living married life, all of it, to the fullest.

He headed back to Fiona's room, stopping at the vending machine down the hall to buy them each a cup of steaming coffee. He was about to turn the corner and enter the room when a soft, sweet voice stopped him.

Jade's voice.

"Peace is flowing like a river," she sang, "flowing out of you and me, flowing out into the desert, setting all the captives free. . . ."

He hadn't heard her sing in nearly a decade, not since that night, a week or so before graduation, when she'd played her guitar so he could hear the newest song she'd written. One line stuck with him, even after all these years: "In your eyes, love,

I see my destiny; when you smile, my whole world is at peace. I have one dream, for all eternity. . .that you'll wrap your lovin' arms 'round me. . . ." He'd thought at the time she'd written it for Hank Berger, and the idea had him gritting his teeth and clenching his fists. He knew better now. She'd written down and sung the words in her heart—words that expressed how Jade felt about him.

Think of all the years you've wasted. Years you could have lived with her, loved her and been loved by her. They'd have three, maybe four kids by now. And a house in the country, like the one Jade had always talked about. *If only you hadn't been so blind, so all-fired dense.*

Riley vowed, right where he stood, not to let another precious second tick by!

Jade had started a new song as he stood musing in the hall, and even without benefit of musical accompaniment, her melodic voice sounded angelic and pure. "We hold a treasure, not made of gold; in earthen vessels wealth untold. One treasure only: the Lord, the Christ, in earthen vessels. . . ."

Silence, then nothing but the quiet creak of the rocker. "Riley," she called softly, "is that you out there casting this giant shadow?"

Chuckling, he looked at the floor, where a six-foot silhouette of himself had slanted across the industrial grade orange-and-green flecked carpeting. "I didn't want to disturb you," he explained, putting one coffee cup on the nightstand beside her. "Your voice is even more beautiful than I remembered."

"That's sweet of you to say," she said, smiling. And looking into Fiona's sleeping face, she said, "but this is real beauty."

"Our sleeping beauty," he agreed. The cherubic face, relaxed in contented slumber, was indeed flawless, with the innocent lift of tiny blond brows and long, lush lashes that dusted round rosy cheeks. The sweet slight smile on her tiny pink mouth told them that Fiona must have be dreaming happy baby dreams.

She stirred in Jade's arms, frowning slightly in her sleep.

"She wants another song," Riley hinted.

"She wants another song?"

"She was fine till you stopped singing."

Grinning, Jade shook her head as Fiona's tiny fingers wrapped around hers. "Well, all right," she grinned. "She loves the tempo and actually knows some of the words to this one."

"Maybe when we get her home, the two of you will sing it for me."

She nodded. "Not maybe; definitely," Jade said, her grin softening to a loving smile.

Heart swelling and pounding with love for her, Riley grinned. "Well, go on," he coaxed, "sing!"

"Bloom, bloom, bloom where you're planted, and you will find your way. Bloom, bloom, bloom where you're planted, you will have your day. . . .

"Look at the flowers, look at them growing; they never worry. . .they never work. Yet look at the way our Father clothes them, each with a beauty all its own.

"Bloom, bloom, bloom where you're planted, and you will find your—"

The sight of a starched white lab coat silenced her.

"Please don't stop; that is by far the loveliest thing I've heard in a long, long time."

Jade blushed and covered her lips with her free hand. "Dr. Stewart," she said, smiling as she nodded at the clipboard he held at his side. "I hope you're that's good news you're holding in your hands."

He lifted it, let it fall. "My dear, I can tell you this: Nothing I can do for that child will equal the healing properties of what you were doing just now."

Perched on the edge of Fiona's empty bed, Stewart shook Riley's hand. "Your wife is quite a talented lady."

"Jack of all trades," Jade began, her blush deepening.

"That's a lot of hooey, and we all know it," Riley countered. "She can draw, too, and make roses grow in sand. And you ought to taste her lasagna!"

The doctor nodded approvingly. "Now there's something you don't see very often these days."

"A perfect woman?" Riley asked.

"The genuine, unbridled love of a man for his woman."

Riley met Jade's gaze and smiled. "Guilty as charged."

Shaking his head, Stewart chuckled.

"Well, it isn't like I was trying to hide it," Riley said, winking at her. He turned to the doctor. "So, what's up, Doc?" he asked, pointing to the clipboard. "Good news, I presume?"

"Seems we have been blessed; little Fiona's meningitis is not severe, and because it's bacterial in nature, we can address it with antibiotic therapy." He looked from Riley to Jade and back again. "If all goes as expected, you ought to be tucking her into her own little bed by this time tomorrow."

"Praise God!" Jade sighed, bowing her head.

"Boom, boom, boom," Fiona said, attempting to sing the notes Jade had just concluded. She thrust a fat little finger between Jade's lips, and frowning slightly, said, "Mama sing?"

A moment of relieved adult laughter bounced from every wall in the tiny room before Jade picked up where she'd left off:

"Look at the love that lies deep within you. Let yourself be! Let yourself be! Look at the gifts you have been given, let them go free; let them go free. . . .

"Bloom, bloom, bloom," she sang as the doctor headed for the door.

"Boom, boom, boom," Fiona crooned in an off-key baby voice.

"Bloom, bloom, bloom," they sang together, their voices blending in a mellifluous duet, "and you will find your way. . .and you will find your way. . . ."

"She looks wonderful, Jade," Amber whispered, peeking into Fiona's room. "She had us all very worried there for awhile. Neil and I prayed for her every chance we got."

Jade closed the door quietly. "Thanks, sweetie."

"So tell me," her sister asked, settling on the family room sofa, "what do you hear from Hank lately?"

"Nothing. In fact, the last time I talked to him was before I left L.A."

"You're joking."

Jade shook her head. "I'm serious as a judge."

"Have you called him? Maybe something happened to him."

She'd poured them each some iced tea before letting Amber peek in at Fiona. Jade picked up her glass and took a sip. "Nothing has happened to Hank Berger." She put the tumbler back on the coffee table. "I called him the night I got here, and the next night, and every night after that for a full week."

"Wasn't he home?"

Another shake of the head. "Nope. Wasn't in the office, either. I left messages with the receptionist at the TV station, on his voice mail at work, on his answering machine at home, with his paging service—"

"Sounds like he was avoiding you."

"And he kept right on avoiding me until the night before Leah died."

"And since then?"

"Not a peep."

"Ha. That makes sense—since I always thought he resembled a plucked chicken."

"Amber!" Jade scolded, laughing. "I'm tellin' Mom!"

Shrugging, she grinned. "What can she do to me? She was the one who taught me I should always tell the truth."

"She also said 'If you can't say anything nice about a person. . .' "

". . .don't say anything at all," Amber finished for her.

The sisters shared a moment of warm laughter that waned into compatible silence.

"So how're you doin', big sister?"

Jade sighed. "I miss Leah. I think I'll miss her till the day I die, but I'm happy, married to Riley, Amber, really happy."

"Why do I hear a 'but' in that statement?"

Another sigh, deeper this time. "If only our marriage was—"

"If only it was what?"

Shrugging, Jade fidgeted, searching for the words that would help her explain.

"Jade!" her sister shouted. "Don't tell me the two of you haven't—You mean you're not—But. . .but it's been three whole months; how can that be?"

Pouting slightly, Jade shook her head. "I sleep in the guest room." She patted the cushion beside her. "And Riley sleeps right here on the couch."

"Now I'm tellin' Mom; you know what she used to say about teasing."

"It's true, every word of it."

"But Jade, the two of you are so much in love. It's written all over both of your faces. Everyone who knows you sees it. I don't understand."

"How can I explain something I don't understand myself? It isn't something we've discussed, that's all."

"That's all? That's all!" Amber clapped a palm to her forehead. "Jade, when are you going to discuss it?"

She shrugged. "I don't know."

"Do you realize that you're missing out on one of the most beautiful things God gave husbands and wives?"

She sighed.

"What about Fiona?"

"What about her?"

"You don't want her to be an only child, do you?"

"I'd love a houseful of children!" she admitted.

Amber buried her face in a toss pillow to muffle her bellow of impatience. "Well, how do you expect to get them," she said, throwing the pillow at Jade, "if you're sleeping there"—she pointed down the hall—"and Riley is sleeping here?" she pointed at the couch. "Osmosis only works on plants, y'know!"

"I know, I know; I've been praying for a solution."

"How do You stand it?" she asked God through the ceiling. And rolling her eyes, Amber hung all eight fingertips from her bottom teeth, she growled with frustration.

Suddenly, she leaned forward, grinning mischievously and wiggling her eyebrows. "Want some advice, big sister?"

Jade laughed at her sister's shenanigans. "I can use all the help I can get."

"You'd better pray harder, or oftener, or something, because I want lots of little tykes to call me Auntie Amber!"

❧

Several hours later, after Amber went home to her husband and little boy, Jade tucked Fiona into the playpen in the corner of the kitchen, where she could keep an eye on her while she prepared supper.

"Mind if I join you?" Riley asked, flopping the evening paper onto the table. "The light's better in here," he explained as he sat.

"Of course I don't mind," she said without thinking. "I love having you so near."

She had her head in the fridge when the phone rang.

"Whatever they're selling," he teased from behind the paper, "we don't want it."

"Not interested in aluminum siding and tilt-in replacement windows?"

"Not interested in lifetime light bulbs that barely last a month or trash bags that can't hold a pound of feathers, either," he added after the second ring.

Jade recognized the voice immediately.

"I can't believe you're still out there," he said. "When are you coming home?"

"Why, I'm just fine, Hank; thanks. And how are you?"

Hank? Riley mouthed. What does he want?

Grinning, she held a finger over her lips as Hank said, "I see you're still the Queen of Sarcasm."

"Now there's a nickname I haven't heard in a while. Can't say I was overly fond of it." Jade paused, then said, "Odd, isn't it, you only called me that when I disagreed with you, because I don't believe you've said anything I can disagree with—yet."

He groaned, and she could almost see him, scrubbing a hand over his face. "Look. I'm sorry. Let's start over, shall we?"

No doubt he's rolling his eyes and bobbing his head from side to side, she told herself.

"So how are you, Jade?"

"Fine. You?"

"Can't complain. How's your girlfriend?"

"Leah?"

"Yeah. That's the one."

"She's—"

"Did you hear? I won the party's nomination; I'll be running for state senate—"

Yes, she'd heard; it had been on the cable news network the week before Leah died. And she knew very well what message his lengthy pause meant to imply: He'd be running, despite the fact that Jade had left him high and dry out there, to do everything for himself. "Congratulations," she said, and meant it. "I'm happy for you."

"Thanks."

"You're welcome."

Another pause. This one, she knew, was supposed to convey criticism, no doubt of what he saw as her blatant self-centeredness.

"You're going to make me say it, aren't you?"

"Say what?"

She heard his deep, exasperated sigh.

"I want you to come home, Jade."

"I am home, Hank."

Riley's brows knitted. Hang up, he gestured, pointing at the empty telephone cradle on the counter.

And Jade shook her head, wagging a finger under his nose.

"You lived here for ten years!" Hank was saying. "This is your home."

"I sold my condo, remember?"

"There are hundreds of properties for sale, and—"

"That doesn't mean I'm in the market to buy."

"Come on, Jade. Surely your girlfriend doesn't expect you to—"

"Leah," she interrupted, angry now. "Her name was Leah. And she—"

"Was?"

"That's right. Was. Leah died three months ago."

"Oh. Sorry." He cleared his throat again. "Why in the world didn't you call? I would have flown out there to—"

"I did call, Hank. But to misquote an old movie, we seem to have developed a failure to communicate. Besides, we managed just fine without you," she ground out.

"We?"

Smiling, she held out her hand, and Riley took it. "Riley and Fiona and me."

"Riley? Not Riley Steele."

"Yes, Riley Steele. I'm surprised you remember him."

"How could I forget him! He was in every issue of *The Wingspan*, and the football coach paraded him out at every school assembly. I don't think there was an election he didn't run for, and win. I was grateful to be a senior when you guys were freshman, let me tell you, 'cause it got me out of that school!"

A moment of silence ticked by, which he ended with, "Look, Jade, maybe I can arrange to take a few days off and—"

"Before you book a flight and reserve a hotel room, I think you should know, Riley and I are married."

For the first time, Jade had no idea how to interpret the quiet. She felt a little guilty for being so abrupt. And just as she was about to apologize for it, Hank said, "I, ah, I guess I'm not surprised." He took a deep breath. "Are you. . .are you happy, Jade?"

She smiled at Riley. "Yes, Hank, I'm very happy."

"Answer me something, Jade."

"What?"

"If I had asked you to marry me, would you have said 'yes'?"

She laughed softly.

The hiss and crackle of the poor connection punctuated his admission. "You should have nagged me to set a date," he said, misinterpreting her reaction.

"Isn't my nature. Besides, it wasn't like we were officially engaged or anything; you never actually proposed, if you'll recall."

"I suppose I should have taken you more seriously."

When she'd been there for him, day after day? Or when she said, the morning she left California, that she wouldn't be back?

"Where's Riley?"

"He's right here. Why?"

"Put him on the line for a minute."

Brows raised, she held out the phone. "Hank wants to talk to you."

Matching her surprised expression, Riley took it from her. "Hank. Hey. What's shakin'?"

"You'd better be good to her, Steele."

Frowning, Riley said, "That's the plan, Berger."

"Because she's a prize."

"A treasure," he corrected. "Not something to be won, but something that, if you're lucky enough to find it, you cherish."

Hank hung up, and none to gently, either. Wincing, Riley put the phone on his other ear. "Gee," he said past the dial tone buzzing in his ear, "I dunno, Hank; that's an awfully big commitment."

"What's a big commitment?" Jade whispered.

Grinning roguishly, he waved her away. "I mean, naming our first kid after you—"

Jade gasped.

Riley continued the charade, "I'm sure it make a great campaign slogan. Yeah, I can see the bumper stickers now: 'Vote for Uncle Hank.' Tell you what, we'll keep you posted; the minute we're, ah, in a family way, you'll be the first to know."

Riley replaced the handset in the cradle and gathered Jade in his arms. "Fiona asleep?" he asked, pulling her closer.

Smiling, Jade glanced at the playpen. "It appears so."

"Good. 'Cause you heard me; I promised Hank we'd consider naming our first kid after him."

She nodded.

Tenderly, he kissed her eyelids, her cheeks, her chin. "And we can't very well do that," he whispered against her lips, "unless we have a kid."

Holding her gaze, he linked his fingers with hers, lifted her hand to his lips and kissed her knuckles, one at a time. "Although, if we did have a kid, I don't know if 'Hank' would be my first choice in boys' names."

"Riley?"

His fingers caressed her face. "Hmmm?"

"Shut up and kiss me."

Epilogue

Seven Years Later. . . .

"Mama," Fiona called, "Zach is crying."

Blinking into the darkness, Jade and Riley disentangled themselves from one another's limbs.

"He probably needs more of that pink stuff on his chicken pox," Riley said around a yawn. "You want me to take care of it?"

"No," she said, stretching. "I'll go. You went last ti—"

"Mama? If you don't make him stop, he'll wake Leah."

Jade smiled and shook her head. "I declare, it seems that child has been talking nonstop since birth. I think the only time she's quiet is when she's sound asleep."

"Even then, her mouth is open," he teased.

"But she's right, you know; if I don't quiet him down, he'll wake the baby."

Riley murmured sleepily against her lips, "Stop calling her 'the baby.' She'll be three in less than a week."

Jade sighed. "I know, I know, but it's a hard habit to break." She climbed out of bed and shrugged into her robe.

He opened one eye. "Hey, it's pretty chilly out there. Aren't you gonna tie it up?"

She laughed softly. "I would if I could, but the belt isn't long enough any more."

"Hang in there, kiddo; a few more weeks and you'll have your flat tummy back again."

"Yeah, right," she said, gently tucking the covers under his chin, "and the sun's gonna shine in exactly one minute."

He opened the other eye, glanced at red numerals of the alarm clock, glowing into the darkness. "But it's only—" He chuckled. "Oh, I get it."

He sat up in bed and held out his arms.

"But Riley, Zach is—"

"Zach is six years old. He'll be fine for one minute more."

Jade climbed back into bed, letting him draw her close.

"You're the most beautiful thing I've ever seen," he told her, "especially when

348

LOREE LOUGH

Loree lives in Maryland with her husband, daughters, and two constantly warring cats. She has written over twenty inspirational novels for adults and children and more than 2,000 articles and dozens of short stories. Loree teaches writing and, even off duty, loves talking about it.

you're pregnant." Gently, he pressed a palm to her child-swelled belly. "If you never got your hourglass figure back again, I'd still love you like crazy."

"Really?" she asked, grinning drowsily.

"You know the answer to that as well as I do." He kissed the tip of her nose. "Now you stay put. I'll dab some more anti-itch stuff on the boy; you go back to sleep."

"Thanks, sweetie."

It was his turn to tuck the quilt under her chin.

"Riley?" she said as he stepped into the hall.

"Hmmm."

"I love you."

"And I love you."

"Hurry back," she added, yawning again, "because I'm feeling a little crampy."

"Crampy?" He all but ran back into the room. "You don't mean—?"

"This one's going to be early, I think."

He slipped his arms around her. "But. . .but we haven't picked a name yet."

"I have a feeling it's going to be a boy. And you still haven't fulfilled your promise—"

"What promise?"

"To Hank Berger, when he called from California all those years ago, remember?"

Grinning, he hung his head. "You know as well as I do that was a bogus promise. Hank hung up long before I made that promise."

"I know," she said, lifting his chin on a bent forefinger.

"You know?"

"I've always known."

"But how?"

She tapped her ear. "Dial tone."

"You heard it?"

She nodded. "I heard it."

"And you let me—"

"I'd been praying God would help us, um, finalize our marriage vows."

"You'd been praying for—?"

Another nod.

He wrapped his arms around her. "Jade?"

She snuggled close. "Hmmm."

"Shut up and kiss me."

A Letter to Our Readers

Dear Readers:

In order that we might better contribute to your reading enjoyment, we would appreciate your taking a few minutes to respond to the following questions. When completed, please return to the following: Fiction Editor, Barbour Publishing, Inc., P.O. Box 719, Uhrichsville, OH 44683.

1. Did you enjoy reading *Maryland*?
   - ❏ Very much—I would like to see more books like this.
   - ❏ Moderately—I would have enjoyed it more if _____
   _____
   _____

2. What influenced your decision to purchase this book?
   (Check those that apply.)
   - ❏ Cover ❏ Back cover copy ❏ Title ❏ Price
   - ❏ Friends ❏ Publicity ❏ Other

3. Which story was your favorite?
   - ❏ *Pocketful of Love* ❏ *The Wedding Wish*
   - ❏ *Pocketful of Promises*

4. Please check your age range:
   - ❏ Under 18 ❏ 18–24 ❏ 25–34
   - ❏ 35–45 ❏ 46–55 ❏ Over 55

5. How many hours per week do you read? _____

Name _____

Occupation _____

Address _____

City_____ State_____ Zip_____

E-mail_____